"CASSIE EDWARDS IS A SHINING TALENT!"—*Romantic Times*

Bestselling author Cassie Edwards has been thrilling readers of historical romance ever since the publication of her first book, SECRETS OF MY HEART. Now, with more than 3 million copies of her books in print and a Lifetime Achievement Award from *Romantic Times*, she has written her most dazzling romance yet— EDEN'S PROMISE. Let yourself be swept away by this swashbuckling tale of wild adventure and wilder passion on the high seas!

PARADISE FOUND

"Make love to me, darling," he whispered, tracing the outline of her lips with his tongue. "Love me with all of your heart."

"I already do," Eden whispered. Her eyes widened when he rose and began removing his clothes. Her gaze swept over the sinews of his shoulders, his rib cage and his flat belly.

Softly feathered with tendrils of crisp, black hair, his chest heaved in rhythm with his heartbeat. His tanned, sculpted face was intense with feeling, his dark eyes midnight-black with passion. . . .

Lead, kindly Light, amid the
encircling gloom,
Lead thou me on!
　　　　—NEWMAN

EDEN'S PROMISE

CASSIE EDWARDS

LEISURE BOOKS ■ NEW YORK CITY

*To my husband, Charlie, who has
filled my life with sweet romance!*
—Cassie

A LEISURE BOOK

June 1989

Published by

Dorchester Publishing Co., Inc.
276 Fifth Avenue
New York, NY 10001

Printed in the United States of America.

Sing me a sweet, low song of night
Before the moon is risen,
A song that tells of the stars' delight
Escaped from day's bright prison,
A song that croons with the cricket's voice,
That sleeps with the shadowed trees,
A song that shall bid my heart rejoice
At its tender mysteries!
And then when the song is ended, love,
Bend down your head unto me,
Whisper the word that was born above
Ere the moon had swayed the sea;
Ere the oldest star began to shine,
Or the farthest sun to burn,—
The oldest of words, O heart of mine,
Yet newest, and sweet to learn.

—HAWTHORNE

Chapter One

Let the rain kiss you, trickle through your hair.

—EASTMAN

1825 . . . May
A few miles down the coast from Charleston, South Carolina

Lurid streaks of lightning flashed brightly against the dark scudding clouds; whitecaps in the ocean rose and fell with the wind. Day had turned almost to night. At Pirate Point Light Station, rain fell in a driving force against the lighthouse windows, yet the light continued to burn steadily in the dark sky.

Spectacular waves crashed with phosphorescent bursts as Preston Whitney, the lighthouse keeper, peered down at the angry sea. "We've needed rain at times, even prayed for it, but I never like gettin' it in one gullywasher," he complained to his daughter, Eden.

Steadfastly, he guided his powerful beacon over the troubled waters of the Atlantic, continually sounding the deafening foghorn to alert ships to the dangerous, rocky shore. "And this ain't the best way to be awakened from a sound sleep," he growled. "I'll not be worth a tinker's damn tonight if I don't get some more sleep today. A man needs his sleep to keep this lighthouse runnin' right when he's awake."

"Surely the storm will abate soon, Father," Eden said. She gave him a half glance. Her reasons for wanting the storm to pass were the same as his: she fervently hoped that he could go back to bed and slip into a sound sleep. His birthday was in a few days. She had planned to go into Charleston this afternoon while he was sleeping to purchase his birthday gift and fresh ingredients for his birthday cake. She couldn't leave on such a venture while he was awake. He did not approve of her going anywhere alone, though she had done so countless times anyhow, whenever she could manage it.

"Pity any ship that gets caught in this weather," Preston said, squinting out over the waves. "My beam can only do so much. The rest is up to the Lord and how he commands the wind and the sea. Makes me feel helpless, Eden. Damn helpless."

More jagged forks of white fire appeared in

the dark sky. Gathering the skirt of her cotton dress around her legs, Eden leaned closer to the window and looked down at the ocean. Its dark water coiled like sea serpents writhing in foaming turmoil. Although the lighthouse trembled and swayed and its iron girders groaned, she reminded herself that the building was designed to withstand such onslaughts from the wind. The lighthouse was secure enough, resting on a huge, submerged iron tube that had a base filled with rubble and concrete.

It had been a part of Eden's life for as far back as she could recall.

Preston gazed at his daughter, proud of her devotion to him. She had been a blessing since the death of his wife. Ten years now. Ten long years since he had lost his dear Brenna.

But somehow Brenna was still there, always with him, kept alive in Eden. Eden was a lot like her mother. She was a sweet and gentle person, and very caring. She even had the same physical attributes that had made her mother special. Flowing gold hair billowed across her shoulders. Her green eyes were soft and kind, shrouded with thick, golden lashes. Her cheeks always dimpled when she spoke or smiled, and her lips were undeniably shaped to be kissed.

Eden had developed into a beautiful woman. Today she wore a cotton frock trimmed with lace, with short puffed sleeves and a high, white collar. Her breasts were round

3

and firm, her waist tiny, her hips perfectly tapered.

Yes, she was a woman. She was his confidante. She was his friend.

But, foremost, she was his daughter, and Preston was preparing himself for the day he would lose her to a man. He knew to expect it soon. She was the right age for marrying. She was seventeen, soon to be eighteen.

Eden squinted her eyes and focused her attention on a movement out at sea. The waves were so high and so fierce that it was hard to tell what she had seen. Her breath caught in her throat when she saw it again. Her hands wove nervously through her hair as she gasped.

"Father, it's a ship," she said, looking quickly over at him and catching him studying her. Of late he had been doing a lot of that. She thought that she understood. With his birthday fast approaching, so would hers. All of her birthdays these past years seemed to be a threat to her father. He knew that he would lose her one day and he dreaded the loneliness that her absence would bring him.

Yes, she understood.

But thus far he had nothing to worry about. No man had caught her fancy. There was no one special. No one who caused her heart to behave strangely. . . .

She was glad when her father's eyes moved back to the sea. It gave her a chance to look at him. He was tall and thin. At forty-five he still had a full head of hair, blond and wavy. His green eyes were sad at times when he was remembering his wife, but usually they smiled as he talked. Denim trousers and shirts were his everyday attire; the smell of pipe tobacco was always on his breath and clothes.

Another bolt of lightning made Eden start with fright. She couldn't help recalling the time when her father had been almost crippled during a fierce electrical storm. He had been on his way up the metal spiral stairway in the lighthouse tower when the stairway had become heavily charged with electricity. He had received a severe jolt from the lightning. Even now the lower half of his body was partially numb from the experience, and he had to walk with a cane.

"A ship you say?" Preston asked, staring out to sea, into the beam of his light. As the gusts of wind knifed around the windows, the lamps flickered, but the wicks, fueled by kerosene, were not extinguished.

"Do you see it, father?" Eden asked anxiously, again looking out to sea. She got another glimpse of sails fighting the wind, then the ship was hidden behind mountainous waves. "Do you think the captain sees your beam?"

Preston's jaw tightened and his lips thinned. He had caught sight of the ship and recognized it. This one time he wished that it wasn't his duty to operate a dependable light. The ship fighting the waves and wind belonged to Pirate Jack, a cursed pirate skilled at eluding the American Naval vessels that patrolled these same waters. The storm was surely the only reason the ship was so close to shore. He and his marauding crew were hunted along the whole shoreline of the Americas.

"Aye, I see the ship and I'm sure it's caught sight of my beam," Preston growled, his hand still on the delicate mechanism that controlled the heavy iron lantern and its full set of lamps suspended by chains.

Eden gave her father a questioning stare. She moved away from the window, relieved to see a separation of clouds overhead. The winds had shifted, and were now more subdued. "Father, you aren't happy about seeing the ship," she said softly. "Or even about sharing your beam with those on board it. Why? Whose ship is it? Do you recognize it?"

Preston gave Eden a troubled glance, not wanting to worry her. For many years there had been little piracy off these shores, but suddenly one final, savage explosion had occurred, and for a decade it had rivaled the Golden Age of piracy in its white-hot intensity. Pirate Jack was one of the remaining pirates, the most elusive of them all. His black devil ship struck fear into all who sighted it.

The fact that the ship was this close to shore gave Preston no choice but to tell Eden, to warn her to be careful when she was alone. He himself was either sleeping during the day, or high in the tower of the lighthouse at night, unable to keep a constant watchful eye on her and the possibility of intruders. She was responsible for her own well-being.

"Father, it's not like you not to answer me," Eden said, placing a gentle hand on his arm. "What is there about that ship that causes you to behave so strangely?"

Preston hesitated a moment longer, then looked Eden square in the eye. "Daughter," he said, patting her hand. "That damnable ship belongs to Pirate Jack. I've heard it described by many who have spoken of pursuing it at sea."

"Father, surely you are wrong," Eden scoffed. She laughed softly. "There have been no pirates in this part of the Atlantic Ocean for years, surely not since the massacre of pirates by the Navy right here in this cove in 1798."

"Were that only true many a captain and crew of plundered ships would still be alive," Preston said. "But what I have told you is true enough. Be warned, Daughter. If any strange men approach you while you are alone and they do not give you a civil answer as to why they are there, use that pistol I gave you for your protection."

"But, Father, surely no pirate would ever drop anchor in this cove again," Eden argued softly. "Or even near it. The lighthouse beam is as deadly as cannon fire. The beam would lead the naval vessels to the pirates and another massacre would occur."

"Eden, though the lighthouse casts its light over the grave of many a pirate in these waters, don't ever think any pirate is too cowardly to come ashore here if he thinks he has a reason to," Preston said flatly, frowning at Eden. "Pirates are called many things, but never cowards."

An iciness crept around Eden's heart as she recalled what she had planned once her father was fast asleep. Was it safe for her to go into Charleston? Were there pirates there, lurking in the shadows of the buildings, ready to abduct an innocent miss? Or was her imagination running away with her?

Picking up a spyglass, Eden placed it to her eye and watched the movement of the ship. The storm had abated, and she could get a good view of the vessel. She knew that her father would be glad to see it moving farther out to sea.

"My beam still reaches the devil ship," Preston said, chuckling. "I imagine every pirate on it is cussing me and my light. Perhaps a naval vessel will show up and blast the black sonofagun clean outta the water."

"Doesn't it frighten you to know that the crew of the ship realizes that you've spied them?" Eden asked. She lowered her spyglass, a sudden feeling of foreboding troubling her. "What if they return to ki—"

Her words died on her lips. She didn't want to say the word "kill", much less think of the lighthouse being a cause of danger to her father or herself.

"They'll be gone soon enough," Preston said, his fingers cramping on the controls. His eyes burned with the need to sleep. "They're smart to hightail it out of here. They have to know that every Navy captain in Charleston Harbor would give a year's wages to chase and corner that sonofagun.''

The clouds had dissipated and the sun was crowning the sea with its golden light. Preston stretched his arms over his head and yawned. He moved shakily to his feet, silently cursing his weak, partially numb legs. He grabbed his faithful cane and hobbled around the small room, extinguishing the lamps.

"I think it's safe enough for me to return to my bed," he said, going to the trapdoor that opened to the staircase. He yanked it open and let it rest against the floor as he began maneuvering his clumsy legs onto the stairs that spiraled around inside the lighthouse to the ground. "I'm going to go and dream of that Fresnel lens that I want for my lighthouse. I hear that its beams are visible up to twenty-four miles away."

"Yes, that would be grand," Eden said, following him through the trapdoor and down the stairs. Her heart ached to see how much effort it took for him to move down the stairs. It never got easier, not for him to walk or for her to watch.

"I hope you can have the lens one day," she said quickly. "I know what it would mean to you. A powerful lens is the pride of many a lighthouse."

The descent to the ground was always a tiring one, even for Eden. Footsteps and the thump-thump of the cane echoed on the steps. The trapped, unpleasant smell of mildew and kerosene stung Eden's nose. The heat of the small space was almost stifling.

When they finally reached the bottom landing, Eden was glad to step outside. She inhaled deeply the air fresh with rain and earthy scents. A low breeze disturbed the silence, bringing with it the fragrance of flowers.

She walked alongside her father down the pebbled path that led to their cottage, then stopped beside him as he took time to admire her well-tended flower garden.

"At least your flower garden benefited from the rain," Preston said, his gaze taking in the variety of flowers. Tulips, primroses, irises, and a generous number of grape hyacinths and daffodils filled the colorful, lush borders of the garden that sat close to the cottage. Chives, parsley, mint and other herbs were planted in the corners.

But ferns were Eden's true obsession. She had a separate garden filled with the woodsy green plants.

"Your ferns are thriving exceptionally well this spring," Preston said, smiling over at Eden. "Though flowerless, they are pleasing to the eye."

Eden bent over and touched a delicate fern frond. "Yes, this year the ferns are so green, so rich," she said, touching another delicate frond. "Father, don't you see? Their beauty lies not in flowers, but in their intense color and fascinating shades."

She straightened her back and rose to her

full height, smoothing wrinkles out of her skirt. "There's a kind of mystery about them," she said, sighing.

"With your manual for identifying the ferns you bring back from the forest, I don't see how they can keep their mystery for long with you," Preston said, chuckling. He turned and headed toward the porch. "If you're not filling your garden and our house with ferns, you're pressing and preserving them."

"Yes, I know," Eden said, moving to his side as he reached the steps. She looked down at her fingernails, showing them to her father. "If I don't have dirt beneath my nails from working the earth in my garden, then I have oil beneath them from working with you at the lighthouse. I surely look far less than ladylike."

Preston leaned hard against his cane. He grunted with the effort of mounting the steps, groaning as he lifted one foot and then the other. "To hell with your nails," he said. "There's much more of you to look at than your damn fingernails. Take a look in the mirror, Eden. You're as pretty as a picture." He swallowed hard. "Just like your mother. Just like your mother."

Eden laughed softly, flipping her golden hair back from her shoulders. "Of course, you wouldn't be prejudiced, would you, Father?" she said, her eyes twinkling.

"Like I said, take a good look in the mirror," Preston said. "No woman in Charleston can compare with you."

Eden started to open her mouth to dispute that statement by mentioning his recent show of interest in Eden's close friend Angelita Llewellyn. But she reconsidered. It was best not to say anything. If her father was infatuated with Angelita, it was for him to tell her of his own accord. He knew as well as Eden how flighty Angelita was. Surely he could see that she was not someone who would settle down with one man, especially a man twenty years her senior, and . . . half crippled.

Nearby, corn swayed in the gentle breeze; sprigs of oats, pea vines and hills of potatoes stretched out in a neatly kept garden. A cow bellowed from a small barn that sat not that far from the little four-roomed keeper's cottage.

A goat roamed in a fenced-in area outside the barn. Fresh goat milk and big brown eggs from Eden's chickens were always available for her weekly baking of breads and cakes.

Leaning hard on his cane again, Preston stepped up onto the porch and lumbered toward the door. "Be sure and awaken me in time for us to check the wicks before it gets too dark this evening, hon," he said. "Ah, I have at least seven good hours of sleep ahead of me."

Eden nodded. She hoped that seven hours would give her enough time to go into Charleston, shop, and return home before her father awakened and realized that she was gone. It was more important than ever that he never discover her trips into Charleston while he slept. If there was danger of pirates on land as well as at sea, even she had cause to wonder about the wisdom of wandering about unescorted.

Yet, didn't Angelita come and go as she pleased? Sometimes she was escorted, but most of the time she wasn't. Eden's father had said nothing about Angelita going about on her own. But, of course, Angelita wasn't his daughter and she wasn't seventeen.

But going into Charleston was Eden's only escape from the drab life of a lighthouse keeper. She lived on a lonely seashore where the loudest noise was the splash of a wave as it rolled shoreward, or the caw of a sea gull as it searched the near shore for food. Eden loved the smells and sounds of the city. She loved to go shopping.

Most of her rainy days were taken up with studying her botanical specimens under a microscope and pressing fronds in diaries. She intended to purchase a new diary today, along with her father's birthday present.

No. Nothing could stand in the way of her excursion into Charleston. Nothing.

Eden followed her father into the cottage. She watched him lumber off into his bedroom, closing the door behind him. Then she began pacing, hoping that she would hear him snoring very soon.

Looking around, she was reminded of the paltry four hundred dollars a year her father earned as the lightkeeper, and of the small amount he paid her for assisting him. There was no room for much luxury on such a salary, but she had done her best to decorate the cottage within their means. It was sparsely furnished, but cozy. The wooden floors were kept golden from fresh waxings. The windows were draped with a length of sheer cotton fabric in which rosettes had been gathered by hand, tied in place with twine and hung from small nails.

The living room furniture was upholstered with a cheerful mix of floral patterns in green and seashell pink. The scent of lemon-oil polish lay pleasantly in the air, and the oak tables beside the sofa shone, proof of the daily use of the polish.

Logs burned pleasantly on the grate of an oversized stone fireplace that filled one whole outside wall of the living room, its chimney dressed with a delicate draping of dried herbs and flowers. Eden's late grandmother's silver candlesticks stood alone on the stone mantel.

Off the living room at one end was a small kitchen with built-in cupboards; drawers and bins for flour and sugar were tucked underneath them. At the other end of the living room were two bedrooms.

Eden went to her bedroom, where delicate white lace adorned her window and canopied her four-poster oak bed and was draped across her dresser. She took a hooded cape from a peg on the wall and eased it around her shoulders. Going to a drawer in her nightstand, she swept a tiny, pearl-handled pistol up into her hand. She silently studied it for a moment, recalling her father's warnings. The pistol had always seemed more of a threat to her than an instrument of protection, for she hated the idea of being forced to carry a weapon for any reason.

But today, it seemed right to slip it into the pocket of her cape. After seeing the pirate ship, she had been made to realize just how vulnerable she was. A man's strength against a lady's could only be stopped with a bullet.

Shuddering at the thought, she dropped the pistol into her deep cape pocket, then leaned her ear against the wall that adjoined her father's bedroom. Her eyes sparkled and she smiled when she heard a steady drone of snores.

"He's sound asleep," she whispered. It was safe enough to leave now. Her father would never know that she had gone into Charleston until she gave him his birthday present. And she was hoping that she would find him a very special pipe to ease his anger at her.

Tiptoeing from her room, she headed for the front door, her pulse racing.

Chapter Two

Her wonder like a wind doth sing.
                                    —O'BRIEN

The country road was scarred with muddy
potholes, formed by the ravages of the recent
rain. Eden clung to the reins as she maneuvered her horse and buggy along the pitted
road. Frowning, she whispered an unladylike
curse beneath her breath when one of the
buggy wheels slammed down into a pothole
and jumped out again, jostling her so much
that her teeth clicked together painfully.

The heat of the sun burned its way through
her dark cape. She looked up at the sky, her
frown deepening.

Directing her eyes back on the road, Eden
dreaded the long avenue of potholes ahead of
her. Shaking the hood of her cape from her
head, she sighed with relief when her freed

hair was lifted from her shoulders by the gentle breeze. She felt that it was safe enough to display her womanly features along this stretch of road. Rarely did anyone but Eden and her father travel it. It was known to everyone as the Lighthouse Road, for there were no homes or plantations yet established along its lonely wake.

Relaxing her tense shoulders, Eden let herself enjoy these few hours of freedom away from her daily chores. She didn't dare try this often, for there was no sense in pushing her luck too far. Either she would be found out by her father, or trouble of some sort would find its way to her.

Yes, while she could, she would enjoy these rare outings and feel blessed for them.

The ocean stretched out to the horizon to her left. She noticed that the tide had gone out quietly, leaving the mudbanks bare and glistening.

Her gaze roamed to the great pine forest and salt marshes to her right. Spring had brought out the azaleas and their riot of color and the delicious-smelling magnolia blossoms. Huge cypress and oak trees shaded banks of camellias. The marshes seemed silent, still, until a red-winged blackbird arrived with his clackerlike call.

Eden was jolted abruptly as the buggy wheel dropped hard into another pothole. This was followed by a loud snapping noise; the wheel shimmied and shook as it threatened to go rolling free from the buggy.

Eden drew the reins tight. "Whoa!" she screamed.

She tried to stay firmly on the seat, but she was being tossed from side to side by the wild bumping of the buggy.

Finally the horse came to a shuddering halt. Eden's chest heaved as her breath came in short, exhausted rasps. Perspiration dampened her brow, her face was flushed. But she was relieved to be seated in her buggy and not sprawled out on the road.

Gathering her composure, she took a long, shaky breath. She then became aware of the precarious tilt of the buggy. The wheel must have come close to dislodging itself completely. She realized just how lucky she was not to have been injured.

The task at hand was not an easy one. It would require more muscle than she could muster to repair the buggy. Untying her cape, she let it flutter from her shoulders to the seat. Feeling all too isolated from the lighthouse and Charleston, she climbed disconsolately from the buggy.

After carefully viewing the situation, she groaned when she saw that the wheel was broken almost in two from the drop into the pothole. It was beyond any repair that she would know how to do. It would take someone with knowledge of this sort of vehicle to make the necessary repairs. Perhaps she even needed a new wheel.

No matter what, it would be costly . . .

Grimacing, she looked down the road one

way and then the other. There was no one within miles who could give her a helping hand. She had only two choices. She could walk the horse back home and confess her misfortune to her father. Or she could chance going on to Charleston and hope that someone would return with her to repair the buggy.

"The money meant for my father's birthday and for my diary spent on a broken wheel?" she moaned. "It's unfair."

Placing her hands on her hips, she felt the hem of her cotton dress whipping around her tapered ankles as the breeze blew more briskly from the sea. Eden studied the road again, trying to decide what was the best thing for her to do. If she went home and awakened her father, she would have more than a broken wheel to explain. She would have to admit to her jaunts alone into Charleston. He was wise enough to know that this wouldn't have been the first time.

But he would see to it that this was most certainly the last.

If she even made it to Charleston by foot, she—

Eden's heart skipped a beat when she caught a movement on the road in the direction whence she had just come. It was a horse and buggy. It had been hidden from view earlier by a curve in the road. Relief flooded her. She would no longer have to consider returning home to face her father. Surely assistance was on its way.

Then her heart skipped another beat.

Where were the travelers coming from? No plantation or any sort of house had been built along this stretch of road. The land was low. There was always a threat of flooding.

"Who can it be?" she whispered. She cupped her hands over her eyes, shielding them from the brilliant rays of the sun so that she could see better.

Her breath caught in her throat. Fear grabbed at her insides. The buggy approaching her was now close enough for her to see that a lone man occupied it. She had expected —had hoped for—a husband and wife. Alone on an isolated road, with only a man to ask for help, she felt much too vulnerable.

"My pistol," she whispered. She looked over her shoulder at the cape crumpled up on the seat of the buggy. "I must get it just in case."

Her father's warning about pirates flashed through her mind. Could this traveler be a pirate? Pirates had to come on land sometimes for supplies . . . and women.

Something shining on the road close to the buggy reflected in Eden's eyes, drawing her attention. She gasped and turned around with a jerk. Her pistol had fallen from her cape pocket and now lay in the road. She started to stoop and pick it up but was drawn around quickly when she heard the horse and buggy stop close behind her.

"What have we here? A damsel in distress?"

The man's voice was smooth and deep. As he stepped from his buggy and moved toward her, Eden was stunned by his appearance. All thought of his being a pirate disappeared. This man could never be mistaken for such a loathsome sort of person. It was not only the smartness of his clothes that made her believe he was quite respectable and most surely dependable, it was the wholesomeness of his features.

His face was sun-bronzed, with lean, smooth features framed by thick, midnight-black hair worn to his collar. He had eyes almost as deep a black as his hair, and so friendly they made Eden feel warm all over. He had a straight, aristocratic nose, a square jaw and most seductive lips.

His broad shoulders filled out the white linen coat he wore over a white, ruffled shirt, and he sported a lace-edged cravat at his throat. His fawn breeches were snug-fitting, his black boots dust-free and shining.

In short, his handsomeness stole Eden's breath away. It was a first for her, this reaction of total awe over a man. And, oh, what an awkward time for it to happen! She was wind-blown and sweaty. Her dress was quite plain, so as not to draw undue attention from gentlemen while she was in Charleston, alone.

If she had guessed that she would be meeting a man who melted her heart this way, she would have prepared for hours for the meeting. She would have made herself so attractive he would never want to turn his eyes away from her.

"Sir?" Eden finally blurted, now also spying a pistol belted at his waist as the breeze lifted the tail of his coat away from it.

"Zachary Tyson at your service," he said,

his dark eyes slowly assessing Eden. He had to assume that she was from the lighthouse cottage, for no other houses stood on this stretch of road. He had heard that the lightkeeper had a daughter, even that she was quite beautiful. But never had he ventured to guess that she could be this lovely.

He drew his eyes away from her long enough to look at the broken wheel. "It seems your wheel gave out on you," he said, his gaze moving back to her. He could not help but look her slowly up and down. It was as though she were sweet pollen in a flower, he the bee, drawn irresistibly to her. Surely one taste of her would be pure heaven.

Zach cleared his throat nervously, casting such foolish thoughts aside. He had been without a woman for too long! That was surely why this beautiful lady was affecting him so strangely.

"But it looks as though you were lucky," he quickly added. "You weren't harmed by the mishap."

He couldn't stop looking at her. With her long, flowing golden hair worn past her shoulders, her green, luminous eyes and pink oval face blessed with lovely dimples, she was ravishing. He dared not stare long at her body, but even in a brief second glance he had seen her well-rounded breasts straining against the cotton fabric of her dress, and the tiny waistline that accentuated her perfectly curved hips.

For the first time in years, Zach felt a burning desire to get to know a lady better.

Until now his way of life had been a barrier to any commitment he may have wanted to make with a woman.

But now he was free.

Well, as free as he could ever feel.

Eden felt as though she were on display. Zach's eyes not only appraised, but branded her. A blush grew hot on her cheeks as she shifted her feet nervously. "Do you by chance have the means with which to repair my wheel?" she asked, her voice lilting and soft. "I would like to be on my way to Charleston. I don't have much time for wasting."

She could not help herself. She had to know more about him! Knowing his name was not enough. She wanted so badly to ask him where he had come from, why he was traveling on this particular road. Perhaps fate had drawn them together.

"Let me take a better look at that wheel," Zach said, moving past Eden.

She turned and watched him as he knelt down beside the buggy. She gasped and placed her hands to her throat. She had forgotten about her pistol, which still lay in the road. He had seen it and was reaching for it, even now.

"Hmm. What's this?" Zach said. He picked the firearm up, the pistol dwarfed in the large palm of his left hand. He turned his head and eyed Eden questioningly. "This must be yours. It's too clean to have been here on the road for long. Ma'am, have you had problems other than broken wheels while traveling this road?

Is that why you felt the need to have a pistol with you? Your father, the lightkeeper, surely does not approve of your traveling unescorted. If I had a daughter like you, I would guard her with my life."

Eden was aghast at his presumptuousness. And how did he know about her father? She hadn't even told him her name.

"Mr. Tyson," she said, interrupting him. "Can you or can you not repair my wheel? It should matter not to you why I am alone or why I choose to carry a pistol for protection."

She felt a strange giddiness at the thought that he might be genuinely concerned about her welfare. Deep down, where her desires were formed, she was not truly angry at him. She was thrilled by his attentions.

Pretending to be unnerved by his questions, Eden held out a hand. She hated it when she could not control the trembling of her fingers. "My firearm, please," she said, lifting her chin haughtily. "I still may need it. One never knows what sort of person one may meet on this lonely stretch of road."

Chuckling beneath his breath, Zach placed the pistol in the tiny palm of her hand. His loins reacted strangely when their flesh came into brief contact and their eyes momentarily met and held. "No," he said, his laughter fading on the wind, his eyes dark with feeling. "One never knows whom one may meet."

Eden's flesh tingled where his fingers had momentarily touched her. She could not define the wondrous, even dangerous sparks of desire firing her insides. She knew not how to cope with them. These were new feelings for her, feelings both sweet and painful.

"Why are you traveling this road? I can think of no conceivable reason why you should be," she blurted out. "It is usually used only by me and my father and those who come to visit us."

Zach smiled at her, then turned and knelt down beside the buggy. Methodically, he began removing the bolts that held the wheel in place. "First, let me remind you that my name is Zachary but you may call me Zach," he said. One bolt was removed, the others dangling. "Second, am I expected to answer your questions when you have refused to answer mine? Why, I have yet to be told your name."

"If you already know so much about me— that I am the lightkeeper's daughter—I am surprised you don't know my name," Eden said stubbornly. She moved to the other side of the buggy and drew her cape into her arms. She slipped the pistol into the pocket and slung the garment around her shoulders.

"Had I known you were so beautiful and feisty I would have made it a point to learn your name," Zach said. With smiling eyes, he peered over his shoulder at Eden. "I would have come calling." He paused for a moment, their eyes once more holding. "Would you have let me? Or would you have sent me on my way?"

Eden couldn't believe what was transpiring on this lonely road with this handsome man, a man of both wit and charm. Even in her wildest fantasies she could not have conjured up such a meeting.

"Eden," she said suddenly. "Eden Whitney."

Zach widened his eyes and gazed up at Eden. "Oh?" he finally said. "What a lovely name."

He was intrigued by her name. His eyes danced, and he smiled slowly up at her. "The name Eden conjures up all sorts of images in my mind," he said, unable to quell the huskiness in his voice.

Blushing, yet used to being teased about her name, Eden lowered her eyes. Again she was at a loss for words and was embarrassed by it. There had hardly been a time in her life when she wasn't able to carry on an intelligent conversation. Why, oh, why, did she have to be floundering now? She must look like some sort of mindless ninny.

Zach's amused smile faded and an eyebrow rose when he saw Eden's blushing innocence. He was attracted to her all the more. These past years he had been acquainted with hard women who were loud and boisterous. Eden was a refreshing change.

Zach unscrewed another bolt, forcing his eyes to the wheel. "Would you?" he asked, his voice thick.

Eden raised her eyes quickly. "Sir?" she said, arching an eyebrow. She was still in a state of semi-shock at having told him her name in such a way. What had gotten into her? What was there about this man that made her behave so strangely?

Zach looked up at her again, his eyelashes heavy over his penetrating dark eyes. "Would you have let me come to call on you?" he asked softly. "Will you?"

Eden found herself speechless again. This situation between her and the stranger was getting more intense by the minute and she still had no answers from him other than his name—and her own discovery of his obvious attraction to her.

"How can I say yes?" she murmured. She walked back around the buggy, to stand beside him. "I don't know you at all or even where you make your residence. I most certainly haven't been able to find out why you are on Lighthouse Road."

The wheel dropped clumsily to the ground as the last bolt fell away. Zach placed the loose bolts in Eden's buggy, then turned to face her. Withdrawing a handkerchief from his rear trouser pocket he began to slowly wipe his hands on it.

"I live on this road," he said. He frowned down at Eden, knowing that his statement would surprise her. "Several miles from the lighthouse. The house was completed only a week ago. The fields are cleared and I hope the crops will be planted soon. I'm going into Charleston today to see if I can acquire some slavehands for my plantation."

Eden's eyes widened with surprise. "You built a house on Lighthouse Road and I never saw you taking supplies there?" she gasped. "Nor did my father. He would have mentioned it."

"I moved by day. Being a lightkeeper, your father works at night, doesn't he?"

"Yes, that is so. But how could you have moved by day without me seeing you?"

"That would have been quite impossible."

"Why would it? I don't understand."

"Because all of the supplies and the furnishings for my house were brought by ship."

"By . . . ship?" Eden said softly. She was puzzled by his declaration, yet shamefully elated to know that he lived so close. "But still, father or I would have seen your house by now from the lighthouse."

"No. That would have been impossible, also."

"How can you say that? We can see for miles from the great height of the lighthouse. And, also, no other houses have been built along this stretch of road because of flooding. Our cottage is protected by a great wall of rocks along the shoreline. It was built up on a slope of land. Perhaps you've done the same?"

Zach returned his handkerchief to his pocket. He lifted the broken wheel and carried it to his buggy, placing it in the back. "My house was built a safe distance from the shoreline and, yes, on the crest of a hill," he said smoothly. He turned and eyed Eden speculatively. "As for why neither you nor your father have seen it . . . I cut only enough live oaks to make room for my house and the slaves' quarters. They're all well hidden in a grove of giant trees."

"But you mentioned that fields are being cleared," Eden said.

29

Then her words froze on her lips as she recalled puzzling about the thinning of trees she'd noticed not long ago. It had been growing dark that evening when she had accompanied her father to the lighthouse. While he had been oiling his lamps she had entertained herself with his spyglass, scanning the sea, and then the land. She had seen the cleared land, but darkness had fallen much too quickly for her to examine her findings more closely.

By the next day she had forgotten her discovery.

"So you're the one . . ."

Zach's jaw tightened; the gentleness in his eyes changed to warning. "What do you mean, I'm the one? The one who what?" he asked before she had the chance to finish her question.

A sudden fear struck at Eden's heart. Zach's mood had changed so quickly. Was she discovering that he had a mysterious side? It was strange how he had built his house without so much as a word of introduction to her or her father, his only neighbors for miles.

And now? He was behaving as though she was ready to accuse him of something sinister. Perhaps his wit and charm were a facade, a front for something quite different lurking beneath his handsome exterior.

"I noticed from the lighthouse the thinning of trees in the distance," she murmured. "You're the one responsible for it. That's all that I was about to say."

Suddenly uneasy with him, Eden eyed her

wheel, which he had placed in the back of his buggy. "Am I to assume that you are going to take my wheel into Charleston for repairs?" she asked.

"Would that make you happy?" Zach asked, his jaw relaxed again, his eyes smiling.

"Only if I am invited for the journey, also," Eden said, smiling slowly up at him, relieved to see that his lighthearted mood had returned.

Zach performed a mock bow for Eden. "Please be my guest," he said, thanking fate that he had chosen this day to make his first appearance in Charleston. With a lady at his side he would draw less attention. They would mingle with the crowd as though Eden and he were man and wife.

And he thanked fate that the lady was Eden. There was no doubt that she was special.

He looked over at Eden, his eyes shadowed by thick lashes. For a moment, he had almost let her see the side of him that he had hoped he could leave in the past. But the past was not that easily forgotten. Could Eden perhaps lead him to Angelita? Sweet and adorable Angelita Llewellyn? How many years had it been since he had last seen her? Until he was with her again, a corner of his heart would forever bleed.

"How gallant of you," Eden said, laughing. Lifting the hem of her dress, she moved toward his buggy. Her heartbeat thundered when Zach turned toward her and offered her his hand. Her fingers trembled as she lifted them toward him. When their flesh touched, it was as though every fiber of her being was awakened to rapture.

"Sir . . ." she began softly.

"Please call me Zach," he said, interrupting.

"Zach," Eden said, her pulse racing. "You never mentioned a wife . . ."

Eden's face grew hot with a blush. But this man had drawn her into saying many things without thinking. She had just met him. She had seen a mysterious, perhaps even a sinister side to him, yet she could not help her openness with him.

Zach took not one, but both of Eden's hands and clasped them tightly. This lady with the face of an angel and the body of a goddess would surely make him do many foolish things. Perhaps she could even make him forget his past.

But even being with her was dangerous. Not only for him, but—God!—most surely for her! He was a danger to anyone who grew to care for him—even Angelita. He usually fought close relationships. But with Eden, he was finding it hard. He was driven to kiss her . . . damn it, he must.

"No, I didn't mention a wife," he said thickly. "For, my dear, there is none."

Eden's eyes widened and her lips quivered into a pleased smile.

She swallowed hard as his mouth lowered toward hers. Her head began a crazy spinning when their lips touched. . . .

Chapter Three

Kiss me sweet with your warm wet mouth.

— WILCOX

Melting beneath the kiss, Eden twined her arms around Zach's neck as though drawn there by some unseen force. She clung to him. She even gasped low, and shamelessly strained her body into his as his fingers wove through her hair, drawing her closer. She was enveloped by a strange and wondrous desire, acutely aware of his hard body pressed against hers.

But when his mouth forced her lips apart and his kiss grew more passionate, a warning shot through her and she somehow found the sense to jerk away from him.

Stepping shakily backwards, touching her fingers to her lips in wonder, Eden looked up into Zach's dark eyes and saw a puzzled, silent

33

apology. She gazed back at him, breathless. She was confused. This man who had stolen her reason had most surely also stolen her heart.

"I don't know what got into me," Zach said, raking his fingers through his midnight-black hair. "You must think I am some sort of rogue whose prime interest is women. Let me assure you that is not so. Please accept my apologies, Eden."

Eden took a shallow, shaky breath. "There is nothing to apologize for," she said, nervously smoothing her hands down the skirt of her dress.

She looked over at Zach's wagon, then back at him. "Perhaps it would be best if we got on our way?" she said softly. "Time is of the essence. I must get back home before my father awa. . . ."

Zach's eyebrows shot up. "Before your father awakens?" he said, interrupting. "So that is why he doesn't know you are going into Charleston unescorted. He's asleep."

Unnerved by his ability to read her thoughts, Eden walked past him and climbed into his buggy. "If you were an only child, a daughter at that, you would see why it is necessary to do things behind a father's back," she said. "I would never be out of my father's sight if he had his way about it."

She watched him guardedly as he climbed onto the seat beside her. She was still trembling from his kiss. She could still feel the press of his hard body against hers, awakening feelings that she had never known before. There were dangers in those feelings. There were dangers in having to depend on him for too many things today.

Zach lifted the reins and slapped them against the magnificent chestnut gelding. The horse neighed and began ambling along the road. Zach then draped the reins loosely between his fingers, rested his elbow on his knee and gave Eden a half glance.

"You speak of a father who cares too much," he said hoarsely. "Eden, be thankful that you have a father at all."

When the buggy found one of the many dreaded potholes in the road and tossed Eden about, she grabbed for the seat to steady herself. She gave Zach a pensive stare. There was a terrible sadness in his voice.

"Your father is no longer alive?" she asked, hoping she was not reopening fresh wounds. There were times when she herself felt an almost physical pain when she thought about her mother and how very much she missed her.

Zach stared ahead, trying to guide his horse around the worst of the holes in the road. "My father died some time ago," he said, his jaw tightening. "So long ago I sometimes find it hard to make out his face in my mind's eye. You see, one has to learn to adjust to losses in life." He gave her a quick glance. "But you are one of the fortunate ones. You still have your father. Feel blessed, Eden. When your father is gone, it can be pure hell sometimes."

Eden looked at him quickly, ready to say that yes, she still had her father, but what of her mother?

But this wasn't the time to think of her own hurts. The sadness in Zach's voice had turned to bitterness. Was it because he missed his father so much, or was it because he hated his father for having died?

Either way, it was evident that Zach was hurting inside.

"Tell me about your plantation," she said, eager to change the subject. "What sort of business were you in before you decided to come to the Carolinas?"

The same guarded look she had seen before flashed in Zach's eyes. A feeling of foreboding soared through her at the thought that he might not be what he seemed to be. What if he was a man who could not be trusted?

She had waited forever to find a man who stirred passion inside her heart. Now that she had, what of the future? Was she foolish to believe there could be one with him? If he was not trustworthy, what then? She had only just met him. She knew nothing about him except that he had just established himself on a plantation and that he had lost his father.

That was hardly enough to be letting her mind conjure up thoughts of building a future with him.

"When my father died, I became quite wealthy, for you see, I had no mother to benefit from my father's death," he said slowly. He was not used to blatantly lying, but he knew that the truth would condemn him in her eyes.

He paused and a haunted look darkened his eyes as he sighed heavily. "I have been a world traveler for some time now," he continued. "But when I reached the age of twenty-seven I decided it was time to fulfill a lifetime dream of mine. I have become a land owner. I wish to raise cotton and perhaps indigo."

"That sounds grand," Eden said, smiling over at him. She was relieved when the gentle side of his nature returned as he smiled back at her. "And you are now on your way into Charleston to acquire slaves?"

"Yes," Zach replied reluctantly. "I don't take much to enslaving men and women in any capacity. When I acquire slavehands, they will soon discover that I am not a master who forces workers to perform beneath lashes from a whip."

Eden found herself falling more and more in love with this man whose gentle side outweighed his hints of mystery. "I am sure your workers will repay you in kind and make your plantation one of the best and most profitable in these parts."

Zach smiled over at her again. "I hope so," he said thickly. His eyes gleamed into hers. "I have heard that the plantation owner's main problem in the Carolinas is General Green."

"General Green?" Eden said, raising an eyebrow. Then she laughed, tossing her hair back from her shoulders with the flip of a hand. "Oh, yes. That general. General grass. Grass is a problem because of the way it takes over a field if not fought daily with the hoe."

"Enough talk about me and my plans," Zach said, snapping the reins again. "Tell me about yourself. What do you do to pass the time when you're not sneaking into Charleston?"

Eden stretched her arms above her head and yawned lazily. "Oh, I just sleep all day," she teased. "I've no chores whatsoever to do. Now what do you think of that, Zach?"

Zach looked over at her, letting his eyes roam from her head to her toe, then back again. "My dear, you do not look the sort to lie around all day doing nothing," he said, chuckling. "First, I notice that your hair is bleached golden by the sun. Secondly, is that a trace of oil beneath your nails? I would wager that when you're not outdoors doing your daily chores you are in the lighthouse assisting your father while your mother takes care of things like cooking and cleaning." He raised an eyebrow at her. "Am I right?"

A stab of loneliness tore at Eden's heart. She lowered her eyes. "My mother has been dead for ten years now," she murmured.

Her fingernails came into view and she sucked in a wild breath when she recalled what Zach had just said about them. He had seen the damnable oil that she could not remove from them no matter how hard she tried! She had always been self conscious about this, but she had been so taken by this man she had forgotten to try to hide her hands from him.

Clenching her hands into tight fists, she looked up at him, smiling awkwardly.

"I'm sorry about your mother," Zach said quietly. "I see the hurt in your eyes at the mention of her. Would you like to tell me about her? Sometimes it helps to talk hurts out of the heart, at least for the moment." He smiled at her again. "I'm a good listener, Eden."

Eden nodded silently, returning his relaxed smile. "Yes, I'm sure you are," she said softly. "And, yes, I would love to tell you about my mother. She was very special to me." She cleared her throat and stared ahead. In her mind's eye she was seeing her vivacious mother as she was those ten years ago.

"My mother was very kind and sweet," Eden began. "She was beautiful. But she worked too hard. When she wasn't being a wife and mother, she was my father's assistant lightkeeper. She would stand her watches and when not actually tending the lamp she would sit at the open door at the bottom of the spiral stairway and sew by the light that came down through the clockwork weight hole in the deck of the lantern."

Eden swallowed hard.

"Mother did everything with energy," she continued, her voice strained. "She did not hesitate to make dozens of trips a day up and down the lighthouse stairs."

Eden clasped her hands tightly in her lap and looked down at them.

"One day while mother was hurrying up those stairs, she collapsed," she said, a sob lodged in her throat. "But it wasn't the fall that killed her. It was her heart. Her heart would not continue to keep up. She must have had a weak heart all along, but no one would have guessed it from the pace she kept up. It . . . just . . . quit beating that day."

"I'm so sorry," Zach said, having heard the pain in her voice. "How tragic for you." He placed a forefinger to her chin and turned her face toward him. "I was wrong. I shouldn't have encouraged you to speak of your mother. I had no idea it would cause you such pain. Forgive me?"

Eden wiped a stray tear from her cheek. She laughed softly. "Yes," she said. "You're forgiven."

Zach toyed with the horse's reins. "Eden, you never answered me before when I asked if you would allow me to come and call on you," he said. "May I?"

A slow, happy blush rose to Eden's cheeks. She thrilled inside as never before in her life. There was a curling heat at the pit of her stomach, as though a burst of sunshine was touching her all over.

Her dimples deepened into exquisite pools as she smiled up at Zach. "Yes, I would love for you to," she murmured. "Oh, so very much, Zach."

Zach's eyes sparkled. He straightened his

back proudly, returning her smile. "Then I shall," he said, nodding. "Tomorrow, Eden. Tomorrow."

"I shall look forward to seeing you," Eden said, lowering her eyes bashfully.

"You never did tell me how you spent your days," Zach said, drawing in a leisurely breath, pleased with himself. He would not let anything spoil this newly found happiness. Not even fear that Eden might discover his past. His past could not continue to haunt him forever.

"How much time do you spend in the lighthouse?" he quickly added. "Are you your father's assistant?"

Eden was again conscious of her stained nails. She smiled at Zach, glad that he had not made mention of them a second time.

"Yes, though it is considered a man's job, dangerous and rugged, I am the assistant keeper," she said softly. "At times I've even thought I might one day assume the title of Keeper of the Light."

She lowered her eyes. "But at other times I think that isn't at all what I would like to do with my life." She looked quickly up at him. "It's not at all a womanly career, is it?"

She unfolded her fingers and stared down at her stained nails. "It's not the cleanest profession in the world either," she said wistfully.

Zach glanced down at her. "Well, as to whether or not being a Keeper of the Light is a womanly career, I guess that depends on the woman," he said hoarsely.

He looked back at the road, his spine suddenly stiff. "Some women might choose the career of homemaker and wife." He gave her another quick glance. "Yes, I would say it depends on the woman."

Eden looked slowly up at him. "And which would you think is best suited for me?" she asked, her voice quavering.

Zach turned to her. Their eyes met and held. "Which is best suited for you?" he said thickly. "Whatever your heart leads you into doing. If it leads you into being a 'Wickie', I'll be the first to stand behind your decision. If it leads you into being a wife, I hope I'll have reason to congratulate you on your choice of husband."

Feeling that the conversation was becoming much too personal, Eden cleared her throat nervously. "So many people do use the term 'wickie' when talking about the keepers of lighthouses," she said, attempting to change the subject. "Of course, they call the keepers 'wickies' because of their constant vigilance in caring for their lights."

Thoughts of the storm earlier in the day came to Eden's mind, and then the memory of the pirate ship fighting the heavy waves. She turned her eyes quickly to Zach. "Zach, during the storm today, my father's beam found a ship battling to keep afloat in the raging sea."

She turned and faced him, clasping her hands together on her lap. "Zach, it was a pirate's ship. Can you imagine? There are still pirates in these waters. And so close to our lighthouse! What if it had sunk? The pirates would have been forced to swim to shore. My father and I would have been forced to rescue them and to give them shelter. I wonder if the pirates would have killed us?''

Zach's eyes had grown cold as she spoke, and now she shivered beneath his gaze. Then she breathed more easily as an apology replaced the ice in their dark depths.

"You said that you saw a pirate ship," Zach said smoothly, his heart thundering wildly within his chest. "How can you be certain?''

"There is much gossip about Pirate Jack's ship having been sighted in these waters," she said softly. "The description of Pirate Jack's ship matched the one we saw exactly. There's no doubt at all that it was he.''

Eden was now wondering over the anxious look etched on Zach's handsome face. Was he afraid of pirates? Was this the reason he was so suddenly ill at ease? He was a powerful-appearing man. Surely nothing would frighten him. Not even pirates.

"Zach, does it bother you much that Pirate Jack is near?'' she asked guardedly. "Do you fear him? Do you hate the pirates as much as I do?''

Zach laughed throatily. "Afraid?'' he said. "No. I'm not afraid of pirates, and no, I do not hate them. These are men whose lives are cloaked in the sea mists, as mysterious as the sea itself. Crude and violent though they often are, they can be abundantly generous to those whom they like and trust.''

43

He paused and looked over at her. "Some pirates have been known to shower jewels and Arabian gold on the liquor traders," he said, as though in deep thought. "Shipmates who have lost eyes or limbs in combat have been allowed to live on board for as long as they chose. Some pirates are sort of Robin Hood figures, giving to the poor, taking from the rich."

Eden's eyes were wide with wonder, in awe of how much Zach knew about pirating.

Again he seemed a man of mystery, yet she could no more turn her back on him than deny herself another breath. She was mesmerized by him, by all the facets of his personality. She knew that he was going to bring excitement to her life. He already had.

Zach sensed Eden's wonder. He reached out and took one of her hands. "My dear, never judge anyone until you actually get to know him," he said hoarsely. "That could apply even to a pirate." His dark eyes became fathomless. "Can't you understand how a man can be lured by the far horizon? The promise of a new tomorrow?"

Eden blinked her eyes and swallowed hard, recalling that he had said he'd been a world traveler. Piracy took men all over the world.

Oh, but surely he hadn't been . . .?

"Charleston shouldn't be far ahead," Zach said, changing the subject. He suddenly feared that he had spoken too knowledgeably of piracy. He had to learn to be more careful.

"What do you say we leave your wheel for repairs?" Zach suggested. "Then we can part long enough for me to go to Ryan's Barracoon to attend the slave auction, and for you to do whatever you came to Charleston to do."

"I've come to get a gift for my father's birthday and fresh supplies so that I can make him a cake," Eden said. "And I want a new diary for myself."

Zach looked over at her with interest. "Oh? Do you keep a daily journal of your feelings and activities?" he asked.

Eden laughed absently. "No. Nothing like that," she said, smoothing a windblown lock of hair back from her eyes. "I use diaries for logging my collection of ferns."

"Oh? You are a horticulturist as well as an assistant lightkeeper?" Zach said, admiration in his voice. "You are a busy woman, at that."

"My passion is mainly ferns," Eden said.

"Oh?" Zach said, chuckling at the word she'd used. "I see."

"As I was saying," she continued, moving uneasily on the seat, "I love to grow and study ferns. I find that my rewards are spiritual. You see, there is a difference between producing something that sustains the body and something that sustains the soul. In my fern garden there is nourishment for the soul."

"How interesting a comparison," Zach said, impressed. "It's good to see a person live life to the fullest and enjoy what she does."

Eden's attention was drawn away from Zach and talk of ferns. Ahead, Charleston loomed before her like a city in a fairy tale, and today her visit would be enhanced by the man at her side.

Chapter Four

Thy smiles can make a summer.
                    —JEFFRYS

The air was seductively soft as it blew in from Charleston Harbor, a trace of ginger mingling with the salt scent of the sea. Wide-eyed, Eden watched the houses pass beside her as the horse's hooves struck the cobblestones along the narrow, oleander-lined, sun-drenched streets. The old houses by the sea were large and airy, built mainly of wood. Many of them were two- and three-storied, with piazzas running the length of the upper stories. They had been built gable end to the streets with ornate, wrought-iron gates opening into private walled gardens.

"It's a quaint, beautiful city, isn't it?" Zach said, his pulse racing.

Yes, to him the city was beautiful, but his troubled past in Charleston wasn't. Everywhere he looked he was seeing familiar streets that he had roamed barefoot and penniless as a child. He was seeing doorsteps on which he had stood, begging.

If he let himself, he could still hear his aunt screeching at him before she whipped his bare bottom. His brow beaded with perspiration even now to recall how he had suffered.

And then there was the part of his past that was warmed by the presence of Angelita . . .

Eden sighed. "Yes, Charleston is beautiful. I love it," she said, interrupting Zach's troubled thoughts. "Each time I come I find myself falling in love with it all over again." She gestured with a hand. "Just look at the churches and the public buildings. Don't they look just like the Greek and Roman temples you see in books?"

"Much of this city reminds me of Spain," Zach said, glad to turn his thoughts elsewhere. He was glad to be able to recall his travels, which had taken place after he had been set free from his aunt's bondage. During his wandering days he had known happiness for the first time in his life.

He looked toward the bay. "Many a ship moored at the quay has been to Spain and back. Since the 1790's sailing ships from Europe have followed the trade winds in a wide southern loop through the West Indies. I am sure this harbor has seen its fair share of ships that come from America."

As they moved farther into Charleston, Eden again became swept up in viewing the city. She admired anew the pink and white and pale blue houses with their bulging iron grilles at the windows, the balconies and arcades and tiled roofs. The town crier was making his rounds and a bell in a church tower rang with a familiar tone.

The buggy rattled along the cobblestones and passed beside Charleston's huge open-air market where street vendors were busy selling their wares. Vegetables were piled high on carts in all shapes and colors. Flies crawled over the meat in sun-splashed booths, making Eden shudder with distaste.

"I have heard that a potion made from a cactus plant is sold in one of these open-air markets, with a guarantee of dulling homesickness," Zach said, giving Eden a slow smile as she looked quickly over at him. "Would you like to try a sample? Or would you like a glass of wine from one of those vendors?"

Eden laughed, flipping her hair back from her shoulders. "No, I don't care for either wine or a potion," she said. "But I do feel the need to get to the blacksmith shop." A feeling of anxiety struck her. "What if the blacksmith can't even repair my wheel? I can't afford to purchase a brand new one. What if I am forced to return home without my buggy? I fear my father would never forgive me."

Zach reached over, took her hand and squeezed it affectionately. "Don't fret so," he reassured her. "If your wheel can't be repaired I will see to it that you have a brand new one to take its place."

"You would do that for me?" Eden murmured. "Truly?"

"Truly," Zach said, laughing softly. "Didn't you take me seriously when I said that I would come calling tomorrow? That should tell you how much I care for you. And when I care for a lady, I will go to the ends of the earth for her."

Jealousy stung Eden's heart. "Oh, so you have been involved before with a special lady?" she asked.

Zach's brow creased into a frown. "No, none," he said thickly. "Eden, you are the first." He winked at her as he drew rein beside the blacksmith shop. "Do you think your intriguing name has something to do with my fascination?"

Eden's lips parted, then she laughed. "I believe you are going to tease me about my name forever," she said. She shrugged casually. "But I am used to it. If only mother had named me something more ordinary— perhaps Jane or Susan. Surely there would be no reason to wonder over such a name as that."

"No, no reason at all," Zach said, stepping down from the buggy, "unless it happened to belong to a woman as beautiful as you."

Zach went to Eden and placed his hands on her waist. Lifting her from the buggy, his eyes met hers and held. "You are so damn beautiful," he said hoarsely, still holding her as she stepped down onto the road. "After our business is tended to, will you have tea and perhaps something wickedly sweet with me? It would be nice to spend a quiet moment alone before heading back home."

Eden's pulse was racing. "That would be lovely," she murmured. It had been so long since she had accepted any sort of invitation from a man. And this invitation was from Zach . . .

The sound of the blacksmith's hammer and the neighing of hobbled horses drew Eden from her reverie. She winced when, out of the corner of her eye, she saw sparks fly from the shop behind her. With a start, she turned and saw a blacksmith fabricating an object out of iron by hot and cold forging on an anvil.

"I'll get the wheel," Zach said, swinging away from her. "Be careful of the sparks if you go into the shop."

Eden nodded, then slowly walked inside, intrigued by all of the activity there. The odor of scorched steel burned her nostrils. She placed her hands over her nose and stopped to watch the blacksmith at work. She recognized him. It was Smitty, the man who owned the shop and who had knowledge of lighthouse mechanisms. Whenever repairs were needed at the lighthouse, Eden's father always called upon this man for quality workmanship.

She remembered Smitty well, but she doubted if he knew her. When Smitty was at the lighthouse, Eden's father ordered her to stay in the cottage away from him. Her father trusted the man to work on his lighthouse, but not to be around his daughter. The man was a most filthy, undesirable person.

Eden had always done as her father had told her and had kept her distance from the man. She had only watched his comings and goings from the parlor window.

Busy shoeing, Smitty was sweating freely. His face was pinched and rugged, and his ankle-length apron black with grease and mire. He first cleaned and shaped the sole and rim of the horse's hoof with a rasp and a knife. Then he selected a U-shaped iron shoe of appropriate size from his stock and heated it red-hot in a forge, modifying its shape to fit the hoof. Cooling it by quenching it in water, he then affixed it to the hoof with nails.

Eden turned and, with a smile, welcomed Zach as he came to stand beside her, the broken wheel in his hands.

When Smitty was finished shoeing the horse, he glanced up at Eden and Zach. "What can I do for ye?" he asked, wiping his hands on his apron. He eyed the wheel and stepped closer, studying it.

"The wheel," Zach said, placing it on the ground before him. "Can it be repaired?"

Smitty bent to his knees and ran his fingers over the breaks in the wood. "Yup, it can be fixed," he said, nodding. "Ye gonna wait? Or come back later?"

Eden clasped her hands together behind

her. "Sir, how much will the repairs cost?" she asked.

"Well, as close as I can figure, it will be about—"

"The cost isn't important," Zach said, interrupting Smitty. He didn't want to worry Eden. This was her day to be carefree away from the isolation of lighthouse life. He placed an arm around her waist, looking down at her with a soft smile. "Just get it fixed. We'll be back in a couple of hours. Can you have it done by then?"

Smitty lifted the wheel. "Sure's hell can," he said with a merry grunt. "It'll be as good as new, too."

"So? Do you feel better about things now?" Zach asked, guiding Eden away from the shop. "You can go on your way and enjoy yourself, can't you?"

"Only because of you," Eden said, smiling up at him. "You are so very, very kind. How can I repay you?"

"Well, first by having tea with me in a little while and then by letting me come to call tomorrow," he said, winking down at her. "But of course you have already promised both of those things to me." He placed a finger to his brow and looked heavenward. "Now let's see, what else can I ask of you?" He brought his lips to her ear. "A kiss would do just fine."

Eden's eyes widened as she looked up into his gleaming eyes. "Now?" she gasped, blushing. "Here? In front of everyone?"

Zach threw his head back with a laugh, then swung away from her. "Not now," he said. "But I'll be sure to tell you when."

"Heaven forbid," Eden giggled.

Zach looked down the busy thoroughfare, seeing a crowd assembling around Ryan's Barracoon, the building where slaves were housed while awaiting sale. He did not look forward to the auction, but knew that he had no choice but to get slavehands for himself. No plantation survived without them.

He looked down at Eden. "I must be on my way," he said. "And you? You never did tell me what you planned to get your father for his birthday."

Eden's eyes sparkled and she lifted her chin proudly. "I hope to find the most special pipe in all of Charleston for my father," she said. "The stem of the one he uses now is riddled with teethprints because he has used it for so many years. He would enjoy a new pipe more than anything else that I could possibly buy for him."

"Well, then, good luck to you," Zach said, squeezing her hand one last time. "Shall I meet you in two hours here at the blacksmith shop?"

"I shall keep close watch on the time," Eden said, pleased to be making special plans with him. "I shall not be one minute longer." Her eyes sparkled. "I, too, look forward to having tea and that shamefully wicked dessert that you promised me."

"And shamefully wicked it will be," Zach

said, laughing along with her. His laughter faded and he gave her a lingering look.

"Till then, Eden," he said, turning to stride quickly away from her.

Eden's eyes followed Zach, loving the way the muscles of his legs flexed with each step and the way his shoulders filled out his suit jacket so powerfully. She already knew his strength. When he had held her in his arms, it was like nothing she had ever felt before.

When he was lost from view among the throng of people at the auction block, Eden turned away and went in the opposite direction, the skirt of her cape blowing in the wind.

Zach stood among the crowd, watching as each slave was brought to the front to be displayed. His insides grew cold when he saw how the men and women cowered and hung their heads as strange hands explored their bodies, their ankles in the grip of irons.

Dreading it, but knowing that he must, Zach took his turn to touch a man, feeling the sleekness of his dark body and the muscles rippling just beneath the flesh. He flinched when his fingers crossed welts inflicted by a whip, reminding him again of the many times he himself had been lashed.

Thank God he had been spared the scarring. His young flesh had healed quickly.

Dark eyes suddenly implored Zach as he caught sight of a young black woman waiting to be placed on the auction block. His insides were stirred with a keen resentment of a society that made slavery a thing to be taken so casually, as though one life was not as precious as another, no matter the color of the skin.

Stepping back, his jaw tight, Zach watched as the tall, statuesque woman stepped into place before the crowd. He admired her proud stance. She held her chin high, and her eyes were filled with fire as her dress was ripped down the front, letting her breasts fall free in their magnificent ripe roundness.

The crowd gasped. Men's mouths watered and their eyes became filled with lust as they waited a turn to touch and fondle her. Zach stood his ground, and her eyes once again met his, a soft pleading in their depths. At that look, an idea was born in Zach's brain.

Slipping his wallet from his hip pocket, Zach stepped forward. When he got to the woman, he held the wallet in one hand, while reaching inside her dress to touch the smooth flesh of her back with the other.

He stepped away from her and again looked up into her eyes. She had stiffened at his touch, but had stood still beneath his hand. There were no marks on her back. Though she showed defiance in her eyes, she had to have done something to save herself from the whip. No doubt her former master had bedded her.

Yes, she was smarter than most. She had a lot of fight in her, yet knew when to use it for her own benefit.

The bidding began. All the while he was bidding for her, Zach's and the woman's eyes were locked in silent battle. He went higher each time someone raised the bid. Over and over again he shouted out a figure.

And then suddenly there was silence, and she was his.

After paying for her, Zach waited for her to be brought to him. Once the irons had been removed from her ankles, leaving raw imprints in her skin, Zach ushered her away from the crowd. He sensed that he would have his hands full getting her home; he would not bid for any more slaves today.

"What's your name?" he asked, giving her a sideways glance.

"Sabrina," she said, her voice sultry, yet void of emotion.

"Hold your dress together in front," Zach said, moving close to her. "I think you've drawn enough attention for one day."

"Attention I nevah' asked fo'," Sabrina drawled. "You got yo' eyes full 'nuff, didn't you?"

"Only because I had chosen to bid for you," Zach growled, glad the blacksmith shop was in sight. Everyone was stopping to stare at this tall, statuesque slave who walked as proudly down the middle of the sidewalk as any white woman dressed in her best finery.

"But of course you have your own plans fo' me," Sabrina spat, looking at Zach with eyes of fire. "Why else would you have taken me and no Bucks? I sho' nuff hope you don't plan fo' me to do all of your plantin', fo' let me tell you, I ain't that much good in the fields."

She smiled slyly at Zach. "Sabrina has ways that no white woman knows, and it ain't in the fields," she said haughtily.

Zach glanced over at Sabrina, his eyes settling on her heaving breasts. "I'm sure you do," he said thickly. His eyes shifted upward. "But I hope I won't disappoint you when I say that I don't intend to discover the truth of your claim. I have someone else who just might, though."

Sabrina winced. She halted in her steps. "I sho' hope you don't have no crazy person waitin' for me," she said. "I would like to have you. No one else. I see kindness in yo' eyes that I mos' time don't see in a white man."

"You do speak your mind, don't you?" Zach said, shocked that she was so open.

"I ain't one to keep my mouth shut, if that's what you mean," Sabrina replied.

"Yes, that's exactly what I mean," Zach said. When he saw Eden walking toward him, blood rushed to his cheeks, for it was obvious that she was shocked to see him with Sabrina. Eden had known that he had gone to purchase slaves, but she would have expected him to have bought several, not just one—and a beautiful one, at that.

He watched Eden's gaze move slowly to Sabrina and then back to him. Surely she would come to the same conclusion as Sabrina. That he had chosen a female slave for all the wrong reasons.

Chapter Five

A heart whose love is innocent.

—BYRON

Her arms heaped with packages, Eden gaped openly at Zach and the woman at his side. Never before had she seen such a beautiful woman. Was this the true reason Zach had come to Charleston? To get himself not only field hands, but a special slave to play with during the long, lonely nights? It was no secret that some plantation owners bedded their female slaves.

The thought of Zach being that sort of man caused a weakness at the pit of Eden's stomach. Had she been wrong to think that he was so gentle, so kind? It was hard for her to believe that he was capable of forcing himself on a woman he had bought as though she were a piece of furniture.

Yet, did Eden truly know him at all? She had only just met him.

Eden stopped in front of the blacksmith shop as Zach and the slave made their way down the sidewalk. Her face turned crimson as her gaze lowered. The woman's breasts were all but exposed where her dress had been ripped down the front.

She looked quickly back at Zach. Had he ripped the woman's dress? Had his powerful hands cupped and kneaded the large breasts? Had his hands gone even lower, to feel the woman's intimate center?

Hardly able to bear any more thoughts of what Zach might have done, or planned to do once he got the slave to his plantation, Eden turned away quickly with a sob. She refused to look at him. It hurt too much. She had expected more from this man. She had envisioned herself running along the beach holding his hand, laughing with him. She had wanted this and oh, so much more.

She no longer knew how she felt about Zach. But one thing she did know. He could not have it both ways. He would not woo Eden one minute and bed the helpless slave the next.

Zach had seen Eden's reaction and understood only too well what she must have concluded. Hadn't it been in everyone's eyes? Every man and woman who had seen them walking together down the sidewalk had envisioned him taking this lovely wench to bed, forcing himself on her.

He cursed himself for not having bought a whole passel of slaves at today's auction. He could have hidden the beauty among the others and no one would have thought anything of it.

Since Eden was so obviously ignoring him, Zach stepped on past her. Sabrina trailing along behind him, he went into the blacksmith shop. He was intent on concluding the business at hand so that he would be free to explain things to Eden. She was still ignoring him, standing outside as stiff as a board, her face pinched with hurt.

He stepped up to Smitty. "Is that wheel repaired?" he asked, removing his wallet from his rear pocket.

"I said it would be, didn't I?" Smitty said, his eyes roaming over Sabrina, slowly up and slowly down.

Zach slapped several dollars into Smitty's hand. "This ought to pay for the wheel," he said. He looked over at Sabrina, then remembered promising Eden to go have tea. He looked back at Smitty. "I have business to attend to here in town. Will you keep an eye on my slave for a while? I paid you well enough to cover the inconvenience."

Zach made eye contact with Smitty. He didn't like the lust that was evident in his expression, but Zach had no choice but to chance leaving Sabrina with him. He needed time alone with Eden. He had a lot to explain to her, especially before he placed her and Sabrina in the same buggy for the journey from Charleston. Jealousy could cause a woman to do anything, and Eden was most definitely jealous.

Smitty counted the money, then slipped it in his rear pocket. He nodded. "I guess I can babysit your black wench for awhile," he said, leering at Sabrina. "You got yourself a beauty at the auction. Cain't understand why her last master decided to give 'er up." He wiped some drool from the corner of his mouth. "Perhaps she was just too hot for him to handle?"

Zach circled his hands into tight fists. He stepped closer to Smitty. "If you so much as touch her, so help me I'll knock your rotten teeth down your throat," he growled. "She's mine, bought and paid for, and if you have any trouble with that I'll not leave her here with you. I won't chance having her pawed by your greasy hands."

"I'd watch that mouth, lad," Smitty growled, his eyes squinting with anger. "It'll get you in a peck of trouble." He reached for Sabrina and yanked her to his side. "Now you paid to have her watched. Get on with you. She won't be damaged none. She'll be as good in bed tonight as she was last night."

The fact that Eden was waiting for him was the only thing that kept Zach from hitting Smitty. He turned on a heel and stormed from the blacksmith shop. He took a deep, shaky breath as he stepped to Eden's side.

She turned slowly and looked up at him, swallowing hard. "You came away from the auction with only one woman and no field hands," she said softly. "Zach, she cannot, alone, plant your crops."

She lowered her eyes. "But she can supply a man's other needs," she murmured. "Tell me that is not the reason you bid and paid for her, Zach. Tell me."

Zach clasped his fingers around her shoulders. She looked slowly up at him again. "Eden, I hate slavery," he said earnestly. "Slavery of all sorts. But I am forced to take part in it because I own a large piece of land that needs tending to. The reason I came away from the auction with only one slave today is that I have an overseer who is damn lonesome. He lost his wife and child on the way over from Africa. I'm hoping this woman will fill the void in his life. He is a kind man. He won't force himself on her." He smiled slowly down at her. "You see, he's one handsome fellow. She'll be the one who won't be able to stay away from him."

Relief washed through Eden like soft, effervescent waves sliding peacefully onto shore. "Oh, how wonderfully sweet of you," she said, dropping her packages to throw herself into his arms. "Zach, I knew you couldn't be guilty of anything ugly. You just couldn't."

Easing his hands around her waist, Zach held her to him. His brow was furrowed, wondering what she would think if she ever discovered the deeds of his past. She would be quickly disillusioned about him. She might even despise him. If God was fair, she would never, never know.

"Let's go and get that tea and dessert I promised you," he said in a hot whisper against her cheek. "Surely you're famished after your shopping spree."

He released her and stooped to collect her packages from the sidewalk. "And did you find exactly what you wanted while shopping?" he asked, smiling up at her.

Eden's heart missed a beat. She reached for the package that held the pipe she had purchased for her father. Had the stem broken off when she dropped the package?

Her anxious fingers opened it. She sighed with relief when she withdrew the pipe and saw that it was still in one piece. She held it out for Zach to see, proud. "Isn't it just too perfect?" she said anxiously. "The bowl is made of briarwood, the root of a species of heather." She placed it to her nose and sniffed. "Doesn't it smell heavenly?" Again she held it out and admired it. "And see how it is so beautifully carved? My father will adore it!"

Zach chuckled. "Men don't adore things," he said. "Only women adore."

Eden giggled and slipped the pipe back into the package. "Anyway, don't you think the pipe is perfect?" she said, gathering some of the packages back in her arms so that Zach would not be burdened down by them all. "Do you think my father will like it?"

"Yes, I think it's a perfect birthday gift,"

Zach said, sweeping his empty arm around her waist and guiding her away from the blacksmith shop.

He glanced over his shoulder, unable to shake a feeling of uneasiness at having left Sabrina with the lecherous smith. But he did want this time alone with Eden.

His friend Joshua was not the only lonesome man at Zach's plantation. . . .

The inn was dark and intimate. Candles were burning low on tables draped with lace tablecloths. Hot tea in delicate porcelain cups and a pâte sucrée crust crowned with sugar-frosted grapes and served with a dollop of lightly sweetened whipped cream, sat on the table before Eden and Zach.

Eden's eyes twinkled at Zach. She placed her hands primly on her lap. "Zach, I have the distinct impression that life with you would never be boring," she said softly. "Am I wrong?"

"Perhaps you are right," Zach said, his lips lifting in a slow smile.

Eden's breath was stolen away when he took her hand and entwined his fingers through hers. Her pulse raced, her cheeks flamed with excitement. She was feeling foolish for having doubted Zach. Never had she met such a sweet man. He was exactly what she had dreamed of when conjuring up fantasies of white knights on dashing charges! He could surely be no less gallant.

"So you enjoyed your shopping spree,"

Zach said softly. "I'm glad. At times you must feel confined at Pirate Point Light Station. I doubt if the lighthouse cottage is all that could be desired, either. Most are small and cramped."

"I have learned to cope with all sorts of situations," Eden said, smiling over at him.

"I'm sure you have," Zach said, nodding. "You can even cope with rogues such as I."

Eden's lips parted in a slight gasp. "I don't think of you as a rogue," she said. "I am sorry if I made you think that I did. But when I saw that you had bought that beautiful slave, I—"

"Yes, I am sure everyone who saw us together made the same assumption," Zach said. He eased his hand from hers. "But I have learned not to be concerned about what others think. I do as my conscience leads me to do."

Zach speared a sugar-frosted grape with his fork. Eden scarcely breathed when he placed the grape to her lips. Her heart raced as she took the sweet morsel into her mouth.

While she chewed it slowly, she picked up her fork and speared a grape from her own dessert, then placed the grape to his smiling lips.

Eden's insides quivered strangely when Zach opened his mouth and swept his tongue out for the tasty morsel, then drew it inside, chewing slowly.

"It tastes almost as good as you look," he said huskily. "Wonderful."

"How kind of you to say that," Eden said, fighting a blush.

"I only say what is true," Zach replied, taking a sip of his tea.

"Always?" Eden asked, raising an eyebrow.

Zach laughed throatily. "Well, now, perhaps sometimes a little white lie is necessary."

Eden was reminded of her own white lie today—her journey into Charleston without her father's permission.

"They say that gluttony is one of the seven deadly sins," she said quickly, to forget her guilty feelings. "It's certainly one of my weaknesses, especially when it comes to sweets. And you?"

"One of my many," Zach said. Then, haunted by thoughts that had been troubling him all day, he asked a question he would not have felt free to ask anyone but Eden. "Do you know a woman named Angelita Llewellyn?" he asked her, reaching out to secure her hand within his. "She makes her residence here in Charleston."

The spell surrounding them was shattered instantly by his questioning her about another woman. Eden's throat went dry and an empty feeling invaded the pit of her stomach.

"Angelita?" she whispered, wondering why Zach had reached for her hand. Was it because he felt something special for her? Or was it because he wanted her to feel that he did, only to get answers from her about one of Charleston's most ravishing beauties? Eden's very best friend!

Her eyes flashed as she looked over at him. "Yes, I know Angelita," she said, her voice quavering. "Quite well." She wanted to ask him why he was asking, but she did not want him to know that she was jealous.

"How well do you know her? She's never been married, has she?" Zach asked, imploring Eden with watchful eyes. He could tell that his questions were unnerving her, but he had to continue. It was imperative that he knew if Angelita was all right. One day he hoped to be free to explain everything about him and Angelita to Eden. At present, he wasn't.

"No, Angelita is not married and never has been," Eden said, easing her hand from Zach's. She wanted to tell him that she knew Angelita very well and that Angelita was spirited and flirtatious and already had too many men dangling on a string for Zach to try to get involved with her. Eden even suspected that her father was infatuated with Angelita, though he was many years her senior.

But she couldn't find the words to tell Zach. If she did, he would see that she was jealous. If he was not interested in her in the way that he had claimed, then he must never know that she had special feelings for him.

"You speak of Angelita as though you know her very well," Zach said, picking absently at his dessert with his fork.

"Yes, you might say that," Eden said dryly. "Though Angelita and I are nothing alike and she is a few years older than I, we have become best friends. We met in a shop one day. We were both purchasing microscopes for examining fern specimens. You see, she has the same hobby as I. We've shared many outings in the forest while searching for unique ferns."

Zach's eyes shot up. His jaw went slack. "Angelita is your best friend?" he gasped. "Eden, I didn't know."

"Didn't you?" she said, her eyes wavering. She was just about to accuse him of many things, but her thoughts were interrupted when an old friend of her father's came into the inn.

Eden looked up and smiled at Sefton Pryor, a well-known Charleston judge. "Good afternoon, sir," she said.

Then her smile faltered when she realized the position she was in. If Judge Pryor told her father that he had seen her, then all future jaunts into Charleston were doomed.

She cringed when he stopped at the table and tipped his tall, dark hat to her. The diamond stickpin pinned into the satin cravat at his throat sparkled in the light of the candle.

Attired in a dark suit with an embroidered vest, he flaunted the wealth that he had amassed in his earlier life as a sea captain. He was short and squat, his hair graying. A scar on his upper lip, that puckered as he spoke, made him look as though he had a harelip.

"Why, Eden, it is you, isn't it?" Judge Pryor said, smiling down at her. "Is your father in town? I have a few things I'd like to discuss with him. He told me something about wanting a Fresnel lens for your lighthouse. I'm fascinated by that lens myself. Only a few lighthouses are using them."

Zach's insides were frozen as he waited for Eden to introduce the Judge to him. He couldn't afford such introductions. Recognition could be fatal! Slowly he inched his chair back. If he recognized the Judge after all these years, surely the Judge could recognize him, as well.

Zach cupped a hand over his mouth. In order to hide his identity behind the hand, he pretended to be choking on something. He coughed, then excused himself and rushed from the inn, leaving Eden gaping after him.

She slid her chair back, grabbed her cape and packages and hurried after him. "I'm sorry, Judge Pryor," she said over her shoulder. "My friend is suddenly ill. I must go to him. I will talk with you later."

"Give your father my regards," Judge Pryor said, waving after her. "Tell him I'll drop by soon for a chat."

Eden's shoulder muscles tightened. She did not respond to the Judge. With any luck he would forget their brief meeting by the time he called on her father again. The Judge's visits had become rare since he had become involved in state politics. He had his eye on the Governor's mansion. He was doing anything and everything to draw attention to himself. She had not known that he could be so aggressive. Some now even called him dangerous.

Then her heart skipped a beat. Oh, but how could she have forgotten? The Judge had been invited to her father's birthday party! The Judge would be at the cottage in only a few days. Would he reveal her venture into Charleston without knowing how much he would be condemning her by doing it?

Brushing the worry aside for now, Eden stepped outside into the rush of people along the busy thoroughfare. She looked desperately from side to side, searching for Zach.

When she saw him walking hurriedly toward the blacksmith shop, she rushed after him. She was more confused now than ever before about him. First there were the questions about Angelita, then there was his strange reaction to Judge Pryor. Zach had not fooled her at all by pretending to be choking on something. He had wanted to flee from the Judge.

But why?

Catching up to Zach, Eden clutched his arm. "Zach, what was that all about?" she asked, breathing hard from running. "Are you all right?"

"I'm fine," Zach growled. He glanced down at her with a wounded look in his eyes. "Don't ask me to explain why I had to leave the inn so quickly. I had no choice."

"It had to do with Judge Pryor, didn't it?" Eden persisted. "Why, Zach? Please tell me. My father and the Judge have been friends for years."

Zach groaned and shook his head. "That's

nice to hear," he said, raking his fingers through his hair.

"Zach, what is it?" Eden asked again. "Perhaps I can help you if you tell me what the problem is."

Zach looked over his shoulder in the direction of the inn. He saw the Judge at the window, looking at him. Had the Judge recognized him? If so, Zach's new life would not be worth a tinker's dam. The first time they'd met, years ago, the Judge had been a sea captain. Zach had been a—

Grabbing Eden by the elbow he rushed her into the blacksmith shop. He turned her to face him, grabbing her shoulders. "Eden, I know I don't make much sense half of the time," he said thickly. "All I ask is that you trust me. Will you?"

Eden's eyes wavered. "I want to so badly," she murmured.

"Then do it," Zach said, desperation in his voice. "Eden, I need you. Damn it, I need you."

"Oh, I so want to believe you," Eden said, a sob in her throat. "But, Zach, why—oh, why must you be so mysterious?"

A commotion from somewhere behind them drew them apart. Zach searched for Sabrina, feeling a cold rage seize him when he saw neither her nor any of the blacksmiths.

Storming past the anvils and neighing horses waiting to be shoed, he went into the back room and faltered when he saw Sabrina on a bunk against the far wall. She was being held down by two young men, her dress hiked up past her waist. Smitty was standing before her, his breeches unfastened and hanging past his knees.

Eden rushed into the room, then felt faint when she saw Smitty about to rape Sabrina. She closed her eyes and swallowed back a bitterness that had risen into her throat, turning her back to the horrible scene.

Zach's mind was spinning. The first thing he felt inclined to do was to kill the blacksmith. But he was remembering Judge Pryor. If Zach caused a disturbance here with the blacksmith, he could kiss his own freedom goodbye.

He had no choice but to settle this peacefully, though every fiber of his being cried for action. He longed to slam his fist into the blacksmith's fat jowls.

"Let her up," Zach said in a low growl that reverberated around the room. "Get away from her, you sonofabitch. You forget who paid top dollar for her today. It sure as hell wasn't you."

Eden was trembling. She turned slowly around and looked at Zach, puzzled by his coolness. She'd expected him to physically attack all three men.

Sabrina looked up at Zach, her eyes empty of emotion. When the blacksmith moved away from her and the two young men released her wrists, she dropped her dress to hide her nudity and rose shakily to her feet. With her chin held high she pulled her dress together in front to hide her breasts and went to stand beside Zach.

"Let's get out of here," Zach said in a low growl, flashing Smitty a look of fire. It took all the willpower he could muster not to bash the blacksmith in the face when Smitty smiled smugly at Zach, fastening his breeches as though he had done nothing wrong.

"You poor thing," Eden said, sidling closer to Sabrina as they left the blacksmith shop. "How horrible for you."

Sabrina looked straight ahead, silent. Zach lifted the repaired wheel into the back of his buggy, then helped Sabrina in the back with it. Taking Eden's elbow he helped her up onto the buggy seat, then strode angrily to the driver's side and sat down beside her.

Zach slapped his horse with the reins. The buggy rattled away from the blacksmith shop over the cobblestone street. He grew cold inside when he saw Judge Pryor outside the inn, his eyes following Zach until the buggy made a turn and went rumbling down another street, away from the business district.

Eden had seen Judge Pryor watching Zach so intently.

She could not help but wonder why.

Judge Pryor stood over a desk littered with papers and ledgers. He cleared a space and splayed his hands against solid oak, leaning closer to Admiral Johnston's face.

"I know a way to rid the seas of Pirate Jack," Judge Pryor said dryly, his gray eyes gleaming. The scar on his lip drew up as he smiled. "Have you a ship and crew to spare? If you go along with my plan, I would like to know I have both a ship and crew at my disposal to do with as I see fit."

Admiral Johnston, a man of distinction in both appearance and speech, looked up at the Judge. Sliding his chair back from his desk, he rose. He went to a liquor cabinet and poured wine into two tall-stemmed glasses. He took one to the Judge and kept one for himself.

"Tell me your plan, Judge," he said, easing back down in his chair. "And why you are willing to become involved in this vendetta against the old pirate." He smiled slowly up at Judge Pryor. "No. I don't think you need to tell me your reason for doing this. It's all political, isn't it? It would be a way to put yourself in a favorable light with voters."

Judge Pryor reached a hand to the scar on his lip. "No, the reason is not all political," he growled. "It's personal."

"Well, whatever the reasons," Admiral Johnston said, twirling the wineglass between his fingers. "Let's hear the plan. I'm sure I won't have trouble with it. I'm damn sick of that pirate. Whatever it takes, I want the seas rid of him."

"Then you will agree readily to what I have to propose," Judge Pryor said.

Chapter Six

To love and be beloved!
                    —EMERSON

Eden stood beside her buggy while Zach attached the last bolt, firmly securing the wheel. She glanced over her shoulder at Sabrina, who still sat in the back of Zach's buggy. She had not breathed a word since they had left Charleston. Her eyes were locked straight ahead.

It gave Eden a feeling of emptiness to think of Sabrina being exposed to Smitty, the man who had often worked so closely with her father making repairs at the lighthouse. Smitty was nothing but a vile, sick man—one she hoped never to come face to face with again! To think what Sabrina must have been through during her short lifetime sickened

Eden. Sabrina was surely not much older than she was.

"I think your buggy is as good as new," Zach said, wiping his hands on his handkerchief. "It didn't get you to Charleston but it will get you back home safe and sound."

"I can't thank you enough for helping me, Zach," Eden said, transferring her packages from his buggy to hers. "I don't know what would have happened had you not come by when you did. I even dread thinking about it."

"Well, I did come along and I'm glad you don't think you're worse off because of it," Zach said, placing his handkerchief back in his rear trousers pocket. He took Eden's hand and drew her around to face him. "I hope the invitation holds for tomorrow. I'd like to come and call on you."

Eden looked up at him, recalling all of her doubts about him. Why had he asked so many questions about Angelita Llewellyn? Why had he become so alarmed by the presence of Judge Pryor in the inn? Why had he known so much about pirates?

There were too many things about Zach that confused Eden, yet she could not deny that she wanted to be with him. Hope was rising inside her again. If he was truly infatuated with Angelita, wouldn't he be asking to see her, not Eden?

Eden would not believe that he was asking to see her again because she was Angelita's best friend! He was not the sort to be bashful with women. He would have no reason to court the friend of a woman he was infatuated with. He would go straight to the source.

"Yes, do come tomorrow, Zach," Eden blurted out, then frowned up at him. "But when you come, please pretend that you have stopped by to introduce yourself as our new neighbor. My father must not know about my trip to Charleston."

In Zach's mind's eye he was seeing Judge Pryor and recalling that Eden had said he was a friend of her father's. How good a friend? Was Zach taking a chance by going to meet Eden's father? Would her father tell the Judge about him?

It was a chance that he would have to take. He could not keep his head hidden in the sand like an ostrich for the rest of his life.

"I think I can manage that," he said.

"Wonderful," Eden said, her eyes brimming with happiness. "You can have tea with me and father, and if you like, you can go up in the lighthouse. Most people find it fascinating and want to see how it works."

She paused and measured her next words very carefully, wanting to see his reaction. "Why, Zach, you might even get a glimpse of the elusive pirate ship," she said softly. "You know—the ship owned by the damnable Pirate Jack."

Zach's jaw tightened and he eased his hands from hers, his eyes darkening. "Yes, that could be interesting," he said smoothly, realizing that he was being baited and not liking it one damn bit.

But it was not Eden's fault that she had been given cause to doubt him. He had foolishly spoken too openly of his feelings about piracy. He could see in her eyes, he could tell by how she spoke of piracy to him now, that she had suspicions of his having been a pirate himself. It was up to him to erase all doubts and wonder from her mind.

Tomorrow he would be given that opportunity and he would grab it. With each breath and heartbeat, he was beginning to realize how important Eden was to him.

He must have her.

And he would.

Eden had sensed Zach's withdrawn attitude over her mention of the pirate again and this made her suspicious that Zach's life had been touched somehow by pirates. Had it been a pleasant encounter? Or had he been forced into something ugly?

She hoped he would confide in her. She would give him every reason to, tomorrow. With each breath and heartbeat, she was beginning to realize how important he was to her.

She must have him.

And she would.

Without warning, Zach swept Eden into his arms and feathered soft kisses along her delicately chiseled features. "Until tomorrow," he breathed against her parted lips. "It's been a day to remember, Eden."

Drowning in ecstasy, Eden wove her fingers through Zach's hair and drew his lips into hers. Wondrous feelings ravaged her as he kissed her passionately. The years of waiting for the right man, of anticipating what it would be like to be in love, heightened her desire.

As Zach placed a hand to her breast and slowly caressed it, she could feel her body ache in places no one had ever touched before. . . .

Trembling, afraid, Eden broke away. Her face was flushed, her eyes were wide; she wondered how she could be capable of such feelings. She tried to control the nervous pounding of her heart by taking a deep breath.

Zach clasped his fingers to her shoulders. "Though I promised never to do that again, I could not help myself any more than you could help responding. There is no reason to be alarmed over our feelings for each other," he whispered. "There is something between us that cannot be denied. This is new for me. I can tell that it's new for you. Doesn't that tell you something, Eden?"

"So very much," Eden said in almost a whisper. "But is it truly right? We only met this morning. How can we feel so strongly, so quickly?"

"Because it is meant to be," Zach said in a sigh. He gave her another brief kiss, then looked over at Sabrina. "I truly must go, Eden. I've someone else to tend to now. I may have bought myself a handful with that one over there."

Eden looked over at Sabrina, glad that Zach was not going to lay claim on her other than being his slave.

But a reminder of another woman teased her senses. What was his interest in Angelita? Oh, dear Lord, what? Eden knew Angelita too well, knew her seductive ways with men, and she wondered how she could hold onto Zach once he met Angelita.

When Angelita wanted a man, she got him.

"Sabrina seems calm enough," Eden said, nodding a silent thank you to Zach as he helped her up into her buggy. "I'm sure she won't cause you any problems. She will soon know what the word gentle means." She placed her hand to Zach's cheek. "Just as I have today."

Zach winked up at her, then turned and went to his buggy and climbed onto the seat. Taking the reins, he gave his gelding a quick flick, then nodded a good-bye to Eden.

Eden waved, feeling warm inside when she thought of tomorrow, and what it would bring her. She would be with Zach again.

Then she frowned. What if her father didn't believe that Zach had come only to introduce himself? What if her father, in his wisdom, figured out by the way Zach and Eden behaved toward each other that they had met before? Would he even be able to tell that they were already in love?

Sighing, not wanting to let anything spoil the wondrous feelings flowering inside her, Eden slapped her reins against her own horse.

She made a wide turn with her buggy in the road and headed toward the lighthouse.

Zach guided his gelding into a long lane lined by a row of large oaks on each side, and at the far end saw his great, white-columned mansion. He squared his shoulders proudly and slapped the reins harder against the horse's back, sending him into a faster trot. How many years ago had he thought that he would die young and poor? How many lashes had he bent beneath before finally finding some measure of freedom aboard a great pirate ship?

Oh, how he had dreamed of the day that he would be his own man—have his own home! Along with his pride and freedom, all that had been stolen from him the day his father died. But his strong will to live had never died. Nor had his ambition.

And now? Could it be taken from him so quickly again? Would Judge Pryor send the law after him? Or would he let the past stay dead?

"You is a wealthy man, isn't you?"

Zach was jolted from his thoughts when Sabrina suddenly chose to say her first word since leaving Charleston. With a forked eyebrow, he looked at her over his shoulder. "So you have regained your ability to speak, I see."

Sabrina flashed him a sour glance, flipping her long, thick, windblown hair back from her face. She clung to the side of the buggy, on her knees behind him. "Sometimes Sabrina talks, sometimes she doesn't," she spat. "Mos' white men I've eva' known don't want me to talk. You say you have no plans to use me." She laughed sarcastically. "Of course that's a lie. You're filled with passion. I could hear your heavy breathing while you kissed your woman. Such passions must be released in ways other than kissing. Tonight you'll use me. You knows it."

"Sabrina, first you don't talk at all, and then you talk much more than should be allowed," Zach said, frowning back at her. He truly was not angry at her for being so open. In fact he admired her for it. Being imprisoned in the mind was even worse than being imprisoned by chains. He understood both sorts of imprisonments. He admired her courage, yet with some who might have owned her, it could have proven fatal.

"And for this you will be the first to scar my back?" Sabrina hissed, realizing that she was being disobedient, as she had been to her past masters. But she was not afraid. She had discovered with even her first master that behaving in this way got her more privileges than cowering down to him.

Somehow, her pride in herself had made the men admire and respect her. Most had felt so strongly about her that eventually she had begun to threaten their own existence. Men had wanted her so strongly that they had wanted her to live with them as a wife, yet had known that this was not possible. Any white man who took a black woman for a wife would be disgraced. It had been easier to sell her into slavery again . . . and again. . . .

Zach did not respond to Sabrina's question. His eyes were directed to a dark man riding toward him on a strawberry roan. Seeing Joshua so tall and free in the saddle consumed Zach with memories of the first time he had seen the slave. He choked back a tightness in his throat when he remembered Joshua manacled to the wall in the hold of the slave ship. His eyes had been wild, his dark, muscular body covered with sweat and grime. His wrists and ankles had been covered with blood where the irons had cut into his flesh, and rats swarmed in the filth at his feet.

"Zach!" Joshua shouted, waving, his strawberry roan growing closer to Zach's buggy.

Zach's thoughts were drawn from that day he had removed Joshua from the pits of hell to live the life of a normal man as Zach's friend, and now his overseer.

"Hello there, friend," Zach shouted. "It's been one helluva day. You should've been with me."

Zach saw Joshua's expression when he caught sight of Sabrina, her chin held proudly high. He frowned, realizing that getting Joshua to accept this woman he had bought for him would not be all that easy. Joshua had not been the only one imprisoned on that slave ship. His wife and three-year-old daughter had also been there—and had died there.

After Zach had set him free, Joshua had lost

count of how many days his loved ones had lain dead, with rats chewing their flesh. Zach could hear Joshua scream out in horror even now in the middle of the night as he relived those last ghastly days on the ship.

No, it would not be all that easy for Joshua to love another woman, for he had loved his wife too much. But he would. He needed a woman to rid him of the horrors of his past.

Drawing his reins taut, stopping the gelding, Zach looked up at Joshua as he wheeled his roan to a stop beside the buggy. It was there, the same haunted look in Joshua's eyes, as he looked down at Sabrina. It was evident that he was vividly recalling much that was unpleasant to him.

But suddenly Joshua's dark eyes softened and his jaw went slack as he stared at Sabrina, seeing her as any man would—lovely, vivacious and very seductive.

"You went to get fieldhands and this is what you bring home?" Joshua said dryly, looking Sabrina slowly up and down. It had been a long time since a woman had made a slow itch begin in his loins. But this woman and her sleek, firm body, with breasts that begged to be kissed, was causing Joshua to suddenly feel life again where, for so long, that part of him had lain dormant.

But he would not give in to such feelings. His wife was still too much on his mind. If he reached out and touched this seductive woman, surely it would be the same as being unfaithful, even now.

"Like I said before, it's been one helluva day," Zach said, looking from Joshua to Sabrina and back to Joshua again. "She is all I managed to get. I'll go back another day soon."

"She won't be able to plant much cotton seeds," Joshua said, his eyes still on Sabrina. "Why, I doubts if she eva' planted one seed in her life. As I sees her, most seeds have gone into her. I'm surprised she ain't got a youngun hangin' on her breast even now."

Sabrina wriggled from the back of the buggy and crawled to the front. She rose up on her knees and placed her hands on her hips, glowering at Joshua. "I have you know, Mista' Knows It All, that I ain't neva' had chillens." She spat angrily. "Nor will I have yours."

Zach groaned and rolled his eyes to the back of his head, knowing that Sabrina had said the wrong thing to Joshua. He looked over at her. "Sabrina, I think you're about to learn that you've met a man who won't take to your mouth all that much," he said. He turned and watched Joshua ride briskly away, toward the mansion. "I would choose my words very carefully with Joshua. He has many a deep hurt to trouble him. Talking mean and spiteful to him isn't going to work. He needs soft talking."

Sabrina plopped down on the seat, folding her arms stubbornly across her chest. "I don't care none about what he needs," she said, staring at Joshua as he rode away from her, watching his muscled form. His body filled out his cotton shirt and dark trousers so much that the fabric strained at the seams. His long, dark hair had framed a handsome face, his lips wide and sensual, his cheekbones high and firm. She had seen much in his eyes as he had studied her. He had liked her, yet he had been cold toward her.

She wanted to warm up to him, yet not too quickly. She still wanted to have the upper hand with a man—even a man of her own skin coloring.

Flicking the reins against the gelding's back, Zach rode on to the house. When he swung himself from the buggy, Joshua was there, waiting, his jaw set.

Zach went to the back of his buggy and withdrew a small package, which he slapped into Joshua's large hand. "Take this and deliver it for me, Joshua," he said flatly. "It goes to Angelita Llewellyn, just like the others we've sent. Be careful when you leave it on her doorstep. You know the dangers in being caught."

"Is it another necklace, Masta' Zach?" Joshua asked, weighing the package in his hand.

"No. This time it's a bracelet."

"Masta' Zach, did you see Angelita while you were in Charleston?"

Zach's eyes clouded with remembrances of Eden. "No, another lady was on my mind today," he said thickly.

Joshua glared over at Sabrina. "Her?" he said sourly.

"No. Someone else. I'll tell you about her

later," Zach said, going to Sabrina and looking her up and down. "For now, we'd best get this one settled in, don't you think?"

Joshua said nothing, just looked at Sabrina, fighting the feelings that were invading him. It had been so long since he had been with a woman. Oh, so long.

"Come on, Sabrina, I'll show you your cabin," Zach said, nodding for her to follow him. "Your torn clothes will have to make do today. I'll try and get you a change of clothes tomorrow. I think Eden won't mind parting with something for you."

He felt Joshua's eyes following him and Sabrina, wondering what was truly on his mind.

Feeling unusually vibrant and alive, Eden rushed into her bedroom and fell to her knees beside the bed. She lifted the spread and shoved her packages beneath the bed, then rose to her feet and sighed with relief. She had returned home before her father had risen from sleeping.

Slipping the cape from around her shoulders, then easing the pistol from its pocket, she replaced the firearm in her drawer, slung her cape over the back of a chair and hurried back out of her bedroom.

Her footsteps faltered and she took a shaky step backwards when she almost ran bodily into her father as he left his bedroom, yawning and leaning heavily on his cane.

Her palms grew clammy when she watched

as his eyes shot upward and he looked at her questioningly.

Preston immediately noticed something different about Eden. He tried to put his finger on just what it could be. Was it the sparkle in his daughter's eyes? Was it the rosy color of her cheeks? Or was it an aliveness about her that he had never seen before?

Or were all of those things making her especially vivacious this late afternoon?

Preston backed away from her, chuckling. "Eden, where were you going in such a rush?" he asked, squinting his eyes as he once again looked her over. "And what have you been up to while I was sleeping? There's something different about you."

Eden felt a pinprick of fear enter her heart. She had always known how observant her father was and had hoped that just this once he wouldn't be. But surely how she felt did show on her face, as though it were the mirror of her soul. How could she help it? She could not forget Zach's last kiss. It had lit up her insides like a torch and she doubted if anything could ever extinguish it. Even knowing he was subject to mysterious mood swings did not quell the nervous beat of her heart whenever she thought of him.

And how could she so blatantly lie to her father? What could she say just to hide the truth from him?

"What have I been up to?" Eden said, lowering her eyes. She glanced down at her fingernails and saw the stains. So often the soil from her garden joined the oil beneath her nails.

"I was doing many things," she said, challenging her father's studious stare with one of her own. "I was outdoors most of the time."

"Oh? You were gardening?"

"Well, some."

"I would've thought the ground would be too wet after the rain."

Eden's heart skipped a beat. She laughed awkwardly, then lifted her fingers for her father to see. "Yes, and I have learned to wait for the sun to dry the soil," she said. "I have gotten my fingernails into quite a mess."

She had not actually come right out and told him a lie. Not yet, anyhow.

Preston nodded, then reached for Eden and hugged her. "Well, at least the sunshine did you a passel of good," he said, patting her back. "I've never seen your cheeks as rosy."

Eden sighed heavily.

Judge Pryor stood at his office window that overlooked Charleston Harbor and the magnificent ships that were moored there. In his mind's eye he was recalling a day several years before when he had been on such a powerful ship, its proud captain, and pirates had overtaken it. While all of the pirates had been actively removing everything from the ship that was worth taking, he had been face to face with Pirate Jack, awaiting execution.

But it had never come. A younger pirate, a handsome man with dark hair and even darker eyes had spoken up in his behalf. Because of this young lad, Judge Pryor was alive today.

"But Pirate Jack still roams the seas," he growled, running a finger over the scar on his lip that the pirate had been responsible for. Though saved from being executed, he had not been spared a wound from the old pirate's knife.

"And what about the man you saw this afternoon?" Sheriff Collins asked, moving to stand beside the Judge, pistols heavy at both his hips. "A Zachary Tyson, didn't you say?"

Judge Pryor turned cold, gray eyes to Sheriff Collins. "Yes, Zachary Tyson, a name that has stayed with me through the years," he grumbled. "I discovered today that he must make residence close to Charleston. He was with Eden Whitney. Perhaps they are neighbors?"

"Do you want me to send some men to question Preston Whitney about the man, since Eden was seen with him today?" Sheriff Collins asked, his teeth sparkling white against his dark tan. "She could lead us to him if you are determined to talk with the man."

"Determined, yes, but cautious," Judge Pryor said, smoothing his hands over his graying hair. "This retired pirate must not discover that I intend to seek him out for questioning. I'm afraid that even the lovely Eden Whitney couldn't hold him at bay if he knew. He'd skip the country faster than you could wink an eye."

He turned and faced Sheriff Collins. "I can't allow that to happen," he said. "He's the only one that can lead me to Pirate Jack. And I must find that sonofabitch pirate. He must be stopped and not only because he's wreaking havoc all up and down the coast of America. I could be awarded a special commendation from the Navy if I were the one responsible for the old pirate being stopped." He smiled slowly. "Just think of the attention I'd get. It would be in all the newspapers."

"And? Besides political? What other reason do you have for wanting to rid the seas of that marauding pirate?" Sheriff Collins asked, taking a pistol from his holster, shining its barrel with his handkerchief. "That scar on your lip—didn't you once tell me the old pirate is responsible?"

Judge Pryor smoothed his fingers over his scar again, frowning. "Yes, the old pirate is the one who made my appearance anything but desirable to the ladies," he growled. "My wife grew used to it but now that she's dead, I find it hard to approach a beautiful lady because I feel that she is repelled by my appearance."

He doubled his fists and pounded them on his desk. "That pirate must be stopped!" he shouted. "Do you hear? Stopped."

"How can you get your hands on this man you saw with Eden today if you are hesitant in going to Preston or Eden to question them about him?" Sheriff Collins asked, flipping his gun back into his holster. He settled down in a sprawling chair beside the desk. He picked up a letter opener and began to run his finger down its smooth edge. "Even if you do find where Zachary Tyson lives, what do you plan to do about it?"

"Eden is going to lead us to the retired pirate without even knowing it," Judge Pryor said, sitting down at his desk. "Sheriff, send some of your men to go and keep a close watch on the lighthouse and cottage. Watch all comings and goings. See who comes and goes and if you see a man who fits the description I give you, let me know and then I will decide how to get him to give me the answers that I need."

"And if he refuses to cooperate with you?" Sheriff Collins asked cautiously.

"We'll have to lock him in jail until he does," Judge Pryor said, shrugging casually. "It won't take him long to talk after wallowing in that filth for a couple of days."

"We should get the cells cleaned up, you know," Sheriff Collins said, laughing throatily.

Judge Pryor smiled slowly over at him. "Yes, I know," he said slyly. "I know."

Chapter Seven

Leave me a little love.
——SANDBURG

The day was deepening to sunset. Downcast, Eden looked from the lighthouse window. Usually she admired the afternoon sun as it cast its last, rich light over the ocean.

But this evening she could not enjoy it. It meant the end of a day that had not produced Zach at her door as he had promised.

What had changed his mind? Had he not intended to come at all? Had his kisses and promises meant nothing? Had he pursued his interest in Angelita? Had he gone to her and found his own answers about her?

Remembering how she had so easily slipped into Zach's arms and had given her lips to him so willingly made Eden feel somehow soiled. Never had she given her affections so freely, or so unthinkingly. Never would she again. Let him have Angelita Llewellyn. He would find out quickly that Angelita tossed men away as though they were nothing but toys to discard when she tired of them.

Angry, she returned her attentions to her duties at hand. Rubbing furiously, she continued washing the glass of the lanterns with spirit of wine.

Preston paused from tending to the light mechanisms to study Eden. Earlier in the day she had been highly spirited and gay, flitting around the house while cooking breakfast as though it were going to be a special day. When Preston had started to go to bed, she had begged him not to go so soon, as though she had special plans for him this day.

To please her, he had waited up and had worked around the house and in the garden with her as long as he could keep his eyes open.

But by noon he had given in to his need for sleep and had left her alone, already seeing a change in her mood.

Even then he had wondered why.

"Eden?" Preston said, placing his key aside. He picked up his cane and walked over to her and took the bottle of spirit of wine from her. "At that rate, you're going to polish until there's no glass left."

He looked at her, seeing a seething anger in the depths of her eyes.

Or was he misreading her?

She was behaving as though someone had hurt her.

But who could have caused such a hurt?

Preston set the bottle of spirit of wine aside and kneaded his chin; none of Eden's behavior made any sense. He had noticed her sullenness when he had arisen from his afternoon sleep. She had been quiet and withdrawn, and at supper she had scarcely spoken a word to him.

"Want to tell me what's bothering you?" Preston asked, placing a hand to Eden's shoulder and turning her to fully face him. He smiled at her, seeing a smudge of grease on her face. He smoothed it away with his thumb. "You're not yourself at all, Eden. Has something happened that you're not telling me? Usually we have no secrets from each other."

Feeling shame for having deceived him more than once with her jaunts into Charleston, and even worse shame for yesterday, when she had let a perfect stranger embrace and kiss her, Eden swallowed hard and lowered her eyes. "Father, I . . ."

The sudden sound of footsteps on the staircase, moving upward, made Eden's words fade and her heart skip a beat. Both Eden and her father looked toward the closed trap door, then looked at each other questioningly.

"Seems we have an unexpected guest," Preston said, turning away from Eden. Leaning his full weight on his cane, he grabbed hold of the handle of the trapdoor and swung it open widely, letting it rest against the floor. He squinted his eyes, trying to see the visitor, but the approaching darkness had already stolen most of the light from the small spaces in the staircase.

Eden's breathing had become shallow, her heartbeat anxious. Could the person climbing the stairs be Zach? Was he keeping his promise after all? Had something delayed him through the day? Or had he remembered that her father slept until early evening?

Each footstep coming closer made Eden's pulse race just a bit faster. Nervously, her hands swept down the front of her fully-gathered cotton dress, hoping that she looked beautiful enough in such a common, ordinary garment. She had known not to dress any way special today, for her father would have noticed.

But she had chosen a frock that displayed some gathered lace at the end of the sleeves and at the bodice, and she had looked petitely feminine enough to please herself when she gazed in the mirror.

All day long she had thought that she had wasted her energies on worrying over how she had looked! Now she felt foolish for having wasted energies on doubting, possibly even hating Zach.

"Hello, up there!" Zach shouted, seeing light shining through the trapdoor overhead as it was flung open. "I hope you don't mind if I made myself at home and came on up to introduce myself. You weren't at your cottage so I knew you would be in the tower, perhaps readying your lamps for the night."

Eden drew a ragged, excited breath; just the

sound of Zach's voice melted her insides. He had come. He did care. Oh, how was she going to hide her feelings for this man in front of her father? She was guilty of always wearing her feelings on her face; she would be condemned for sure if her father looked at her now.

"Come right on up," Preston shouted down the stairs. "But watch your footing. If you're not used to these dang stairs you could slip real easily on them. I've been known to do it myself."

"Light a lantern, Eden," Preston said. "Hand it to me. Let's be hospitable to the visitor. I don't recognize his voice. He must be new in these parts."

With trembling fingers, Eden lifted the chimney of a kerosene lantern. Striking a match, she placed it to the wick and watched impatiently as the fire burned along the top until finally there was a steady flame.

Replacing the chimney, she hurried to the trapdoor and held the light over the opening, her heartbeats almost swallowing her whole in her anxiety to see Zach.

But she must remember to pretend that she had never met him. She must act as though this was the first time, even if every fiber of her being would be crying out to move into his arms for the wonders of his embrace. Her lips burned with the want of his kiss.

"Thanks for the light," Zach shouted, now more steady on his feet. He peered upward, the pit of his stomach stabbed with desire when he saw Eden's face illuminated beautifully by the lantern's glow.

His pulse raced, having thought of nothing but her the entire day. It was going to be hard to pretend that he did not know her. When they were close, it was as though a magnet were drawing them even closer together.

"Visitors are always welcome in my lighthouse," Preston said, now able to make out the features of the visitor and seeing that he was a healthy, very handsome young man. It was evident that he was wealthy in the way that he was dressed. He wore a brocaded vest, a double-breasted white linen frock coat and fawn-colored breeches. He was deeply tanned, with midnight-black hair, and he had an honest face.

"Zachary Tyson's my name," Zach said, stepping through the trapdoor opening. He extended a hand to Preston. "But, sir, everyone calls me Zach."

Eden stepped back away from them, sitting the lantern on a shelf, finding it hard to control her heart. It was beating so profoundly, surely her father could hear it. She saw this moment as perhaps the most dangerous of her life. If her father had any suspicion at all that this meeting was all pretense, how disillusioned he would be with her!

Preston steadied himself with his cane and gripped Zach's hand, giving him a firm handshake. "Son, my name's Preston. Preston Whitney," he said, again admiring this fine figure of a man. He glanced over at Eden. "And that's my daughter, Eden." He nodded at Eden. "Come here and make this young man's acquaintance, hon."

Eden's knees were weak and her face was undeniably hot as she cautiously approached Zach. As he removed his hand from Preston's grip to extend her a courteous handshake, she had to try with all of her might to keep her hand from shaking as she extended it toward him. Surely one touch would ruin everything, for she knew how his touches affected her.

"Sir," she said, keeping her voice politely soft. She felt a jolt to her insides when Zach's fingers encircled hers. "I'm pleased to make your acquaintance."

"Likewise," Zach said, his eyes gleaming down into hers. "Your name is Eden?" His lips lifted into a slow, purposely teasing smile. "How fascinating a name. It's intriguing, to say the least."

Eden smiled stiffly back at him, having hoped that he would refrain from teasing her about her name again, especially in front of her father, who was watching much too closely. "Yes, most do find my name quite unusual," she said tersely.

Preston looked slowly from Eden to Zach, feeling something in the air, a sort of electricity flowing between his daughter and this stranger. It unnerved him to feel that he was on the outside looking in, an unwanted observer.

But this was foolish. Eden had never met the man before.

Leastways, she hadn't told her father about it if she had.

"Well, now, Zach," Preston said, taking him by an elbow and guiding him away from Eden.

"Are you new in these parts? Or have you just decided to take a jaunt from Charleston to inspect my lighthouse firsthand?"

Zach gave Eden a nervous glance across her father's shoulder. Then he moved with Preston to stand before the wide window that displayed the glorious splash of the sunset spreading over the ocean like some great orange flower.

"I moved here only recently," he said softly, wincing when Preston groaned as he tried to lift his legs to sit on a stool. Eden hadn't told Zach that her father was partly crippled. But of course she wouldn't. She was probably too used to it to even think about it on a regular basis.

"I live down Lighthouse Road," Zach added quickly, not wanting Preston to notice that his lame legs had drawn attention. "My house was completed only recently or I would have come earlier to make the acquaintance of you and your lovely daughter."

Preston sat down on the stool and leaned his cane against his legs. He eyed Zach closely. "How is it that I haven't been aware of any activity along Lighthouse Road?" he asked guardedly. "Surely you needed supplies from Charleston quite often in order to build your house."

Zach glanced over at Eden, recalling her own initial wonder. He then smiled at Preston, maintaining the cool and collected demeanor that was required to quell suspicion. Slowly, but calculatingly, he repeated the same tale that he had told Eden. He was relieved when her father seemed pleased enough with the explanation.

"Eden, perhaps Zach would like some tea," Preston said, lifting his cane toward her, motioning with it. "Go on and prepare some. We'll be there soon."

Preston arched a brow as he looked over at Zach. "You do have time to take tea with us, don't you?" he asked. "I don't have long, myself, though. I must be sure and get the lamps all lighted by the time the sky fully darkens."

Eden glanced down at her father's legs, and then up again. "Father, why don't I go and prepare the tea and bring it here?" she asked softly. "I see no reason why you should make such an unnecessary trip up and down the stairs. I do so worry about you."

Preston slapped his legs good-naturedly. "These legs are in better shape than those of some younger men I've met in my day," he chuckled. Then his smile faded. "It's you I worry about on those steps, Eden. If your mother hadn't traveled the stairs so often, perhaps she . . ."

Preston's words faded and he stopped himself from finishing the words that always cut into his heart like a knife. Even though ten years had passed, it did not seem right to talk about his wife being dead.

Eden went to her father and embraced him. "I'm fit as a fiddle and you know it," she assured him. "Please let me bring the tea to you."

"I won't hear of it," Preston growled, pushing her gently away from him. "Now go and get the tea ready. It'll be dark before you know it and I'll have to return to be with my lamps."

"Yes, sir," Eden said, flashing Zach a nervous smile as she brushed on past him in the small confines of the room. "I shan't be long. Come and drink it while it's fresh and hot."

"We'll be there, hon," Preston said, waving her away with his cane.

Eden was breathless, not from the descent on the stairs, but from what she had just been forced to endure. It had been hard to pretend that she didn't know Zach when all along her heart was crying out to him.

But she had gotten through these first moments without her father detecting her true feelings.

Surely it would get easier . . .

Finally at the foot of the stairs and outside, where the air was fresh and dew was already tipping the grass with its diamond droplets, Eden hurried to the cottage and on into the kitchen. She placed a kettle of water on the stove. Trembling fingers took three of her finest teacups and saucers from the cupboard. With bated breath she folded three crisply starched linen napkins. Then her eyes grew wide and she looked toward the door when she heard the approach of a horse and buggy outside in the drive.

Placing the napkins aside, Eden went to the front door and opened it. Everything within her grew cold when she recognized Angelita Llewellyn in the buggy with a male escort.

Gripping the edge of the door to steady

herself, knowing this was the worst time of all for Angelita to arrive unannounced, panic rose inside Eden. What if Zach should come down from the lighthouse now, just in time to meet face to face with Angelita? Up this close he would see just how beautiful and vivacious she was. He would no longer have cause to ask questions about her. He would see for himself.

Eden thought it was not at all fair that Angelita should arrive at this precise moment, when Zach was there. But perhaps she was about to find out the true reasons Zach had questioned her about her best friend.

Stepping back into the living room, Eden began to pace nervously, then spun around when Angelita burst into the room without knocking.

"Eden, I've only a minute," Angelita said in a seductive purr, carrying a long, narrow, gift-wrapped package with a yellow bow tied neatly around it under her arm and a wicker basket filled with cinnamon rolls thick with white icing in her hand. She pushed all this into Eden's hands. "Though I plan to attend the party, I have brought your father's birthday gift ahead of time. The cinnamon rolls are for both your breakfasts tomorrow morning."

Angelita stifled a giggle behind a gloved hand, looking toward the door. "I'm with Roger Dawson tonight. He's going to take me to the theater." She clutched Eden's arm. "Isn't that romantic, Eden? I wish you could get a beau and go with us some of these times."

Eden was scarcely breathing, keeping an eye on the door, listening for the thump-thump of her father's cane, which would warn her that Zach would also be coming into the door any minute.

Then she forced a smile as she looked into Angelita's dark eyes feathered over by thick, black lashes.

"Thanks for thinking of Father and for bringing the cinnamon rolls," Eden said softly. "And I'm glad you're coming to the party." She laughed lightly. "You do have a way of livening up a gathering."

"Sometimes I feel that I embarrass you when I flirt so with the gentlemen," Angelita said, her eyes dancing. "Do I, Eden? Do I?"

Eden placed the gift and wicker basket on a table beside the sofa and smiled at Angelita, seeing how beautiful she was this evening in her frilly blue silk dress with its low bodice displaying a generous amount of her large breasts, and with a waistline so small any man could place his hands around it and make his fingers meet, tip to tip. Her thick, long black hair was held back by diamond-encrusted combs, her cheeks and lips were bright, and she was wearing such a lovely gold necklace and bracelet. Had her rich aunt purchased them for her? Or had one of her men callers?

"No, you don't embarrass me," Eden finally sighed, embracing Angelita. "It's just in your nature to be more flighty than I." Purposely, she slipped an arm around Angelita's waist and began ushering her toward the door.

"Like tonight, Angelita—you made your gentleman friend drive you clear out here and now he must wait for you. What will he think?"

"Oh, Roger?" Angelita giggled, flipping her hair back from her shoulders. "I do believe I've stolen his heart." She leaned closer to Eden and whispered. "I'm not sure if that's good. So often after I know a man desires me so intensely, I care not for him any longer. The challenge is gone. Do you know what I mean, Eden?"

Eden laughed to herself over how fickle her friend was and how often she seemed to get away with it. No matter how many men she discarded, there were always more at her doorstep, begging for an hour of her time.

Perhaps even Eden's father, if given a chance?

Eden didn't know Angelita's secret and had never cared to find out. She did not like the idea of flitting from man to man. Serious relationships could never be made that way. And that's what Eden wanted. A serious relationship with Zach.

Smiling at Angelita, Eden was glad to have managed to get her at least as far as the porch. "Well, I'm not sure, when you talk of challenges in the same breath as you talk of men," she said. "But as long as you know what you're doing, I guess that's all that matters. I only want whatever makes you happy, Angelita."

Eden squeezed Angelita's hand and

frowned. "How is your aunt?" she murmured. "Is she faring better these days after her stroke? Is she still paralyzed?"

"Auntie is holding her own," Angelita said softly. "She seems to hang on when most would just give up and die."

Angelita's eyes grew suddenly wide. She reached for a gold necklace at her throat. "Why, Eden," she gasped. "I almost forgot to show you." She held the necklace out away from her flesh, so that Eden could get a better look at it. "Would you just look at what someone left at my doorstep?" She held up her wrist so that Eden could see her bracelet. "I have a secret admirer. He left both the bracelet and the necklace just outside my door for me to find. One day I received the necklace. Another day I received the bracelet. I wonder who could be doing this? Though I have had many men interested in me, none have ever left me gifts in such a way, especially without signing their names. Men want me to know when they are interested in me. Who could not? Surely it is a man of mystery."

Looking at the beautiful gold jewelry, a reminder of the questions Zach had asked about Angelita scorched her like a branding iron. He had acted like someone who was infatuated with a lady! Could he be the secret admirer? Wasn't he, in a sense, a man of mystery? There were many things about him that she did not understand.

She bit her lower lip and turned her face away, tears stinging her eyes.

Angelita noticed nothing, and turned with a

flip of her dress. "Well, good-night, Eden," she said spiritedly. "I mustn't keep Roger waiting."

Sniffling, Eden turned and waved. "Good-night, Angelita," she said, her voice breaking with emotion.

Angelita turned with a bounce and looked up at Eden. "Please tell your father that I said hello." She clasped her hands before her. "He's such a wonderful, kind man."

Something grabbed at Eden's heart. More and more she had noticed Angelita's budding interest in her father. Lord, the last thing her father needed was to know that Angelita might be just as infatuated with him as he surely was with her. Angelita would surely be as fickle with him as with any other man and he deserved much better. He deserved another woman exactly like his first wife.

"Yes, I'll tell him," she said stiffly. "Have fun tonight, Angelita."

"I always do," Angelita said, giggling as she climbed up beside her companion. "Bye, bye, Eden."

Eden nodded and watched until the horse and buggy moved out of sight, then stiffened when she heard voices echoing down the lighthouse staircase.

Wiping a tear from her eyes, she hurried inside and hid the gift and took the cinnamon rolls into the kitchen.

She rushed back into the living room and forced a smile as her father and Zach came through the front door, chatting as though they were old friends.

Chapter Eight

Miss you, miss you, miss you!

—CORY

Sitting stiffly, seething inside with suspicion, Eden sipped her tea while her father and Zach went on talking like long-lost friends.

A fire simmered low on the grate, the sunset was turning the wall opposite the fireplace a soft orange. Zach and Eden's father sat on the sofa facing the fire, and she was in a rocker, slowly rocking and listening.

Yet her mind could not help but conjure up thoughts of Zach and Angelita together. Wouldn't they look as though they were meant for each other—he so masculine with his sharply chiseled features and she with such a perfect face and body? People would say it was a union made in heaven. They even resembled each other in their eyes and hair, as dark as all midnights.

Jealousy ate away at Eden's insides. She glanced toward the kitchen, having purposely awaited the right moment to bring the cinnamon rolls in to serve with the tea and announce who had brought them. Zach would be the first to sit up and take notice of the name. It was a name that he knew well enough.

But why didn't he know the lady? What was holding him back from finding out all the secrets about her firsthand? Why ask Eden?

No. None of it made any sense.

"So, lad, you haven't told me what you did before coming to the beautiful Carolinas," Preston said, sitting forward, eyeing Zach admiringly.

Preston liked Zach more by the minute. He saw him as a tall and powerfully built young man with intense eyes and a likable personality. It was a bit mysterious how Zach had so quietly built his mansion down the road from the lighthouse, but Preston would not let suspicions cloud his sudden liking for the man. It was good to have a neighbor at last— and one that carried on a decent conversation, as well.

Preston gazed at Eden. It was good to have a decent prospect for a husband for his daughter, too. He arched a thick eyebrow and drummed his fingers nervously on his knee. What was wrong with Eden? He could see a quiet anger in her eyes.

Zach shifted nervously in his seat. He

placed his teacup and saucer on the table beside him and looked at Eden. His eyebrows arched, wondering what was causing her to look so seethingly angry. Nothing could have possibly been said to cause her to behave in such a way. When he had first arrived, she hadn't behaved in this way. What could have happened since?

He shook his head slightly and turned his gaze back to Preston. "For the past several years I have been a world traveler," he said dryly. "In a sense, I was following a route at sea made by my father."

"Oh?" Preston said, placing his cup aside. "Was your father a seaman?"

"Yes, at first he was only a sea merchant," Zach said, feeling a strange coiling at the pit of his stomach, for he was not used to outright lying. But it seemed that one lie begot another . . . and another. "But then he became the owner of a vast fleet of ships. When he died, I took over the business."

Eden cocked her head, curious; she had not heard this exact version of Zach's past before. Why did she get the distinct impression that he was lying?

But why would he?

Unless he had something important to hide.

That thought gave her a queasy feeling at the pit of her stomach. Had she fallen in love with a man with a questionable background?

Glancing at Eden and seeing her guarded expression, as though he was not convincing her at all about his past, Zach saw the need to change the subject.

He looked at Preston and at the cane resting against a knee. "Sir, enough about me," he said. "Tell me about yourself. I noticed the cane. Did you injure your legs on a fall? Perhaps on the lighthouse stairway?"

Preston sighed. He patted his knees. "You might say the stairs are the cause," he said. "But the partial numbness isn't from a fall. It's from lightning. Now whenever it storms I know damn well not to get on the stairs. They can become charged with electricity. That electrical charge went up into my legs some years back. Slowly my legs are regaining their feeling. But only slowly."

"I've never heard of such a thing happening," Zach exclaimed. "I guess you could call that a freak of nature."

"Yes, guess so," Preston said, nodding. He looked from the window into the sky all orange with sunset. "Yesterday we had such a storm. But the only unusual occurrence brought about by that storm was an unwanted visitor in these Carolina waters."

He glanced back at Zach, chuckling. "Seems you've moved to these parts in time for some excitement," he said. "We've an old pirate asking to get his ship blown clean out of the water. My beam spotted ol' Pirate Jack yesterday. He wasn't flying his skull and bones flag, but anyone'd recognize that damnable black ship. It's been described by the authorities often enough."

Zach shifted nervously in his seat and sucked in a deep gulp of air. Glancing from

114

Eden to Preston, he knew that he had better act naturally or both would see that the mention of Pirate Jack was alarming to him. He had already spoken too much of pirates to Eden. If he did again, questions would be asked that he would not be able to answer.

"A pirate, you say?" he said, hating it when his voice sounded strangled. "Well, I'll be damned. I would have thought piracy was out of fashion."

"Perhaps piracy is never out of fashion," Eden said, finally getting a word in edgewise. "Isn't the thought of pirates being this close intriguing, Zach?"

"Quite," he said softly, nodding, knowing that she was toying with him again over his earlier mention of pirates.

Preston studied the sky. "Well, perhaps I'd best make that trip up the stairs and see to my lamps," he said, picking up his cane.

Desperation rose inside Eden, thinking that perhaps she had waited too long to bring up another subject that might cause Zach even more distress. She rose quickly to her feet.

"Father, you have a moment longer," she interjected. "Let me refill your cup. You see, I forgot to serve you the cinnamon rolls that Angelita brought while you were still in the lighthouse with Zach. Surely you want to eat at least one of them before going to work. You know how hungry you get at about midnight."

She turned her eyes slowly toward Zach. An ache troubled her heart, for she could see how the name Angelita had affected him again. He was pale and withdrawn, and his jaw was set. There was no denying that he had hidden feelings for Angelita.

But why were they hidden? If he was infatuated with Angelita, Eden needed to know now rather than continue making a fool of herself over a man whose heart belonged to another.

"Oh? Angelita was here?" Preston said, his blood and heartbeat quickening at the mere mention of her name. He rose shakily to his feet, leaning his weight on his faithful cane. "Why didn't you tell me sooner?"

Eden lowered her eyes. "It slipped my mind," she murmured.

"Did she say how her aunt was? Is she faring better?" Preston asked, moving toward Eden.

Zach's heart skipped a beat at the mention of Angelita's aunt. In his mind's eye, he was recalling when he was a small boy, being forced to eat bread and water. He was feeling the sharp pain from the whip. . . .

Eden raised her eyes. Something made her look toward Zach before answering her father. She was taken aback by the sudden pain that she saw reflected in his eyes as he gazed down at the fire, as though lost in deep thought.

Oh, yes, there was much that he wasn't telling her.

And Eden suspected that most of it was not pleasant.

"Angelita's aunt is faring well enough," she murmured. "I forgot to ask if her aunt has regained her memory. The stroke stole most of it away, you know."

Zach looked quickly over at Eden. He almost spoke up, but his questions would have brought too much attention his way. Those questions would come later, after Eden had put more trust in him.

But it was evident that she was trusting him less and less. He would have to do something about that. And soon!

Preston shook his head as he moved toward the door. "Martha was so happy with her second husband, and not just for the riches that he bestowed on her and Angelita. She just couldn't hold up under the pain of losing him. Too bad he had to die. Broke Martha's heart, it did."

Eden moved briskly toward her father as he opened the door. "Father, you aren't staying for more tea and one of Angelita's cinnamon rolls?" she asked, a tone of desperation in her voice. She suddenly didn't want to be left alone with Zach. She was afraid of attacking him with accusations that would perhaps reveal too many truths if he defended himself.

"No, I need to get up to my beam," Preston said. He nodded toward Zach. "Zach'll eat my share, won't you, Zach?"

"Well, sir, I am partial to sweets," Zach said, rising to go to Preston. He stretched out his hand. "Sir, I cannot tell you how much I enjoyed meeting and talking with you. Shall we do it again soon?"

"Most certainly," Preston said, shaking

Zach's hand. "And call me Preston. Sir is far too formal, don't you think?"

Zach laughed softly. "Well, yes, I guess it is," he said. He shifted his feet nervously.

"Preston, I'd like to come calling tomorrow, if that's all right," he said, easing his hand to his side. "I'd like to invite your daughter to go horseback riding."

Preston nodded toward Eden. "Son, it's perfectly fine with me," he said, chuckling. "I'm sure it's all right with Eden. The fresh air and exercise'll do her good."

Eden gave Zach a tight-lipped look when he turned and smiled at her.

"Well?" he asked softly. "Will you?"

Eden exhaled a nervous breath. She knew that her father would not understand her hesitation, and she did not want to reveal all of her suspicions to her father, so she said a quick "yes."

"It would be fun," she said, her eyes meeting with and holding Zach's. "Yes, I would enjoy going."

"Well, then, that settles that," Preston said, laughing. He walked out onto the porch.

Eden raced after him. She had one more thing to say about Angelita in front of Zach, to see his reaction. "Oh, father, wait a minute," she said, placing a hand on her father's arm. "You should have seen the necklace and bracelet that Angelita was wearing. They were brought to her doorstep and left there by a secret admirer. Can you imagine? Isn't that exciting?"

Preston shook his head, not at all amused. He could not deny the jealousy that ate away at him every time he thought of Angelita and all the men swarming around her. If not for his damn legs, he would tell her exactly what he thought of that. And of her. He wanted her. Oh, God, how he wanted her.

"That woman," he said, his voice drawn, "has every man in the county sniffing after her skirts. Perhaps it's the perfume she wears."

He walked away, his hurtful forced laughter following after him.

Eden turned slowly and looked at Zach, her lips pursed tightly together.

Glad to see the sun lowering in the sky so that she could see the end of her work day, Sabrina stopped scrubbing the floor of yet another slave's cabin to go to the door and get a breath of fresh air. She folded her arms across her chest and stared at Joshua. He was in the fields, laboring as though he were a hundred men instead of just one. Since daybreak he had been busy with the hoe, the many neat furrows along the land evidence of his obedience to his master.

Even now while the sun was setting, he continued to ready the land for planting cotton. He hadn't asked for Sabrina's help. He had shoved a bucket of sudsy water in her one hand, a scrub brush in the other, and had told her to ready all of the cabins for the rest of the slavehands that would one day occupy them.

Even though the cabins had been built only

recently, he still made her scrub them, most surely to keep her away from him.

Sabrina's eyes and mood softened as she watched Joshua so diligently at work. Though he treated her as though she had the plague, she could not help but see him as special. There was much pride in the way he held his head high on his broad shoulders. He was thin-flanked, tall and lithe. His dark breeches hugged his body like a glove.

There was no denying that Sabrina's pulse raced as she let her eyes devour his naked chest and back. Sleek with sweat, his muscles corded and flexed magnificently every time he lifted the hoe and slammed it back down into the black, fertile earth, creating more furrows across the land.

To Sabrina, he was powerful.

To Sabrina, he was beautiful.

"And he don't want to be bothered with me," she said, her lower lip forming a pout. "I wonder if he hates all women?"

Lonesome for the friends she had made at the last plantation before the master had stripped her away from them to sell like a dog, Sabrina took one last lingering look at Joshua, then moved back into the cabin.

Dropping to her knees, she placed the scrub brush into the water and then swung it out again and began moving it in circles across the floor. She blew back a strand of hair from her eyes, glancing down at her attire. No wonder Joshua had no eye for her. The dress that she had worn at the auction had been ripped open by grubby, unfriendly hands. Surely every time Joshua looked at her he could see all of those men's hands on her, familiarizing themselves with the shape of her breasts, the flatness of her stomach, and the feathering of dark hair at the juncture of her thighs.

But surely he could not find that any more distasteful than she did! She had been the one abused, not he.

"No, it's somethin' more," Sabrina whispered to herself, shaking her head. "I sees it in his eyes. He's missin' someone. It mus' be his woman. There's always that same hauntin' look in a man's eyes when he's missin' a woman."

The sunset spilled through the door and window. Sabrina swirled the scrub brush and water along the wooden floor. Tired, filled with melancholy, she suddenly lost her balance on her knees and fell clumsily sideways.

Shoving a hand to the floor, Sabrina caught her fall. Her eyes widened and she cried out as a sudden jolt of pain shot beneath one of her fingernails as she scooted her hand along the floor to right herself.

The fingernail pulsing, Sabrina held it up to the light. Tears streamed from her eyes and she sobbed painfully when she discovered that a huge splinter was lodged beneath the nail of her thumb on her left hand, imprisoned between the nail and flesh.

Trembling, she rose to her feet and went to the door of the cabin where she would have more light. She tried to get hold of the end of the splinter, but she only managed to cause her finger to throb more intensely.

"Lordy, what am I to do?" she cried, tears stealing paths down her cheeks, salty in her mouth as they settled there.

She held her wounded hand with her other hand. Crying, she began to rock back and forth from her bare toes to her heels. She looked through her tears at Joshua, not wanting to ask him to help her. If she troubled him, wouldn't he hate her even more?

But she had no choice. The pain was worsening. The throbbing was no longer only in her finger, but in her entire hand.

"Mercy, mercy," she sobbed. "I mus' go and ast him to help me. That thing hurts wors'n anything I can remember."

Still holding her hand, her eyes red from crying, Sabrina left the cabin and began walking barefoot across the cleared, black land. She stepped over one furrow and then another, until she was standing behind Joshua who had not even noticed that she was coming to him.

"Don' you even care that I'm cryin'?" Sabrina sobbed, staring at his massive, dark back, waiting for him to turn and face her. "You is a cold-hearted man, isn't you?"

Joshua turned on a heel and glowered down at her, then his expression softened when he saw the pain in Sabrina's eyes. He looked down at the way she grasped her hand, then back up into her eyes.

"It's a splinter lodged beneath my nail," Sabrina cried. "It hurts so."

Joshua reached for her hand. "Little Momma, let me see that finger," he said softly, his defenses crumbling. A woman's tears always did that to him—especially when they came from a woman who most generally only showed a strong, courageous side.

In Sabrina, he was seeing many of the characteristics of his late wife. She could be soft and vulnerable at times. She could be firm and brave. It was the best of combinations for a woman—especially one who was enslaved by the white man.

Joshua already knew that he was going to love Sabrina.

Sabrina looked up at Joshua, wide-eyed. She sniffled. Surely she was making a fool of herself. Hardly ever did she let a man see her cry. Surely Joshua would hate her even more for it, for showing that she had such a weakness.

"What sort of man would leave gifts for a woman without including his name, Zach?" Eden asked, shuffling on past him, into the kitchen. She plopped cinnamon rolls on two separate saucers and handed these to Zach as he followed her into the room. "Please take these into the living room. I shall bring the tea."

Zach stepped aside as she walked past him, carrying the teapot. He watched her hips sway seductively and how she held her chin high. It was evident that she was playing a game with him and he had no choice but to go along with her for now. He would not reveal any truths to her just yet. He couldn't. As long as Pirate Jack was anywhere near, Zach's past would always be there to haunt him.

"What sort of man would leave gifts for a woman without including his name? From the sound of things, he seems just the sort of man Angelita Llewellyn would attract," Zach said, sitting down on the sofa before the fire. As Eden sat on the sofa beside him, he handed her a cinnamon roll as she handed him a freshly filled cup of tea. "Is her reputation scarred by so many admirers? Surely she has one man she is most fond of."

Eden was beginning to do a slow burn. "Angelita?" she said tersely, looking heatedly over at Zach. "Hardly."

Zach took a bite of the cinnamon roll. "Well, one thing for sure, she knows how to cook," he marveled, taking another quick bite. "These are delicious."

"Angelita did not bake those," Eden snapped, scooting her dish aside, refusing to have any part of the cinnamon roll. "Her cook did the honors. Why, I am sure Angelita does not even know how to boil water."

Zach almost choked on his next bite, amused by Eden's pure show of jealousy. He set the dish aside, along with the teacup, and reached for Eden's hand. "Eden, your behavior surprises me," he said. "Darling, you're placing too much emphasis on my asking a few simple questions about Angelita. Please trust me that I have good reasons to and none of them are romantic." He lifted her hand to his lips and kissed her palm. "It's you I want to share romantic moments with. Only you."

Eden's lips parted in a gasp. Her face grew hot with an anxious blush, and she was temporarily speechless. Then she could no longer hold back the questions that had been hammering away at her brain.

"How can I believe anything you say?" she blurted out, jerking her hand away and rising to her feet. "First you talk of another woman, ask all sorts of questions about her. Then you show an obvious interest in piracy! It was even in your eyes that you felt some alarm or danger when Angelita's aunt was mentioned." She waved a hand in the air. "Zach, why? I'm so confused."

Zach moved swiftly to his feet. He drew Eden into his arms and held her close, even when she struggled to get free. "Trust me, Eden," he said hoarsely. "I would never do anything to hurt you. Never. Be patient. In time I will reveal everything to you. Until then, will you please just trust me and let me show you how much I love you?"

Eden's head was spinning. She sighed heavily, reveling in the feel of his arms and the warmth of his breath upon her cheek. Oh, how badly she wanted to forget all of her misgivings about him. He did sound so sincere in his pleadings.

"Eden?" Zach whispered, weaving his fingers through her hair, directing her eyes to meet his. "Will you go riding with me tomorrow?"

Swallowing hard, Eden's heart guided her into nodding to him. "I said yes earlier," she murmured. "I haven't changed my mind."

"Eden, there's something else," Zach said, his eyes dark with feelings.

Eden tensed. "What?" she murmured.

"Do you have a spare dress that I could borrow?"

Eden's eyes widened as she looked up at him with surprise. "A dress?" she gasped. "You want to borrow one of my dresses?"

"Yes, a dress," Zach said, nodding. "It's for Sabrina. The one she was wearing at the auction was ripped. I don't want to go into Charleston again this soon to buy her a replacement."

Eden smiled slowly up at him. She placed a hand to his cheek. "Yes, I believe I have a dress for you to give to Sabrina," she said softly. "How kind of you to care."

"Darling, I care," Zach said, drawing her lips to his mouth. "Oh, how I care. I care so very deeply for you."

Their lips came together with a gentle passion. Eden's heart soared, for the moment forgetting everything but that she could not help loving Zach.

At that moment there was no Angelita. There were no mysterious secrets.

Sabrina winced as Joshua gently ripped some of her fingernail away, giving him better access to the large splinter beneath her nail. She cried out when he tried to pull the splinter free, as the skin grew more and more sensitive beneath the nail.

"Little Momma, there's one more way I can try to get the splinter," Joshua said, raising her hand close to his lips. "Just bear with me."

Sabrina nodded anxiously, then grew wide-eyed when he placed her thumb to his lips and began sucking on it, centering on the splinter. The pain was suddenly no longer a prime factor. His lips, the suction of his mouth on her thumb, were creating a sensation of euphoria within her, for while he was doing this, he was looking into her eyes, setting her afire inside. His dark eyes seemed to be reaching clean into her heart, sending messages of desire to her brain.

When his teeth began nibbling on the tip of the thumb while trying to get hold of the splinter, it was as if something had awakened inside her that until now was dormant. Sabrina's heart began to pound. Her pulse raced.

But too soon he stepped away from her, presenting her with a thumb free of the splinter.

"That's that," Joshua said, nodding. He held the splinter up between his fingers for Sabrina to see. "You'll be all right now."

"Thank you," Sabrina said, breathless. She rubbed her sore thumb, mesmerized by a man for the first time in her life, and not knowing what to do about it. She shuffled her feet nervously in the dirt and smiled clumsily up at Joshua. "Well, I best get back to work."

"No, you best not," Joshua said, frowning down at her. "You mustn't get your finger in the dirty water. It'll only hurt worse." He nodded toward the porch. "You go sit down. Relax them pretty bones."

"Yas'sa," Sabrina said, moving backwards awkwardly. She giggled when she tripped on a furrow, then turned around and hurried to the porch. Plopping down on a step, she watched Joshua as he resumed hoeing the land. Again sweat began to shine on his muscled back. Again he beat at the land with the hoe, as though there were no tomorrows.

Not able to take seeing him laboring so hard alone any longer, and not caring about her own hurt, Sabrina went and grabbed another hoe and started working alongside Joshua. She smiled at him as he stopped to marvel over her, wiping beads of perspiration from his brow.

"Stop your gawkin', handsome man," Sabrina drawled, flashing him her most seductive smile. "Don't you knows this woman can do more than scrub floors?"

Joshua smiled slowly over at her. "Little Momma, nothin' you do surprises me," he said, winking at her.

Sabrina's heart sang with joy for the first time in her life.

Chapter Nine

Clasp me close in your warm, young arms.
— WILCOX

Two horses thundered along the beach, spitting sand up from beneath their hooves. Zach held his head high, enjoying the air rushing against his face, warm and exhilarating. The sun was high, and the sky was a brilliant blue, with only a few puffy white clouds scudding along the horizon.

At times like this Zach felt truly free. Ah, but if it were only true! The past two nights he had had nightmares about Judge Pryor and the suspicious look in his eyes as he had watched Zach riding along the streets of Charleston.

In the nightmare, Judge Pryor had come after Zach and had placed him in a place of squalor, where rats tumbled over his feet while he hung manacled to the wall. He could feel the pain of the whip on his bare chest. He could feel the blood trickling down his body.

Shaking himself from such ugly thoughts, his heart pounding as though even now he was imprisoned in the cell, Zach still could not stop thinking about Judge Pryor.

He had recognized Zach, and now he was playing a waiting game.

Would Judge Pryor leave him in peace? Or did he hate all pirates and was he ready to condemn Zach for his own confused past?

If fate allowed Judge Pryor to recall the one time that his life had been saved because of Zach, he would be the free man he had always ached to be. If Judge Pryor had a decent bone in his body, he would still be thanking Zach.

Her hair flying in the wind, Eden clung to her horse's reins, numb with fright but not admitting it. She had never liked to ride horseback. She had only learned how because her father had explained the importance of her doing so. Isolated on Lighthouse Road, vulnerable, the horse would be a faster escape into Charleston than a mere horse and buggy if the need arose.

Before her father was partially crippled, he had gone riding with her, teaching her the skills that were required, but since his accident, she had gone riding only a few times, and those skills were rusty.

"You ride beautifully," Zach said, looking proudly at Eden. His gaze roamed over her, seeing how the wind blew against her white, long-sleeved blouse, molding it against her breasts, defining her nipples so clearly. However much she tried, she could not keep her riding skirt from hiking up, revealing a good portion of the calves of her legs. His loins were burning; he had wanted her from the beginning, and he wanted her even more now.

"We should do this often," he added, his pulse racing.

Eden groaned to herself, giving him a furtive glance. This time Zach had not been able to read her thoughts. If he knew how she truly hated riding, he would never put her through such torture again.

"Yes, often," she said, forcing a smile. She would not let him know how clumsy she felt in the saddle. She wanted him to believe that she could do anything that she tried. He seemed the sort to like a woman who could do anything she set her mind to.

She thought how handsome he looked in his loose cambric shirt that revealed the frothing of hair at his powerful chest, and how his dark riding breeches fit his muscled legs the way a glove fits a hand. His high-topped boots shone as though freshly waxed. His wind-tossed hair made him look wild, free, and untamable.

Her heart raced, knowing that at this moment, when she was not letting her doubts plague her, there was nothing more important than to impress him.

"Have you had enough for the moment?" Zach asked, sidling his horse closer to Eden's. "Want to stop and take a rest? I brought a bottle of wine and two glasses in my saddle-bag.''

Eden flashed him a look of surprise. Perhaps he had read her thoughts after all. It would be sheer heaven to have her feet on the ground again.

"Yes, I believe I do need a bit of refreshment," Eden said, laughing softly. She would not say that it was her poor, aching bottom that needed the reprieve from the horse.

And, oh, how her thighs ached. Could she even straighten her legs to walk normally again? Surely they would retain the shape of the horse's back. If she had been more lady-like and ridden sidesaddle, perhaps she wouldn't be suffering so.

"This looks as good a spot as any," Zach said, having purposely chosen an isolated place on the beach far from Eden's cottage. With her father sleeping at this time of day, away from the lighthouse they would have complete privacy. Zach needed this sort of privacy to convince her that he loved her.

Yet could he tell her the truth about Angelita just yet?

Only Joshua knew the truth and Zach had found it hard to tell even him. The past was not a pleasant thing to ponder over to himself, much less speak of aloud.

Up to now, he had felt that it was enough to give Angelita secret gifts to make up for some of the hardships of the past. Perhaps that was the way it should remain. He had been wrong to ever mention Angelita's name to Eden.

Until he chose to tell her the truth, he would refrain from mentioning Angelita again. He had already caused too much doubt, too much hurt.

Eden followed Zach's lead and drew her mount to a halt. Moaning, she slowly lifted her leg over the saddle, placed a booted foot in a stirrup, and slipped down to the sandy beach. Rubbing her sore behind, she marveled at the grace with which Zach swung himself out of his saddle. Though he was a man of the sea, he looked comfortable on land, even riding a horse.

Apparently he was a man of many talents, most of which Eden would never know about. This not knowing troubled her, but at this moment she wanted only to enjoy being with him.

Loving for the first time in her life, she wanted nothing to spoil it.

It felt too wonderful.

Zach unfastened his saddlebag and lifted a bottle of wine from inside it, then two very carefully wrapped glasses. Turning to Eden, he held them up in the air. "Nourishment for my lady," he said. Eden smiled as she took a folded blanket from her own saddlebag.

Feeling suddenly ill at ease for being so totally alone with him on this isolated strip of beach, Eden shook the blanket out onto the sand. Kneeling on the blanket, she smoothed out its corners until it lay perfectly flat.

She settled down on the blanket, and her lips quivered into a smile as Zach sat down beside her. Her pulse racing, she felt at a loss for words and hated herself for this awkwardness. This was a moment to be cherished! She was alone with the man she loved. Everything within her wanted to be kissed by him. She hungered for his arms.

So why did she feel so awkward with him?

Then she suddenly knew the cause.

Wasn't this a perfect spot for a seduction? Didn't it make sense that Zach would try more than to kiss and embrace her today? There were such strong feelings between them, it was only natural that he would attempt to draw her into a total seduction.

Would she allow it?

Could she not?

Lord help her. She wanted him with every fiber of her being. . . .

"You hold the glasses and I'll pour the wine," Zach said, holding out the long stems of the glasses supported between two of his fingers.

Taking the glasses, Eden held them out before her. "Very rarely do I drink wine. Normally tea is my preference," she said, laughing softly. She was relieved that she had gotten back her ability to speak. "With you, drinking wine could become a habit."

"You don't see it as a nasty habit, I hope," Zach said, slowly pouring the wine into the glasses. He arched a dark eyebrow as he glanced up at her. "Just as I hope you don't see me as a nasty habit you are forced to endure because of my persistence."

A shimmer of sorts raced across Eden's flesh; his eyes mesmerized her. "Never," she murmured, her voice a trace too husky for her liking. Embarrassed, she lowered her eyes.

Zach worked the bottle into the sand beside the blanket, balancing it so that it would not tip. He clinked his glass against hers. "To your health, darling," he whispered.

Hearing him call her darling, and so very sincerely, made Eden's gaze move slowly upward. Without even touching her, he was evoking wonderful sensations inside her. Her entire being throbbed with awakening desire, frightening her. Never before had she wanted a man in this way. And more than likely she never would again. She had fallen madly in love with Zach.

"To us," Zach added, moving closer to Eden. He took her free hand and squeezed it affectionately.

Her heart feeling as though it were throbbing in her throat, Eden smiled seductively at Zach over the rim of her glass and sipped the wine slowly. His hand was setting her flesh aglow where his fingers entwined with hers. His eyes were two points of fire, silently seducing her into breathlessness.

Suddenly their moment of magic was interrupted when a great flock of sea gulls appeared overhead, sweeping and diving down over them. Eden looked at their grayish-white bellies and large, dark eyes, and flinched at their threatening screeches.

"What's wrong with them?" Zach asked,

setting his glass down on the blanket. He rose quickly to his feet, watching the frantic movements of the gulls. "What do they want?"

Eden set her glass aside and rose to her feet beside Zach, then she laughed softly when she was able to understand what was wrong with the birds.

Cupping a hand over her eyes, she scanned the long avenue of the beach to her left. "I believe we're intruders," she said, recalling the one other time she had been there. "We're too near the gulls' nesting area. If we moved just a bit farther up the beach we would see thousands of eggs lying about on the sand. I've gathered these eggs before, to use in my cakes and bread dough."

Wanting to see the eggs again, Eden looked over her shoulder at Zach as she began to run toward the nesting area. "Come on," she shouted, "I'll show you."

Zach looked nervously up at the soaring birds, then back at Eden who was determined to explore the nests. "Eden, perhaps we'd better not," he shouted, holding his ground. "Come on back. We'll move our blanket and wine farther away."

"Oh, come on, Zach," Eden cried. "You're not going to let a few birds scare you away, are you?"

Shaking his head, Zach followed and soon caught up with her. He grabbed her hand and ran alongside her, his eyes dancing as he looked down at her. She looked no more than a child with mischief on her mind. She was giggling, and her green eyes sparkled as she glanced at him.

He loved the way her waist-length hair lifted from her back and caught the breeze, some tendrils whipping around, across her face. He loved to watch her firmly rounded breasts bounce as she ran, the blouse straining against them. He loved her dimples, as her giggles faded into a soft, seductive smile.

Unable to refrain from kissing her any longer, Zach swept an arm around her waist and stopped her by drawing her to him. Breathing hard, he pinioned her against his body, then framed her face between his hands and lowered his mouth to her lips and fully consumed them.

When she did not object, but grew limply pliant within his arms as she returned the fiery kiss, he began lowering her slowly to the sand. Once there, he straddled her. While kissing her long and passionately, his fingers began unbuttoning her blouse, his knee probing her legs apart, then inching her skirt up.

Fully aware of what was happening, Eden could no more tell him to stop than to tell herself to stop breathing. It seemed natural. It seemed right. So many moments, so many shared glances and touches had been leading up to this. As he peeled her blouse open and her breasts sprang out, free and throbbing with the need to be touched, she was melting into a sweet surrender.

Zach's hands trembled as he moved them over her breasts, sucking in his breath with desire as he felt how soft they were against his hard palms. He began gently kneading them, his thumbs and forefingers tweaking the nipples into tight, dark peaks.

Sighing, growing heady with pleasure, Eden parted her lips, welcoming his tongue as it speared inside her mouth. The sensation this evoked caused her to moan and she hated it when he drew away from her.

She looked up into his dark, fathomless eyes as he began to remove her blouse, leaving her with only the warm sand pressed into her back.

"Tell me you need me," Zach said, his hands unfastening her skirt, smoothing it down and away from her. He went to her feet and began removing her riding boots. "Eden, tell me."

Her face flushed, her eyes devouring Zach's handsome face, trying not to feel that what they were about to share was wrong, Eden nodded. "Oh, how I need you," she said, goosebumps traveling across her flesh as she realized that she was now lying completely nude in the presence of a man for the very first time in her life. "I love you, Zach. From the very first moment, I knew that I was destined to love you."

Zach's fingers moved slowly over her body with an exquisite tenderness. When a hand cupped her at the juncture of her thighs, where her tendrils of hair guarded the secrets of her desire, she flinched and gasped slightly.

But when he began to stroke her softly and soothingly, arousing that part of her that had never been touched by a man before, she closed her eyes and let the euphoria take hold. Her heart beat faster when she felt Zach's lips feathering kisses along her body.

"I don't think I can wait much longer, Eden," Zach whispered into her ear. "Darling, tell me that you want me to make love to you. Tell me."

Eden's eyes opened wildly. She swallowed hard, fear suddenly a part of these moments thus far so filled with bliss. There was only one time in a woman's life when she could lose her virginity to a man. If she did not marry that man, then the one she did would look at her as whorish.

Dared she take that chance?

Did Zach love her enough to marry her?

Was this the time to question him, or would that break that magical spell that had woven between them?

She looked up at the heavens, feeling herself an extension of the sky, the sun, the clouds. She looked at Zach, feeling an extension of him. She truly could be if . . .

Twining her arms around his neck, Eden drew his lips close to hers. She kissed him softly, her pulse racing. "Yes, make love to me," she murmured. "Tell me to make love to you."

Zach kissed her hotly, his fingers probing between her thighs, trying to ready her for that initial burst of pain that would shoot through her when he plunged himself inside her that first time.

"Make love to me, darling," he whispered, tracing the outline of her lips with his tongue. "Love me with all of your heart."

"I already do," Eden whispered. Her eyes widened when he rose up away from her and began removing his clothes. She was only half aware of the sea gulls landing on the sand around them, gawking as though with human curiosity. She was wholly aware of Zach's body as it was slowly being revealed to her. Her gaze swept over the sinews of his shoulders, his rib cage and his flat belly.

Softly feathered with tendrils of crisp, black hair, his chest heaved in rhythm with his heartbeat. His tanned, sculpted face was intense with feeling, his dark eyes midnight-black with passion.

And then he lowered his breeches, giving her that first look ever of this part of a man's anatomy. Her heart skipped a beat. He was swollen with need, much larger than she would ever have imagined. And as he knelt down over her, letting that part of him touch her inner thigh, her breath was stolen away. Though large and hard, his manhood had the feel of velvet.

Zach was thankful that the birds had stopped their squawking. "Do you think they mind sharing their mating area with us?" he asked thickly.

"We've an audience for sure," Eden said,

laughing lightly. Zach reached for her hand. He guided it downward. "Touch me," he said huskily. "Familiarize yourself with that part of me that is going to take you to paradise and back. Move your hand over me."

Scarcely breathing, her heart having gone crazy with unleashed passion, Eden's eyes locked with Zach's as she circled her fingers around his hardness.

"Move your hand up and down," Zach said softly. "Give me pleasure, Eden. In turn, I will do the same for you."

Unashamedly, Eden began moving her hand, intrigued by how his largeness felt within her fingers. She thought she could feel a strange sort of throbbing against her flesh. It was as though that part of him had a life of its own.

Zach closed his eyes and held his head back, pleasure soaring through him. He trailed his hands over Eden's soft body, then again centered his fingers at the juncture of her thighs.

In time with her hand movements, he stroked her. He could feel her coming more to life beneath his touch. He could hear her breathing becoming erratic.

Moving her hand away from him, again looking into her eyes, Zach moved his hardness to the core of her womanhood. "Darling, it's time . . ." he whispered, and made one quick plunge downward, into her. . . .

Chapter Ten

Heart, soul and senses need you, one and all.
—ALFORD

Bubbling with happiness inside, Eden laughed softly against Zach's bare shoulder as he lay beside her in the sand. She clung to him, then unashamedly strained her body into his.

"I doubt if I shall ever feel as wonderful again," she marveled, kissing Zach's sleekly wet chest. She wove her tongue around one of his nipples, evoking a thick groan from deeply inside him. "Loving and being loved is so beautiful."

Zach sucked in his breath when Eden nibbled at his nipple with her teeth, then suckled on it, drawing its hardened tip within the warm recesses of her mouth. "If you continue to do that we'll never leave this place," he said huskily, his hands slowly caressing the soft-ness of her buttocks.

Feeling himself hardening again, pleasure spreading like wildfire within him at the mere touch of her, he moved her beneath him and opened her legs with a knee. His eyes gleamed down at her, his lips lifted into a soft, teasing smile. "Darling," he said softly. "Sometimes when you play with fire, you get burned."

Eden's face was flushed with desire. She twined her arms around his neck, looking up at him adoringly. "Do you truly believe that I am playing?" she murmured. "Zach, can't you see? Though it may be wrong, I shall never stop wanting you. Never."

Zach caressed her breasts. The heat of his gaze was scorching as he looked down at her. He wove his fingers through her hair and drew her mouth to his and kissed her wonderingly.

But he knew that he could not spend the whole day making love to Eden, much as he wanted to. He had left too much undone at his plantation to be with Eden this morning. He still had to make plans to buy more slavehands. Though dangerous, another journey into Charleston was necessary.

His steel arms enfolded Eden and lifted her up from the sand. Smiling mischievously down at her, he began to carry her toward the ocean.

Puzzled by his abrupt halt to their lovemak-ing, Eden fluttered her lashes nervously as she looked up at him. She smoothed her hair back from her eyes. "Whatever are you doing?" she gasped.

She looked over her shoulder; Zach was already in the outer edges of the water. She looked wildly up at him, then began giggling. "Zach, put me down," she said, squirming in his arms. "I hate saltwater. I hate it."

Zach chuckled. "You live by the ocean, even make a living by it, and you hate saltwater?" he said, his eyes dancing. "God, woman, you're full of surprises. Don't you know that I noticed how you hated every minute on the back of that horse? I can read every expression on that lovely face of yours as though it were a book. What else don't you like that you want to keep from me? I know that you love me. I know that you enjoy my kisses. I know that you don't like being teased about your lovely name. . . ."

Shaking her head and laughing, Eden doubled a fist and pummeled his chest with it. "You fiend," she said. "I knew you had the power of reading my every thought. You've proven that more than once to me. As for my feelings for you—you have seen it in my eyes and felt it in the way I always respond to you. You know that I love you passionately. Except for one thing. . . ."

The water lapping at his knees, Zach stopped and stared down at Eden, his thick brows arching. His lips lifted into an amused smile. "Except?" he said, leaning his face closer to hers. "Except what?"

"Except that I'll hate you if you lower me into that saltwater," she blurted out. Then she looked pleadingly up at him. "Truly, I hate it. It stings my flesh. Please don't dunk me into it,

Zach. I'll break out into all sorts of horrid little bumps if you do. Sometimes even the saltwater spray irritates my skin."

"You're as delicate as a flower, are you?" Zach teased, holding her out away from him as though he was going to drop her in the water. "You'll wilt if I drop you?"

Eden clung onto his arm for dear life. "No I won't wilt, you imbecile," she screamed, laughing. "I'll turn into one large bump."

"But, darling, we both need cooling off," Zach teased her. "We've already taken too much time in making love. We can't again."

He eyed the water, then Eden. "And yet . . . I've never made love in the ocean before," he said, his eyes dancing. "To hell with bumps! I'm going to seduce you in the water."

Eden sighed heavily. She threw her head back, shaking her hair so that it hung in golden streamers toward the water. "I see that I can't win with you," she murmured. "Take me if you must." She raised her eyes to his and smiled seductively. "But suffer the consequences. You will have to sacrifice weeks of loving me, for, my dear, I will be too horrid to look at and to touch. The last time I came into contact with saltwater I was quite a monster to look at."

She screwed up her mouth, twisted her nose to one side with a forefinger, and squinted up at Zach. "I looked like this," she teased him, crossing her eyes to add to the picture.

"God," Zach said, laughing. He began carrying her from the water. "I think I can take a hint." He kissed the tip of her nose as she let her face relax to its natural loveliness. "And I most certainly wouldn't want to do anything that would cause you pain."

Eden cuddled close to his chest, twining an arm about his neck. "Zach, this has been a most beautiful day," she murmured, feeling melancholy for having to draw it to a close. "I wish it could last forever."

Zach set her on her feet, then drew her into his arms. He feathered kisses across her face, relishing the touch of her soft breasts against his hard body. "It could, you know," he whispered, his breath hot on her cheek. "Marry me, Eden. Be my wife."

Eden's heart lurched. Her knees grew weak. She leaned back, surprise in her eyes. "Marry you?" she gasped. "Zach, tell me that I am not imagining things—that I heard right. Tell me that you did ask me to be your wife."

Zach chuckled. His lips swept down and he kissed first one breast, then another. He knelt on one knee and kissed her navel, his fingers splayed against her abdomen. "Yes, I proposed," he said huskily, his lips now at the triangle of golden hair at the juncture of her thighs. He kissed her there, then rose to his feet again. He placed a forefinger to her chin, tilting her face upward so that their eyes could meet and hold. "Will you? Will you marry me?"

Soaring with happiness, Eden touched his cheeks wonderingly, then his lips. "Nothing would make me happier," she murmured. But then the memory of her doubts about

Zach and his mysterious side surfaced again and began stabbing away at her consciousness.

Remembering Angelita, her eyes wavered. Recalling Angelita's exuberance over having received gifts from a secret admirer made her feel a pang of jealousy around her heart.

Yet, there was no proof that the secret admirer was Zach. Surely it wasn't. Why would he send Angelita gifts and not the woman he professed to love—even asked to marry?

No. She would not question him about Angelita, nor anything else, for that matter. For now it was enough that he was proving his love to Eden Whitney. No man married one woman with another woman on his mind—a woman who was even more available at that.

"Oh, yes, I would be happy to become your wife," Eden said, lunging into his arms. She closed her eyes tightly, trying to force doubts from her mind. She hugged him fitfully, having never thought it possible to love a man so intensely. "I love you so, Zach. Oh, so very much."

"Then let's go and tell your father," Zach said, lifting her up into his arms. He swung her around, laughing. "I don't think he'll be too disappointed in your choice, will he? He may question how quickly the decision was made, but he surely knows that it is possible to fall in love at first sight. I bet he fell in love just as fast with your mother." He kissed her softly on the lips as he put her to her feet again. "Especially if she looked like you."

Eden smiled up at him, tears in the corners of her eyes. "Everyone who knew my mother marvels over our resemblance," she murmured. "But I don't see how I could ever be as lovely as she was. As I remember her, she was the most beautiful woman in the world. She was a most perfect mother."

She lowered her eyes. "And father says that she was a most perfect wife," she said softly.

"Eden," Zach said, again lifting her chin with a forefinger. "You are the most beautiful woman in the world. You are gentle. You are caring. I feel the same for you as your father felt for your mother."

"Oh, Zach," Eden said, snuggling into his arms. "Always love me as much."

"Always."

He drew away from her and gathered her clothes up into his arms. "Let's hurry and get dressed," he said. "By the time we reach your cottage your father will be awakening for his long nightly duty in the lighthouse. We'll give him something to think about all night. Of course, he will be sad to think that he will be losing you to another man, but we will make sure that he never has cause to be lonely. In fact, we'll pester the daylights out of him by visiting him so often."

Tears once again surfaced in Eden's eyes. She touched Zach's cheek meditatingly as he placed her clothes across her other outstretched arm. "Darling, you are so kind, so generous," she murmured.

Zach smiled down at her, yet his insides were troubled. There was so much to tell her and he was fearful of it. If she became disillusioned with him because of his past, would she be so anxious to become his wife? Would she even turn her back to him forever, seeing him as nothing but a rogue with no morals? Sometimes when he looked at himself in the mirror, that was what he saw.

Would he ever be able to forget?

He doubted it.

Would she, if he told her?

He doubted it.

Silently, they hurried into their clothes.

Horses whinnied and stamped their hooves nervously as Joshua went from stall to stall, scooping more straw into them. Shirtless and slick with sweat on his bare chest and back, his muscles rippled across his shoulders as he lifted the pitchfork full of straw, then lowered it slowly, his eyes and thoughts elsewhere. Through the wide-opened door of the barn he saw Sabrina hanging Zach's washed clothes on the line, looking so graceful.

Wiping a bead of perspiration from his brow and leaning his full weight on the handle of the pitchfork, Joshua continued to watch Sabrina. He was fighting his feelings, but it was useless. He had been without a woman for too long and this woman was not like any other he had seen for a long time. He liked everything about her, especially her spirit. She knew her own mind and she did not hesitate to let you know it.

If not for the color of her skin and her bare feet, it would be impossible to know that she was a slave. Anyone who happened along and saw her in the yard, so beautiful in the dress that Eden had kindly given her, would see only that she was a part of the household, free and answering to no one.

Shifting his weight on the handle of the pitchfork, Joshua continued to watch Sabrina. The cotton dress, with its tiny yellow rosebud pattern against a white backdrop, fit her snugly on top, revealing her generous breasts straining against the fabric. Her tiny waist was accentuated by tucks, leading Joshua's eye to a fully-gathered skirt. It was blowing in the wind now, lifting to reveal tiny ankles. Every now and then even a thigh was revealed until she slapped the skirt back down and resumed pinning clothes to the line.

Lifting his eyes, Joshua admired Sabrina's long, thick hair, and then her perfect profile. Her dark eyes were lazy and sure today, as if she found her new home way more pleasant than her last.

Letting the pitchfork fall to the straw-covered floor, Joshua ambled out of the barn. He walked toward Sabrina, wanting her. It had been in her eyes earlier in the day when they had met for breakfast that she had special feelings for him, also.

With him, loving would come naturally, not forced. He would give her a gentle loving. Never would she feel forced again as long as he was around to protect her. She hadn't been brought here to bed with a white man. Only dark hands would touch her from now on.

Sabrina felt Joshua's presence even before

151

she heard his footsteps approaching her. It was his eyes. They were burning into her, causing her to turn slowly toward him.

Dropping a clothespin, she smoothed the skirt of her dress down as the wind once again whipped it up, revealing her shapely legs. Her heart began to beat soundly. She was becoming breathless, her eyes locking with Joshua's, knowing what he was asking her without words.

Swallowing hard, she held out a slender hand and melted inside when he gathered it into his thick, callused fingers. Drawing her to his side, he led her toward the barn.

"Sabrina, tell me you need me as much," Joshua said thickly. "Tell me you've been as lonesome."

"Sabrina do need you," she murmured. "Sabrina's been powerful lonesome, Joshua."

"Neither of us will be lonesome again," Joshua said hoarsely. "And I'll make sure no one uses you again. I'll protect you. You'll see."

Sabrina sighed and cuddled against him as they stepped into the barn. "It'll be good to have someone lookin' out for my welfare," she whispered. "Since I was a child, I've had to look out for my own." She lowered her eyes. "That wasn't enough, Joshua. Too many hands on my body made me realize I wouldn't be big enough, eva', to fend fo' myself. I learned just to let myself go all dead inside when I was bedded by my masters." She looked slowly up at him. "But with you, it'll be different."

"Little Momma, you're soon to see just how different it's gonna be," Joshua said, smiling down at her. "I'm going to make your sweet little heart sing."

Bashfully, she lowered her eyes again. "I knows it," she whispered. "I knows it."

Riding along the road, the cottage and lighthouse in view, Eden felt as though what was happening to her was not real at all. It was too much like a fantasy, something that she might read about in a book. Things like this happened to other women. Not her.

The man riding at her side had actually proposed to her! They were going to be married.

Radiantly happy, she could hardly bear not to touch Zach at this very moment. She had to see if he was real, to be certain that he was not a figment of her imagination. She wanted to hug him to her and never let him go. To be separated from him for even one hour would be too much.

"Eden, darling Eden," Zach shouted, "let's not wait long before setting the wedding date."

Eden looked at him, again amazed at how he could so easily read her thoughts. Only a moment ago she had worried about being separated from him. "Darling Zach, tomorrow would not be too soon," she shouted back, throwing her head back and closing her eyes dreamily. "Oh, if only we could be married tomorrow. Wouldn't it be heavenly?"

"I think it can be arranged," Zach said, sidling his horse closer to hers. "I'll see what I can—"

Zach's words were drawn to an abrupt halt when suddenly, from behind a thick cover of oak trees at the side of the road, appeared several men on horseback, pistols drawn. Zach grabbed Eden's reins and stopped her mare as he brought his own gelding to a shuddering halt.

Eden's eyes were wild with fear; her throat was dry. She grabbed for Zach's arm and clasped it, her fingernails digging through the material of his shirt, into his flesh. "Sheriff Collins!" she gasped. "What does he want?"

Zach glared at the sheriff. He understood too well who had to be behind this roadside escapade. Judge Pryor.

"Darling, just keep quiet and whatever you do, don't panic," Zach said, glancing over at Eden. He eased her hand from his arm. "I'm sure you won't be harmed. It's me they're after."

Eden looked slowly at Zach, feeling coldly numb inside. Was she about to find out why at times she had seen a mysterious side to the man she loved? He seemed to believe that these men were there to take him away. Why? What could Zach have done to put himself in such a compromising position?

Her hand to her throat, Eden felt panic rise inside her. She once again recalled how Zach had spoken so favorably of pirates. She knew his love of the sea. Could he be—?

"Zach, please tell me what this is all about," she cried. "You know, don't you? You know why these men are here?"

Sheriff Collins separated himself from the others and rode up to Zach.

"If you leave with us without causing any problems, the lady will be permitted to return home, unharmed," Collins said, giving Eden an uneasy glance. Then he looked back at Zach, no obvious hate in his eyes. "Zachary Tyson, we want you. No one else. Go into town with us peacefully. Do you understand?"

Seeing at least a dozen pistols aimed at him, Zach chuckled low and nodded. "Seems I have no choice, doesn't it?" he said, tightening his hands on his reins. He looked at Eden. "Darling, it seems I waited too long to explain some things to you. Now perhaps it's too late."

He reached a hand to her cheek. "Go home," he said thickly. "Forget about me. I should never have drawn you into my life in the first place. I knew it was dangerous. I just hoped that it was finally possible for me to have a decent, normal life. With you, it would have been wonderful."

Tears burned at the corners of Eden's eyes. She choked back a sob. She clutched Zach's hand. "Zach, I'm so confused," she cried. "This can't be happening. Only moments ago, we—"

Zach placed a finger to her lips, sealing the words inside them. "Shh," he said. "Just let it be. You have no other choice."

Eden brushed his hand aside. "How can

you expect me to just ride away from here, to go home and forget about you and me?" she cried. "Can you forget? Can you?"

Sheriff Collins nudged Zach in the ribs with the barrel of his pistol. "Enough of this," he growled. "Come on, Tyson. It's time to take a ride into town."

Eden looked wild-eyed at the sheriff. "Where are you taking him?" she screamed. "Why are you taking him?"

"Lady, if you know what's best for you, you'll do what this man advised you to do," he said flatly. "Go home. Forget you ever knew him. He's not worth any lady knowin'. Don't you know there was so many women in his life when he traveled the seas that you are just another one to gloat over?"

Zach doubled his hands into tight fists. His eyes narrowed with anger, but the pistol in his ribs made him hold back an angry retort. He had no choice but to do as the sheriff said. As he saw it, he had just lost all choices in life again. And he had lost Eden.

He looked at her, his eyelids heavy over dark, penetrating eyes. He could see her parted lips and her look of confusion over what the sheriff had just said. There was no use trying to explain that, when he had told her she was the first woman he had truly loved, he had been telling her the truth. It was in her eyes that she would not believe him now, or perhaps ever again.

Setting his jaw firmly, he turned away from her and rode away with the armed men, his heart aching for having lost Eden after just having found her.

Eden gaped openly at the men who still kept their pistols drawn on Zach, as though he was too much of a threat to their safety to holster their weapons.

Sobbing hard, her heart feeling as though it were being shredded into a million pieces, she wheeled her horse around and headed quickly for home. She wanted to go to her father for help, but at the same time she did not want to trouble him. He barely got around well enough to take care of his own problems.

"And this problem is mine," she said, licking salty tears from her lips. "I must find some answers, some explanation of what has happened today. Even though Zach has obviously lied to me about his past, I must try to help him."

Tightening her reins and drawing the horse to a halt, Eden looked into the distance, where she could still see dust rising from the road where the horsemen and Zach traveled away from her.

"Judge Pryor," she whispered harshly. "I'll go to him. Perhaps he can help me. He's the only one I know who knows about things like this."

She looked toward the lighthouse and at the dimming light in the sky as the sun neared the horizon. "But I can't now," she whispered. "Father will be up soon. I'll have to risk going into Charleston after dark."

A fearful tremor coursed through her at the

thought of traveling Lighthouse Road alone at night.

But she knew that she must. For her sanity, for Zach's life, she must.

Stretched out on a soft bed of straw with Sabrina at his side, Joshua smoothed his hands along her nude body, savoring its softness. "Little Momma, did I makes you feel good?" he asked huskily, cupping her breasts in the palms of his hands. When she sighed and curved her body into his, he knew her answer without hearing her reply.

Then he lurched forward and looked toward the barn door, something causing him to feel suddenly torn inside. He eased away from Sabrina and leaned up on one elbow, the uneasy feeling inside him quickening.

Sabrina saw the sudden panic in his eyes. She leaned up and touched his cheek. "What is it?" she asked softly. "Did you hear a noise outside?"

Joshua kneaded his chin, his brow furrowed. "No, no noise," he said. "It's just somethin' I feels. I feels like somethin' is happenin' but cain't put my finger on it." He looked toward the empty stall that usually housed Zach's gelding. "I has this crazy feelin' that Zach's in some sort of trouble. It's hard to explain. But I've known him for so long now, it's like we're brothers. When he hurts, I hurts. When he's feelin' good, I'm feelin' good. Right now, I have this terrible gut feelin' that he's cryin' out to me somehow."

Sabrina wove her body against his and

urged him down on his back. "Now, handsome man, you're bein' foolish," she said, laughing softly. Her fingers played along his flesh, tormenting him. "You know he's with Eden. They're probably makin' love this very minute. That's what is probably bein' communicated to you. He's probably this very minute soaring in the heavens while locked in the arms of the one he loves."

Joshua frowned, finding it hard to shake the foreboding feeling seizing his insides. He scooted Sabrina away from him and drew on his breeches. He went to the barn door and looked into the distance. "When he comes ridin' down that oak-lined drive, only then will I feel betta' about things."

Sabrina looked up at Joshua, a shudder encasing her, for even she was beginning to have a premonition of doom. But surely it was only because it was rubbing off Joshua onto her.

Slipping her dress over her head, she went to Joshua and eased into his arms. "Things'll be all right," she purred. "He's too kind a man for anything to happen to him. You'll see."

Joshua nodded. "He is sho' nuff a kind and generous man," he agreed, but in his mind's eye he recalled when Zach was known far and wide as a pirate. To those who did not understand his ways of pirating, he was akin to the devil. Those were the ones Joshua feared. It was those who would find delight in seeing Zach dead.

Chapter Eleven

Oh, memories that bless—and burn!
——ROGERS

Eden had left a pot of soup simmering over the fire, so she did not have to stand over a stove and prepare supper when she returned home from her outing with Zach. She thought she would have retched if she'd had to cook. Even now, as she sat at the supper table forcing herself to eat the soup and to look as though nothing terrible had happened, she felt nauseated.

She stared down at the soup as her mind swirled with questions and despair washed through her. How could the world be so perfect one minute, then tumble down around her the next? Zach had asked her to marry him and she was not even free to tell her father. As far as she knew now, there would never be a marriage.

"Eden, what's going on inside that head of yours?" Preston asked, laying his spoon aside. He leaned closer to her, over the table. "When I asked you if you had a pleasant day with Zach, you said that you did. If so, why the long face? Why are you so quiet? This isn't like you at all. Tell me, Eden. Did something happen between you and Zach that you don't feel free to tell me? Did he—"

Eden looked quickly up at her father, panic grabbing her. He was about to ask if Zach had approached her wrongly. She could not bear for him to ask, for it had been a mutual seduction. Knowing now that Zach had been far from honest with her made her realize that she should have never allowed this afternoon to happen.

"No, father," she lied. "Nothing like that happened." She forced a smile. "It was a wonderful day. It's just that I am tired. You know how I hate to ride horses. I feel as though every bone in my body is wracked with pain."

Preston laughed softly. He picked up his spoon and resumed eating. "That explains it all," he said. "I should've known you'd come home all out of sorts." But then he paused with his spoon halfway to his mouth. "Hon, I'm glad you made the effort to please that nice young man. I like him a lot. I see him as special."

Eden winced. A choked feeling invaded her

throat. She looked away from her soup, feeling sick again. She knew that she would not be able to eat or sleep until she had some answers about Zach. As soon as her father was busy in the lighthouse, she would choose something as masculine as she could find and ride into Charleston on the dreaded horse and go to Judge Pryor and ask him to help her. It was useless to go to the jail herself to see if Zach was there and demand his release if he was. Sheriff Collins would only send her away.

Then her throat constricted when she recalled Zach's reaction to Judge Pryor that day in the inn. He had most surely fled because of him.

Oh, Lord, was Judge Pryor the one who had sent Sheriff Collins to arrest Zach? If so, he was not the man to go to for help.

Yet, she knew no one else that well who had such power.

"What're you going to do tonight while I'm working?" Preston asked, taking a sip of coffee. "Or need I ask? Surely you are going to soak yourself in the tub and fall into bed exhausted."

Eden raised her eyes slowly and smiled awkwardly at her father, then nodded. Guilt plagued her for having to lie to him again.

But he would never understand any of what had happened.

She didn't, and she was a part of it!

Shirtless and manacled to the wall in the cell, sixteen-pound irons weighing down his wrists and ankles and eating into his flesh, Zach winced as he tried to move his arm. Pain shot through him; he looked somberly around him, and shuddered. The place was so verminous and the stench was so overpowering that his nostrils burned, clear down into the lining of his throat.

The slap-slap of waves outside, washing up onto shore close to the wharves, filled Zach with memories of days not so long past, when his life had centered on weeks and months at sea. He had just begun to leave his sea legs behind, had just seen the promise of a wonderful future on land with Eden at his side, when Judge Pryor had seen and recognized him. If Zach had been smart, he would have fled.

But he had already found a measure of happiness in his new way of life and he did not want to leave it now. He could not run from the law the rest of his life!

Candles dripping wax burned in rusty sconces along the walls. Footsteps approaching down the corridor drew Zach's quick attention. He peered through the bars of his cell, knowing who it must be—Judge Pryor. When he was brought to Charleston, Zach had been taken directly to the Judge and questioned. The Judge had made demands on Zach that he would not comply with. Confining him in the filthy cell was the Judge's way of forcing Zach to agree to his demands.

But it was apparent that Judge Pryor did not

know Zachary Tyson very well. No one forced this retired pirate to do anything.

No one!

The days when he could be forced were long past.

He would die first!

The white frills of the Judge's silk shirt, the embroidered waistcoat, and the diamond glittering in the folds of the cravat at his throat mocked this damp darkness called a jail, as Judge Pryor stopped before Zach's cell. Squinting, he smoothed his hands over his gray hair as he gazed expressionlessly at his prisoner.

"Well? Have you had time to reconsider?" Judge Pryor asked, slowly looking Zach up and down. "You don't seem to fit in here with the drunken derelicts that inhabit the other cells. They are brawlers, dragged out of the saloons and off the streets of Charleston. There are sailors too young to even blow their noses, who got a bit too rowdy. And you? Seems you've been living a good life since you gave up pirating. If you want to return to that way of life, do as I've asked and you'll be free to."

"I'd rot in hell first," Zach said, spitting at the Judge's feet. "Though I don't approve of what Pirate Jack has been up to these past months, I respect him too much to turn him over to you. He gave me a chance when nobody else gave a damn. I owe him for that."

Judge Pryor stepped fastidiously out of

Zach's range and clasped his hands together behind his back. "I think you have someone else to consider now, don't you?" he said, smiling slowly at Zach. "When you were captured today, you were with Eden Whitney. You've been with her quite frequently, haven't you?"

Zach frowned deeply. "That's none of your damn business," he growled.

"Don't you think she's worrying her pretty little head over you just about now?" Judge Pryor said smugly. "I was told that she was very upset when you were wrenched away from her. Should I go and enlighten her and her father about your past?"

"You leave Eden out of this," Zach growled. "She's already been hurt too much. Leave her be."

Judge Pryor began pacing in front of the cell, wincing when the lice and roaches crunched beneath his highly polished black shoes like shells along the shore. "I think she should see you in irons, in this squalor," he said, smirking. "Cooperate with me or I'll be forced to bring Eden here. Cooperate and I'll release you immediately."

The thought of Eden seeing him in this hellhole made Zach's stomach turn, but he knew the Judge was a good friend of Eden's father, and there was a slight possibility that the bastard wouldn't chance losing the friendship by pulling Eden further into this scheme of his.

"Cooperate with you?" Zach said, laughing throatily. "Never."

Judge Pryor began kneading his chin. "Now let's go over it once more," he said with exaggerated patience. "Very few pirates succeed at getting away with their ill-gotten gains by settling down into respectability as landowners. Most are captured and brought to justice for the crimes committed at sea. But, young man, you are going to be given a chance for a life of freedom. You are going to make amends for your past wrongful deeds. All I'm asking of you is to return to the sea just one more time."

Judge Pryor stopped and clasped his hands onto the bars, glaring, with an evil grin now, at Zach. "If you don't agree to what I ask, you will be hanged or left to rot in this cell," he warned. "You're an ideal choice for the deed that needs to be done. You know the ways of pirates. You know where Pirate Jack makes his residence when not at sea, looting and killing. You must go to Pirate Jack and kill him. Only by doing this will you ever be a free man again."

"Ramble on," Zach taunted. "You're wasting your breath. I won't kill anybody for you. Especially not Pirate Jack."

"Damn you!" Judge Pryor stormed, his eyes wild. "On account of Pirate Jack, ships are having to leave Charleston harbor in convoys, under Navy escort. Insurance rates are astronomical because of that damn pirate. He must be found and killed at all cost. It is up to you to do it, for no one knows him and his habits as well as you."

"Like I said—no thanks," Zach said, grimacing when a rat began sniffing at his bare feet. "And what's all of this to you, anyhow? You're no longer a man of the sea. You're a judge. It makes no sense at all that you're involving yourself in this."

He gazed at the scar on the Judge's lip. "Is it because of your lip? Because Pirate Jack made it ugly?"

Judge Pryor self-consciously covered his lips with a hand. He cleared his throat nervously. "Why I do this is no concern of yours— but that I will see that harm comes to Eden if you don't cooperate, is."

Anger flared in Zach's eyes. "You wouldn't," he growled. "Her father is your friend."

"Sometimes friendship gets in the way of ambition," Judge Pryor said dryly.

He leaned closer to the bars of the cell. "Perhaps I can entice you into cooperating with the knowledge that the Navy has agreed to let you have one of its fastest ships to take to sea in your search of the old pirate," Judge Pryor said, his voice low and strained. "The ship will be readied with a crew, though most will be taken from the jail cells since the Navy can't spare both a crew and ship. You will be in charge of the ship's welfare. Your reputation precedes you, Tyson. Everyone who has ever heard your name knows that you are one damn good sailor. What a pity you wasted your talents on piracy. You could have been an admiral in the American Navy!"

"You flatter me," Zach said sarcastically.

Judge Pryor frowned up at Zach. "Word will be spread that your ship will never be fired upon by the Navy," he continued. "Pirate Jack will be the only one not familiar with it— until he discovers that his old friend has gone back to pirating. Pirate Jack will never suspect that you are out to kill him."

Zach laughed throatily. "You have it all figured out, don't you?" he mocked. "You even have the Navy cooperating with your damnable scheme. You even offer me one of their ships. Damn it, man, don't you know I have enough money to buy every ship in the harbor? To hell with the Navy and the drunken sod crew you offer me. To hell with *you!*"

"I was hoping I could convince you without making a bloody mess out of you," Judge Pryor said. He turned his back to Zach and snapped his fingers, alerting two armed men who had been half hidden in the dark corridor. "I think this man needs convincing."

Zach's heart skipped a beat when he saw the two burly men approach him. He scarcely drew a breath when the Judge unlocked his cell, but tightened himself back against the cold, clammy wall, veins throbbing on his brow and in the tightness of his throat. When the first blow came on his face, his head jolted back with a snap. Over and over again he was hit in the face, chest and stomach but he did not cry out or agree to what the Judge had asked.

Finally the men stepped away from him and left the cell, nodding to the Judge.

Wracked with pain, Zach glared at the Judge. "You bastard," he breathed, looking through swollen eyes. He tasted his own blood as it trickled into his mouth. "I should've let Pirate Jack slit your throat that day I spoke up and saved your life."

"But you didn't," Judge Pryor said, laughing. He slipped his hands into his pockets, letting his thumbs hang over the front. "Now let's get back to business at hand. I'll ask you again and you will agree to go after Pirate Jack or the performance I just witnessed will be repeated. We have all night."

"And I'll refuse you all night and all tomorrow," Zach said stubbornly. "Nothing will change my mind. Even before I became a pirate, I learned to endure much in life— even daily beatings."

In Zach's mind's eye he was recalling his hellish aunt and how she had smiled as she had beat him when he was just a boy. He closed his eyes and thanked God that his precious sister had been spared such treatment.

He tightened his muscles when he heard the hefty men approaching him again. He clenched his teeth together so that he did not cry out with each of the blows to his body. Slowly his head began to spin until a black void of unconsciousness claimed him. . . .

Judge Pryor snapped his fingers. "That's enough for tonight," he said. "We'll try again tomorrow."

He turned and walked away, ducking his head. He had not wanted to go this far. He admired Zachary Tyson. He owed Zachary his damn life.

But he couldn't pass up this chance to draw attention to himself. Everyone would praise him for being responsible for ridding the seas of the damnable Pirate Jack. When he announced that he was going to run for governor of South Carolina, all votes would be his.

Yes, at all cost he must assure himself of that special recognition.

Judge Pryor reached a hand to his lip, smoothing his fingers over the wretched scar. Finally, too, revenge would be his.

The moon was hidden behind a thick cover of clouds as Eden drove herself desperately on. Riding a dependable, magnificent chestnut, she slapped the horse with her reins, commanding it to gallop faster. The night was so black, dark and still that she seemed to be riding into emptiness. The only sound was the constant drone of mosquitos. She had never felt so alone, so vulnerable.

Yet she had chosen well her attire for the journey into Charleston. She was dressed in a pair of coarse pants that she sometimes wore while working in the garden, and her leather riding boots. She had borrowed an old dark jacket from her father's closet, along with a wide-brimmed hat that he had not worn in years.

The hat hung almost to her nose because it was several sizes too large for her, and Eden had to keep pushing the brim up from her eyes. With her hair coiled tightly and hidden beneath the hat, she felt that she could pass for a man. If she could travel the streets of Charleston unrecognized, surely she could get to Judge Pryor's stately residence without being accosted. It was imperative that she get his help. If he were truly a friend, he would keep her visit in confidence and not tell her father. Eden hoped he was not the one who had given the orders to arrest Zach. Why would he, after all?

A victim of many emotions, Eden felt her throat tighten. The stark, blackened woods at one side, the rush of the ocean at the other seemed to make her fears rise up to choke her.

Every gust of wind brought whistles and moans. From the marshes came the rustling of the tiny fiddler crabs searching for food.

Glad to see some light flickering ahead, knowing the city was near, Eden ignored the musky smell of rich earth, and the thick, heavy shrubbery forming huge, looming shapes at the side of the road. She tried to concentrate on the hope of seeing Zach soon and gaining his release.

"Oh, Zach, if you had only been truthful

with me from the beginning," she said, a sob catching in her throat. "I wouldn't feel so helpless—so betrayed! Should I be chancing everything now to try and help you? Are you even worth it?"

Riding into Charleston, Eden traveled along the jumbled, narrow streets, wincing as her horse's hooves struck upon the cobblestones much too loudly, echoing into the night. She glanced from side to side. The hour was late and not too many people were on the streets; the houses looked cozy with the golden light of their lamps spilling from their windows. The strong aroma of smoke was in the air as it puffed up from fireplace chimneys.

When she came to the business district, she cowered over the mane of her horse, hearing the boisterous activities in the saloons and in the houses that were known to be used as brothels. Women in slinky dresses and color-fully painted faces paced the walks outside these establishments. Men guffawed and teased them as they rode past on horses or in fancy carriages. One of the women even raised a hand at Eden, motioning for her to stop.

A chill rode up and down Eden's spine. The woman thought she was a man. She was ready to lift her skirts to Eden for money.

Eden's eyes lit up suddenly. She smiled. If she fooled one of the whores of Charleston, surely she was fooling all of the men. She could ride on through the city without being afraid of being accosted because she was a woman wandering loose in these ungodly hours of the night.

Straightening her spine and squaring her shoulders, Eden slapped the reins against her horse's back and made a turn in the street that would take her away from the business district and toward Judge Pryor's fancy townhouse by the sea. She remembered well how to get there. She had gone with her father only a few months before to have tea with the Judge, who had also lost a wife some years back. He was a pleasant enough man, but was he kind? Was he trustworthy? Would he keep the secret that had brought her to him in the night, begging for help?

It was a chance she had to take. She must go to Zach. She must beg for his release! She had to have the answers he had denied her.

"But what if I'm too late?" she whispered, panic seizing her.

Riding along an oleander-lined street, with townhouses on both sides—two-storied, tall and statuesque, with gingerbread trimming and horseshoe-curved porches—Eden urged her horse into a soft trot.

Breathless, filled with fear as much over having to approach Judge Pryor in such an indelicate way as having been forced to dress like a man, she locked her eyes on his house. Studying its windows, seeing that lamplight was still evident in most rooms, she eased her horse to the white picket fence that surrounded it.

Her knees weak, she swung her leg over the saddle, stepped into the stirrup, and bounced to the ground. Her fingers trembling, she twisted and turned the reins around a fence post, then went to the gate and began to open it.

Jumping with alarm, Eden screamed when a large Collie bounded across the yard, barking incessantly at her, baring its teeth as it stopped on the other side of the gate, growling menacingly.

Eden calmed herself. She placed a finger to her lips. "Shh," she urged. "I'm a friend. Please. I must see Judge Pryor."

Her eyes moved slowly upward when the front door of the townhouse opened and there, silhouetted in the doorway, was a tall, lean man holding a lantern high over his head.

"Who is there?" the man said, his voice booming.

Eden knew that it wasn't the Judge. The Judge wasn't as tall and his voice wasn't as deep. This man was surely the butler.

"I've come to see Judge Pryor," Eden shouted, forgetting to disguise her voice to go with the man's outfit that she wore. She realized it the moment she spoke! But it was important now to reveal her true identity. The disguise was meant only to get her to the Judge's house.

"Judge Pryor isn't here," the butler said flatly. "Now, you ruffian, get on your way, or I'll have to turn the dog loose on you."

Eden's throat went dry. She glanced down

at the dog, its large brown eyes narrowing in on her. Again he growled and revealed his sharp teeth.

Desperate, Eden looked back at the butler. "Sir, just tell me where Judge Pryor is," she begged. "I'll leave you in peace. Please tell me. I must talk to him."

The sound of a carriage approaching made Eden turn with a start. Her heart beat anxiously in her chest, for she recognized the Judge's stately carriage as it pulled up beside her.

"What is this?" Judge Pryor said, opening the door and stepping down from the carriage. He looked intently down at the waif who stood at his gate. The night was too dark to make out the young man's facial features, but his clothes were enough to let the Judge know the lad was dirt poor. "Lad, what do you want at my house this time of night? If it's a handout, come back at a decent hour. I think my cook can scrape up something for you." He waved a hand in the air. "But for now, get on with you. You know better than to come around here this time of night. You could be shot, you know."

Eden was stunned for a moment from having been mistaken for a street urchin, even though the Judge should have noticed that she had traveled to his house on a magnificent horse that cost more than any urchin could afford just to feed.

Then she smiled to herself. Yes, she had disguised herself well.

Jerking her hat from her head, she removed her combs and shook her hair so that it tumbled down across her shoulders, then down her back.

"Judge Pryor, it's me. It's Eden!" she exclaimed. She clutched his arm. "Sir, I've come for your help. A dear friend of mine has been arrested. Oh, please help me find out what has happened to him."

Judge Pryor squared his shoulders, feeling smug. Eden had stepped right into his trap! She was the answer to getting Zachary to crumble beneath his demands.

But not yet.

Zachary Tyson must be made to suffer one more night. After the rats and lice had their way with him, he would be more easily persuaded!

Judge Pryor placed his hands on Eden's shoulders. He looked her up and down, and then into her eyes. "Eden, does your father know that you're here?" he said smoothly. "But of course, he doesn't. He wouldn't allow it. And you wouldn't be dressed in such garb."

Eden paled. "Sir, please don't inform my father of this," she begged. "This is my own private battle. It doesn't concern him." She lowered her eyes. "And I don't want to worry him." She raised her eyes quickly and implored him, "Please help me, sir. I must find out about Zach. Will you go to the jail and see if he is there, and if so, if he is all right? Will you help me see to his release? I know that he was arrested unjustly. He must be set free."

"Zach?" Judge Pryor said. He kneaded his chin, trying to pretend that he didn't know Zach. "Who is this Zach? What is he to you?"

Tears pooled in Eden's eyes. She swallowed hard. "Sir, Zach asked me to marry him today," she murmured. "A short while later Sheriff Collins arrested him! The Sheriff gave no reason why he did this. He took Zach away. Oh, Judge Pryor, I must know if he's all right."

Judge Pryor looked down at the street, shuffling one of his feet across the smooth cobblestones. "This man," he said slowly. "Is he the one who was with you at the inn?"

Eden grew numb inside. "Yes," she murmured.

"Let me ask around," he said, smiling smugly. "I'll see what I can do."

Unable to hold herself back, Eden lunged into his arms and hugged him. "I knew you would help me," she cried. "Thank you. Thank you."

Judge Pryor eased her away from him and looked down at her. "But not tonight, Eden," he said. "It's late. I had planned to come tomorrow morning for your father's birthday celebration. I'll tell you what I've found out then."

Eden's heart skipped a beat. "Lord," she gasped. "I had forgotten about tomorrow! Oh, how can I go through with it? How can I pretend that nothing has happened? But I must. Father is counting on this party."

Tears began flowing down her cheeks.

"How can I stand to wait until tomorrow to find out about Zach's welfare?" she cried.

"It seems you have no choice," Judge Pryor said, drawing her into his arms. He gave her a false, comforting hug. "Now, Eden, I'm going to ride along with you tonight, to see that you get home all right. But, young lady, you must promise never to do anything as foolish as this again. The jail is brimming with all sorts of vermin. There's more like them on the streets. Any of them would enjoy getting his hands on a pretty young thing like you."

"How horrible," Eden said, visibly shuddering with the thought of Zach being among those sorts of men in the jail.

"The world is filled with despicable men who deserve to be imprisoned," Judge Pryor said flatly.

In his mind's eye he was seeing Zach, unconscious and bloody. Perhaps tomorrow, when Eden was taken to him, the young man would stop the suffering that he had chosen over freedom.

Chapter Twelve

Oh barren gain—and bitter loss!

—ROGERS

A day that was supposed to have been wonderful was now shadowed by a cloud of gloom. Eden couldn't get Zach off her mind. Was he being mistreated? Was his life in peril? Would she ever see him again?

Glancing from the window, she eagerly watched the road. Perhaps Judge Pryor would bring good news with him. Perhaps she could tear him away from the other guests long enough for him to tell her his findings without others hearing.

Sighing heavily, she untied her apron, and draped it over the back of a kitchen chair, then went into the living room. Bending to one knee, she placed another log on the fire, then rose and stood with her back to it, absorbing the warmth through the cotton of her dress. She became melancholy with thought.

She had risen at the crack of dawn to bake her father's birthday cake before he came down from the lighthouse to get a few winks of sleep before his party. He had been asleep now for about two hours and guests were to arrive at any moment. A morning party had been planned so that he could have the rest of the afternoon to catch up on his sleep.

And while he slept in the afternoon, she would go into Charleston and see Zach. She could not bear another day of not knowing how he was . . . or where he was. . . .

Eden went to her bedroom and stood before her mirror. She smoothed her hands over her cheeks. She had slept scarcely a wink all night, and dark circles had formed beneath her eyes; they were red from crying. Her father had been too tired after working a full night in the lighthouse, and he had not noticed. But when he awakened, he surely would. There would be others who would notice, also. Angelita. Angelita Llewellyn. She noticed everything about everyone.

Her hair drawn back with a yellow satin bow that matched the small yellow polka dots on her fully gathered dress, Eden turned away from the mirror, her hands doubled into fists at her sides. "Angelita!" she said between clenched teeth. "Zach surely lied about his feelings for her, also. He must care for her, or he wouldn't have shown such concern."

But he would not have been arrested because of Angelita. There was something else in his past that had caused him to be treated so cruelly.

She went to the window and leaned the palms of her hands against the windowsill, peering out at the sea. "Could he have been a pirate?" she whispered. "If so, what crimes did he commit?" She grew cold inside. "Did he even commit . . . murder?"

Covering her eyes with her hands, she emitted a low, torturous sob, then jerked her hands from her face when she heard footsteps enter her bedroom. Everything within her grew numb when she saw Angelita there, sashaying into the room in her gorgeous maroon velvet dress that clung to her curves seductively.

"Angelita," Eden gasped, trying to wipe away the tears that were stinging the corners of her eyes. "I didn't hear you come in."

"I knocked and knocked," Angelita said, her dark eyes flashing, her midnight-black hair drawn up above her head into a loose swirl secured by diamond-encrusted combs. She rushed to Eden. "Eden, you've been crying. Do you want to tell me what's bothering you? It's not like you to cry. I've hardly ever seen you cry."

Eden shook her head. Angelita was the last person on earth she wanted to confide in. She didn't even want to mention Zach's name to

Angelita. What if Angelita recognized the name and laughed about Zachary Tyson having been one of her earlier conquests? The knowing would make Eden die a slow death inside.

"Why, Angelita, there's nothing at all wrong with me today," Eden said, forcing a laugh. She flipped the skirt of her dress around as she stepped on past Angelita. "Come along. Let's wait in the living room for the rest of the guests. Father will be rising soon. It should be such a nice morning."

Angelita hurried after Eden. "Eden, I saw tears," she fussed. "Now are you going to deny that you were crying?"

Eden went into the living room and stood at the window, watching the road for Judge Pryor's arrival. "I was just feeling sentimental," she said softly. "My father is a year older. So shall I be a year older soon."

Angelita plopped down on a chair. "Yes, we are all getting older," she said, groaning. "Even I will be seeing my next birthday soon. I shall be twenty-two. I must seriously consider settling down soon with one man or I shall qualify for the title of spinster. Heaven forbid, Eden. I shan't let that happen."

Eden moved from the window and sat down opposite Angelita. "The secret admirer?" she said dryly. "Perhaps you will one day meet and marry him." She cleared her throat nervously. "Angelita, have you received any gifts from him lately?"

Angelita removed a lacy handkerchief that

had been tucked up in the sleeve of her dress. She began twisting it around her forefinger. "It's strange that you should ask," she said. "For days I received wonderful gifts, and then the past two days I've received nothing."

Eden felt as though someone had stabbed her in the heart, realizing that Zach couldn't have sent any gifts to Angelita under the present circumstances. Oh, surely he was the admirer! Why then had he asked Eden to marry him?

Perhaps she would never know.

"How is your aunt?" Eden asked, to direct the conversation elsewhere.

"She's about the same," Angelita said sullenly. "But I think she will begin recognizing me soon. She's been doing a lot of mumbling to herself." She lowered her eyes and released a little sob. "I sometimes believe that when she's mumbling, she is speaking of my brother."

Eden scooted to the edge of the chair. "Angelita, always in the past when you've begun to speak of your brother, you stopped after only a moment," she said softly. "There is always such pain in your eyes when you mention him. But never have you told me his name or why he is no longer with you. Angelita, is he dead?"

"Eden, I don't know," Angelita said, her voice shallow. "Though I do owe my aunt so much for the kind way she treated me after my parents' death, she treated my brother intolerably! She even—"

The sound of a carriage and several horses coming down the lane stopped Angelita from confiding any more to Eden, and, anxious to see if Judge Pryor was one of the new arrivals, Eden did not even notice. She rose quickly to her feet and rushed to the door and flung it open.

When she saw Judge Pryor stepping from his carriage, a dizziness swept through her, so anxious to see what he had to say.

Yet, how long would it be before they could be alone to talk in private? Perhaps not until after the party was over. The waiting would be sheer agony!

"Well, what have we here?" Preston said from behind Eden. He moved from his bedroom, leaning heavily on his cane. "Am I almost too late for my own birthday party?"

Eden had to forget about questioning Judge Pryor for the moment. Her father had to be the prime focus for now. Going to him, she hugged him fiercely. "Happy birthday, Father," she murmured. "I can hardly wait for you to see the gift that I bought for you."

He patted Eden's back. "You are gift enough for me, honey," he said softly. "Always remember that."

"And Angelita," Preston said, moving toward her, his eyes feasting on her loveliness. "I'm glad you found time from your busy social calendar to come to an old man's birthday party. It's nice to have you here."

Angelita placed a hand to her throat and giggled, fluttering her lashes up at Preston.

186

"Preston, you knew that I'd be here," she said. "And, gracious me, you are not an old man." Her gaze swept slowly over him, seeing his golden hair with not even a hint of silver among its threads, and a handsome face with no trace of wrinkles.

Her gaze lingered on his legs a moment longer, her heart aching because of his misfortune. Remembering him so vividly before the accident, when he was still strong and vital was enough for Angelita to still see him that way, instead of half crippled.

She raised her eyes and smiled sweetly up at him. "Why, if I met you only today and had to guess your age, I would say you are no more than thirty," she said in a seductive purr.

Eden's mouth gaped open, shocked over how Angelita was so openly flirting with her father. And by the look in his eyes, he was being taken in by her sweet talk.

Frustrated, Eden swung away from them and began greeting everyone at the door. One by one the guests filled the room. When Judge Pryor entered the cottage and took Eden's hand and kissed it ever so politely, his eyes locked with hers and her heart skipped a beat. Oh, if she could only talk with him about Zach now! How could she wait? How?

Her eyes followed the Judge as he walked across the room and settled into a chair. She jolted with alarm when her father came to her side and looked down at her with questioning eyes when it was apparent that everyone who was going to come was there.

"Where's Zach?" he asked. "You invited him, didn't you?"

Eden swallowed a fast-growing lump in her throat. "Father, he had to attend to business," she said hoarsely. "I'm sorry. But he did send his regrets. He even said that he would be bringing you your gift later."

"Well, isn't that thoughtful of that nice young man?" Preston said, his eyes lighting up.

Judge Pryor and Eden exchanged glances. Her pulse raced, seeing something in the Judge's eyes that made her more impatient than ever to talk with him. He had seen Zach. He knew his condition. . . .

The last gift was opened. The pipe that Eden had given her father was clamped proudly between his teeth as she hugged him.

"Now when did you go shopping for this pipe?" he asked, patting her on the back.

Eden tensed, glad that Judge Pryor interrupted.

"Preston, will you lend me your daughter for the rest of the afternoon while you're catching up on your sleep?" Judge Pryor asked, stepping up to Eden's side. "I have some tulip bulbs I'd like to give her. Also, my gardener found some rare ferns while exploring in the forest the other day. I'd like to show them to Eden. Can you spare her?"

Eden slipped from her father's arms, scarcely breathing. She glanced from Judge Pryor back to her father, awaiting a reply.

Surely the Judge was going to take her to Zach!

The thought made her insides quiver. How would she find Zach? Would he be all right? Did she even truly want to know? If he was harmed in any way, she wasn't sure she could bear it, for no matter how much he had lied to her, she would love him forever.

Preston's eyes gleamed as he smiled at the Judge. He leaned on his cane with one hand and clasped the other on the Judge's shoulder. "What have we here?" he chuckled. "Am I to gather from that invitation that a man my own age has eyes for my daughter?"

Judge Pryor gave Eden an uneasy glance, then smiled at Preston. "Would you give me your blessing if that were true?" he teased. Then he laughed. "No, Preston. I've nothing in mind except to give Eden pointers on how to brighten up her flower beds. That's all."

"Well, Sefton, I guess I can manage to let her go with you," Preston said, smiling at Eden. "That is, if you'll get her home before sunset. I don't like her out after dark. Pirate Jack could have some of his scruffy crew wandering these back roads, looking for female companions to take on board his ship. I don't want that to happen to my daughter."

"She'll be home in time to help you light your lamps in the lighthouse," Judge Pryor said, his voice drawn. "I guarantee it. And I'd like to come back myself when I have more time. You've got to tell me about that Fresnel lens you're considering for your lighthouse.

Sounds interesting. Perhaps I can find a way to see that you receive funds for the lens."

"How thoughtful of you, Sefton," Preston said, shaking the Judge's hand heartily. "I'd appreciate whatever you can do for me."

Judge Pryor smiled at Preston, then eased his hand away. He stepped to Eden's side. "If I'm to get you back before dark we'd best leave now," he said.

"All right," Eden said, her pulse racing.

Angelita moved to Eden and embraced her fondly. "I've really got to go, also," she murmured. She turned to Preston and looked up at him, smiling. "Happy birthday, Preston. I hope the new cane I bought you is to your liking."

"It's just fine," Preston said. He patted Angelita on the back, hungering to do more than that. He wanted to draw her into his arms. He wanted to warn her about traveling Lighthouse Road without an escort. But he wasn't free to scold her or to love her. He was nothing to her but an invalid friend.

"And don't wait so long to come back visiting, do you hear?" he said. "You have a way of brightening up a place."

"I'll see to it that you'll get tired of my face," Angelita said, giggling. She swished her full skirt around and rushed from the house; everyone else took her lead, filing after her until all were gone but Judge Pryor.

"Now, Sefton, you take care of that daughter of mine," Preston said, following Eden and the Judge to the door. "See to it that no roadside scalawag grabs her away from you."

"She'll be just fine in my company," the Judge said. He placed a hand to Eden's elbow, helping her down the stairs.

Eden gave her father a quick smile over her shoulder. "Father, are you sure it's all right?" she said pensively. "Today's your birthday. Perhaps I shouldn't be leaving."

"I'm going to bed as soon as you leave," Preston said, waving. "You just have a good time." He smiled as he glanced up at the wide, open heavens, so blue it was as though the sky was a mirror of the ocean. "I've never seen such a beautiful day. It's nice that you've been asked on an outing."

"Yes, nice," Eden said, stepping up into the carriage. She waved, then grew tense as the Judge sat down beside her. She glanced over at him. "Lord, this has been the longest morning. Sir, now that we have the chance to talk, please tell me. Is Zach all right?"

Judge Pryor closed the carriage door. The driver directed the vehicle around in a half circle, then down the long lane that led to Lighthouse Road.

"My dear, there's so much I have to say to you," Judge Pryor said quickly. "I'm sure you won't understand much of it, but you must be told. You won't rest easy until you know. And I understand. If you love the man, love can make one do crazy things."

"Like trust a man?" Eden said stiffly.

"Yes, like trust a man," Judge Pryor said, avoiding her eyes. "Perhaps you trusted Zachary Tyson much too quickly."

Eden's heart bled, dreading to hear what the Judge was about to tell her, for she now knew that none of it could be good.

But she had to know.

"Sir, please don't dilly-dally any longer," she blurted. "Please tell me everything. I do love Zach. I need to know."

"First, let me tell you that he was not at all the man you thought him to be," Judge Pryor said. "Surely you would have never fallen in love with a pirate."

"A . . . pirate?" Eden whispered, paling. "Oh, Lord, I had guessed as much. I was right?"

"He's a retired pirate," Judge Pryor continued. "He rode the high seas on the black devil ship with Pirate Jack. Eden, it was I who sent Sheriff Collins to arrest him. Tyson alone can lead to the dreaded, damnable Pirate Jack. That is why I had him arrested. I'm trying to convince him that for his own health and happiness he must agree to go and kill Pirate Jack. If he doesn't agree to cooperate, he'll never be a free man again."

Eden's head was spinning. She hung her face in her hands. The man she loved had been a part of Pirate Jack's crew. He was a retired pirate. Judge Pryor had himself ordered him to be arrested.

"Last night?" she said, her voice thin and

drawn. "You knew last night, yet you did not tell me?"

"Yes, even last night," Judge Pryor admitted. "I couldn't take you to him last night. It wouldn't have fit into my plan. Taking you to Zachary today does."

Eden glared at the Judge. "What plan?" she said icily. "Why are you even involved? Why are you so eager to have Pirate Jack slain? It is the problem of the Navy. Not yours."

"You'll soon see why I've chosen to make it my problem," Judge Pryor said, still evading her eyes.

"You call yourself a friend," she hissed. "Sir, from this day forth you are not my friend, nor shall you be my father's."

"And so you plan to tell your father about all of this?" Judge Pryor asked, finally looking at Eden. "He'd be very disappointed in you, Eden, if he found out how you have deceived him."

"My father will forgive me," she spat. "But never you. You became a part of the deceit the moment you chose to include me in your schemes."

She folded her arms across her chest and stared ahead, her heart beating furiously with fear for Zach. Oh, how she was torn. She could not hate him for deceiving her, for at this moment he might even be dying.

She lifted her eyes to the heavens and spoke a long, silent prayer.

Chapter Thirteen

My hand is lonely for your clasping, dear.
——ALFORD

The stench made her stomach lurch and she was gasping for air as Eden followed Judge Pryor down a steep staircase that led to the jail cells. She emitted a soft cry and lifted the hem of her dress up past her ankles when a rat scurried by her. She did not want to think about what might be on the floor beneath her feet. It was as though she were entering the pits of hell, and it tore at her heart to know that Zach had been forced to endure a full night there already.

"We're just about there, Eden," Judge Pryor said, giving her a quick glance over his shoulder. "Be prepared for a sight that isn't too pleasant. But remember—it's of Zachary's choosing. He could have made things much easier if he had just cooperated."

"Yes—if he had only agreed to act as your executioner for whatever reason you still refuse to tell me," Eden said dryly. "Though I am sure the world would be a much better place without such a man as Pirate Jack, I can understand why Zach refuses to kill him. He isn't the sort to just go about aimlessly murdering people."

"Aren't you the naive one," Judge Pryor said. "Just what do you think Zachary did when he rode the seas as a pirate? Do you think he was saintly and gave blessings like a priest to all those aboard the ships that he and Pirate Jack plundered? Eden, he has the blood of many a man on his conscience."

He stepped back to Eden's side. He had to be prepared for an assortment of reactions from her when she saw Zachary. She might faint. He could not allow her to fall into the grime of the floor. If she returned home all filthy and stinking, he would have her father to answer to.

It was imperative that her father know nothing of this scheme to shock Zachary into cooperating after seeing Eden there in the jail, so vulnerable!

A friendship hung in the balance here.

Eden's feelings were torn. She did not want to think of Zach being a pirate. She could not bear to think of him as a man who could take another man's life, for any reason.

Yet, she could not help but recall the moments when she had seen a dark, sinister side to him.

A sob froze in her throat. All of this was almost too much for her to bear. The next few moments would surely be etched onto her brain for eternity, as a leaf becomes fossilized into stone. Surely if Zach were ever released, a life with him would be impossible. How could she let a man who had killed innocent people touch her?

Judge Pryor took Eden by her arm as they came to the foot of the steps and approached the dark gloom of cells. Eden's knees were weak and her breathing was shallow as she began to walk past the cells that lined each side of the dark, long corridor. Something clutched at her heart when she heard the moans and groans of men all around her.

Sheriff Collins had been trailing along behind Eden and Judge Pryor with a lantern. He suddenly took a wide step around them and hurried to one cell in particular. He held up the lantern, giving Eden a full view of the man manacled to the wall. She gasped and felt a lightheadedness seize her when, through the blood and grime, she recognized Zach.

"No!" she screamed, wrenching herself free from the Judge's firm grip. She ran to the cell and clung to the bars, crying. Her gaze swept over Zach, scarcely believing he could still be alive. He was manacled at both the wrists and ankles. In an unconscious stupor, his head was hanging forward; his face was swollen and covered with blood. Bruises were evident on his bare chest and stomach. His breeches were covered with dried blood. Even his bare feet were blood-covered.

"Zach!" Eden cried, hysteria rising in her voice. "Darling, what have they done to you? Wake up, Zach, I'm here for you. Tell me you're not going to die."

Judge Pryor took a wide step toward Eden. He pulled her hands from the bars and held her by the wrists. She had seen enough and he could tell by the way Zachary was stirring that he was regaining consciousness and had heard enough to make him aware of what he must do. It was obvious that seeing him was tearing Eden apart inside. Zachary would know this and surely want to be set free because of her. Seeing her would be a clear reminder of the threat that Eden would be bodily harmed if he didn't come to his senses and cooperate.

Judge Pryor smiled to himself. He could already see himself behind the grand desk at the Governor's Mansion. . . .

Yes, for Eden's well-being, Zachary Tyson would now surely agree to all his demands.

Taken bodily away from Zach's cell, Eden fought to free herself. "Let me go!" she screamed. "I want to stay here. I want to be with Zach."

"No, Eden," Judge Pryor said, half dragging her along the corridor, Sheriff Collins following along behind them with the lantern. "It's time for you to return home. Forget this man.

No decent woman would want any part of him. Especially not you, Eden—especially not you."

"Leave me alone!" Eden screamed, pulling at her wrists until they pained her. "Let me go. You're the fiend, not Zach."

"Eden, I'm seeing to it that you are taken home," Judge Pryor said. "Just forget everything that happened today. Especially what I forced you to see. Do you understand?"

Unable to fight back any longer, Eden's body went limp. She turned pleading eyes to the Judge. "Sir, please, I beg of you," she cried. "Turn Zach loose. Forget this scheme of yours to have him kill a man. Can't you see? Zach was living a peaceful life, not harming anyone. Why can't you let him go back to that life? He was no threat to anyone."

"No, not so much a threat," Judge Pryor said smoothly, guiding her up the stairs. "More like a convenience. Because of him, if he cooperates, I will be commended for ridding the seas of Pirate Jack, and my standing in the community will be considerably enhanced. Soon I shall be governor of this fine state!"

He ran a hand over the scar on his lip. "And I will finally get revenge," he growled. "Pirate Jack should never have used the knife on me that scarred me for life."

Eden stared at his scar, stunned to know how he had acquired it.

Then she looked into his eyes, aghast over his scheming ways that, in truth, would profit only him! It did not matter that a lovable, kind man's life lay in balance—Zach's life.

"Tell your father I will be seeing him soon about that Fresnel lens," Judge Pryor added in a monotone. "I would like to be the one who sees that your father gets it for his lighthouse."

Eden still stared at him, in awe of how in one breath he was so evil, and in another so kind. Surely no one knew the true man! Definitely not her father.

She found one last burst of energy that had not been drained from her. She yanked at her wrists, wincing with pain when the Judge clutched them harder. "Zach!" she screamed, her voice echoing down the steep staircase. "Zach! No matter what you did, I love you! I shall always love you!"

"Damn it, woman, get control of yourself," Judge Pryor said, stepping outside into the fresh air. "There's no need for the whole city of Charleston to know about your affair with that rogue."

Sheriff Collins stepped forward, giving the lantern to the Judge. "I'll see that she gets home safely," he said, giving Eden a reassuring look. "Ma'am, you can trust me."

"Use my carriage," Judge Pryor said, releasing Eden's wrists. He turned to her. "If it is any consolation to you at all, Eden, I wager that Zachary will be released from jail in the next few moments. All he has to do is agree to my demands—and something tells me that he's ready now." He smiled devilishly at her. "You see, it was my plan that Zach see you so

200

upset. Now he will cooperate with me just to be free to come to you to explain everything, and to see that you are willing to forgive."

Eden looked disbelievingly up at the Judge, then hung her head, empty inside. She did not believe that Zach would be set free. He would never agree to murdering a man in cold blood—not even to be free to come to her!

"Oh, and by the way, Eden," Judge Pryor said. "You'll find those tulip bulbs I promised you for your garden at the back of my carriage. I had them with me all along, knowing we wouldn't truly be going to my townhouse. It's best for you to have the bulbs when you get back to the cottage, or your father will wonder about it."

Eden sighed, never having thought the Judge could be such a scheming man. She went with Sheriff Collins and climbed into the carriage and rode through the city, feeling defeated. She had found a love so sweet and now she had lost it so quickly.

She was not sure she could live with the loss.

Wracked with pain, his stomach growling from intense hunger and his mouth dry from lack of water, Zach watched as Judge Pryor returned to his cell, alone.

"You bastard," Zach growled, looking through swollen eyes at the smug judge. "You planned it well, didn't you?"

Judge Pryor clasped his hands together behind him and rocked slowly back and forth from his heels to his toes and back again. "Yes, you might say that I did," he said. "Clever bastard, aren't I?"

Zach licked his parched lips. "You knew that Eden comes first in my life, didn't you?" he said hoarsely. "If you can go as far as bringing her to see me in this squalor, you sure as hell wouldn't stop at harming her!"

He stopped and inhaled a shaky breath, then continued, "You knew that when I had to choose between the welfare of the woman I love and Pirate Jack, the old pirate would be the loser. Well, you were right. Release me. I'll do as you ask. I can't bear the thought of Eden's being hurt by all of this."

"You've made a wise choice," Judge Pryor said, nodding. "Your ship and crew await you. You can raise the anchor as early as the coming hour. From that point on, do with your time as you see fit. Go and see Eden. Go and find the damnable pirate. You will be free to make choices again."

Judge Pryor glared over at Zach as he fished in his pocket for the key to the cell. "But remember that you are only free because of your decision to search out the pirate and kill him," he said flatly. "That is of prime importance. I will expect you to be far out to sea by midnight tonight."

"You have a ship and crew ready?" Zach said, glowering at the Judge. "You knew all along that I would agree to do this thing."

"I knew Eden was the answer," Judge Pryor said, unlocking the cell. He swung the door open and went to Zach, unlocking the irons at his ankles.

Zach scarcely breathed as he watched the key turning in the locks of the irons at his wrists. As soon his hands were free, he dropped his arms limply to his sides, waiting for the blood to begin circulating in them again. As he felt the strength returning, he took a step toward the Judge and doubled a fist. With one powerful blow he hit Judge Pryor in the jaw.

"Now I feel better about things," Zach said, watching with satisfaction as the blood trickled from the Judge's mouth. He rubbed his raw knuckle. "Show me to my ship. I think I can command it with vigor now."

Stepping out of his blacksmith shop for a breath of air, Smitty watched a stately carriage pass briskly by down the street. He slipped his hands into the pocket of his coarse, dark breeches as he recognized Eden Whitney through the small window. He smiled to himself, having just heard the news of her lover's incarceration with the rest of the slime of the city. This left Zachary Tyson's new slave, Sabrina, without a master. It would be a good time to go and get her. He had some unfinished business with her.

Tonight. Past the midnight hour, when everyone would be asleep, he would abduct her—and pity anyone who tried to stop him.

Chuckling throatily, he turned back into his blacksmith shop and resumed shoeing a horse. His loins were on fire with the thought of having that soft body yielding to his every whim and desire. If she refused him anything, he would give her a dose of snake and teach her how a whip felt against her dark, bare flesh.

Joshua watched the sun lowering in the sky, his dark brow furrowed with a frown. He stared into the empty stall in the barn for a few moments, then went outside and peered disconsolately up the oak-lined lane.

"He ain't nowheres in sight, Joshua," Sabrina said, coming from her cabin to stand at his side. "I been watchin'." She hugged herself with her arms, a chill coursing through her. "Don't it seem strangely quiet? I don't hear any birds in the trees or nothin'. Is that a bad omen, Joshua? It makes me afraid."

Joshua slipped his powerful arm around her shoulders and drew her close to him. "Little Momma, I suddenly is afraid, also," he said. "I fears that somethin' terrible has happened to Masta' Zach. It ain't like him to stay away unless he tells me he's goin' to. I fears he's run into bad luck."

"He was with Eden the last we knows," Sabrina said, her eyes wide as she looked at Joshua. "Maybe you should go and ask her if she knows where he's at."

"No'sah," Joshua said, setting his jaw firmly. "I ain't leavin' this place. There ain't nothin' a poor colored fella can do. I'm condemned to silence by all the white folk 'cept for Masta' Zach. I can't go around askin' questions. I might get locked up for what the white folk would say is insolent behavior for a slave."

"Yes, ah knows," Sabrina said, cuddling close to Joshua. "Hold me close, handsome man. Hold me close."

Joshua drew her around and hugged her mightily, his eyes still on the lane, watching . . . hoping. . . .

Zach was amazed at how Judge Pryor seemed to think of everything, how he had planned all along that he would agree to go and kill Pirate Jack. Even now, Zach stood on the deck of a powerful ship in a fresh change of clothes. They had been placed in his cabin by the Judge. The long, flowing sleeves of his shirt fluttered in the breeze as he watched his crew scurry around, readying the ship to be taken out to sea.

A brace of pistols held in loops on slings of leather were worn across his shoulders and his hair was drawn back from his face and secured in a pony tail by a leather thong. Zach felt as though he was a true pirate again. Besides his brace of pistols and his flowing shirt, he wore glossy black boots with high, wide tops and black leather breeches that molded his muscled legs like a second skin.

He was filled with the same sort of excitement that being aboard a ship always created inside him.

Looking around, he gazed at the fine ship that had been given him for his venture at sea. She was of a full-rigged design, one of the latest in fighting vessels. Designed for speed, maneuverability and firepower, the swift sloop was a near-ideal vessel for pirates. A rapier-like bowsprit almost as long as her hull enabled her to mount a parade of canvas that made her more nimble than any schooner or brigantine.

In favorable winds, a square topsail would give her an extra measure of speed—up to eleven knots if he needed it. Though not so shallow in draft as the schooner, this one-hundred-tonner would draw eight feet of water carrying a crew of fifty and fourteen cannons.

Earlier, upon close examination of the ship, Zach had found that, aside from the captain's cabin and a nearby cubby for the first mate, the interior of the ship was spartan in the extreme. Except for the Captain's cabin, there were no crew quarters as such; at night the men would have to cram into her hull, curled up wherever they could. They would have to relieve themselves by clambering onto the bowsprit. There was no galley, just a gigantic stewpot and a bricked-in hearth used only in calm weather and located far from the powder stores.

In the hold, the shot locker, with its six tons of shot for the cannons, and the huge water casks, each weighing a ton, were located amidship to help ballast the ship.

To survive close-quarters combat, each of the crew had been issued what most would call a walking arsenal. Each had been given a musket, blunderbuss, cutlass, boarding ax, pistol and dagger.

In the hands of these men who had been freed from the Charleston jail cells, the dangers were great—except that they all knew the price of mutiny.

Even Zach could not help but think of what the power of this ship could mean to him. He could blast the entire American Navy clean out of the water.

But a future with Eden, if she would even have him after realizing what sort of a past he had, made him think only of the chore that lay ahead of him. Pirate Jack could no longer be a consideration in Zach's life. Zach had paid his dues. Now perhaps it was time for Pirate Jack to pay his. Pirate Jack had become greedy. He had begun to plunder and kill for the fun of it, keeping all of the booty for himself.

Zach swallowed hard. The world would be a better place without Pirate Jack and Pirate Jack would be better off if Zach killed him. It would be quick and painless. If anyone else caught the old pirate, he would more than likely be tortured endlessly before he died.

Anxious to get on his way, knowing that he must take the ship down the coast a little way first, in order to land to go and assure Joshua and Eden that he was all right, Zach leaned his full weight on the rail of the ship.

"Hove up anchor!" he shouted. "Then once at sea, everyone come and listen to what I have to say. I will run a tight ship here! Remember that!"

He listened to the clanking of the anchor chain as it slowly pulled the anchor from the sea. Melancholy set in as he recalled the many wondrous hours he had spent at sea, loving the smells, the sights, the freedom. . . .

Then he was brought back to reality when his crew moved in close to him as the ship began inching away from the harbor.

Placing his hands on his hips, Zach looked from man to man. "Now hear this!" he shouted. "These are the laws that govern all men while on a ship commanded by me! If any man robs another while aboard my ship, he shall have his nose and ears slit and be put ashore. Lights and candles should be put out at eight at night and if any of the crew desire to drink after that hour they shall sit upon open deck without lights. Each man keeps his piece, cutlass and pistols at all times clean and ready for action. No boys or women are to be allowed amongst you. Any man found seducing any of the latter sex and carrying her to sea in disguise shall be put to death. I will allow no fighting on my ship between any of my crew. If an argument needs to be settled amongst you, it will be by sword or pistol on shore." He nodded and clasped his hands tightly together behind him. "That is all."

Conversation buzzed among the men as they disbanded. Zach turned and watched as Charleston was left behind. He turned and looked toward the lighthouse in the distance. "Eden," he whispered. "Oh, Lord, Eden, how I wish I could have spared you."

Chapter Fourteen

There are no stars tonight but those of
memory.

—CRANE

Eden paced the parlour floor, wringing her
hands and watching her father's bedroom
door. He had overslept and she could not find
the courage to go and awaken him. One look
into her eyes would reveal far too much to
him.

For many reasons she could not reveal any
of this afternoon's activities to her father. He
would become a disillusioned man if he ever
discovered the truth about those he admired
and loved. In Zach he had seen something
special that he had not seen in any of Eden's
other gentlemen callers—but he did not
know it was something sinister too. He did not
know his close friend, Judge Pryor had a cruel

side. Even his daughter was finding it so easy to deceive him!

"And he will find out," Eden murmured, cringing at the thought. "But as for his feelings about me, I must take this one step at a time. I must perform grandly this evening. I must behave as though nothing terrible happened today."

Making it through this day, unable to shake the memory of Zach covered with blood and manacled in the grimy cell, would be the hardest thing Eden had ever been forced to endure.

Going to the window, she peered up into the darkening sky. Soon she would be traveling in the dark along Lighthouse Road again. First she would go to Zach's plantation to tell Joshua what had happened. If Judge Pryor hadn't released Zach and he wasn't there, she would go to Charleston. If Zach was still in that damnable jail she was going to plead with Judge Pryor just one more time for his release. If the Judge didn't comply, she would make him do so at gunpoint.

She loved Zach and believed with all her heart that no matter what he had done in his past, he had to have had his reasons for his behavior. The man she had gotten to know could not go around murdering and pillaging. She had seen too gentle a side to his nature. But why hadn't he trusted her enough to confide in her? Why?

"Well, I shall give him that chance again," she whispered, tightening a hand into a fist at her side. "I just can't be that bad a judge of character. I saw so much more good in Zach than any possibilities of bad. . . ."

"Eden?" Preston said suddenly from behind her. "Are you missing Zach so much that you've taken to talking to yourself?"

Startled, having dreaded this moment all afternoon, when her father might read the despair in her eyes, Eden turned around with a jerk and faced him. She was glad that he was busy slipping suspenders over his shoulders, not even looking her way.

"What do you mean—missing Zach so much?" Eden murmured, stiffening her back. Did he already know? Had someone come and told him that Zach was imprisoned? If so, how could he be taking the knowledge so casually?

His suspenders in place, Preston went to the fireplace mantel, picked up his new pipe and slipped it into his shirt pocket. "Lord, Eden, it's only been a day since you've seen him," he chuckled. "Now you've got to get used to that young man's absence. He has a plantation to run. He doesn't even have any slavehands yet, only an overseer. He might have gone into Charleston to choose a few today."

Eden swallowed hard, breathing easier. "Yes, I'm sure it's something as simple as that," she murmured. She started toward the kitchen, still trying to evade her father's eyes.

"Honey, I seemed to have overslept, so I'm not going to take time to sit down to supper with you," Preston said, walking toward the front door. "Just dish me up whatever you prepared and bring it to me later." He chuckled and gave her a quick glance. "Much later. I'm still full of that damn good birthday cake you baked for me."

Eden turned slowly around, having to look his way. The flames in the fireplace cast a glow in her green eyes, turning them golden. The faint light from the one candle that she had lit was struggling to fill the spaces in the room as it grew darker outside.

Eden forced a smile, yet could not control the hammering of her heart, for she had only another moment or two to perform her act of dutiful daughter.

"I'm glad you liked the cake," she said. She looked at the pipe thrust into his shirt pocket. She didn't dare mention it. That might remind him again to ask when she had bought it. When there were many guests around, it had been easy to evade his one question about it.

Now, it was only her. It was only him.

"Yes, it was the best cake you've ever made," Preston said, opening the door. "Oh, by the way, Eden, did you get some prize tulip bulbs this afternoon from Sefton?"

He chuckled and gave her a fleeting glance over his shoulder as he stepped out onto the porch. "Knowing you and how you love your garden, I bet you already have them planted," he said proudly. "Just like your mother. You can do anything you set your mind to."

Feeling it safe enough to follow him outside, where the fading light of day cast shadows on her face and hid the emotion in her eyes, Eden clutched the porch rail to steady herself. It pained her so to see her father struggling with his cane on the stairs. It pained her to know that she would soon be betraying him again!

"The bulbs are quite nice, but not anything extra special," she said dryly, not wanting to give the Judge credit for anything. "I may plant them tomorrow."

"If Sefton gave them to you from his garden, you will see just how special they are when they begin blooming next spring," Preston said, walking along the pebbled path toward the lighthouse. "He's a fine man, Eden. I wish he were a few years younger. Though I see great possibilities in Zachary, Sefton Pryor could give you everything in life I've not been able to."

A chill coursed through Eden. "But he is too old, father," she shouted after him as he approached the lighthouse. Then she whispered to herself, "He's too old and too scheming. If you truly knew him, Father, you might even hate him."

She leaned forward and a slow ache circled her heart when she heard the echoing of her father's cane on the lighthouse steps as he moved slowly up them. "He needs me so much and I continue to deceive him," she sobbed, hurrying back inside the house. If she did not take him his supper later as he had requested, he would finally discover just how deceitful she was. She would be gone.

"I can't allow father to find out," she cried. She hurried into the kitchen and began put-

213

ting together a tray of food. She would take it up to her father now and say that he needed his strength and she wanted him to eat the beef stew while it was fresh from the pot!

She looked toward her bedroom. Awaiting her escape into the night was her cape and her pistol hidden in the depths of its pocket. When her father had given her the pistol, he had not expected her to use it to help a man escape from jail. It had been for her own protection.

"Can I truly shoot someone if it becomes necessary?" she whispered. This time she would be traveling into Charleston dressed as a woman, for she would not go to Judge Pryor dressed as a man again. Her dignity would not allow it.

Carrying the tray, she left the house, looking guardedly about her. It was now dark. Fear grabbed at her heart when she saw the beckoning shadows of night dancing around her as the trees blew and whistled in the breeze.

His ship tied up at the dock he'd built by his plantation, Zach ran through the thick grove of trees toward his mansion. He had to reassure Joshua that he was safe, and he had to send Joshua on a mission. These past several days, Zach had not sent Angelita any gifts. Even tonight there would be no gifts. Instead, there would be a lengthy note delivered to her doorstep.

Zach hoped he would be able to see Eden to

explain everything to her before he sailed away. But he did not have much time to spend on his private affairs. He had spied a small ship tailing along behind his vessel and expected it to continue hounding him until he took himself out to sea. Only then would the Judge believe that Zach was going after Pirate Jack. To be sure that Eden came out of this safely, Zach had no choice but to cooperate with the Judge.

But, just in case he missed Eden for whatever reason, he would have a note written to leave at her doorstep also. Even if her father got the note before she did, that was all right. No doubt her father already knew about everything, or would soon. Word of these sorts of things ran rampant through a community. Even as far as an isolated lighthouse!

Rushing down the long avenue of oaks, seeing a faint whisper of lamplight in the windows of the first floor of his mansion, Zach's eyes brimmed with tears. He had had such hopes of a decent, peaceful future in that house that had been built with his sweat— even his blood! All those years of fighting for his mere existence had gone into building that house. He deserved a serene life, but now it was being denied him.

"How can I be expected to kill Pirate Jack?" he softly cried. "He gave me back my life, my respect."

Swallowing back a fast-growing lump in his throat, he hurried on. When he got closer to the house he stopped short, seeing something that warmed his insides. Without letting Joshua know he was there in the shadows, watching, Zach silently observed him and Sabrina. They were standing side by side, obviously drawing comfort from being with each other. Zach knew that Joshua had hungered for a woman for a long time now. It seemed that Sabrina was filling that need.

But he had little time to waste. Zach rushed on toward the house, the moonlight flooding down on him as he ran from the cover of the trees.

"Joshua!" he shouted, waving his arms. "Joshua!"

"The captain's been gone long enough," one pirate whispered to another on Zach's ship. "Let's go now while we have a chance. Let's go find us a wench to have a little fun with while the others are sleepin'."

"Y'know the penalty for bringin' a woman aboard ship," the other pirate argued. "I ain't ready to have me hide skinned fer no lady."

"No one will know about 'er. We'll hide 'er in the hold of the ship. We'll tie and gag 'er. No one'll ever know she's there."

"I don't like it, Mike."

"Clarence, yer a goddamn chicken."

"Mike, the first time ye called me that and I did what ye wanted, I got thrown in the brig. The second time I got thrown in jail. I'm outta both hellholes now and I'm stayin' out."

"If ye don't go with me, Clarence, I'll stick ye with me knife when ye least expect it. Now what's it to be? Do ye want to go with me, or do ye want to have to wonder when I'm gonna stick ye?"

"Mike, ye wouldn't truly do that, now would ye?"

"If ye don't give me no choice, I will."

"Some goddamn friend ye turned out to be."

"I ain't yer friend no longer if ye don't go with me tonight. The sweet flesh of a wench is more important than a friend who ain't no friend at all."

"Where in hell would ye find a woman out here?" Clarence argued. "It's isolated as hell."

"Don't ye see the beam of that lighthouse yonder? Don't ye know that most lighthouses have cottages next to them? Let's go see if there's a wench in the cottage that we can steal away."

"If we get caught, we won't live to see another day," Clarence argued.

"If we don't get caught because ye don't go with me, ye won't live to see another day, anyhow," Mike chuckled. "Come on. Time's a wastin'."

The two pirates moved stealthily across the upper deck of the ship and down the gangplank. The moon was hidden behind a small dark cloud, aiding their flight.

Hiding her identity beneath the hood of her cape, her pistol close by in her pocket, Eden sat square-shouldered in her buggy, riding along at a brisk clip. The moon was elusive tonight. First it was shining a path down the middle of the narrow road for her, and then it was hiding behind a cloud.

But either way, she felt way too vulnerable on this lonely stretch of road.

"Just how far is Zach's plantation?" she whispered to herself. It seemed that she had ridden forever. What if he wasn't even there and she had all of this road to travel again to get to Charleston? She was tempting danger with every heartbeat.

The cloud slipped away from the moon, again brightening everything with its silver light. Eden sighed with relief, able to make out the trees on one side, the ocean on the other, where only moments ago there had been only dark shadows in the night.

Then she screamed and drew her reins taut when two men stepped from behind a thick stand of brush at the side of the road and daringly stood in the way of her buggy.

Fear grabbed Eden's insides. She grew weak all over as her buggy swayed dangerously as her horse reared and snorted, then came to a fearful stop as the strangers grabbed the bridle. Clarence took the reins from Eden's hands. Mike approached her with a drawn pistol.

Scarcely breathing, her eyes holding Mike's, Eden inched a trembling hand toward the pocket of her cape.

"I wouldn't do that, missie," Mike said, grabbing her wrist. He looked down at the bulge in her pocket. "What'cha got there? Some toy of a firearm?" He yanked her down from the buggy and held her close. "Clarence! Over here. Reach inside the lady's cape pocket and fish out the firearm. Toss it in the weeds. We won't have no need for her toy."

Small and wiry, Clarence moved stealthily toward Eden. In the moonlight she could see a face covered with dark whiskers. As he sneered at her, she saw that several of his teeth were missing, and that those that weren't were jagged. He wore dark, filthy clothes, and his red hair hung in greasy strands down to his shoulders.

When he got close enough for her to get a whiff of him, her insides churned in revolt; never had she smelled such a vile odor! Even the jail where Zach had been imprisoned hadn't smelled as bad.

"Who are you two?" she finally found the courage to ask. She flinched when Clarence reached into her pocket to get the pistol, taking his time, to first move his hands familiarly over her curves through her cape and dress.

"She ain't bad, Mike," Clarence said, with a snort. "Now I'm glad ye talked me into comin'. Once we get 'er on the ship we'll have ourselves lots of fun."

"We'd best get on our way," Mike said. "Put 'er back in the buggy. We'll use the buggy to get us back to the ship faster. When we get a little ways from the beach we'll ditch the buggy and the fool horse into the sea."

He looked coldly at Eden. "And if she don't cooperate, we'll just throw 'er in with 'em." He moved to stand over her, large and burly, with a bald head shining beneath the moonlight. He patted her cheek menacingly. "Do ye hear that, little lady? Ye cooperate or yer dead."

"What do you want of me?" she asked, her voice quivering. "What ship are you taking me to? Are you a part of Pirate Jack's crew? Has he decided to bring his ship closer to land after all?"

They didn't answer her, instead placing her bodily in the buggy and climbing aboard themselves, pinioning her between them. Eden looked desperately from one to the other. She turned and slapped Clarence in the face and tried to scramble over him to escape, but a blow to the back of her head stopped her.

She slumped low on the seat, a veil of blackness taking her into unconsciousness.

"Now why'd she have to go and do that fer?" Mike growled, snapping the reins. He guided the horse off the road and began following the same path that had brought them there. Already the lights of the ship were in view.

"In case someone sees us returnin' to the ship, we'll carry our little prize on board all wrapped up in that black cape of 'ers and no one will think it's more than a rolled up blanket that we've taken from some innocent soul," Mike said. "No one on board is gonna question us havin' left the ship fer some fun, now are they? I'd be surprised if some of the crew didn't take the opportunity to escape and never come back. If we were smart, that's what we'd have done."

"That'd be dumber than grabbin' this woman and takin' 'er to the ship," Clarence growled. "You know Judge Pryor and Sheriff Collins. They stick together like glue. They hunt down anyone that escapes and make life miserable for them in the jail. There's enough irons there for all the men ridin' the high seas today. I don't want to spend the rest of my life manacled to the wall of that stinkin' hole."

Now close to the ship, but not close enough so that anyone could see their activities, Clarence carefully wrapped Eden in the cape, then lifted her from the buggy and slung her across his shoulder. Guffawing, he watched as Mike sent the horse and buggy into the sea. His eyes feasted on the struggling horse. He laughed when all that was left were bubbles along the water's surface. . . .

"Let's go," Mike said, hunching his shoulders as he moved stealthily along the beach. A cloud once again gave them the cover they needed to use the gangplank without being noticed.

Breathing hard, Clarence carried Eden down the companionway ladder. When they reached the hold of the ship, they felt around in the darkness until they found a secure corner to hide her in.

"Tie 'er and gag 'er and we'll come back later fer our fun," Mike flatly ordered. "We'd best make an appearance on topdeck or suspicions will be aroused."

"Yeah, later." Clarence said, chuckling low.

Smitty lay on a bunk in his private quarters at the back of his blacksmith shop, his head spinning from the whiskey he had consumed. Leaning up on an elbow, he took another swig, then dropped the bottle to the floor. He would sleep his drunken stupor off, then go to Zachary Tyson's plantation. The later the hour the better. Everyone would be asleep.

Yet, did that truly matter? He wasn't afraid of Zachary Tyson. Gossip had spread earlier in the day that Zachary had been practically beaten to death in the jail. If he did survive, surely he would be mindless.

"Just a few winks of sleep," he whispered, wiping whiskey from his lips with the back of his hand. "Then I'll get me a handful of woman."

His laughter faded into snores.

Chapter Fifteen

Life is short, so fast the lone hours fly.
—ALFORD

Zach and Joshua embraced, then Joshua's dark eyes grew wide when, beneath the splash of the moonlight, he saw Zach's blackened eyes, bruised face and cut lip.

"Masta' Zach!" he gasped, taking a shaky step backwards. "Who done this to you? Where you been?" He looked past Zach, down the oak-lined lane. "Where's your horse? Why have you come here on foot?" He stared at Zach again, gaping openly at his pirate's attire and shoulder brace of pistols.

Zach clasped his hands onto Joshua's shoulders. "I've lots to say and have so little time," he said. He glanced at Sabrina, then back at Joshua. "It looks like you and Sabrina will be alone here for a while."

"I don't understand," Joshua said. "Where you been? Where you goin'? What am I to do? We don't have enough hands to plant the crops."

Zach patted Joshua on the shoulder. "There will be another year, another growing season," he said hoarsely. "I've waited these many years to see my dream come true . . . I can wait a little longer."

He motioned for Joshua to follow him into the house as he climbed the stairs to the porch, then nodded at Sabrina. "Both of you come on in the house," he said. "I'll explain what's happened and where I'll be for a while." He looked at Joshua. "And, Joshua, you have a couple of errands to run for me tonight."

"Yas'sa, whatever you says," Joshua said softly.

"I want you to deliver two notes," Zach said, stopping on his wide porch, surveying the land that was his, but not his to be enjoyed just yet. He placed his hands onto the porch rail and leaned his full weight against it, his heart aching. "I had planned to attempt to see Eden tonight, but on second thought I think it's best if I write her a note, asking her to trust and be patient with me. If I saw her in person I might not be able to wrench myself away from her. As it is, I must go to sea, Joshua. I have no other choice."

"Go to sea?" Joshua gasped. "Why would

you want to be goin' to sea?''

''It's not that I want to,'' Zach murmured. ''As I was saying, Joshua—you take the note to Eden's cottage and slip it beneath her door. You'll do the same with the note I'll be writing to Angelita. Just make sure no one sees you. You know the risks. You could be accused of doing something sinister.''

''Yas'sa, Masta' Zach,'' Joshua said, nodding. ''Anything you says, I do.''

''Come on into my study,'' Zach said, turning to the door. ''Both of you. I'll write the notes and then I'll explain what's happened. I'm damn mad about it all, but my hands are tied. Sometimes there comes a time in a man's life when he is forced to do things against his will. I ought to know. I've been there many times. I guess I can endure it one more time and learn to live with the results.''

He opened the front door and stepped into the spacious foyer. He refrained from looking around at the plush furniture in the parlor to his right, or at the priceless paintings that lined the corridor and staircase. They were there to be enjoyed—but not yet.

Eden awakened with a start. She looked wildly around her, seeing nothing but total darkness. Quickly, though, she became aware of other things. Her head was throbbing unmercifully. Something had been tied around her mouth, gagging her, and her ankles and

wrists were bound. She could hear the
squeaking of rats from somewhere close. A
putrid aroma burned her nostrils and her
stomach was becoming queasy.

But other things were too much on her
mind for her to dwell on her discomforts. She
was recalling the men who abducted her. She
remembered them mentioning a ship.
She was on that ship now. She could hear the
slap-slap of the water against the hull. Was
the ship already out to sea? She could hear the
shuffling of feet overhead and the laughter
and joking of the crew.

Tears streamed from her eyes. What ship
was she on? Pirate Jack's? How soon could
she be expected to be raped by not one, but
perhaps many? Where were the two men who
had abducted her?

Terrified, Eden cowered against the damp
wall behind her. She stared into the dark, her
thoughts straying to Zach and how he was
faring. She felt as though she had failed him
more than he had failed her by not being
truthful with her. Now neither of them might
ever get the chance to make things up to the
other. . . .

Zach walked up the gangplank, his heart
anywhere but in the chore that lay ahead of
him. He went onto the ship and began handing out orders to his crew, causing them to
scurry around, preparing the ship for going to
sea.

Going to the rail, he gazed longingly toward

land for a few minutes, wondering when he would return. Then he turned and gave the command that would wrench him from his new way of life.

"Hove up anchor!" he shouted. "Take her out to sea!"

After the anchor was cranked up and secured and the sails began filling with wind, Zach turned and looked toward the lighthouse as its beam swam across the deck and lit up the filled canvas. His gut twisted and he swallowed hard, envisioning Preston there in the tower, surely wondering about this ship and crew that were so close to land.

If he only knew.

He would never guess that Zach was the appointed captain of this ship of mismatched sailors, some even pirates who had been jailed for months, awaiting death by hanging—only to be spared for this strange voyage.

Zach's eyes wavered when his thoughts went to Eden. Was she still distraught over seeing him in the cell? Perhaps he should have gone to her after all, to show her that he was all right.

But would she truly care now that she knew that he had not been truthful with her?

Eden was becoming more and more petrified. She had heard the anchor being lifted from the water. She could feel the motion of the ship as it moved out to sea. She had heard a voice shouting out commands, but it had been too muffled to make out whether the captain was young or old. Surely it was Pirate Jack, having sent two of his crew out in the darkness to find a plaything for them all while they were out at sea.

Yet, if these men had been commanded to take her aboard, why had they hidden her away?

No. Something told her that she was not there at the orders of someone with higher authority. She had been stolen in the night for use by the two filthy seamen, perhaps even then to be dumped overboard when her usefulness ran out.

Tears made a path down her cheeks. She struggled with her bonds, but they only cut deeper into her flesh, sorely paining her. She began scooting across the damp floor, wanting to get away from where the men had hidden her. She must find another place to hide. When they returned for her, at least she would make them hunt for her first.

She scooted, then rested awhile, then scooted some more.

Then, exhausted, she stopped and leaned her back against what seemed to be a barrel. Now she had to wait and see what her fate would be.

Feeling the aloneness closing in on her, now that Joshua had left to deliver the notes, Sabrina huddled under the blankets on her bed in her cabin, afraid to go to sleep. Being so alone, away from everyone, she felt a sense of foreboding hang over her like a dark cloud.

But she was so sleepy.

Slowly her eyes closed. It felt wonderful to drift off into sleep—until she began having nightmares. Sweat beaded on her brow as she dreamed of being whipped, of feeling the whip cut into her flesh like a knife. . . .

Jolting from her sleep, Sabrina sat up in bed and tried to catch her breath. She looked wildly around her. The moon was streaming through the window, creating dancing shadows on the walls as the trees outside blew in the breeze. There was an eerie stillness in the air.

"Hurry back, Joshua," she cried, then slumped back down on the bed and drifted into another fitful sleep.

Joshua dismounted and moved stealthily through the darkness toward the lighthouse cottage. Seeing no lights, he had to believe that Eden was already asleep. Moving up the steps to the porch, he crept toward the door. Taking the note Zach had written to Eden, he slipped it beneath the door, relieved that the wood was, as usual in these parts, warped from the dampness blowing in from the sea, leaving space at the bottom of the door.

Hurrying from the porch, he mounted again and rode away into the darkness, on to Lighthouse Road. He leaned low over the saddle, sending his horse into a hard gallop. He felt uneasy about having to leave Sabrina alone. He had promised her that he would protect her, that he would let no more harm come to her. He wanted to be able to keep that promise!

He rode hard for what seemed like hours, then sighed with relief when he came to the outskirts of Charleston. As always before, when going to Angelita's house he took side streets. It wouldn't look right if anyone saw him riding a horse as though he owned it, him being a slave and all, and he was glad when he came to Angelita's house by the sea.

Grand, with massive gingerbread trimming and live oaks guarding it like sentinels, the two-storied white house glittered beneath the moonlight. Joshua looked cautiously from window to window as he slipped from his saddle. There was lamplight in only one of the windows upstairs. If he was careful, he would not be heard.

Moving quietly onto the wide porch, he found that again he was in luck. There was just enough space beneath the door to slip the note inside the house.

His mission completed, Joshua mounted his horse and turned it in the direction of home.

A gun holstered at his hip and ropes thrown in the back of the buggy—enough to tie and hold Sabrina in place once she was abducted —Smitty slapped his horse with the reins, then a whip, having wasted too much time already in getting to Zach's plantation. He had asked around and found exactly where the land had been cleared for the retired pirate's plantation. Just down the road from the light-house, off Lighthouse Road.

Slashing at the horse unmercifully with the whip, Smitty began shouting at him too. Now that he was out of the city, he could make all of the racket he wanted and no one would be the wiser. Since he had sobered up enough to think more clearly, his loins ached fiercely for the want of that dark skin against his.

For what seemed hours to him, Smitty pushed the horse onward, cursing when the wheels of the buggy fell into the occasional potholes in the road. But he had already passed the lane that led up to the lighthouse and was on a close lookout for another lane.

His pulse raced and the blood ran hot through his veins at the thought of getting Sabrina all to himself. He would show that damn Zachary Tyson to talk down to him. Smitty had been humiliated in front of his employees by Zachary when the retired pirate had taken the wench away from him just as he was going to get his pleasure from her.

"I'll show him," he grumbled. "I'll show 'em all. Especially that black bitch."

He smiled crookedly when he saw the gap in the trees just ahead to his left. He urged his horse onward and wheeled the buggy onto the lane lined with massive oaks.

Soon the moonlight illuminated the mansion at the end of the lane.

Having driven himself and the horse hard, Joshua looked up the lane that led to the lighthouse and cottage, wondering if Eden or her father would find the note first.

Either way, he hoped that Eden would do as Zach had asked—that she would be patient. One day she would know all about Zach's troubled past and would understand and love him all the more.

Who couldn't love the man?

He had gone to hell and back to try to carve out a peaceful existence for himself.

Also for Joshua, and now Sabrina.

Sinking his heels into the flanks of his horse, Joshua pushed him into a faster pace.

Smitty slipped down from his buggy, looking from one slave cabin to the next. Ropes dangled from where he had tucked them into the waist of his breeches as he moved stealthily through the night toward the first cabin. When he reached it, he raised the latch and pushed the door open slowly. His loins burned with hungry lust when he looked across the room and saw the moon spilling down onto Sabrina, her face visible above the blanket pulled up to her chin.

His hands trembling, his heart racing, Smitty tiptoed across the room. When he reached the bedside, he scarcely breathed. He bent lower, then lower—and clasped one hand over Sabrina's mouth as he grabbed her wrists together with the other.

"Now don't you scream or nothin', bitch," Smitty hissed, seeing that he had startled her awake. "You let out a squeal when I take away my hand, I'll kill you, swear to God. Do you understand?"

Sabrina was cold with fear. She nodded her head, then stifled a sob of fear in the depths of her throat as he pulled the ropes from the waist of his breeches.

"I'm goin' to take you with me," he said, chuckling. "After gettin' a taste of what you had to offer the other day, I knew I had to get more."

"You'll be sorry," Sabrina finally found the courage to say in a shallow breath. "Masta' Zach—"

Smitty slapped her across the face. "Shut up," he growled. "I don't want to hear nothin' about any master Zach. You've just got yourself a new master. You'd best learn to accept that and be obedient to me or you'll be the one who'll be sorry."

Sabrina choked back another sob, then her eyes grew wide when she saw a tall shadow suddenly looming in the doorway behind Smitty. She gasped when the sound of a whip cracked and she saw Smitty's body lurch with pain. He screamed and turned around to face Joshua's furious eyes. Joshua came farther into the room and raised the whip, bringing it down across Smitty's face.

Smitty yowled with agony, but his senses were not stolen away so much that his reflexes did not work. He whirled a pistol from his holster and clamped a finger on the trigger. The burst of gunfire and the stench of gunpowder filled the air. Joshua dropped the whip and grabbed at his right arm. Blood gushed from it.

Sabrina screamed and ran to Joshua. She reached for him, crying, "Joshua! Joshua!"

"Get away from that damn sonofabitch," Smitty screamed, the pain on his face and back biting clean into his soul, it seemed. "I should finish him off! But that's not good enough. I'm going to see that he rots in jail for usin' the whip on me, a white man. Let the rats feast on his flesh. That's better than shootin' or hangin' vermin like him."

Sabrina cowered as Smitty motioned with his pistol toward Joshua. "Like I said, wench, get away from him," he said thickly, blood streaming from the wounds on his face. He tasted the salt of the blood as it trickled into his mouth. "You stay here while your friend goes with me to the buggy."

"No! I won't do as you say!" Sabrina screamed, clinging to Joshua whose eyes were blank from shock. He was losing far too much blood!

Smitty stormed at Sabrina and slapped her across the face again, so hard this time that it threw her across the room. She fell in a loud thump against the wall, stunned.

Grabbing hold of Joshua, Smitty dragged him outside to the buggy. "Climb aboard," he growled. "If you make one wrong move, I'll end it for you here and dump your body in the ocean—let the fish make a feast of your black skin!"

Sabrina rose from the floor, her body aching. She inched toward the door, then bit her lower lip with despair as she looked toward Joshua. There was nothing she could do to help him. She must think of her own survival. She must escape into the forest while Smitty was too busy to notice.

Taking a deep breath, mustering up enough courage for the escape, Sabrina then made a mad dash from the cabin, hurrying around to the side away from where Smitty had left his horse and buggy. Tears streamed down her face as she ran, barefoot, across the furrowed land.

When she reached the forest, she continued to run. She flinched when her bare feet picked up thorns in their soles. She guarded her face as she ran beneath low-hanging limbs. Sobs tore from her throat as she despaired over Joshua. Surely he was going to die. Where was she to go then? Without Masta' Zach or Joshua to protect her, her own fate was in question.

Ducking her head, she ran ahead, toward the lighthouse cottage. She would seek help there!

His arm throbbing, the loss of blood making Joshua lightheaded, he acquiesced to Smitty's demands. Shock having set in, he stumbled into the buggy, too groggy to even think clearly.

Sabrina?

Sabrina?

Where was Sabrina?

Securing Joshua with a rope to the inside of

the buggy, then tying his wrists and legs together, Smitty went back inside the cabin. His heart skipped a beat when he found it empty.

He rushed outside and looked around him. Seeing no signs of Sabrina, he realized that he had let her slip through his fingers.

She had escaped!

The night was too dark, the marshes too threatening to those who were not familiar with them, and already having Joshua complicating things, Smitty sighed heavily and gave up on Sabrina. He could hunt for her the entire night and would probably only find himself lost in the marshes. She wasn't worth it.

Going back to his buggy, he glared down at Joshua. He would drop him off at the jail and say that he was an escaped slave. He would tell the sheriff that he had found him hiding in his blacksmith shop. Smitty would say that he had received the wounds on his face and back as he was capturing the slave. No one would believe the ramblings of a wounded slave if Joshua regained consciousness and tried to explain what had truly happened.

Downcast, Smitty drove away from the plantation. He wondered if anyone would believe Sabrina if she told what had happened here tonight. What it boiled down to was who would be believed. A black slave—or a white businessman whom so many depended on for his services?

He smiled smugly. No one would ever take

the word of a slave over his! That just wasn't the nature of things.

Eden listened intently to the sounds on the ship. The vessel had been out to sea for some time now. Everyone on deck seemed to have quieted down. She hoped that meant they had gone to sleep for the night. That would give her at least a short reprieve from the hands of rapists.

Her throat went dry. Suddenly there were footsteps in the hold of the ship. They were drawing closer. Surely it was the two sailors, coming to claim their prize!

The hold became awash with light as a lantern was lit. Eden held her breath and watched its soft glow draw closer. . . .

Chapter Sixteen

The midnight hears my cry.
                                    —TAYLOR

Eden was almost faint with fear as the light drew closer. It was useless to try to hide. Any moment now she expected to be attacked by the two vile men who had abducted her. She was defenseless against them. If she ever did manage to flee this ship, would any man ever want to touch her after she had been defiled? If Zach ever managed to be set free, would he love her less because other men had used her body?

Tears splashed from her eyes. She could not stifle a sob that escaped from her throat, against the cloth that was bound around her mouth.

Then her heart skipped a beat, realizing that the noise she made had caused whoever was approaching to stop, for the reflection of the light was no longer wavering along the ceiling, but had stopped dead still.

A voice broke through the silence. "Is someone there?"

The voice was not familiar. It didn't belong to the abductors. Could she dare to hope that she would be rescued from this fate that surely was worse than death itself?

Or were all the sailors, pirates perhaps, on this ship as vile as those who had abducted her?

Eden didn't know whether or not to make another noise, unsure of her fate if she did so. But her fate if she waited for the two abductors to come to her was certain. At least, with this sailor who had heard her emit the soft sobbing sound, she had a chance of being released and treated civilly.

Perhaps even set free!

Though bound at both her wrists and ankles, Eden began inching her way across the filth-laden floor, emitting any sounds she could force out of her throat.

"Who's there?" the voice said cautiously. "Show yourself! Speak up!"

Eden grunted more loudly, her pulse racing as she saw the trail of light once again on the ceiling, knowing that the sailor was approaching her. Her wrists and ankles paining her from the ropes cutting into her flesh, she curled up on the cold, damp floor and waited, her eyes eagerly watching.

"My God!" the sailor gasped, moving toward her with his lantern held out before him. "It's a woman!" He fell to his knees beside her. "Who in hell did this to you?"

Tears streamed down Eden's cheeks when she saw compassion in the depths of the sailor's eyes. He was a young man of no more than sixteen, with shoulder-length red hair and a face covered with freckles. But his clothes proved that he had fallen on hard times. They were tattered and torn and fit him tightly.

"Wait until the captain sees you," the young man said, placing his lantern on the floor. He quickly removed Eden's gag, then touched her gently on her tear-stained face. "I'm Tom. Who are you? How'd you get here?"

"My name is Eden Whitney," she said, licking her parched lips. "Two men from this ship abducted me. They brought me here." She turned her eyes away. "They—they planned to rape me."

"Damn!" Tom said, untying the ropes from around her wrists. "Two sailors from this ship, you said?"

"Yes." Eden rubbed her raw wrists as the ropes fell away. "They were disgusting."

"Did they reveal their names to you?"

Eden twisted her face into thought, but she was finding it hard to recall the smaller details of her abduction. Her hand went to her head, which still throbbed almost unbearably, then winced when she touched the raw, blood-covered wound at the crown. She had suffered a terrible head wound. Perhaps that was why she was finding it hard to remember anything vividly.

"Perhaps they did," she murmured, breathing a sigh of relief when the ropes fell away from her ankles. "But at this moment I can't remember." She closed her eyes when another sharp pain shot through her wound. "One of the men hit me over the head with something. Perhaps his gun?"

"Well, the captain'll find out who's responsible and he'll tend to them," Tom said. "Are you strong enough to walk? I'd like to take you to the captain. He'll do right by you. Though I've only recently become acquainted with him, I can tell that he's the decent sort."

Eden wanted to ask Tom if his captain was Pirate Jack, but afraid that it was, and wondering if the young man was truly that good a judge of character, she chose not to.

"Yes, I am sure I have the strength to walk," Eden said, smiling up at Tom as he placed a hand to her elbow and helped her to her feet. She leaned her weight against him, feeling lightheaded and weak-kneed. "I think I can walk." She laughed nervously. "Lord, I've never felt this weak in my entire life."

"It's the blow to the head," Tom said, lifting the lantern from the floor. "Want me to take a look at it?"

"No, that's not necessary," Eden said, her knees wobbling. "Just help me out of this dreadful hole. I had begun to think that rats would have me for their supper."

"Damn. When I was told to come down

here to get the captain some fresh water for drinking, I never expected to find anything but rats," Tom said, chuckling. "Certainly I'd never have expected to find a lady."

"If I had my way about it, I would be either sleeping in my bed, or up helping my father with his beam," Eden said, breathless as she forced one foot ahead of the other. The companionway ladder was straight ahead. Could she even climb it?

Yes.

Anything to get out of this place.

"Your beam?" Tom said, forking an eyebrow at Eden. "What do you mean?"

Eden swallowed back the lump growing in her throat at the thought of her father and the shock he would have to endure when he discovered her missing. Oh, what would he do?

He would go to Judge Pryor.

But Judge Pryor could not help him. He had no way of knowing what had happened to her.

But what of Zach? Judge Pryor most certainly held Zach's fate in the palm of his hand.

"My father is the lightkeeper at Pirate Point Lighthouse Station, down the coast from Charleston," Eden said proudly, taking her first step on the ladder. "I am his assistant."

"Well, blow me down," Tom said, looking at her with admiration. "Most women I've known don't have the brains or skills to do anything but have babies. You are certainly an exception to the rule."

Eden's jaw tightened. "I know you expect a

thank-you for that remark," she said, "But you aren't being fair when you speak of women in such a way!"

"Seems the head wound ain't holdin' you back all that much," Tom said, smiling at Eden. "You're full of spirit. You're going to be just fine."

Eden laughed loosely, realizing how she must have sounded. "Yes," she murmured. "I do believe I'm going to be all right."

Stepping up on deck, Eden found a path opening for her through the gawking seamen as she was taken to the captain's quarters. Her pulse began to race, wondering who she was about to come face to face with. Whoever it was would determine her fate. She scarcely breathed when Tom knocked on the door that separated her from that man.

Unable to sleep, worrying about her aunt, who was feeling no better tonight, Angelita threw a shawl about her shoulders. She would go downstairs and get a breath of fresh, night air on the porch. There was always something about the breeze blowing in from the sea. It invigorated her, gave her new life.

Carrying a brass candleholder, the candle casting a soft glow upon the stairs, Angelita tiptoed down them. The skirt of her dress rustled around her ankles as she moved toward the front door, where something lying just inside the door drew her quick attention. It looked like some sort of note.

"Who put it there?" she whispered, then

smiled smugly. "My secret admirer is back and has gotten bolder. He has written me a note."

Her pulse racing, Angelita hurried to the note. She plucked it up from the floor and placed her candle on a table in the foyer. Her fingers trembling, she unfolded the note and began to read. Tears brimmed her eyes and her heart began to thump wildly.

"Zachary!" she cried, a sob almost choking her. She held the note to her chest and hugged it to her as though it were a person. "Zachary, my God, it was you all along. You are alive!"

She turned and stared through a veil of tears up the staircase. Should she tell her aunt? Would knowing that Zachary had survived these long years stir her aunt into some sort of consciousness?

But why would it? She had never cared for Zachary. She had even sold Zachary into slavery.

"No, I shan't tell her," Angelita whispered. "She doesn't deserve to know. It shall be my secret. Only mine."

She went to the window and drew the curtain aside, looking toward the glittering sea. In Zachary's note he had said that he was being forced to go to sea just one more time.

But he would return to her.

Soon.

Sobbing, Angelita clutched the note to her chest again. "Oh, God, please protect him," she cried. "Please let him survive this last misfortune. Let him return to me. I so badly want to hold him and tell him that I never forgot him—that I have always loved him."

She covered her face with her hands. "Oh, how I've missed my brother," she whispered. "Only a part of me has been alive since he went away."

"Enter!"

The familiar voice speaking through the closed door of the captain's quarters made Eden's heart lurch. "Zach?" she gasped.

She didn't wait for Tom to open the door. She grabbed the latch and raised it and swung the door suddenly open. Then she took a shaky step backwards, almost fainting from dismay. A lantern hanging from the low ceiling shone down on Zach. He was sitting behind an oak desk, maps and papers strewn across the top. When he saw Eden, he scrambled to his feet.

"Good Lord!" he gasped, grabbing the desk for support. "Eden! Where did you come from?" His gaze swept over her, and he blanched when he saw the strands of her hair that were stuck together with dried blood.

Having gathered his composure, Zach rushed to Eden. He drew her into his arms and hugged her fitfully. "Who did this to you?" he said, glaring over her shoulder at Tom. "Tom, where did you find her?"

"In the hold of the ship, sir," Tom said, his blue eyes wide with wonder. "Like you told me, I was down there to get you fresh drinking water. She was there, tied up and gagged."

Zach held Eden away from him and looked down at her, anger rising inside him. "Who did this to you?" he demanded.

Eden was so stunned by the discovery that Zach was the captain of this ship, that how she had gotten on it was less important to her than that he was there, unharmed.

"Zach, I see that Judge Pryor set you free," she said softly, running a trembling hand across his face. Seeing his contusions made her heart ache. "Are you all right? I had so feared for you."

"Yes, I'm fine," Zach said, once more focusing on the dried blood in her hair. He took her by the hand and guided her closer to the light. "Let me take a look at your head. You must have taken quite a blow."

"Sir, it was done by two men on our ship," Tom said, nervously clasping his hands behind him. "But the lady can't recall their names. What do you want me to do? Question all the men?"

Zach gave him a glance. "No, do nothing," he growled. "I'm sure they saw her brought to the cabin. Let them sweat it out for awhile. Then we'll line all the men up and let her point the guilty ones out to me. They'll pay for what they've done."

"Yes, sir," Tom said. "I'll be going, sir."

"You are dismissed," Zach said, then smiled over his shoulder at Tom. "Good work, lad. Thanks."

"It was my pleasure, sir," Tom said, turning to walk away.

"Tom!" Zach said, stopping him.

"Sir?"

"What crimes are you guilty of that had you in jail in Charleston?" he asked. "That got you placed aboard this ship of misfits?"

Tom lowered his eyes. "Stealing, sir," he said softly.

"Stealing what, Tom?"

Tom's eyes lifted slowly. "A loaf of bread, sir," he said, his voice breaking. "I was hungry, sir. I ran away from home—from my father's temper. Not a day passed when I wasn't beat, sir. I could take it no longer."

Zach swallowed hard. He went to Tom and embraced him. "Lad, if ever we get out of this mess, you have a home waiting for you," he said, patting him on the back. "Mine."

Tears rolled down Tom's cheeks. "Honest?" he sobbed. "You'd do that for me?"

"You'll see, son," Zach said. "If God is willing, and we come through this fracas alive, you'll see. Now you get on your way. Keep to yourself. Don't let any of that riffraff on this ship hurt you in any way. Do you hear?"

"Yes, sir," Tom said, beaming as he stepped away from Zach. "I know all sorts of ways to watch out for myself."

Eden was choked up with emotion, again witness to Zach's kindness. When Tom left the cabin, closing the door behind him, she rushed to Zach and embraced him. "That was beautiful," she cried. "You are beautiful."

"Well, now, I wouldn't go so far as to say

that," Zach said, chuckling. He swept an arm around Eden and took her to the light again. "Let me take a look at that head wound. Then we both have a lot of explaining to do, wouldn't you say? I've kept too many secrets from you for too long, darling. I'm going to reveal my entire life history to you. Perhaps your opinion of me will change once you hear it all."

Eden winced with pain as Zach parted her hair and examined her wound. "Zach, nothing ever again will change my opinion of you," she murmured. "Even without your telling me, I know that you are a victim of your past. I saw it in the way you treated that young man. You were seeing a mirror image of yourself, weren't you?"

"Yes," Zach said. "A reflection of myself. Eden, when you hear of my beatings as a child, you will see how blessed you are to have had a decent upbringing. So many don't have, you know."

He led her to the bunk fastened to the outside wall of the cabin and eased her down on it. "I'm going to cleanse your wound, then we will talk," he said, smiling down at her. "My darling, then if you still love me, I shall be the most lucky man in the world."

"If?" Eden said, smiling up at him. "Never say if when speaking of my love for you. I do love you. I shall always love you, no matter what."

"But you have been filled with such doubts, Eden," Zach said. He lifted a pitcher and poured water into a basin. Sinking a wash-cloth into the water, he wrung it out and knelt over Eden, softly dabbing her wound with the wet, soft cloth. "I am sorry that I caused those doubts to fester inside you. But I was waiting for the right time to tell you everything about me." He cleared his throat nervously. "You see, I was afraid to. Pirates are regarded as evil, vile men. I was never that kind of pirate, Eden. Never."

Eden looked up at him, breathing shallowly. At long last, he was admitting that he had been a pirate. Strangely, she did not withdraw from him as she would have from anyone else who had confessed to being a pirate. She believed him. He could never be vile or evil.

"Tell me everything," she murmured. "Darling, I'm listening."

Joshua lay on the floor of the jail cell, only vaguely aware of rats scurrying over him, sniffing. He was only vaguely aware of sounds around him, of men crying and cursing, even screaming.

But he was sorely aware of the pain. It felt as though his arm were going to throb off his body. He tried to lift it but it was too heavy, too numb.

"Masta' Zach," he whispered. "Oh, God, Masta' Zach, I think I'm dyin'. Please don't let me die."

Drifting off into a soft blackness, he smiled, for he was seeing a beautiful lady, her dark skin as sleek as velvet, dancing around him.

Her eyes were flirting with him as she flipped her skirt around her lovely, long legs. When she threw her head back in a throaty laugh, her dark hair tumbled down her slim back.

Then the beautiful thoughts slowly faded from his mind's eye.

"Sabrina," Joshua whispered, reaching a hand out for her. "Don't leave me, Sabrina."

His body went slack as he once again fell into the merciful grip of sleep, blood seeping only slightly now from his wound onto the floor beneath his arm.

Frantic and disoriented, Sabrina ran blindly through the forest, then tripped and fell into the slimy marsh waters. She groped for a hold on the grass that lined the embankment, but kept slipping in the mud. She prayed softly, in her mind's eye recalling Joshua's lifeless body. Were they both going to die? They had only had a few hours of peace and loving one another! It wasn't fair.

But what in life was?

Finally able to grab hold of a thick stand of grass, she began pulling herself out of the muck and mire until she was lying on the ground.

Exhausted, she was engulfed by sleep. Chilled, she lay beside the water, mosquitos swarming over her.

Chapter Seventeen

I love thee, I love but thee.

—TAYLOR

Her hair clean and fresh-smelling after washing the grime from it, Eden combed her fingers through it, spreading it out across her shoulders and down her back.

Feeling somewhat refreshed after her ordeal, she sighed and eased into Zach's arms as he offered them to her.

"It's a long story, darling," Zach said. "Let's get comfortable." He plumped up a pillow on the bunk. "Rest yourself against this while I talk." As she scooted up close to the pillow, her back against it, he sat down beside her and held her hand. "I hardly know where to begin."

"At the beginning, Zach," Eden said,

squeezing his hand affectionately. "You'll soon discover that I am a good listener."

Zach lowered his eyes. "You'll soon discover that I am a damn good liar," he said. "But the lies were necessary. If on our first acquaintance I had told you the truth about even one thing in the past, it would have led to many more truths that I find very hard to talk about, even now. Eden, I could have lost you that very first day had I told you everything about me before you had a chance to get to know and judge me for the man that you saw for yourself. Do you understand?"

"I believe so," Eden murmured. She reached a hand to his cheek and touched it softly. "Darling Zach, do go on. Tell me everything. Every turn of your life doesn't require an apology to me."

"The one truth I did tell you was that my father was a seaman and I have been a part of the sea myself for many a year," he said, clearing his throat nervously. "The first big lie I told you was that my father was rich and I inherited his wealth. In truth, my father was only a mate on a merchantman trading to the Bahamas. He had the reputation of being a very good seaman, but he saved only enough money to make his family comfortable and to send me and my sister to school."

"Sister?" Eden said, interrupting. "You never mentioned a sister."

"I shall, Eden," Zach said, weaving his fingers through her hair, then again grasping her hand. "I'll tell you about my sister later. But first, let me go on with my tale."

"I'm sorry," Eden murmured. "I shouldn't have interrupted. I shan't again."

"My mother," Zach said, getting a faraway look in his eyes, "was very dear to me. During my formative years she brought me up and bred me in experience of virtue." He hung his head and spoke in despair. "That I ever fell away from my mother's good teachings and became the friend and companion of a pirate is more by reason of harsh circumstance than by inclination."

He cleared his throat again and went on. "My mother died when I was ten, my sister five," he continued. "Shortly after that our father departed on a long sea voyage. My sister and I were placed in the care of father's half-sister, the wife of a small ship's chandler. I was treated well enough until money ran low and news of my father's death at sea arrived. After that, my aunt became harsh and tyrannical with me, yet treated my sister well enough, for she had always wanted a daughter of her own."

He patted Eden's hand, then rose and began to pace back and forth in the cabin. "Shortly after that, my uncle died an untimely death," he said, his voice drawn. "There was hardly enough money to put food on the table. My aunt begrudged every morsel I ate and beat me unmercifully; she punished me by reducing my meals to bread and water in solitary confinement. If she caught my sister bringing me food, she would lock her away in her room. Thank God my aunt never beat her, so that she would never bear the mental and physical scars of the past, as I have been forced to endure."

He poured himself a mug of port and drank it in several quick swallows. He slammed the mug back down on the desk, to pace again. "At length my suffering became more than I could endure," he said. "I ran away but was found and tortured some more. When my aunt had had enough of me, she sold me to a gentleman to work as a slave in his fields. This man eventually sold me to a pirate. The pirate was Pirate Jack."

Eden was filled with compassion and sadness for Zach. Never had she imagined that what he had hidden from her could be so unhappy—so cruel!

Now she understood so much.

How could anyone condemn him for anything? Circumstances had forced him into the life of piracy.

What amazed her was his gentleness, his sweetness in spite of it all. She would have thought that anyone who had been forced to endure such a life would have ended up as evil as those sinister characters he was forced to associate with.

Zach was nothing like that.

Zach sat down beside Eden and took her hand again. "Darling, surely you can understand why I soon began damning those who were governed by laws that could not protect a young man like myself against such people as my aunt," he said. "Alongside Pirate Jack, I learned to plunder the rich, and got pleasure out of giving much of our plunder to the poor. We raided slave ships and set the slaves free. On a ship such as that I found Joshua. If you had seen the squalor in that ship, if you had seen how his wife and daughter died and were left to be fed upon by rats! Joshua chose to stay on board ship with me instead of being set free, on land. We became as close as brothers."

He kneaded his brow and again rose to pace the cabin. "It was not long after being on Pirate Jack's ship that I was taken in by the lure of far horizons, the promise of a different tomorrow and the fantasy of breaking out of the trap of my existence—an existence that until I became acquainted with Pirate Jack had meant pain and disgrace."

He swung around and faced Eden. "But all of this came to a halt when I saw Pirate Jack become too greedy, no longer helping the poor, but thinking only of himself and his riches," he said, his voice breaking. "It was then that I decided it was time for me to retire from pirating. Pirate Jack understood. We split our share of the money that we had accumulated through the years and I bought the land on which my plantation now sits. It was a dream that I had carried with me through my years of pirating. I wanted to return to Charleston and make a home for myself. I wanted to show everyone that the poor boy had become a rich man at only twenty-seven!"

"You say you wanted to return to Charleston," Eden said, rising from the bunk and going to him. She leaned into his embrace. "You are originally from Charleston?"

"I was born and raised there," he said, placing his cheek to hers. "Darling, my aunt still resides there. She just doesn't know yet that I've survived, or returned. I had planned to surprise her one day."

He drew away from her and looked down into her eyes. "Darling, I don't think I shall ever get that chance," he said. "You see, I have learned recently that she has had a stroke. She doesn't recognize her own adopted daughter —my own sister."

Eden looked up at Zach, breathless with wonder. "You have an aunt and a sister who reside in Charleston?" she murmured. "Who, Zach? Perhaps I know them."

"Yes, you know them well," Zach said, nodding. "Angelita Llewellyn is my sister. Several years ago, surely before you met Angelita, when my Aunt Martha married the wealthy Mr. Llewellyn, Angelita was adopted legally and her last name was changed to fit her new status in life. Darling, that is why I had such an interest in Angelita—she is my long-lost sister."

"My Lord," Eden gasped. "Angelita is your sister?"

She was surprised, yet in the same heartbeat, deliriously happy. She had been jealous of Zach's sister!

"I couldn't make myself known to her just yet," Zach said. "I was afraid of embarrassing her, me being a retired pirate and all. She is well known in the community and gossip of a pirate brother could very well ruin her name." He lowered his eyes. "So I spared her a while longer."

"Oh, Zach," Eden said, hugging him. "You could never embarrass anyone. You are so wonderfully kind and sweet. Oh, how thrilled Angelita will be to see you! Whenever she mentioned having a brother to me, it was always briefly, because it hurt her to even think about you, much less talk of you. She never mentioned your name. You see, she thought you were dead."

"Well, she knows about me now," Zach said, chuckling. "I wrote her a note and had Joshua deliver it to her doorstep. At this very moment she could be reading it, discovering that her brother is very much alive. She is awaiting my return from this sea venture."

"Zach, about this sea venture," Eden said, easing from his arms and looking up at him. "I know that Judge Pryor wants you to go and find Pirate Jack, to kill him. He told me only a little of why he is forcing you to do this. Please tell me everything."

Zach explained about Judge Pryor having once been a sea captain. He told her about the time he had saved the Judge from death after Judge Pryor's ship had been boarded by pirates. "I talked Pirate Jack out of killing the man," he said, frowning down at Eden. "Now I realize that I made a mistake. I must hunt down my old friend and kill him, or die myself, or rot in jail because of Judge Pryor." He touched Eden's cheek. "He even threatened that he would see harm come to you if I didn't cooperate."

Eden blanched. "He actually said that he would harm me in some way?" she said, her voice lilting. "Surely he wouldn't. He's my father's friend."

"Friends sometimes turn on friends," Zach said. He sat down on the edge of the bunk, his shoulders hunched. "Look at me. I am a prime example. I am forced to find my friend and kill him. I'm not sure I am capable of such deceit as that."

Hearing the pain in his voice, Eden sat down beside him. "Darling, perhaps things will work out," she tried to reassure him. "I have learned that if you take things one day at a time, many things work themselves out."

Zach framed her face between his hands and drew her lips close. "After all I've told you about me and my past, do you still want to marry me?" he whispered, brushing her lips with his mouth. "Do you still want to go to your father and break the news to him once we are free to do so?"

"Yes, yes . . ." Eden breathed, feeling ecstasy claim her, making her momentarily forget everything but her need of Zach. She twined her arms about his neck. "I love you so. Oh, Zach, once all of this is behind us, I shall give you such a wonderful home life that it will make up for all the ugliness of your past. Your every moment will be brimming with happiness! You'll see—oh, darling, you'll see."

"God, Eden, make it so," Zach said throatily. His trembling fingers smoothed her hair back from her face. His quivering mouth came down upon her lips and kissed her passionately.

Caught in his embrace, a surge of ecstasy welled within Eden, drenching her with warmth. All of her senses yearned for him. Suddenly his hands were everywhere, unfastening her dress, drawing it down from her shoulders. His mouth left her lips and found the nipple of her breast. Her gasp of instant pleasure echoed like thunder through her.

Delirious with sensations, she felt the last vestiges of rational mind floating away, welcoming the euphoria that was washing through her.

Zach drew away from her momentarily and looked down at her with passion-dark eyes. "Would you rather we didn't proceed?" he asked. "You've been through a terrible experience. Does your wound hurt too severely? Darling, I would never want to add to your pain."

Eden smiled up at him. She began unbuttoning his cambric shirt. "You are exactly what I need," she said in a soft purr. "You have already made me feel as though my veins were filled with a magical elixir."

"I worried so that you would hate me after discovering the truth about me," Zach said, letting her slip his shirt away from him. "I gave you cause to hate me, Eden. What would I have done if you did? Though I have endured much in my lifetime, I don't think I could bear losing you."

"Let's not even talk about it," Eden said, her

fingers unfastening his breeches. "Let's grasp what happiness we can when we can. Who knows about tomorrow? You are committed to a cause that could cost your life. If it does, I hope I can die alongside you." Her pulse raced when she pushed his breeches down past his thighs and she saw that part of him that had taught her the mysteries of lovemaking.

Zach pulled off his boots and then his breeches. "I'm taking you home," he said hoarsely. "I won't allow you to travel on this ship with me while I search for Pirate Jack. There may be a battle at sea and I cannot chance your being in the middle of it. I shall return you home as quickly as the ship can travel back to Charleston."

Eden leaned up on an elbow and frowned. "I don't want to go home—" she began, but was stopped when Zach leaned over her and placed a hand over her mouth.

"Hush," he scolded. "We've already said too much." He removed his hand from her mouth. His eyes two points of fire, he began lowering her dress away from her, and after she was lying silkenly nude on the cot, his fingers began tracing circles around her belly, up to her breasts, just missing the nipples so that they strained with anticipation.

Eden shivered. Her eyes met Zach's and locked in an unspoken understanding, promising rapture. When his fingers moved to the juncture of her thighs and began caressing her throbbing center, she thrust her pelvis toward him, only half aware of making whimpering sounds of pleasure.

White heat vibrated through her blood. The air was heavy with anticipation.

Zach moved over her, sculpting himself to her body. He pressed his pulsing hardness gently into her slowly yielding folds.

Eden's body jolted and quivered. She snaked her arms around his neck and drew his lips to hers and gave him a fierce, fevered kiss. Her body arched and met his heated thrusts within her. She locked her legs around him at his waist, drawing him closer . . . closer . . .

Zach could feel the urgency building within him. He crushed Eden so close to him that she gasped. Then he moved with her, stroke by stroke. With her, he could forget all uglinesses of the world. He always saw such promise in the future with her—Eden's promise.

He moved his lips from her mouth and reverently breathed her name against the column of her throat. His hands cupped her breasts, absorbing her creamy softness into his palms. He moaned throatily as he felt the fire rising in his loins, spreading like roaring flames throughout him as the pleasure mounted.

Eden's blood quickened along with Zach's thrusts. His body tightening against hers told her that he was close to the same brink of bliss as she. She abandoned herself to the wondrous soft, melting energy blossoming within her. She clung to Zach, wandering sweetly over the edge into mindless ecstasy as he groaned his pleasure against her throat and his body lurched and lunged wildly into hers.

Holding her for a moment longer, waiting for his heartbeat to slow, Zach feathered kisses along Eden's taut-tipped breasts. He smiled up at her as she moaned with pleasure, her eyes closed, enjoying the sensations.

Then he lay above her, bracing himself with his hands. He kissed her navel, flicking his tongue into it, then went lower, tasting himself as he kissed her bud of womanhood.

"Please . . . don't . . ." Eden said, feeling drugged. "Zach, please . . ."

Zach rolled away from her and lay down beside her, drawing her close. She sighed with joy. "I love you so much," she whispered. "But I so fear for you. Why is Judge Pryor being so unreasonable? Zach, perhaps we could just run away. You and I. Where Judge Pryor could never find either of us."

Zach kissed her brow. "Darling, you know you wouldn't be happy doing that," he said softly. "There's your father. What about him? He needs you. He has no one else."

Eden's eyes shot open. "Zach, my father!" she cried. "In only a few short hours he will be returning to the cottage after his duty in the lighthouse. He will find me gone. It will frighten him so."

Zach looked at her, troubled. "That won't be the only discovery of the morning," he said. "My darling, I had Joshua deliver a note to your cottage. He was to place it beneath your door. Your father will find it and soon discover that I am not exactly what he thought me to be."

Eden's hair cascaded across her shoulders as she turned to Zach. "A note?" she murmured. "What did it say?"

"I did not go into detail about my past," he said, placing his fingers to her shoulders to ease her into a sitting position beside him. "But I did say that I would be gone for a while at sea and asked you to be patient with me. I said I would explain my ugly past to you upon my return."

Eden paled. "Ugly past?" she said softly. "When father reads that he will be filled with wonder."

"And doubts," Zach grumbled, rising to draw on his breeches.

Eden rose from the bunk and began dressing. "Oh, darling, there is truly nothing to worry about," she said, sighing. "He will be filled with such worry about me, he surely will have no thought to spare for your note."

"One damn thing's for sure," Zach said, sitting on the edge of the bunk and pulling on his boots. "He'll know you're not with me when he finds you missing. I won't be accused of abducting you."

A sharp pain stabbed through Eden's head. She pressed her hand to her wound, her moments of sharing love with Zach having made her forget about her experience with the two seamen.

Zach saw her grimace with pain. "Eden!" he gasped. He rose quickly to his feet and reached for her, drawing her into his embrace. "Darling, perhaps it wasn't wise to make love. Did it cause your wound to hurt more fiercely?"

Eden clung to him. "No," she murmured. "Darling, it helped me forget for a while about how it got there."

Suddenly angry, Zach glowered down at Eden as he held her away from him. "I think it's time for you to point out those two scoundrels to me," he said in a hiss. "They'll wish they had never laid eyes on you—or me."

"Zach, what are you going to do to them?"

"It's not what I'm going to do *to* them, it's what I am going to do *with* them."

"What do you mean? What do you have planned?"

Zach dropped his hands to his sides and nodded toward her clothes. "Darling, get the rest of your clothes on," he said. "Tonight you will point out the guilty parties. Tomorrow you will see how they pay for their crime."

Hurrying into her clothes, Eden feared the next few moments. She dreaded facing the two seamen again, yet she had to, to identify them. Something had blocked their names from her brain.

But, of course, *they* had dealt her the blow to her head that had made her forget.

She pressed her lips angrily together. They deserved whatever Zach had planned for them.

Then doubts flooded her. If she could not recall their names, would she recognize their faces? The moonlight had afforded her a good look at both of them, but would that have truly been enough, especially now that she was having trouble remembering?

"Eden?" Zach said, placing his hand on the latch of the door. "Are you ready? Can you identify the men?"

Eden fastened the last snap on her dress and smiled weakly. "I shall try my best," she murmured.

Zach reached for her hand. "Give it your best," he said. "That's all you can do."

Her chin held high, wanting so badly to be able to remember the two rogues, Eden moved out of the cabin at Zach's side. When he released her hand to grab a lantern and hold it high above him, she scarcely breathed. Already, without the men even being ordered to line up for her scrutiny, the seamen were gathering about, staring at her and Zach. She looked from man to man, not yet recognizing any. If she didn't, they would go free and perhaps do the same thing to another innocent woman at the next port. Oh, Lord, she couldn't allow that.

Zach turned to Tom who stood dutifully by his side. "Tom, go and check all of the corners of the ship, even the hold, so that we are sure everyone is accounted for and on deck," he said flatly.

As Tom scurried away, Zach began scrutinizing the men. "Form a single line," he shouted. He gestured toward Eden with his free hand. "As you see, we have a woman aboard the ship. There are among you two seamen who abducted her and brought her here. You know the penalties of such a disobedient act. This woman, who is my fiancée, will pick out the guilty parties. Stand your ground and allow yourself to be studied by her."

The men shuffled their feet while obeying his stiff command.

"Go on, Eden," Zach said, nodding toward her. "Take your time." He handed her the lantern. "Take this with you. Place it before the faces of the men. Point the guilty parties out to me as you come to them."

Tom hurried back to Zach, breathless. "Everyone seems to be accounted for, sir," he said, standing tall next to Zach, his eyes gazing admiringly at him.

Zach patted Tom's shoulder fondly. "Thanks, lad," he said. His gaze followed Eden's as she looked onto the men's faces, studying them carefully; then she turned and he saw that she had recognized one of the faces.

"This one," she murmured. "I even recall his name. His name is Clarence."

"Tom, go and remove Clarence to the brig," Zach ordered flatly.

Clarence squealed and fought Tom's strong grip on his arm. "It wasn't my fault she was abducted!" he screamed. He nodded toward Mike. "He's the one. It was his idea. He forced me to go. He even said he'd slit my throat if I didn't."

"Mike?" Zach said, forking an eyebrow. Just as Eden stepped before the bald, burly man known to most only as Mike, Zach was eyeing him with contempt.

"This is the other one," Eden said weakly. "This is Mike."

Zach yanked Mike away from the others. Eden gasped when, in the brighter light of the lantern, more was revealed to her than that night by moonlight. On Mike's left cheek, close to the nose, he bore a big branded 'T'.

"My goodness, why is the man branded in such a way?" she gasped. She was glad that Zach was holding him tightly by the arm so that he could not grab her, for in Mike's eyes there was a seething hatred as he glared at her.

"My darling, the 'T' on this bastard's face stands for thief," he said. "You see, before he tried his art of stealing women, he was branded for having stolen many other things. This man was taken from the jail and given to me as part of my crew only to save Judge Pryor the effort of placing a noose about his neck. He was a marked man then. He is now!"

Zach shoved Mike toward Tom. "You've got two to lock in the brig for me," he said sternly. He gave Mike and Clarence a dark frown. "You two had better not cause any trouble on your way to the brig." He glanced down at Tom's holstered pistol. "I wouldn't want to mess with this lad's ability to fire a piece." He took a wide step toward Mike and grabbed him by the throat, partially lifting him from the floor. "And if he happens to miss, I'll be here to back him up. What I have planned for you tomorrow at sunrise would be nothing to what I would do to you tonight, if forced to."

Zach jerked his hand free and brushed his

palms against his breeches to cleanse them of the touch of the filthy pirate. "Tom, take them away!" he commanded gruffly. He turned and placed an arm around Eden's waist, walking her back inside his cabin. "I'm hungry. I'll order us up a feast."

"What sort of food does one eat on a ship?" Eden asked. She was glad to be back inside his cabin, away from the stench of the men and their gawking, angry eyes.

Zach closed the door. He turned her to face him. "What does one eat on ship?" he mused. "I think the main course on board ship tonight is turtle meat, or perhaps pigeon."

Eden visibly shuddered, having had a brief look at the cook and the large, dark pot used for preparing the food. "Zach, I don't think I'm all that hungry," she murmured.

"Well, then perhaps a taste of wine will please you?" Zach took two mugs and a bottle of wine and began pouring the red liquid. "I've ale aboard ship, but I don't think you'd like its taste. It's brewed from malt and hops and is usually too bitter for a woman's liking."

"Yes, wine sounds much better than food or ale," Eden said softly.

A sick feeling at the pit of Eden's stomach had taken away her appetite anyway. All she could think of was what the next several days might bring for the both of them. True happiness seemed so elusive, for what happiness she had thus far found with Zach was always too short-lived. She was beginning to doubt if it would ever prove lasting.

Chapter Eighteen

I arise from dreams of thee.
                              —SHELLEY

The sunrise was spreading its glorious golden-orange across the waters of the Atlantic; the black ribbons of night were slipping away. To ward off the chill of early morning, Eden hugged herself with her arms as she stood at the bow of Zach's ship. She was peering at an island that was so small it resembled a whale's still, dark hump thrusting up from the water. Flinching when she felt the drag of the anchor, she grew numb with fear as she watched the longboat being lowered over the side of the ship.

Slowly her eyes went from man to man in the longboat—from Zach to Tom, who sat at opposite ends of the boat, and from Mike to Clarence sitting in the center, glowering. Both men had been stripped of their clothes, which had also stripped them of whatever dignity they might have laid claim to.

The light of the sun picked up the shine of the blades of two cutlasses lying across Zach's lap, both of which might be covered with a man's lifeblood in a short time. Zach held one of his powerful, muzzle-loading pistols pointed at the two condemned men.

Tom's red hair blended well with the sun-drenched ocean behind him. Though only sixteen, he had powerful muscles, revealed when they corded as he drew the oars through the water, taking the longboat and its occupants toward the piece of rock that would no longer be uninhabited.

There was to be a duel fought with swords. One man would surely die quickly. The victor would not be truly victorious, because he would die a slower, agonizing death in the hot sun and without water on this island with his dead friend at his side.

Eden scarcely breathed as she watched the longboat approach the island. Zach was too far away for her to hear what he was saying, but as he climbed from the boat she could hear him shouting as he motioned with his drawn pistol to the men to disembark, while Tom took the cutlasses and left the boat with them.

The whole ship's rail was lined with sailors, many of them pirates, some with only one eye and some emaciated from having been imprisoned for so long. Hardly anyone spoke; the sea whipping its waves against the hull of the ship made the only sounds. The sails lay becalmed in the early morning light, and the stench of greasy food cooking spoiled the freshness of the sea air.

Embarrassed by seeing the two seamen step naked onto the island, Eden turned her eyes away. But the echo of steel ringing in the air as the cutlasses began crashing together in lethal combat drew her eyes quickly back around. She clasped her hands to the ship's rail, somehow mesmerized by those two sleek bodies moving in jerks around each other, the rising sun bronzing their skin golden. Both men seeming to be practiced in the art of sword fighting, and neither had yet inflicted a wound.

Eden turned her eyes to Zach. He stood back from the combatants, his pistol aimed at them, while Tom stood on the other side, his firearm also drawn. Eden could not see Zach's face closely enough to read his feelings, but she could see in the way he held his body rigidly that it was not in Zach's nature to enjoy handing out such punishments. Even while watching two men duel to the death, his mind could be elsewhere—on her, or on the plantation he had been forced to leave behind.

One day soon he must be allowed to return to a decent life, with Eden at his side to look after him. She would never let herself think that he would not come out of this forced journey alive. He had survived too much already in his life to lose now.

A loud scream pierced the air. Eden's stomach lurched and she clamped a hand over her mouth when she saw Mike draw his cutlass away from Clarence, where he had inflicted a horrible wound to Clarence's left arm. Blood streamed profusedly from the wound, yet Clarence did not cry out with pain again. He was approaching Mike, swinging his cutlass more angrily.

Unable to watch any longer, Eden turned her back to the dueling pair and waited with bated breath for it to end.

"Ye sonofabitch," Clarence growled. "I ain't gonna let ye kill me. I ain't."

Mike laughed. "Yer too stupid to understand that both of us are goin' to die anyhow," he shouted. "It don't matter who cuts who now. We're both gonna be left on this chunk o' rock to rot."

"No matter what ye say, Mike, I'm not givin' up," Clarence shouted, the pain from the wound in his arm making him dizzy. "I'm goin' to cut ye good for what ye got me into. I never wanted to go after that woman. Ye forced me."

Zach listened to the dialogue with much interest. He thought Clarence was telling the truth. Facing sure death, no man would think to tell a calculated lie. It would benefit no one.

He lowered his pistol a fraction. Clarence was innocent. Mike was the instigator of the whole sordid plan to steal and rape Eden. Clarence should not even be forced to fight this duel.

Suddenly deciding to stop the duel and take Clarence back to the ship, leaving Mike to die alone and unharmed, Zach opened his mouth to shout out the orders to stop.

But just as his breath brushed across his tongue to speak, he took an unsteady step backwards. In a blink of an eye, Clarence had thrust his cutlass into Mike's stomach, penetrating clear to the other side where it plunged out of the victim's back.

Mike dropped his cutlass and a low gurgle surfaced from deep inside him as he reached out for Clarence, his eyes filled with fear. "Goddamn ye . . ." he hissed, crying out with pain as Clarence jerked his cutlass free and dropped it to the ground.

Mike crumbled to the sandy beach beside his own cutlass, clutching at his belly. He lay there, convulsing, staring wildly up at Clarence.

"Mike!" Clarence said, almost choking on the name. He fell to the ground and hovered over his friend. "Ye made me do it. If I didn't cut ye, ye'd have cut me. Ye wouldn't even have cared."

"Ye moron," Mike whispered, gasping for breath. In one last burst of energy he found the strength to reach for his cutlass and in one quick sweep he ran the sharp blade across Clarence's throat.

He dropped the cutlass and laughed as

Clarence looked down at him disbelievingly, emitting strange gurgles as blood spurted from his wound and from between his fingers as he clutched at his throat.

"My God," Zach gasped. Everything had happened so quickly it couldn't have been prevented. Stunned, he watched Clarence fall sideways next to Mike, his eyes glazed in death. Mike's body convulsed one more time, then lay stone-quiet as he stared lifelessly straight ahead.

Tom and Zach stared at each other for a moment, then Zach slipped his pistol into the waist of his breeches. He began walking toward the longboat, nodding to Tom. "Come along," he said. "Time's wasting. We must turn our sails back to Charleston. I've my lady to deliver to safety."

Preston yawned as he made his way down the steep spiral lighthouse staircase. His cane echoed hollowly as he moved from step to step, leaning his weight on it. It had been one of those nights when his beam had captured all sorts of activity at sea. One ship in particular had been peculiarly close to shore. As his beam followed the vessel, he had caught sight of the lone figure of a man with flowing sleeves looking up at him, as though he was trying to communicate something to him with his steady stare.

Preston laughed to himself. "My, oh, my, how these long nights tend to make my imagination work overtime," he whispered, glad to reach the foot of the stairs. He stepped outside and walked toward his cottage, the sunrise teasingly beautiful on the horizon as the sun crept higher in the sky.

As he grew closer to the cottage, he lifted his nose, testing the air for the smell of bacon and eggs cooking in the kitchen. He could envision Eden there, her face pink with the heat of the woodburning stove, her golden hair drawn back from her face, shining lustrously from a fresh morning brushing.

She would be wearing a lacy apron over her drab cotton dress, yet she would be a vision of loveliness. She was always a wonderful sight in the morning for a man who had spent long, lonely hours watching for ships straying off course in the night.

Discovering no such pleasant scent of breakfast foods cooking that always made his empty stomach growl, Preston frowned. Worried, he looked from window to window of the cottage. Something grabbed him at the pit of the stomach. There were no lights. He looked up at the chimney. There was no smoke. He looked back at the cottage. There were no sounds. Eden would usually have come rushing to him to say a merry hello. She always knew that he was coming by the sound of his cane on the lighthouse stairs.

"Something's happened," Preston said, blanching. His knees trembled as he pushed his legs harder across the pebbled path. He groaned as he climbed the steps to the porch. His heart was thundering inside him as he shoved the front door open. His breath became short and raspy when he heard only dead silence in the house.

"Eden!" he shouted. "Eden!"

There was no response. He knew without even going to Eden's bedroom that she wasn't there. He exhaled a shaky breath, suddenly afraid for his daughter.

Then, something lying on the floor just inside the door caught his attention. It was a note of some sort.

Slamming the door shut, he grunted with pain as he stooped to pick up the note. He held it in the light of the rising sun and opened it. He frowned as he read it.

"Zach? What the hell is he talking about in this note?" he whispered. "He says he'll be gone awhile? Where? Why? What is this about his past?"

He truly didn't care about anything Zach had to write, except that from the note Preston learned that Eden could not be with him.

Consumed with fear for Eden, he tossed the note aside. "Where can she be?" he shouted, flailing his free hand in the air. "Who is she with?"

A scraping noise from outside the closed door made Preston turn with a start and stare toward it. Another scraping noise and then a faint knock made blood rush to his face.

"Eden?" he gasped. "Is that Eden?"

Zach climbed out of the longboat into the ship. Eden turned slowly to face him, having not watched the last moments of the duel. She questioned Zach with her eyes, then looked past him, toward the island. When she saw the two bodies, she covered her mouth with her hand. Gasping, she turned her eyes away again, glad that Zach placed an arm around her waist to steady her. She looked slowly up at him as he began shouting to his crew. One dreadful chore was behind him. What unthinkable deed would come next?

"All of you!" Zach shouted, placing a fist on a hip and spreading his legs. "Get back to work! Head this ship back to Charleston! And if anyone wants to question my authority, let him speak up now! That island is big enough for a few more occupants."

The crew scattered quickly to their duties. Zach turned to Eden. "Let's go to my cabin," he said, his voice drawn. "I'd like to put these last few moments from my mind. I know of no better way than to be with you, darling."

He walked her away from the ship's rail, listening to the chain cranking up the anchor. "Eden, I want you to be assured of one thing," he said, looking down at her. "You have nothing to fear while aboard this ship. The crew understands the penalties now, if they didn't before."

"When I am with you, I am never afraid of anything," Eden said, snuggling close.

Zach's gaze moved to the far horizon, troubled. The sun had been replaced by a low, long line of dark clouds. Lightning was dancing in the sky. Thunder echoed across the waters. "Except perhaps for that storm way out at sea that just might catch up with us?" he said, frowning down at her.

Eden glanced over her shoulder and grew tense with fear. Then her shoulders relaxed when she saw just how far the storm was from the ship. Out on the open sea, the whole sky could be a display of different phenomena. From her time spent in the lighthouse, she knew that. She had watched many a storm far out at sea—storms that never reached the shores of Charleston.

"Oh, darling, that storm will never come this far," Eden said, forcing a laugh. Though she did not want Zach to realize it, she was still unnerved over having seen the slain men, and over Zach having been forced to allow it to happen to show authority to his crew. When in life would he be free of being forced to do anything?

A strong stench of vinegar suddenly rose up into Eden's nose as she walked past a sailor busy scrubbing the deck. She shuddered visibly. "Whatever is he doing using vinegar to scrub down the deck?" she asked, welcoming something besides the duel and the slain men to think about.

"Eden, most merchantmen wash down the decks of ships with vinegar and salt water," Zach said, walking her toward his cabin. "In my pirating days, those aboard our ship were even known to slosh the decks with plundered French brandy if they had a lot of it and the mood seized them."

He nodded toward the companionway ladder. "Below decks, the usual drill on all vessels is to fumigate with pans of burning pitch or brimstone," he further explained. He curled his nose up in distaste. "From the smell of this ship, I think it's been a long time since anyone bothered to clean anything on it." He smiled and mocked a salute to his busy crew. "That's going to change quickly if I have anything to say about it."

Eden looked around her. In the brighter light of day she saw that the wooden sailing ship was a damp, dark and cheerless place, reeking with the stench of bilge water and rotten meat. Surely, no matter the weather, the ship had to leak.

Zach swept Eden into his cabin and closed the door and latched it. A candle was burning in a copper candleholder, casting only a faint glow around the small, cramped spaces.

Zach turned Eden to face him. "I'm sorry you had to be a part of what happened today," he apologized. He touched her cheek softly. "Eden, soon I will deliver you back to your father. We may have only these last few hours together. Can you forget what you just witnessed? Shall we take advantage of being alone while we can?"

Eden moved into his arms. She hugged him tightly, then stepped back away from him and unhooked her dress. Then, looking at each other with promise of rapture in their eyes, Eden stepped out of her shoes as Zach yanked off his boots.

Zach went to Eden. With fire burning in his eyes, he bent down and kissed her parted lips and eased her down to the bunk. His fingers trembling in anticipation, he slipped her dress from her shoulders and on past her breasts, baring them to him. Eden sucked in a tremulous breath as he cupped her breasts within the comforting warmth of his hands. Pleasure spread through her body as Zach's lips trailed kisses from her lips, across the slender column of her throat, and then to her breasts. One by one he flicked his tongue across her nipples, coaxing them into hardened peaks, all the while smoothing her dress down away from her.

Eden closed her eyes and a soft cry of passion rose from inside her as Zach worshipped her body with his lips and her secret places were scorched with the heat of his kisses.

A raging hunger swept through her, wanting today what tomorrow might deny her! She twined her fingers through Zach's hair as he loved her with his mouth and tongue at the juncture of her thighs. The ecstasy that this way of loving her evoked made her urge his mouth closer. Her throbbing center melted as his tongue danced across it. She drew a ragged breath, the heat of passion building.

And then Zach was above her, enveloping her within his powerful arms. His dark eyes smiled down at her as he thrust his hardness inside her. She arched and cried out, having not been aware of him slipping his breeches off while loving her with his lips and mouth. His cambric shirt was still on, but unbuttoned, revealing his powerfully muscled chest. As his lean hips moved on top of her, she splayed her hands across his chest, the dark feathering of his hair there making a soft cushion against her palms.

Sweet currents of warmth swept through Eden as Zach's tongue brushed her lips lightly, his hands taking in the roundness of her buttocks, stroking them.

Then his lips took her mouth by storm. He crushed her to him so hard that she cried out against his lips. Then she clung and rocked with him, his thrusts within her moving faster, in quick, sure movements. She lifted her hips to meet him, shaken with the desire that was consuming her. It was easy to forget the ugliness of the world, the uncertainty of tomorrow. She was nearing that point of being beyond any coherent thought. Their bodies jolted and quivered, then the explosion of ecstasy claimed them both. Zach plunged deeper and deeper, their groans of ecstasy intermingling. They soared above the clouds on wings of bliss, and then became still.

Afterwards, Eden clung to Zach, filled with a great, wondrous calm.

Opening the door with a jerk, Preston looked down, alarmed. Lying at his doorstep was a negress, her dress soaking wet and clinging to her skin, her dark eyes pleading up at him.

"My God!" Preston said, leaning on his cane as he reached down for the lady's arm. He helped her to her feet. "Who are you? Where have you come from?"

"My name's Sabrina," the woman said in a raspy whisper, exhausted from her traumatic night in the marshes. Her flesh was on fire with mosquito bites, and she was chilled to the bone from her wet clothes.

She clung to Preston as he led her slowly into the house. "Masta' Zach. I'se lost from Masta' Zach's. The marshes. They'se cold." She hung her head and choked back a sob. "Joshua. Po' Joshua."

Preston's head was swimming, trying to make sense out of her ramblings. He wasn't familiar with the name Joshua, but he damn well knew who Zach was!

"Do you know where Zach is?" he asked anxiously, easing Sabrina down onto the sofa in front of the fireplace, where the fire of the previous evening had died down to cold, gray ashes.

A sudden chill shook Sabrina fitfully. She hugged herself with her arms, only vaguely aware of Preston's question about Zach. "Ah'm so cold," she murmured, her teeth chattering. Tears rolled down her cheeks. "Po' Joshua," she said, rocking her body back and forth. "It's too late fo' him. It's too late fo' me."

Preston saw how badly she was chilled. Still making no sense out of her ramblings about a Joshua, he turned and bent his numb knees and began hurriedly placing wood on the grate over kindling already spread there for a fire. Striking a match to it, he quickly got the fire going.

Glancing at the note on the floor—the note from Zach to Eden—Preston began thinking about its contents. In that note Zach had asked for Eden to be patient, that he would be gone for a while, but when he returned he would explain his ugly past.

Oh, God, what ugly past? To Preston, Zach had seemed a perfect specimen of a man. Had the man fooled both Eden and her father?

The mystery of who Zach truly was burned at his senses. He could not bear the thought of Eden having even for a moment been infatuated with a man of questionable morals!

Oh, God, where was she now?

Had this man caused her to fall into evil hands?

Wanting to question Sabrina further about Zach, Preston turned around, only to find she had stretched out on the sofa and was already in a deep sleep. Preston gently shook her, but she scarcely stirred.

"Ah's so tired," Sabrina whispered. "So tired."

Seeing that he was not going to get any answers out of her, and worrying that she might catch her death of cold in those wet clothes, Preston saw no other choice but to undress her and get her things dried while she slept.

Uneasy at having to remove her clothes

himself, Preston frowned as he slipped Sabrina's dress over her head. The bites from many mosquitos made large, red welts on her flesh, yet even those could not disguise her magnificent body.

His eyes wavering, unable to deny that looking at this lovely, female body made him recall private moments with his wife those ten long years ago, he hurriedly slipped a blanket over Sabrina.

Then he went to the window, and his mind returned to his daughter. Should he go into the city and report her missing? Should he seek help from Judge Pryor or someone else in authority?

In his mind's eye he was seeing Eden returning home all bruised and battered at the hands of some marauding pirate. If she had been attacked she would need her father there to comfort her.

No. He could not leave the cottage in case she returned, needing his help.

Going into the kitchen, he got a fire going in the cookstove and placed a kettle of water on it for tea.

Then, slouching down at the table, he hung his head in his hands, sobbing.

Chapter Nineteen

The happy sweet laughter of love without
pain.

—EASTMAN

The air was heavy with the aftermath of
pleasure. Their bodies lay intertwined, bare
flesh against bare flesh; Eden sucked in her
breath when Zach's mouth lowered toward
hers, on fire with passion again.

"I must have you again, darling," he whispered against her lips. "My love for you is
unquenchable. Tell me you want me again as
badly."

"You know that I do," Eden said, twining
her fingers through his midnight-black hair.
"Love me, darling. Love me."

Zach molded her close into the contours of
his body, his manhood pulsing against her
thigh as he kissed her hard and long. Eden

returned his kiss, clinging to him. She breathed in the wondrous masculine scent of him as their bodies tangled. She gasped against his lips as he entered her with one bold thrust and began steady strokes within her, each thrust sending a rush of pleasure through her.

With a firm grip around Eden's waist, Zach shifted their bodies so that she was on top of him. "My darling," he whispered, looking up into her passion-filled eyes.

He took his hands from her waist and circled her breasts with them, running his thumbs around each nipple. He thrust his pelvis upward, filling her deeply with his hardness.

Eden was becoming breathless. She held her head back, letting her hair tumble in a golden sheen down her back. Sighing, she sank her fingernails into the flesh of Zach's hips, riding him, ecstasy welling within her. Tremors cascaded down her back as he leaned up and captured a hardened nipple between his teeth, drawing it into his mouth. His tongue circled the taut tip, causing Eden almost to go over the edge into paradise.

Again placing his hands to her waist, Zach slipped her around, beneath him. He surrounded her with the corded muscles of his arms. As before, he rushed her to him so hard, she gasped.

"Perhaps I was too hasty to condemn your abductors," Zach whispered against Eden's lips. "I'm enjoying having you on board ship.

If not for them, you'd be on land, still wondering what sort of man you had lost your heart to."

He smoothed kisses along her brow. "Now you know and do not hate me," he said softly. "That makes me so happy, Eden. So very, very happy."

Eden traced the sculpted lines of his face. "Always feel as though you can confide in me," she murmured. "Please don't keep secrets from me any longer."

"Nor you from me," Zach said, kissing the tip of her nose. "We shall have mutual trust between us."

"Yes, always," Eden said, then trembled with passion as his mouth bore down upon her lips again.

She felt his hardness begin moving within her again, slowly at first, sliding deeper, moving more quickly. She grasped his shoulders, rocking against him, shivering with bliss.

When the magical spasm soared through her, thrilling her from her head to her toes, she clung wildly to him, for his body was jolting and jerking in time with hers.

Waves of energy surged through them again and again, fusing them together as though one.

Afterwards, Zach held Eden close. His chest heaved and his breathing was short and raspy against her cheek. "I hate returning you home," he whispered against her lips. "I will miss you so much. What am I to do when the wide breadth of the sea separates us for the time it will take to settle this thing with Pirate Jack? I'm not sure if I can bear it, Eden."

"Let me go with you," Eden pleaded. "I won't get in the way. I promise."

Zach chuckled as he turned to face her. He stroked her breast, causing stars to sparkle in her eyes again. "No women are ever allowed on a pirate ship," he said softly. "Everyone knows that women are bad luck to a ship's crew."

"This is no true pirate ship. And even if it were, you know that is a lot of superstitious hogwash," Eden pouted, running her hands over the fine hairs of his arm, so lightly, not even touching his skin. "I don't want to leave you. What if I never see you again?"

"Now that *is* a lot of hogwash," Zach said, his fingers tracing circles around her breasts. "I have been involved in many a sea battle, and as you see, I am quite alive."

"And so is Pirate Jack," Eden argued softly. "When the two of you come together for the last time, darling, one of you will be the victor—one the loser."

Zach rose to a sitting position and raked his fingers through his hair. "I am not even so sure that I can bring myself to harm the old pirate," he said, his voice drawn. "Though he is doing things now that I could never approve of, still I find it unbearably painful to think of ending his life. He is such a colorful, interesting old rogue. Should you ever see the true side of him, you would understand just why it is that I am torn."

Eden wrapped her arms around him. "Darling, if it were not for my father, we could run away and ignore Judge Pryor's demands and threats. Oh, but we could be so happy! We could have our own little paradise, you and I."

"But there *is* your father to consider," Zach said, turning wistful eyes to Eden. "And, also, darling, I have grown tired of trying to hide my true identity. I want to be free of running from it."

"Yes, I can understand that," Eden said, nodding. "That leaves us no choice but to do what must be done. Again I implore you—let me go with you, Zach. Please?"

"I can't risk losing the only true, genuine thing in my life," he said, drawing her into his embrace. "No, Eden. I shall deliver you to your father's doorstep very soon. We had not been all that far out to sea when you were discovered. I would say that you will be home very soon."

A crack of thunder outside drew them hastily apart. The bulkheads creaked, and the lurch of the ship made Zach tense.

"That storm that I thought would stay far out at sea must have crept up on us after all," he said, quickly drawing on his breeches. "You'd best get dressed too. It could take hours for the storm to reach its peak, or it could hit suddenly. It's all according to the winds."

Having watched many a ship being tossed about at sea beneath the sturdy light of the lighthouse beam, Eden was gripped in a cold, clammy sudden fear. She slipped her dress over her head, gasping when another terrific clap of thunder echoed through the cabin.

A great burst of thunder awakened Preston with a start. He looked around him, feeling drugged. While Sabrina had slept, he had fought off the urge to go to sleep himself, wanting more answers from Sabrina and sick with worry about Eden.

But drowsiness had claimed him and he had gone to bed, fully clothed, determined only to rest for an hour.

Seeing how dark it was in his bedroom, Preston moved shakily to his feet. Damn. He had slept all day. How could he have, with Eden's welfare in question?

The sound of the clock on the wall chiming the eleven o'clock hour made Preston tighten up inside. God. Had he slept all day and even most of the night away? Could it truly be eleven o'clock at night?

He grabbed his cane and went to the window. Throwing aside the curtain he looked outside—and realized that it was not night at all. A portion of the sky was a brilliant blue, but most of it was dark, piled high with a density of clouds that darkened the daylight. Lightning flashed from cloud to cloud, in almost blinding flashes.

"Damn. This looks like a bad one," Preston whispered.

He leaned against his cane and left his

bedroom. Sabrina was still sleeping soundly, but he had no choice. He had to leave her, to go to the lighthouse and get his lamps ready. Soon the ocean would be a battlefield of crashing waves. Pity any ship that was caught out in such waters.

Preston went on through the parlour and stepped out onto his porch. His body jerked in fear as he looked up at the white cracks of lightning in the sky. This thunderstorm would be the sort that seemed capable of bursting creation. He recalled the one other time the lightning was as fierce.

He looked slowly down at his legs, paling. The stairs could become as charged today as on that fateful day when he had been injured, yet he had to chance it. He ran a dependable beam. If he could lead even one ship to safety, it was worth all the pain he had been through —or might go through again.

He could hear the rumbling of the sea and the howling of the winds as he walked up the pebbled path to the lighthouse. He stepped inside and eyed the steep, spiraling staircase. With trembling fingers he took hold of the rail and began taking the stairs one at a time, his heart pounding each time he heard another crack of thunder outside, and could see the lurid lightning flashes through the small windows that lined the walls of the tower.

When he finally reached the top and pushed open the trap door, he sighed with relief. Hoisting himself up into the little room, he began to check the oil supply, then began lighting the lamps.

One at a time they began to flare.

The whole ship creaked and groaned, laboring under the winds that slammed against it. Zach rushed around, shouting out orders to his crew. The piled-up clouds overhead had darkened the daylight to night.

The rain had just begun to fall, obscuring all visibility. As Zach peered through it his eyes felt as though they were being slashed with steel pellets. Thirty-foot waves were hitting the ship in huge port-to-starboard blows.

Eden couldn't stand to stay in the cabin any longer. She could hear the shrieks and cries of the crew and the creaking of the ship's timbers as they began pitching and heaving in the howling winds.

Her jaw set determinedly, she fought against the door as she tried to open it. The wind was blowing so strongly against it, it felt as though a muscled arm were pressing against the door, holding it closed.

Then, suddenly, she managed to throw the door open—only to be attacked by great sprays of water on her face. Choking, holding onto the edge of the door with all her might, Eden screamed.

"Zach!" she shouted. "Oh, God, Zach. Where are you?"

She tried to see through the pouring rain but could only see blurs of movement. She gasped with alarm when a lurid flash of lightning lit up the sky and the sea, and seemed to set the decks on fire.

Above the sound of the fierce, howling winds, Zach heard Eden's frightened screams. His gut twisted, knowing that she could be carried overboard if she tried to walk on the watersoaked deck.

His heart in his throat, Zach supported himself by ropes as he made his way back to his cabin. Just as he saw Eden, he saw something else there, illuminating her. It was the beam from a lighthouse. They were close to shore. Eden's father was tending to his beams, giving a steady, dependable light.

But Zach doubted if any light would help his ship. He was aware of how many planks had loosened on the frame. The masts were nodding, swaying and bent. Belowdecks, the ship was completely awash! There was a mighty roar as the water crashed and tumbled, the larger waves threatening to roll the ship over.

"Oh, Zach," Eden cried, seeing him approach. Slipping and sliding, she went to him and clung to him. She looked into the beam glowing from the lighthouse, so thankful that they were close to land, and that her father was being obedient to his beam even though he was surely filled with worry over where she was.

Zach shouted above the howl of the wind. "Darling, you are only a heartbeat away from safety," he said, framing Eden's face between his hands. Rain pelted her face as she peered intently up at him. "Thank God your father is tending to his beam, for it is going to be treacherous getting you to shore."

"Perhaps we should wait until the storm dies down a bit," Eden shouted back, licking the rain from her lips.

Zach shook his head slowly. "No, I can't wait that long to get you off this ship," he responded hoarsely.

"Zach, are you so eager to be rid of me?" Eden gasped.

"Eden, oh, Eden, you know better than that," Zach said, drawing her into his embrace. "It's something else. I don't want to frighten you, but you must know. This ship is very likely to capsize. It's reeling dangerously under the lash of the squall."

He swung her away from him and began walking her along the deck, holding her tightly to him when she slipped. "I must get you into a longboat quickly," he said. "Though the waters are fierce, you have a much better chance of surviving if you are no longer a part of this weakened ship."

Eden was numb with fear—not for her own safety, but for Zach's. If she left him on this ship and he sank with it, she could not bear it.

"I shan't leave the ship!" she cried, jerking away from him. She grabbed for a rope and balanced herself. "I can't leave you, Zach. I can't."

"Tom!" Zach shouted, seeing the young man struggling with a barrel that had rolled loose. "Come here. Quickly, Tom. Leave the damn barrel go."

Tom ducked against the wind and rain and hurried to Zach's side.

Zach grabbed Tom by the arm and shouted over the wind, "Tom, I am giving you a mission that you must succeed at for me!"

"What, sir?" Tom shouted, his red hair blowing wildly in the wind. "I shall do whatever I can!"

"Get my lady safely to shore," Zach said, his eyes dark with emotion. "Do this for me, Tom, and you shall stay ashore yourself! Eden will direct you to my plantation. You can introduce yourself to my overseer and tell him that I have given you permission to stay there."

"You are serious?" Tom said, his eyes wide with wonder.

"Tom, I am not much for teasing," Zach said, "Especially under conditions such as these and with the life of my lady being threatened!"

"But, sir, what about Judge Pryor?"

"Tom, if ever I even make it back to shore alive to see the judge, I shall say that I abandoned you on the island with Mike and Clarence," Zach said hurriedly. "No one will be the wiser."

"Sir, I do appreciate what you are offering," Tom said. "But, sir, I feel that I should stay aboard and help you fight the storm."

"Tom, lad, you should have never been placed aboard this ship in the first place," Zach argued. "Landlubbers are not popular recruits on pirate vessels. If a man is going to be a part of the pirate community, he has to be able to tell a marlinspike from a sounding lead and fulfill the normal requirements of a common seaman about the ship."

Zach managed a throaty laugh. He reached a hand to Tom's shoulder. "Now let's get the longboat lowered and pray that you can navigate it safely to shore in these high waves. That will be your last command at sea, Tom. Your last."

"Aye, aye, sir," Tom said, smiling crookedly from Zach to Eden. "I'll try my hardest to get your lady to safety."

Eden began crying softly. She knew that nothing she said to Zach would change his mind. He was determined to see her off the ship. He was determined to die without her, if that became necessary!

Fighting the wind and rain, she followed alongside Zach as he held her strongly to him. She clung to him as Tom loosened the ties of the longboat, then offered her a hand.

"Go on, Eden," Zach urged, giving her over to Tom. "God-speed, darling," he said. "I shall love you forever."

Sobbing, Eden wrenched herself away from Zach and climbed into the longboat. She clung to its sides as it was lowering toward the swirling waters beneath her. She kept looking upward, not wanting Zach to leave her sight. She was so desperately afraid that this would be the last time she gazed upon his handsome face.

* * *

Preston squinted as he tried to see the activity aboard the ship that was battling the waves much too close to land. His pulse raced, fearing for the crew being battered by the stormy waters.

Steadying his beam, keeping the light directed on the ship, he lifted his spyglass and adjusted it when he saw a longboat being lowered from the ship. There was a woman in the longboat, but he could not make out her features.

He was awash with dread and fear, yet the longboat had only a short distance to battle the sea. If God was willing, it would make it.

As for the larger ship, it seemed that God had not been as kind, for no ship battered as much as that ever survived.

Chapter Twenty

Young love, the strong love, burning in the
rain.

—EASTMAN

The swells grew higher. The longboat shuddered as it dropped into the raging seas. Eden
clung desperately to the sides as Tom sank the
oars deep into the water, catching and forcing
it beneath the boat to send it away from the
rocking ship. Water droplets clung to Eden's
thick lashes, and her hair hung in a wet mass
across her shoulders and down her back.

The creaking of the small vessel as the sea
rumbled against its hull sent an icy stab of fear
into Eden's heart. She looked back over her
shoulder, expecting to see the larger, maimed
vessel ripped apart at any moment.

But Zach and his crew had managed to keep
the ship afloat. It was even moving back out to

sea, rising, falling and rolling with the wind and rain. Through the howling of the wind she could hear the wild shouts from the deck of the ship. She could hear the crash of the water, the creak of ropes. She could hear the sails being ripped in shreds as the gallant masts bent in the wind.

Choking back a sob of despair, Eden hunched over, leaning into the cold rain. She focused her eyes elsewhere, not wanting to watch if the ship did capsize. With it would go her heart.

Instead she admired how Tom was keeping the longboat afloat, his muscles cording as he maneuvered the oars through the bubbling white water.

She glanced up at the lighthouse, barely discernible except for the beam glowing down on the longboat, and then out at the ship.

"Oh, Father," Eden cried, sobbing. "You can't keep your light everywhere at once. Please keep it on Zach. He is in more danger than I."

"We're about there, ma'am," Tom shouted. A great bolt of lightning whitened the sky and sea and made him flinch. "And none too soon I'd say. I've never experienced such fierce lightning in my life. I fear it more than I fear the sea. We could be struck at any moment."

As the longboat drew closer to shore, it shuddered dangerously. The roar of water crashing and tumbling onto shore in great, massive waves was deafening. Each wave threatened to topple the longboat as it rose and fell into them. The winds were harsher, shriller as the storm seemed to increase in intensity.

"We're there!" Tom shouted, guiding the longboat onto a spit of sand that jutted out from the beach. He dropped the oars and turned and reached for Eden. "Hurry. I fear we're going to be swallowed whole by those waves."

Eden clasped his hand and rose shakily to her feet. The longboat still tossed from side to side by the churning waters and the wind; at any moment it might be carried back out to sea.

She climbed from the longboat, stepping knee-deep into water. Tom clasped hard onto her hand and half dragged her along behind him until they were out of the water, on more solid footing.

"Thank goodness," she sighed, then looked over her shoulder at Zach's ship. "But what of them?" she cried. "What of them?"

Tom drew her against him, wrapping a secure arm around her waist, and began running her up the beach alongside him, toward the lighthouse. "The captain'll do his best," he shouted. "All we can do is offer a little prayer, ma'am."

Eden cried softly, biting her lower lip in frustration. Her whole body ached from the thrashing of the cold rain and wind. Yet how could she worry about herself when Zach was fighting for his life?

Oh, was there anything fair in life? If he

died, she would never believe in anything again! Never!

Finally at the lighthouse door, Eden broke away from Tom and rushed inside. Lifting the drenched skirt of her dress into her arms, she began running up the stairs, her breathing harsh, her lungs aching from the exertion.

She looked upward and kept her eyes locked on the trapdoor that her father hadn't closed. The soft lamplight flooding down from the open space was more a beacon of safety to her than the larger beam that lighted the seas. Soon she would be held within the wonderfully firm arms of her father. He would give her all the reassurances that she needed to believe that Zach would survive this latest ordeal in his troubled life. And wouldn't he be wondrously happy to see that she was all right? Her absence had surely caused him much despair.

"Eden, wait!" Tom shouted, climbing the stairs behind her. "In your haste you may fall. The captain has handed you over to me to keep you safe. Please listen to what I say. I don't want to disappoint the captain. He's become a godsend to me."

"Tom, don't worry yourself so." Eden shouted back. "I am quite practiced on these stairs, remember? My father is the lightkeeper, and I am his assistant."

The wind was howling as though the pits of hell had been opened up and had released condemned souls from its bowels, but Preston heard the commotion on the stairs, then heard Eden's name being called. He even heard her voice.

Good God, she was there, alive and well! Could she have been the one brought to shore in the longboat? Had she been on that ship being ravaged by the sea?

Oh, God, had she been abducted by pirates and then set free after they had grown tired of using her?

Ignoring his beams, his heart racing, Preston grabbed a lantern and held it down low, over the stairs. Tears flooded his eyes when he saw Eden looking up at him, drenched to the bone, but very much alive and, it seemed, even well.

"Eden!" Preston said, setting the lantern aside. He gathered her into his arms as she came up off the stairs. "I could hardly stand not knowing what happened to you. Where have you been? Who were you with?" He held her back away from him, eyeing her closely. "Were you the one brought in the longboat from that ship?"

Eden nodded, choking back the urge to burst into tears. She looked anxiously at the steady beam of light directed out to sea. "Father, you see that I am safe and well," she said, rushing to the window. She peered down into the raging sea, searching for Zach's ship. "Allow me to explain everything later. But now please tell me—how is the larger ship faring? Do you think it will ride out the storm?"

Preston moved to the window and began scanning the foaming waters with his light. Eden placed a fist to her mouth when she finally caught sight of Zach's ship. It was leaning first one way and then another, its sails dangling, whipping loosely in the wind. "And, father, Zach is still on the ship. Please tell me that he's going to be safe."

"Lord, Eden, are you saying that Zach is on that ship? And you were on the ship with him?" he gasped. "Why? However did that come about? Zach sent you a note. In it was revealed enough to me to know that you weren't with him."

Tom stepped up from the stairs, into the small tower room. "Sir, she was abducted by two pirates," he said, slicking his wet red hair back from his eyes. "She was taken on board ship without the captain's being aware of it. But she is safe now." He went to the window and leaned against it. "But what of the captain? Will he survive?"

"Pirates? Abducted? Zach is the captain of a pirate ship?" Preston said, stunned by all these disclosures. His gaze moved up and down the young man. "And who the hell are you? Another damn pirate?"

Eden reached for Tom's hand. She wove her fingers around it. "This is Tom," she said, smiling at Tom. "And, no, he's not a pirate. He's a friend. A true friend."

Preston shook his head, not understanding

any of this. But for now it was enough that Eden was home, that Eden was safe.

He looked quickly back out to sea and his heart lurched when he saw that the ship was losing its battle.

"I hope you have some energy left after all you've just been through, young man," he said, grabbing a lantern and thrusting it into Tom's hand. He lit two more and gave one to Eden and kept one for himself. "Soon we'll have some rescuing to do. It doesn't look at all good for that ship and its crew."

Eden felt faint. She clasped hard to the handle of the lantern and followed Tom and her father down the steep staircase.

Suddenly she noticed something. Her heart skipped a beat and joy leapt through her. Her father wasn't walking with the aid of a cane. Had the shock of missing her, then seeing her so suddenly, given him back the full use of his legs?

"Father!" she cried. "Haven't you even noticed? You are walking without a cane! Oh, father, you are suddenly well!"

Preston's heart seemed to leap clear up into his throat as he looked down, seeing how his legs were moving all on their own, the numbness miraculously gone! He blinked his eyes disbelievingly, then let out a loud whoop of joy.

"I don't know how it's happened!" he shouted, looking back at Eden with tears in his eyes. "But, Lord, honey, I welcome it!"

Eden blinked tears from her eyes. She said a

soft prayer, asking that another miracle be performed this night.

As Zach clung to the helm, he watched the monstrous swells crest and thunder toward the ship. Each one was capable of swamping, capsizing, or destroying the craft.

Suddenly a violent williwaw—a white squall—smashed against the ship broadside. With a great crack the mainmast broke, the overstrained tiller splintered.

Reeling under the lash of the squall, the boat began ripping apart.

Zach jerked himself around, white with fear. "Abandon ship!" he screamed. "Every man for himself. God be with you!"

The ship suddenly rolled over on her starboard side, paused for a moment, then began sliding sideways into the sea. Zach dove into the murky water, the crests of the waves all about him whipping into whitecaps.

Making contact with the icy water, he plunged into its dark depths. As he fought to climb back to the surface, he felt a great sucking sensation on his body.

Panic rose inside him. This great suction was caused by the ship as it began sinking to the bottom of the sea not all that far from him.

His lungs felt as though on fire and the muscles of his legs and arms throbbed as he fought to stay clear of the whirlpool created by the ship's descent. A lightheadedness was sweeping through him. He feared that he was losing the battle!

Suddenly he felt a hand grab hold of his arm. He was being pulled to safety. As he popped to the surface, he choked and wheezed as he gasped for air. Treading water, his vision cleared and the beam from the lighthouse revealed who had rescued him.

"Tom!" he said hoarsely. "My God, Tom, you're supposed to be with Eden!"

Tom grabbed the main hatchway door as it floated past. He moved it within Zach's reach so that he could cling to it. "She's safe. She's with her father," he shouted, grinning at Zach. "I couldn't let the captain go down with the ship, now could I?"

"Tom, all I can say is thank you," Zach said, smoothing his wet, dark hair back from his eyes. He looked desperately around him. "Are there any more survivors? Do you see any?"

"None as far as I can see," Tom said, peering across the water that had become a massive grave. "We're lucky, captain. Damn lucky."

The lightheadedness was again claiming Zach. He had swallowed a lot of saltwater while struggling to free himself from the whirlpool that had drawn the ship into the depths of the ocean. Each breath he took was a struggle.

"Tom, there may yet be one less survivor," Zach said, his head spinning. "I think I'm going to black out. Hang onto me. Don't let me follow that damn ship to the bottom of the sea. Hang onto me!"

Tom grabbed hold of Zach as his eyes closed

and hung onto him with all his might as he looked anxiously toward shore. A rogue wave could claim him and Zach at any moment. He shouted at Eden and Preston to get their attention. They had surely lost track of him after he had dived into the water to save Zach. As far as they knew, he had been drowned and Zach had gone down with the ship!

"Eden!" he shouted. He waved his free hand. "Over here, Eden! God, can't you hear me?"

A wave momentarily blinded him.

Eden held her lantern high. She had lost sight of Tom. Oh, Lord, had he also drowned while trying to save Zach? Once he swam away from shore, that had been the last she had seen of him.

But suddenly she heard a voice. She scarcely breathed, listening.

When she heard it again, she recognized that it was Tom's. She lifted her lantern higher. Her pulse was racing as she peered through the torrents of rain toward the sea.

Then her heart skipped a beat. For a moment she had seen two men on a piece of debris float into the lighthouse beam, but just as quickly they disappeared from sight as a wave pushed them away.

Again she saw the two clinging men! She took a step towards the ocean. "There they are!" she shouted, looking back at her father. "There are two of them. One of them is Tom. I heard his voice. I know it was him."

Preston stood firmly on his revitalized legs. He lifted his lantern higher. "Keep a steady light on the water. When the men get close enough for me to reach them, I'll go and help them to shore."

The rain was only a slight mist now. The wind was settling down into a gentle breeze, and the waves were subsiding. But Eden's heart had never beat more soundly than now. She chewed on her lower lip, frantic with fear. Was her and Zach's love never meant to be and would he die because of it?

"He's got to be all right," she whispered, pacing. Then her heart faltered when she saw the two men dangling from a piece of debris from the ship. Her heart was beating so quickly and her throat was so constricted from anxiousness that she could hardly point the men out to her father.

But that wasn't even necessary. He had placed his lantern on the ground and was already running toward the water.

Moving into the water up past his knees, Preston steadied the battered hatchway door so that Tom could get a steady footing on the sand. He then reached for Zach and swung him away from the debris, slipping one of Zach's arms around his shoulder, dragging him to shore while Tom stumbled alongside him. He lay Zach gently on the sandy beach.

"Is he going to be all right?" Tom asked, gasping for air. "Is he?"

Eden fell to her knees beside Zach. She dropped the lantern to the ground, sobbing, then placed her hands to Zach's cheeks, feeling their utter coldness. His lips were purple and his teeth were chattering. His eyes were closed, as though he was in death's grip.

"Father, it's Zach," she cried. "Tell me he's going to live. Tell me!"

Preston gave Eden a pensive stare. "I don't know what the hell's going on here," he growled, wiping his wet face with the back of his hand. "But now isn't the time for explanations. If Zach is going to make it, he'll have a much better chance if he's out of those wet clothes and into a warm bed."

Preston nodded toward Tom. "Give me a hand, lad," he said flatly. "Let's get him to my cottage. We'll do what we can for him." He glanced at Eden. "And then I think there's a lot of explaining to be done, daughter."

Eden gulped hard. "Yes, sir," she murmured. "Indeed there is, sir."

Preston and Tom lifted Zach from the beach and carried him to the cottage. Eden trailed along beside them. She shuddered, thinking how fate had so many twists and turns.

Chapter Twenty-One

There's a strange, sad silence 'mid the busy
swirl.

—CORY

Eden hurried into the cottage after her
father and Tom. The fire had died down only
to embers. There would not be enough heat
radiating from it to warm Zach quickly
enough.

"Take Zach to my room!" she urged. "We
must get him beneath a thick layer of blankets.
Getting him warm is of the utmost importance!"

Preston gave Eden a concerned glance.
He had yet to find out why Zach had been on
the ship and why Eden had been on it with
him. Did he even want Zach in his house
now?

"Father," Eden persisted. "Zach must be
taken to my bed so that yours will be free for

you to get the rest you need to care for the lighthouse. Please! We must see to Zach now. He must have swallowed an awful lot of water to still be unconscious."

Preston had never turned his back on anyone in distress, so he hesitated no longer and, with Tom, took Zach into Eden's room and lay him on the bed. He blanched when Eden hurried into the room and began undressing Zach, as though it were nothing at all that she would soon see the man in his nakedness. She was as though half crazed, her fingers trembling as she tossed his wet shirt aside.

"Father, please go and get me some hot water and a washcloth," Eden said, pleading to him with her eyes. "I want to bathe Zach with the hot water. We must get some heat circulating in his veins. He shouldn't still be unconscious. Not unless—"

Preston placed a hand on Eden's shoulder. "Eden, you had best think of yourself," he said. "You are soaked to the bone, also. Go get into some warm, dry clothes and I will tend to Zach." He motioned at Tom. "You can find the kitchen. Get a fire going in the cookstove and put a kettle on."

"Aye, aye, sir," Tom said, turning to leave.

"Young man, I ain't your sea captain," Preston said dryly. "Save your salutations for when you're back aboard a ship. Call me Preston."

"Yes, sir, Preston, sir," Tom said, shifting his feet nervously. He frowned down at Zach, worry etched on his face. "But I'm not going to be aboard any ships again. Zach promised me that I could go and stay at his plantation. He told me to tell his overseer, Joshua, that he gave me permission to go there." He swallowed hard. "But now I'm not sure if it would be proper. What if Zach—?"

Eden went to Tom and took his hand. "Don't even think about Zach's dying," she said, her voice quavering. "Tom, you get the water on the stove, then go on to Zach's plantation. Once you get off our lane, and onto Lighthouse Road, take a right. Zach's plantation is up the first lane to the left. There are no other plantations along this stretch of road. You surely won't have trouble finding it."

Preston was kneading his chin, the name that Tom had spoken so casually troubling him. Joshua. Joshua was the name of Zach's overseer? Joshua was the man that Sabrina had mentioned in her ramblings.

"Sabrina!" he said in a rush. He looked toward the door that led into the living room. "Lord, I forgot all about Sabrina! When we came in just then, the living room was too dark to see if she was still sleeping on the sofa!"

Eden turned with a start. She looked at her father, puzzled. "What are you talking about?" she gasped. "What did you say about Sabrina?"

"She's here. She came here, all worn out

from being lost in the marshes," Preston said, then glanced down at Zach as Zach began to cough and choke. He fell to his knees beside the bed and began loosening more of his clothes. "But we'll deal with her later. We'd best get along with caring for Zach."

Preston glanced up at Tom. "But on second thought, Tom, we can deal with Sabrina now," he quickly added. "Take her to Zach's plantation with you. Take our horse and buggy. Sabrina was mighty weak when she arrived here. She can't be faring much better now."

He frowned up at Tom. "Treat her with respect, young man," he said. "She's another man's property. She was bought and paid for by Zach."

Preston cleared his throat nervously. "And I hope you find everything there is all right," he said, his voice drawn. "Sabrina kept rambling on about something to do with Joshua. She never did make any sense about him."

Eden didn't understand at all why Sabrina would be there, but now was not the time to look for answers. Zach was her prime concern.

Going to her wardrobe, Eden grabbed a change of clothes. She rushed from her room to go to her father's room to change into them, but stopped short and stared at Sabrina, who was crouched down on the sofa, a blanket draped around her naked form.

"Sabrina?" Eden gasped, looking at the clothes that were clutched in her arms.

Sabrina swallowed hard. She looked toward

Eden's bedroom door, having been awakened by the voices and commotion as Zach was carried into the cottage. "Masta' Zach?" she murmured, her eyes wide. "He ain't goin' to die?"

Eden sighed heavily, still too driven with fear over Zach's welfare to stop and question Sabrina about how she had gotten lost in the marshes and ended up there. "Sabrina, I don't know," she said, rushing on past her towards her father's room. "Slip into your clothes. You'll be returning to Zach's plantation with one of Zach's friends. Zach will come as soon as he is able."

"Joshua?" Sabrina said, scurrying to her feet. "Oh, Miss Eden, Joshua! He—"

"He'll be glad to see that you are returned safely," Eden said, stopping before closing the door so that she could dress in private. "I don't know how you happened to stray from the plantation, but I am sure Joshua will be very happy to know that you are all right."

Sabrina reached a hand to Eden and opened her mouth to explain about Joshua and his misfortune, but the closed door too soon separated them. Hanging her head, feeling empty inside over not being able to get anyone to listen to her about Joshua, Sabrina dropped the blanket and slipped her dress over her head.

She looked blankly at Tom as he ran past her, into the kitchen. He seemed to be a gentle, understanding boy, but Sabrina had now decided that the only person to tell about

Joshua was Zach, for Zach loved the man as though he were a brother.

But Zach might not even be alive long enough to go and see to Joshua's rescue.

Tears rolled down her cheeks. She looked toward the window. The dark storm clouds had broken up, releasing streamers of sunshine across the wooden floor of the cottage. Sabrina wanted to see the promise that sunshine after a storm brought to the world, but today she could not see anything but darkness ahead.

Keeping vigil at Zach's bedside, Eden breathed much more easily. He had awakened long enough to say her name and smile weakly up at her, and then drifted back to sleep. She had brought his temperature up to normal with hot compresses, and he now lay beneath blankets, scarcely seeming to breath in his stupor.

Eden flipped her hair back from her shoulders as she heard footsteps enter the room. She smiled up at her father, then went and hugged him. "You don't know how good it is to see you walking without the aid of a cane," she murmured. "Father, it is nothing less than a miracle. I'm so happy for you."

Preston patted her fondly on the back, looking over her shoulder at Zach. "As for the young man, what are your thoughts on him?" he asked. "Are you ready to do some explaining?"

Eden slipped from his arms and turned to look at Zach. "If I must, I must," she whispered, clasping her hands nervously behind her. She looked quickly over at her father. "Father, he's sleeping too soundly. I'm afraid for him."

Preston went to stand over Zach, studying him. "You were right when you said that he must've got a lungfull when he was in the water," he said. "But he's breathing much more easily now. And you'll notice, he's not coughing any more."

He reached down and touched Zach's brow. "He doesn't have a temperature, either," he said, nodding. "I'd say you'll see this young man's eyes opening again very soon. He'll be just as full of spirit as before."

Preston took Eden's arm and guided her from the room to the sofa in front of the fire. "Sit down and tell me what all of this is about," he commanded. "And don't leave out one damn thing. Do you hear?"

Eden smiled weakly up at her father, then glanced toward her bedroom door. "Should he be left alone?" she asked softly. "What if he awakens choking?"

"We're not that far away that we won't hear," Preston said, easing down beside her. He rubbed his knees, enjoying being able to feel something for the first time in years.

Yes, it was nothing less than a miracle.

He looked at Eden. "Go ahead, Eden," he said. "I'm listening."

Eden stared into the fire, glad that her father had built it, for she still felt chilled from her ordeal in the torrential rain.

"Oh, how do I begin?" she said, screwing her face up into a frown.

"I'd say, at the beginning," Preston said, drumming his fingers on his knees impatiently.

"The beginning?" Eden said. "I guess that would be when I met Zach that first time."

"You can pass on that," Preston grumbled. "You met him the same time I did. I saw nothing consequential in the meeting, except that after that day all hell seems to have broken loose in our lives."

Eden shifted uneasily on the sofa. "Father, I want to tell you everything and that means I must reveal my true first meeting with Zach," she said in a rush of words. She saw his face grow pale, as he slowly realized that she was guilty of deceiving him.

"Please don't hate me after I tell you," she pleaded. "You see, I only went into Charleston that day without you because I wanted to buy your birthday present and fresh ingredients for your birthday cake. Never had I imagined that a wheel would become damaged on the buggy and that I would have to seek help from someone. Oh, father, that someone was Zach! I met him on Lighthouse Road the day before he came to introduce himself properly to you. Father, he helped me in my time of trouble. Because I knew you would be angry at me for having gone into Charleston alone, I asked him to pretend that we had not yet met when he came here the next day."

Preston was taken aback by her confession, yet he was not surprised. She was cooped up alone with him too much in the lighthouse and cottage. It was her nature not to be stifled, even by her father.

"How often have you done this, Eden?" he asked. "Aren't you aware of the dangers?" He stormed to his feet and circled his hands into fists at his sides. "But, yes, you are. You only today escaped death on that ship. Damn it, Eden, how did you get on the ship? Why was Zach on it? What's this about pirates?"

Eden stood and placed her hands to his cheeks. "Father, please sit back down and listen," she implored him. "I will tell you everything, even about Zach and his tortured past. When I am through, you will surely see why I cannot help but love him as I have from the first moment I saw him. Give me a chance to tell you. Listen with an open mind and heart, as I did when Zach explained it all to me."

Preston shook his head sorrowfully. He was tense as she began her story. When he heard that Zach was a retired pirate, he became enraged. A pirate was a pirate! All were filthy, murdering thieves!

When he heard of Judge Pryor's deceit, he was hurt.

He was torn with many emotions as Eden continued her story, but only up to the point of her being abducted by the seamen. Then he could no longer just sit by and listen. His eyes blazed with anger.

"If not for that man in there, none of this would have happened to you!" he shouted, gesturing toward Eden's bedroom. "And you want me to pity him? Eden, he is nothing but trouble! And a pirate to boot? It's a miracle you came through being alone with him without being raped or having your throat slit."

Eden grabbed her father's hands tightly. "Father, what a horrible thing to say!" she gasped. "Please let me finish. After you hear everything, you will feel differently. I know you. You are a caring man. You will have pity for Zach. You will even want to see that things are made right for him."

Preston shook his head again. "Eden, I just don't see how . . ." he began, but her soft hand was on his lips, hushing him.

"Shh," she whispered. "Please? Listen?"

Preston sighed and nodded.

Eden drew her father back down on the sofa beside her. She went into Zach's past and told every sordid detail about his beatings, about his having been sold into slavery and handed over to Pirate Jack.

When Eden was through, she could see the change in her father by the softening in his eyes and jaw.

"Angelita is his sister?" Preston said. "Her Aunt Martha is Zach's aunt? She's the one who beat Zach and sold him into slavery?"

"Yes, it's all true," Eden said, sighing heavily. "Now do you understand? Can you sympathize with Zach?"

"I would be a hard man not to," Preston said softly. His eyes were drawn to the door just then when Zach called out from the bedroom for Eden.

Eden's heart lurched. Her face filled with warmth. "Zach!" she whispered, placing her hands to her cheeks.

Preston nodded toward the bedroom. "Go to him, honey," he said. He looked toward the sun drenched window. "It's cleared up outside. I'm going to go out on the beach and see if anyone else has been washed up on shore."

Eden's knees were trembling and the pit of her stomach felt strangely weak when she rose to her feet. Then she heard Zach cursing, obviously trying to figure out where he was. It was quite apparent that he was going to be all right!

Eden rushed into the bedroom. A sob of happiness froze in her throat when she saw Zach sitting on the edge of the bed, a blanket dangling across his lap. "Darling, you're going to be all right," she said, happiness bubbling inside her at the sight of him.

She sat down on the edge of the bed beside him and twined her arms around his neck and hugged him tightly, her mouth brushing his lips in a light kiss.

Zach wove his fingers through her hair, drawing her lips into his with force. He kissed her ardently, drawing her breath away, then leaned her away from him.

"I just about went down with that damned ship, didn't I?" he said, coughing as a pain stabbed his lung. "That wasn't too smart of me, was it? The ship didn't even belong to me."

"It's understandable," Eden said, raining kisses along his face, deliriously happy that nothing seemed all that much damaged from the drenching in the sea. "You were dedicated to the sea for so long, you could not let a ship go down that easily. You would fight to the end. You did, Zach. You did."

"After I saw that you were safe, that was all that mattered to me," Zach said, licking his parched lips. He looked around him. "Where am I?"

"Darling, under any other circumstances you might feel victorious," Eden teased him. "You see, you just spent several hours in my bed, in my bedroom."

Zach chuckled, his eyes twinkling. "Perhaps I'd best take advantage of a good thing while I have the opportunity," he said. He swept her closer and kissed her again, cupping her breasts through her dress. "Darling, perhaps we have that second chance at love. Can we truly be that lucky?"

"We are, darling," Eden said, ecstasy swimming through her. "Oh, Zach, we are so very lucky!"

"It may be short-lived, Eden," Zach said. "You know that Judge Pryor will manage to have another ship commissioned to me, don't you? He won't be happy until I kill Pirate Jack. His dream of living in the Governor's mansion is stealing his common sense away. How many lives must be lost for that fool to gain the recognition he feels that he needs to become Governor? How many?"

Eden placed her hands on his shoulders and guided him back down onto the bed. "Don't weaken yourself by talking so much about that crazy man," she said. "And as for your being commissioned another ship, you're staying right here for now and letting me nurse you back to health. As long as you're here, Judge Pryor won't give you orders to do anything. And I'm going to keep you with me as long as I can."

Zach's aching lungs made him aware that he could honestly humor Eden for at least a little while. He did need to rest.

He had no choice but to face Judge Pryor again sometime soon. He had to get this ordeal behind him for good, in order to begin a normal life again—a life that he would spend with the woman he loved. With Eden.

Just as Preston left the porch to go to the beach, Angelita Llewellyn swung her horse and buggy to a halt beside him.

Preston gazed at Angelita and smiled. As always, seeing her made him feel young again. She was so full of life, so spirited. All dressed up in lacy finery, a fancy bonnet hiding her dark curls, she was a vision of loveliness, and it made his old heart flutter as though he were a boy. He had had twinges of feelings for her in the past, but today it was a powerful burst of emotion.

Angelita hopped from the buggy and met Preston as he moved on down the porch steps.

Her dark eyes danced as she looked him up and down. Suddenly she lunged into his arms and hugged him tightly.

"Preston, oh, Preston!" she cried. "You are walking without a cane. That's wonderful. Wonderful."

Awkwardly, Preston slipped an arm around her waist and returned her hug. He hoped that she could not feel the furious pounding of his heart. For so long, he had fought against these special feelings creeping up inside him for Angelita. She was young enough to be his daughter. Hardly a man in Charleston would not kill to take her out for an evening on the town.

He had listened to her bragging about the parade of men at her doorstep until it had become pure agony for him at times. At first he had thought it was because he had feared for her safety and respect.

But now he knew that it was because he had been jealous. He could love her, if given the chance. No lady had felt as good in his arms since his wife had laid claim to them.

Because of his damn numb legs, he had rejected any feelings for any woman.

But now he was a whole man again and was ready to play the part to the hilt!

"Yes, I've got the feeling back in both my legs and can walk as naturally now as I did before the accident," Preston said. "Angelita, I'm glad you're happy for me."

He stepped back away from her, holding her hands tightly. Their eyes met and held. A strong electric current seemed to be flowing between them. He could see a sudden surprised look on her face.

When a blush stole upward onto her cheeks, he understood that she was discovering that his feelings were not those of a friend's aged father, but of a vital, attractive man.

"Yes, Preston, I'm happy," Angelita murmured. "It is so very, very wonderful."

They stood for a moment longer holding hands and looking into each other's eyes, as though discovering each other for the first time.

Then Preston laughed awkwardly and eased his hands from hers. "You didn't come way out here to hear an old fool braggin' about having legs that work," he said, clumsily raking his fingers through his hair.

"Why, Preston, I've told you so often before that I don't see you as old at all," Angelita said, smiling sweetly up at him. "Nor do I see you as bragging. Why, you've much to be proud of. I'm proud for you."

Preston shifted his feet nervously. It had been a long time since he had been forced to make idle conversation with a lady whom he was trying to impress.

Then suddenly he recalled what Eden had just revealed to him—that Zach was Angelita's brother. Zach was inside and she didn't know it!

He gently placed an arm around her waist. "Angelita, come inside," he said, walking her up the stairs. "I think there's someone here that you'd like to see."

Chapter Twenty-Two

Bend down your head unto me.
                    —HAWTHORNE

Zach's clothes lay spread across a chair close to the bed, dry. The sun poured brightly in through the window. Eden tucked a blanket up around him. "I'm going to get some soup started on the stove," she said, taking his hand and squeezing it affectionately. "Though I dread seeing you go, I don't want to be accused of purposely starving you so that you are too weak to leave."

"I'm sure your father is anxious to see me walk out your front door," Zach said dryly. "Does he know everything about me? Have you told him?"

"Yes," Eden said, nodding. "Even that you are a retired pirate."

"A retired pirate being blackmailed into going back to sea," he scowled, drawing his hand from hers. He folded his arms across his bare chest angrily.

"He knows even that," Eden said, bending to kiss his lips. "And, darling, he understands everything. I explained how you were mistreated as a child. He sympathizes with you and the sort of life that the abuse forced you into."

"He knows of Angelita? Of my Aunt Martha?" Zach asked, grabbing Eden's hand.

"Of course," Eden said. "They are your past. Your aunt is the one who hurt you."

Zach swallowed hard and turned his eyes away. "Thank God Angelita was spared such abuse," he said. "For so long I didn't know." He turned his eyes slowly back to Eden. "After I became acquainted with Pirate Jack and had a measure of freedom, I sent out feelers, investigating how Angelita was being treated. If I had discovered that she was being abused, I would have sent for her and taken her away. After I discovered that she was living a comfortable life and being treated exceptionally well by our aunt, I left her alone." Again his eyes wavered. "She only knew me through my gifts."

"But now she knows who sent the gifts," Eden said, relieved herself to know. "When you sent her the note with the explanation, did you not believe you would return alive to tell her yourself?" Her eyes grew wide. "My note! The one you wrote to me! I haven't seen it yet. I must go to father and ask for it."

"The note is no longer important," Zach said. "I've already told you its contents. In it I mainly asked you to be patient until I returned."

"Then you were confident that you would survive this venture forced on you by Judge Pryor?"

"I've lived through worse, I assure you, Eden."

"Then why the need of the note to Angelita? Why didn't you wait and reveal yourself to her, in person?"

"I thought I had waited long enough already. And telling her the truth in writing was much easier than having to do it in person. How could I know what her reaction would be?"

Eden placed a finger to her lips. "I wonder how she did react?" she wondered aloud, knowing that Angelita had loved thinking she had a secret admirer. When she found out that it was a brother . . . ?

She pondered this question for only a moment longer, then smiled at Zach. "I must go and prepare that soup," she said. "Soon you will go wild with the delicious smells wafting in here from the kitchen. I make delicious vegetable soup."

"So you are not only a wonderful lover, horticulturist, and assistant lightkeeper, you are also a cook?" Zach teased, his eyes twinkling. "What else are you good at, Eden?"

"You'll find out all of my secrets once we are married," Eden said, bouncing out of the room. She stopped dead in her tracks when, arms linked, Angelita and her father came through the front door.

"Angelita!" Eden gasped, stunned to see her there. Only a few footsteps away lay Angelita's beloved brother. Only moments ago they had been speaking of her. "What brings you here?"

"Several things," Angelita said, breaking away from Preston. She withdrew a folded note from the pocket of her dress and handed it to Eden. "As soon as the storm cleared, I left Charleston to come and share this with you. Oh, Eden, I'm so happy. I just had to come and share my secret with you and Preston. This note is from my brother. Eden, he was the one who sent all the gifts. It was no secret admirer at all. It was my brother Zachary! He is alive! He is well!"

"How wonderful," Eden said, glancing over her shoulder at her bedroom door, then down at the note being thrust into her hand.

"Read it, Eden," Angelita said excitedly. "Please let me share this with you."

Preston snaked an arm around Angelita's waist and hugged her reassuredly when he saw tears in her eyes—tears of happiness. His insides melted when she looked up at him and smiled softly, clasping a hand over his hand that lay possessively at her waist.

"I've so many reasons to be happy today," she murmured.

Eden was too involved in reading the note to see the suddenly open affection between her best friend and her father. The note told her that she should never have doubted Zach, but somehow it felt better seeing it in print. He had lied to her before about so many things. Perhaps now he would never find it necessary to lie to her again.

The shuffling of bare feet behind her drew her head up with a start. Zach spoke Angelita's name, his voice so filled with emotion that it almost tore her heart apart. He was wearing his dried breeches and shirt, grabbing the back of a chair for support as he walked unsteadily into the room.

"Angelita!" Zach said, tears in his eyes. He reached a hand out to her. "Angelita, it's me. It's Zachary."

Angelita gasped and grew pale; she swayed as though she were going to faint from the shock, yet Eden's father was there, supporting her.

For the first time Eden noticed that there was more in the embrace than merely supporting a friend who seemed ready to faint. There was something in her father's eyes as he looked down at Angelita—a look that Eden had seen so often in Zach's eyes when he looked at her!

When could it have happened? When had her father allowed himself to fall in love again? Should she be happy, or wary? She knew Angelita's fickle ways. But so did her father and they seemed no longer important.

"Zachary?" Angelita said, breathless. She moved slowly away from Preston and toward Zach, looking him up and down. Though puzzled by the bruises on his face, and by his being in Eden and Preston's cottage, she was looking more closely for a resemblance to that little boy she remembered. It just did not seem real that they were coming face to face again after all of these years. She so desperately wanted to embrace him, yet something held her back. She wanted to be sure.

"Angelita, it is me," Zach said, inching toward her. "Why do you doubt it?"

Angelita began sobbing, seeing so many of her own features in Zach.

Yes, it was him.

"Oh, Zachary, how I've missed you," Angelita cried, rushing to him. She embraced him so hard he teetered, then steadied himself against her as he returned her hug.

"Why did you wait so long?" Angelita sobbed. "Why didn't you reveal to me many years ago that you were alive? I've been so lonesome without you. I've done everything to try and banish my loneliness. I looked for you in all the men who have courted me."

Eden glanced at Preston, realizing that Angelita's last statement had touched his heart, for now he knew, as she did, why it had been necessary for her to flirt with so many men. Perhaps now she could be happy with just one.

But could it be with a man twice her age? Could Angelita truly care for someone that much older? Or—perhaps that was just what she had needed all these years!

The room was charged with emotion—

with love and with happiness! She wiped away a stray tear, then went on into the kitchen, her father behind her.

"I think everything's going to be all right between those two," Preston said, going to the window to stare out of it. "Now perhaps Angelita can be truly happy. I never knew that she was so tormented over missing her brother."

Eden slipped an arm around his waist. "When you get to know Zach better, you will understand why anyone would be tormented to have, and then lose him," she said softly. "Father, I would want to die myself, if anything happened to Zach."

Preston turned Eden's face up to his. "How could you love that man so quickly?" he said, imploring her with his eyes. "You have known him such a short time, Eden."

"Love is not measured by the amount of time one knows a man," she said, "nor by the amount of time one knows a woman. Just how long have you known Angelita, father? How long have you loved her, yet would not admit to such a loving?"

He chuckled. "So you have seen something between me and Angelita today, have you?"

"Who could not?"

"I'm sure I am expecting too much. I will play this deck of cards very carefully, Eden. Very carefully."

Eden lunged into his arms. "And, father, you will win," she murmured. "Who could refuse you anything? Especially love! You are so very, very special."

Night had fallen. A candle burned low on the nightstand in Eden's bedroom. Still fully clothed, Zach sat on the edge of the bed. He handed the empty soup bowl back to Eden. "Yes, I would say I will be getting a bargain by marrying you," he said, smiling up at her as she took the bowl from him. "You've proven that you can also cook. That vegetable soup was the best I've ever eaten."

Eden set the bowl aside and sat down beside Zach. She traced his handsome features with her forefinger. "Darling, I'm glad you enjoyed my soup, but what I want to hear is how things progressed between you and Angelita. How is she taking knowing that you were a pirate? Does she plan to tell your aunt about you?"

"Shh, Eden," Zach said, weaving his hands through her hair, drawing her lips close. "You are asking too many questions that surely you already know the answers to. Didn't you see how happy Angelita was when she left? Isn't that all that matters? I'll deal with my aunt later. That is, if she ever fully regains her senses after her stroke."

Eden touched the bruises on Zach's face, chilling inside with the memory of how he must have suffered while imprisoned. "And, of course, you told her about how you happen to have those terrible bruises," Eden said, screwing her face up into a frown. "Judge Pryor ought to be horsewhipped!"

"She knows everything," Zach said, lowering Eden down to the bed and hovering over her. "Even that I plan to marry you, my darling."

"Even that?" Eden said, melting beneath his eyes. "And when do you plan to tell my father? If Angelita knows—Lord, Zach, the whole world will soon know! She is not only flighty, she is also incapable of keeping a secret."

"Before I go into Charleston to meet with Judge Pryor, to reveal the fate of his ship and crew, I will speak with your father," Zach said, raining kisses across one of Eden's cheeks and then the other. "I don't think I can manage tonight. He's already gone to the lighthouse for his nightly duty and I'm damned if I have the strength to climb those stairs."

Zach's hand slipped up the skirt of Eden's dress, making her thrill with desire as he caressed his way up to the juncture of her thighs.

"Zach," Eden said with a trembling sigh. "Surely you don't have the strength even to finish what you are starting here. Do you . . . ?"

"I'll certainly do my best," he said with a chuckle.

Eden sucked in her breath when Zach cupped a hand fully over her throbbing center. When one of his fingers began to softly probe within her, she felt herself surrendering to the torrents of feelings sweeping through her. "Oh, Zach, are you truly well enough?

337

Only a few hours ago you were laboring for your every breath!"

"My lungs are still paining me," he said, kissing the hollow of her throat as she threw her head back in ecstasy. "But, darling, there is a part of me that is on fire." He reached for her hand and placed it to his hardness that was straining against his breeches. "Make the pain go away, Eden. Touch me where I throb so unmercifully."

His eyes drugged her, darkening with the depth of his emotion, and Eden did as he asked. She unfastened his breeches and slipped them down off his hips. As he kicked them off, she moved her trembling fingers to him. She did not have to do anything more, for he began to move his body, just as if his hardness was inside her, but instead it was cupped within the soft confines of her hand.

Breathless, her blood spinning hot through her veins, Eden felt desire spreading through her. When his lips came to hers, they were with an explosive kiss—a kiss of total demand. She parted her lips as his tongue surged between her teeth. She arched her hips as his fingers stroked the core of her womanhood more vigorously.

Intense pleasure was within reach, but Eden wanted more. She wanted the feel of his entire body against hers. It was even more exciting because they were making love on her bed—as if this were something forbidden!

Scooting away from Zach, Eden left the bed and beneath the soft splash of candlelight, began loosening the snaps of her dress from behind. She smiled down at Zach as she began slowly revealing herself to him. When they were on the ship, she had feared they might never experience these wonderful moments again.

But, blessedly, they had been spared. She would not let herself think of the hours that lay ahead, when he would be facing Judge Pryor. Would the Judge forget about Pirate Jack now that a ship and crew had been lost? Or would he keep pushing Zach into doing this until Zach was killed too?

No. She would not think of anything like that at this moment. She had Zach to herself. She would savor every touch, every kiss, every embrace!

Zach's heart beat wildly as he watched Eden undress. As her ripe, sinuous body spilled from the dress, he could not get enough of looking at her, from her tantalizingly full breasts, to her narrow and supple waist, across the gentle curve of her stomach, to the golden valley between her legs. His body tightened with want of her and when she drifted toward him and lay down beside him, he surrounded her with his arms and pressed her body into his.

With exquisite tenderness he kissed her, his fingers running down her body, caressing and arousing her. The tenderness grew quickly into a wild surge of passion. He drew her beneath him as he leaned over her. She arched and cried out as he entered her with one hard thrust. He began stroking within her, feeling her excitement rising in the way she moaned with pleasure against his lips.

Zach's arms slipped around her and drew her closer. He pressed harder into her, so hard Eden gasped with momentary pain that soon blended into something joyously beautiful. His tongue brushed her lips lightly, then he looked down at her, his eyes sheened with passion.

"Darling," Zach whispered, molding her breasts in his hands as she clung and rocked with him. "How can I leave you again?"

"Must you?" she whispered, shooting him a look of sadness through her lashes. "Oh, must you truly leave again? You may not be as lucky a second time."

"Tomorrow I shall see exactly what my plans will be," he said huskily, his lips a breath away from hers. "But tonight there is only you. There is only us."

His mouth seized her lips in another fiery kiss. He went to her, thrusting more deeply inside her. An exuberant passion claimed Eden, a tremor beginning deeply within her. She was breathless as she clung to Zach, then shuddered as her ecstasy crested to match his. Their bodies strained together, their breaths mingled as they moaned in unison. Then they lay still, clinging. . . .

Eden stirred beneath Zach. She touched him almost meditatingly on the cheek. "Darling, you're so quiet," she whispered. "Perhaps you weren't strong enough to make love. Did it totally exhaust you?"

Zach rolled away from her, laughing softly. "My heart is pounding a little too fast," he said, stretching out on his back, his arms thrown out beside him. He sucked in a trembling breath. "But even if I fainted from the effort of loving you, it was worth it."

Eden rose to her knees beside him and splayed her hands across his wide breadth of chest. "You are only teasing, I hope," she said, frowning down at him. "It truly didn't weaken you that much. If so, I would feel so bad, Zach. Tell me you are only teasing."

Zach took her by the wrists and pulled her down beside him. "Yes, I was only joshing you," he chuckled. "If you want to know the truth, I am ready to start all over again. Do *you* have the strength, Eden? I could go on through the night, until your father returns from the lighthouse. What if he caught us in such a compromising position? Surely he thinks we are even now both fast asleep."

His eyes widened and his fingers began tracing patterns along her stomach. "My God, Eden, suddenly your body has small red welts on it," he gasped. "What on earth is it? Is it because of me? Have I hurt you?"

Eden looked down, then laughed softly. "It's not because of you, silly," she said. "It's because of the saltwater. Remember my telling you that I was sensitive to it?"

"What if your whole body becomes one large welt?" Zach asked.

"I believe this is all I will get," Eden said, scratching one of the welts. "Though I was drenched with seawater during the storm, I was also quite wet from the rain. The rain surely helped wash most of the salt from my body.''

"How long will you have them?"

"Since they aren't so bad, surely by tomorrow I shall be as good as new."

Zach reached his hand to the crown of her head and parted her hair. "And your head wound?" he asked. "How is it?"

"Strangely, I'd forgotten it," Eden said. "But with all that has been happening around me, I can see why I would." She ran her own fingers over the place on her head. "It's healing well. It should be no further bother."

"Damn those men," Zach said, drawing Eden into his embrace again. "But they paid for their mistake—just as anyone else would who threatens you in any way will pay."

"I don't want to even think about what has happened since the night of my abduction," Eden said softly.

She drew away from him, brushing a kiss across his lips. "I think I had best leave now and go to father's room, where I must spend the night," she said, her eyes twinkling. "If I don't go now, I may not be able to and he would discover us together in my room—in my bed."

"How shameful!" Zach said, again laughing.

Then suddenly he released her wrists and stared over her shoulder, into space. "How can I make so light of what has happened?" he said thickly, raking his fingers through his hair. "Here I am making love to the woman I love while—while so many who rode that fateful ship with me are in their graves at the bottom of the sea.

"Your father went and checked along the shore late this afternoon," he murmured. "He said there were no more survivors—not even signs of those who had died. Perhaps a few came ashore further up the beach? Perhaps not all of them died."

"If God was willing, more than you and Tom survived the shipwreck," Eden said, moving from the bed. She drew on a robe and slipped her feet into soft slippers. "Tom is very courageous to return to the sea to save you after having reached land safely with me."

"I'm glad you sent Tom ahead to my plantation," he said, sighing heavily. "Joshua will see to it that he is made comfortable. He always sees to things when I'm gone. He's very dependable."

Eden paled. Her throat went dry. The mention of Joshua had made her recall Sabrina! Through all of the excitement of the day, she had forgotten about Sabrina being lost and then finding her way to the lighthouse cottage. Everything else had seemed more important at the time than Sabrina's misfortune. But she was back at the plantation, all safe and sound, by now.

"Zach, I think there's something you need to know," Eden said, settling down on the bed beside him again. "It's about Sabrina."

"What about Sabrina?" Zach said, rising up

on an elbow. His face was shadowed with a sudden frown.

"Well, Zach, she got lost somehow in the marshes and ended up here," Eden said softly. "I truly don't know how she managed to get into the marshes in the first place. I didn't take the time to question her. I was too concerned about you."

Zach rose quickly to a sitting position. "Something's wrong at the plantation," he said. "Joshua wouldn't have let Sabrina out of his sight, unless some sort of trouble was brewing there."

He rose shakily to his feet and began drawing on his breeches. "Damn it," he growled. "I know something's wrong. If Sabrina had got lost, Joshua would have gone and found her!"

He looked wildly at Eden. "God, Eden, I have the awful feeling that something terrible has happened to Joshua. I have to go and see. Now!"

Eden rose from the bed and grabbed his arm frantically. "No," she argued. "You're hardly able to walk, much less get on a horse and ride. I won't let you, Zach."

Zach picked her up bodily and set her aside. "Eden, I'm going," he said firmly. "There won't be any stopping me. And if you don't lend me a horse, I'll walk to the plantation. I have to see if Joshua and Sabrina are safe." He drew on his shirt, then slammed one foot into a boot, and then the other. "And I must find out now!"

He walked unsteadily from the room, then outside, while Eden ran after him. "Zach, don't do this!" she screamed. She watched him enter the barn, then walk out again, leading a horse.

"Oh, Zach, please don't go!" Eden cried as he mounted the horse. "I don't think I can bear it."

Zach rode the horse up next to her. He bent over and reached for her hand and held it, touching it lightly with his lips. "Now, darling, I know I am going against your wishes by doing this, but I want you to listen to what I have to say to you," he said softly. "Don't get involved any further in this. I have much to see to and I want to do it with an easy mind, knowing that you are here, safe and sound. Will you promise me that you won't leave the cottage except to go up in the lighthouse with your father? Will you, Eden?"

"Zach, how can I promise such a thing?" Eden pleaded. "Not knowing what is happening to you will drive me insane!"

"Eden, you must have faith that everything will be all right," Zach said. "Now if you truly love me, you will send me off with a clear mind. Tell me you will behave and stay here with your father until I return?"

"Only if you will promise to inform me if Judge Pryor assigns you to another ship, and you will let me know when you will be going to sea again," Eden said, near tears. "Will you, Zach? Will you?"

"I shall keep you informed as best I can, at

all times," Zach reassured her. He bent lower and kissed her brow. "I really must go now. Keep safe, Eden. I love you. I shall always love you."

Eden stepped back away from the horse and placed her hands to her throat as she watched Zach ride away into the darkness. She watched him until she could no longer make him out in the shadows.

Then she turned toward the sea and glared across its wide breadth, hating it. . . .

"You will come back to me, Zach," she whispered. "You will not let the sea claim you. You are mine! Mine!"

Chapter Twenty-three

I have been proud, and said, "My love, my
own!"
——BROWNING

Dawn was breaking along the horizon. Tall
in the saddle, Zach rode into Charleston. He
thrust his booted heels into the flanks of his
gelding, urging it faster through the narrow
streets, one destination in mind. The blacksmith shop. The day Zach had pulled the
blacksmith off Sabrina, he had noticed that
Smitty made his residence at the back of the
filthy shop.

After riding to his plantation and hearing
Sabrina's account of the blacksmith's attempt
to abduct her, and of how he shot Joshua and
took him away, no aching lungs would keep
Zach from getting his revenge. He had left
Tom behind to protect Sabrina.

If Joshua was dead, pity the blacksmith, for Zach would show the man how pirates made a scoundrel die.

Zach drew his reins tight in front of the blacksmith shop. A pistol holstered at his right side, a knife in a leather scabbard at his left, he drew his horse to a halt. He tied the reins to a hitching rail, all the while keeping an eye out for any signs of movement inside the shop.

Stepping back away from the horse, he looked cautiously from side to side. There were no other travelers at this time of day. Only desultory puffs of smoke rose from chimneys, indicating that people were just rising and stoking their fires.

Pulling his pistol from his holster, Zach ran to the back of the blacksmith shop. He placed his back to the wall of the building and began edging his way toward the door. His nostrils flared as a foul odor stung his nose.

He looked around and found the source of the odor. Piles of horse dung lay everywhere, flies buzzing around them. Garbage lay rotting on the ground, where it had obviously been tossed from the back door. He stepped high and low over odds and ends of twisted iron and broken harnesses.

And then Zach smiled. The latch on Smitty's back door was broken and hung limply to one side. The door was even partially open.

"You're a trusting bastard, aren't you?" Zach whispered, laughing to himself.

With the barrel of his pistol he inched the door open farther. The aroma of scorched horse flesh met Zach as he moved into the dark room. He squinted his eyes and looked slowly around him, in his mind's eye replaying that other time he had been there. Sabrina. Smitty. The other men standing around watching, waiting their turn. . . .

Snores drew Zach's gaze on around the small room. Anger swelled within him when he saw Smitty on the small bunk pushed up against the drab wall, a filth-laden blanket draped over him, only partially hiding the torn underclothing he slept in.

Moving stealthily across the room, Zach bent over Smitty. Then he jerked the blanket away from the blacksmith with the barrel of his pistol and thrust the barrel into Smitty's ribs.

"Wake up, you piece of slime," Zach said between clenched teeth, pushing the pistol harder against the blacksmith's flesh.

As Smitty's eyes flew open in alarm and he gasped, Zach glowered down at him. "I think you've some explaining to do," he said. "You'd better begin now or I will be forced to lower the barrel of my gun and shoot some vital parts of your anatomy away."

Smitty scarcely breathed. He looked down at the pistol, then back up into Zach's eyes. "You're here about your nigger?" he said in a rush of words. "He deserved to be thrown in jail. He'll hang for what he did to me." He dared to move to point out the whip marks on his face and chest to Zach. "No nigger does this to a white man and gets away with it! An example must be made of those who do! He'll be hangin' soon and nothin' you can say or do'll stop it."

"Do you want to take a bet on that?" Zach said, reaching to place his free hand on Smitty's throat. He began to squeeze. "Why don't you practice with me what you are going to tell the sheriff when I take you there? It'll make it easier the second time. Of course, you will have to tell him that you trespassed on my property and went to steal my slave that I had legally bought and paid for. You will have to tell him that you shot the handsome buck while you were on my property. Now are you ready to tell the sheriff that you were the one who actually committed these crimes? If not, I'll just have to inflict some more wounds and they won't be the sort that will heal as quickly as those made by a whip. In fact Smitty, they won't heal at all."

"You wouldn't," Smitty said, breathless with fear. "You wouldn't do that just because of a couple of darkies." His eyes narrowed. "But maybe you would. I heard about you bein' a retired pirate. I also heard about the shipwreck. I thought you were dead."

"I have nine lives, just like a cat," Zach chuckled.

He squeezed Smitty's neck harder. "Now do you cooperate with me or do I begin shooting?" he snarled. "I would enjoy watching you beg me to stop. You're the sort that would beg, you know."

"I ain't beggin' you for nothin'," Smitty said, yowling from fear when he saw Zach lower the pistol, jabbing his loins with the barrel. "Don't shoot! Don't shoot! I'll do anything you say!"

Zach stepped away from him. He held the pistol steady on Smitty. "Get dressed," he ordered flatly. "We've someone to get out of jail."

Smitty stumbled into his breeches. "I knew I should've gone lookin' for that wench when she ran into the marshes," he said, giving Zach an angry stare. "I knew she'd be trouble. I knew it."

"One learns from one's mistakes," Zach said cheerfully. He motioned with his pistol. "Hurry up, damn it. I've got to get to Joshua. If he was wounded as badly as Sabrina said he was, we may already be too late."

Pulling on his boots, his shirt thrust only halfway into the waist of his dark trousers, Smitty winced when Zach jabbed his shoulder with the butt of the pistol.

"Outside," Zach ordered. "Get on a horse. You ride just ahead of me to Judge Pryor's house without any commotion or I'll shoot you in the back."

"Judge Pryor's house?" Smitty said, his voice drawn. "What the hell for?"

"He's my guarantee that Joshua will be released," Zach said flatly.

"But what about the sheriff?" Smitty asked, inching along the wall to the door.

"The sheriff?" Zach said, chuckling. "He's going to give Judge Pryor the key that will unlock the cell to release Joshua, and if I have my way about it, you'll be put there in his place."

"Why would you want to do a thing like that?" Smitty said, stumbling outside. "I'm cooperating! I'm cooperating!"

"It's all according to the condition I find Joshua in," Zach said matter-of-factly. "You had better hope he's fit as a fiddle."

"You can't have any say over what happens to me," Smitty said, stopping to glare up at Zach. "You ain't nothin' but pirate scum."

Zach shrugged. "Like I said, I have reason to believe that Judge Pryor will see to it that whatever I want is what I will get," he said. He nudged Smitty with the pistol, sending him toward a brown mare. "Now get on that horse. Too much time has already been wasted."

He waited for Smitty to mount the horse, then went to his own gelding and swung himself up into the saddle. "Ride ahead of me," he said, motioning with the pistol. "One false move and you will wish you hadn't made it."

Once Smitty was in front of him, unable to see whether or not the weapon was pointed at him, Zach lowered it to his side. He did not want to draw undue attention to himself. The streets were just coming alive with travelers.

He followed Smitty down the narrow, oleander-lined streets, and when the blacksmith drew rein in front of a beautiful white house with gingerbread trim and a white picket fence surrounding it, Zach knew that he had been smart to trick Smitty into guiding him there. Zach had not known where the Judge lived.

Dismounting, he went to Smitty and coaxed him from his horse by the barrel of his pistol. Together they went to the fence gate. They stopped abruptly when a huge collie came bounding into sight, barking and snarling.

"Damn it," Zach thought, looking from side to side. "That's all I need. A damn dog drawing too much attention my way."

His gaze was drawn to the door. Judge Pryor was suddenly there, a pistol drawn and pointed threateningly at Zach and Smitty. Then, when he recognized the intruders, he eased the pistol down to his side and stepped on out into full view. He yelled at his dog and grabbed its collar as it went to him. Slapping the dog's rump, he sent it on into the house. Closing the door behind him, the Judge went to the gate and looked up at Zach, smiling.

"You are a survivor, I see," he said, looking Zach up and down. "I thought you had gone down with the ship. After several survivors came into town, telling of the shipwreck, and you were not among them, I thought the sea had finally claimed one of its own." He chuckled. "I don't know whether to be glad or sorry to see you." He reached over and clasped a hand to Zach's shoulder. "I guess I should be glad. You can still fulfill that mission for me."

Zach stepped away from his hand. "So there were more survivors?" he said. "I'm damned glad to hear it."

Judge Pryor looked at Smitty and Zach's drawn pistol. "Now what, may I ask, is this man's connection with you?" he said, kneading his chin. "Or do you force all blacksmiths by gunpoint to do your work for you? Why do you bring him here?"

"He's responsible for my overseer being in jail here in Charleston," Zach said, giving Smitty a sour glance.

"This overseer. He is white, I presume?"

"No. He's black."

"I see," Judge Pryor said. "And in your eyes he is innocent of the charges that placed him in jail?"

"Quite."

"And what do you expect me to do about it?"

"Judge, you want me to go to sea again for you, don't you?"

"Yes, and I assure you, I have a ship that could be readied at a moment's notice."

"Then, Judge, if you truly want me to captain that ship, you must manage to free my overseer from that jail cell. If not, I'll be happy to join him there and die alongside him, if I must."

Judge Pryor was taken aback by Zach's dedication to a dark-skinned man. He frowned. "And Eden?" he asked. "What of her?"

"Her father will deal with you if you harm her in any way," Zach said flatly. "I don't think I would chance what he might do if something happened to his daughter. I don't think I've ever seen such a devoted father."

"Yes, I have seen it also," Judge Pryor said, then smiled slowly. "I'll see what I can do about your slave." He looked at Smitty. "But what does this weasel have to do with this?"

"He's the one who is responsible for Joshua's being in jail," Zach said. "If you will just go with me now to see to Joshua's release, I will explain on the way."

"I must get my horse and buggy," Judge Pryor said. "You ride along with me. Smitty can hold the reins to your horse and follow alongside us."

"You heard the man," Zach said, tossing Smitty the reins.

Eden placed strips of bacon on a platter, awaiting her father's arrival for breakfast. It was strange not to be listening for the thump-thump of the cane on the porch, but it was wonderful too. At least she had that to be happy for.

As for Zach, she was burdened down with worry. Their sweet moments together had been short-lived. Now how long must they wait to be together again? If Judge Pryor had his way about it, Zach would be riding the high seas again even as soon as today. Zach would have no choice but to comply. Until he got this thing behind him, he could never have even a measure of a normal life.

The sound of a horse and buggy approaching down the lane drew Eden to the window. She drew the sheer curtain aside, then smiled when she saw that the driver was Angelita.

Her smile faded. Angelita had surely come to see two men—and one of them was no longer there. Her disappointment would be no less than Eden's that Zach was gone. He was her long-lost brother. They had only been able to visit for a short time the previous evening before she had had to leave for Charleston, to be home before dark.

Eden's gaze was drawn elsewhere. She warmed all over inside when she saw her father leave the lighthouse. His healthy legs were carrying him quickly to the buggy as Angelita drew it to a halt close to the front porch. Eden clasped her hands together and sighed when she witnessed a wondrous hug between her father and her best friend. When their lips met in a kiss, Eden turned her eyes away, blushing.

When she heard laughter and footsteps in the living room, Eden rushed to meet Angelita and her father, then laughed herself when she saw what Angelita was carrying—a wicker basket piled high with cinnamon rolls topped with thick white icing.

"Lord, Angelita, are you trying to make us all fat?" Eden said, her eyes dancing.

"I thought we would all have a special breakfast this morning," Angelita said, handing the basket to Eden. "Is Zach up yet? I am so anxious to see him and talk with him again. I still can't believe that he is here. Isn't it wonderful?"

Preston glanced toward Eden's bedroom. "I imagine he's still asleep, Angelita," he said softly. "He had quite a tiring day yesterday. He's lucky to be alive."

Eden sat the wicker basket down on a table,

then went to take her father's hand, and one of Angelita's. "Zach is no longer here," she said, her voice drawn. "He left last night." She swallowed hard. "There was no holding him back. He had much to attend to."

Angelita paled and choked back a sob.

The jail was dark, its stench overpowering. As Zach walked down the long line of cells behind Judge Pryor, his spine stiffened as he looked from cell to cell, remembering those hours he had been forced to endure this filth. His stomach turned at the thought of Joshua having to relive those weeks and months in similar degrading conditions aboard the slave ship.

But this time it was different. Much different. Joshua was wounded. He could have died from the loss of blood and no one would even have noticed.

Zach yanked Smitty along beside him. "You had better hope that Joshua is alive," he threatened. "If not, you will pay."

With the permission of the sheriff, Judge Pryor had taken charge of the keys to the cells. He stopped suddenly before a cell at the far end of the corridor. The keys jangled on their chain as he inserted one in the lock.

His knees weak from fear of what he was about to see, Zach stopped beside Judge Pryor. As his eyes adjusted to the semi-darkness of the cell in which Joshua lay, his gut twisted and a bitterness rushed up into his throat.

Turning his head away, he fought the urge

to retch. This man, this special friend of his, was lying asleep on the bare floor in his own body wastes, roaches crawling all over him.

Slowly, Zach looked back at Joshua. He circled a fist at his side as he studied his friend more closely. His heart skipped a beat. He took a quick step into the cell as the door swung open, and almost retched again. It took only one glance at his friend's wounded arm to know that it was beyond recovering. Where the shirt sleeve was ripped away, he could see black, dead skin, a visible line separating the dead tissue from the living.

"Gangrene," Zach said, almost choking on the word as the stench of dead flesh rose up into his nostrils. He turned his eyes away and covered his mouth with his hand. "My God, gangrene."

A rustling of feet made Zach turn with a start. It was apparent that Smitty had seen the gangrenous arm and knew that Zach would be ready to kill him because he was to blame. He was running away as fast as his legs would carry him.

"You bastard!" Zach shouted, raising his pistol, aiming at Smitty's back. "Because of you Joshua will lose his arm! He may even die!"

Judge Pryor knocked Zach's gun aside. "I wouldn't do that," he said. "It would be hard to explain to the townsfolk exactly why you felt you had the right to shoot that man in the back." He nodded at Joshua. "I suggest that you do what you came here for while you have the chance. Take this man with you." He stared down at the arm. "But I'd say it's a waste of time. Chances are he won't be alive long."

"I'll see to Smitty later," Zach said, thrusting his pistol into his holster. He turned wavering eyes to the Judge. "I've got to ask two more favors of you and then I'll be ready to command another ship for you."

"What are they?" Judge Pryor asked, clasping his hands together behind him. "I'll see what I can do."

"I'll be taking Joshua to my plantation immediately and I'll be needing the best doctor in Charleston to look at his arm," Zach said in a rush of words. "Then give me a full night with him before asking me to command a ship. I'm sure he will have to have his arm removed. I want to see him through the agony of it."

"I see no problem with either of those requests," Judge Pryor said, looking down at Joshua. "No. No problem at all."

"Thanks," Zach said, clasping a firm hand on the Judge's shoulder. "Thanks a lot."

The Judge nodded.

Zach dropped to his knees beside Joshua. He shuddered and chills rode his flesh as he scraped the cockroaches away. Then he placed a gentle hand to his friend's dark face. He flinched when he felt how hot it was. Joshua was burning up with fever. There was definitely no time to lose.

"Joshua?" Zach said, leaning down close to Joshua's face. "Can you hear me? Joshua?"

Joshua inhaled shakily. His eyes opened

slowly. He breathed Zach's name only barely loud enough to hear. "Masta' Zach?" he whispered. "Masta' Zach, ah's so glad to see ya." He reached a shaky hand to Zach's arm and grabbed hold. Tears streamed down his face. "Oh, Masta' Zach, I hurts so!"

"I've come to take you home," Zach said hoarsely. "I've come to take you back to Sabrina."

Joshua licked his parched lips. "Sabrina . . ." he said, his eyes slowly closing again.

Zach lifted Joshua up into his arms. The pain in his lungs wasn't as severe as the one in his heart. He carried Joshua up the steep, dark stairs, and then outside, where he placed Joshua in the back of the Judge's buggy, then tied his horse to the buggy and climbed aboard. As he cracked the whip against the horse's back he looked back at Judge Pryor as he ran from the jail, waving his arms and yelling angrily.

"Come back here with my buggy," Judge Pryor shouted.

"Seems I forgot to ask permission to use it, doesn't it?" Zach shouted back, laughing. "Just one more concession on your part, if you know what I mean."

Again he slapped the horse with the reins. He glanced over his shoulder at Joshua, his heart aching. "You're going to be all right," he said beneath his breath, yet knowing that he wasn't.

Joshua would have to lose that arm.

Chapter Twenty-four

We ought to be together, you and I.
—ALFORD

Day was deepening to sunset, the shadows gaining confidence. Eden took her gardening tools into the barn and placed them in their storage bin, then strolled back outside. It was strange how, before she met Zach, evenings had been her favorite time of the day. She had never been all that troubled by loneliness.

But now?

Without Zach, it felt as though the world was closing in on her.

She stopped to stare at the ocean. Hugging herself, she tried to fight off a chill caused by knowing that more than likely Zach would soon be forced to go to sea again. Perhaps he was already there. If Judge Pryor did not give him the opportunity to come and tell her, she might never know for sure what had happened to him.

"And how are things back at his plantation?" she murmured, recalling how apprehensive Zach had been after having heard about Sabrina coming to the cottage, disoriented and afraid.

The breeze lifted her hair from her shoulders. "I hope Zach found everything all right there, for he has enough troubling him now without adding to his worries."

She was again overcome with a sudden chill. Shaking it off, she looked toward the lighthouse. It was now dark enough for her to be able to see the beam's soft glow. Dedicated to his craft, her father did not always wait until it was totally dark to send his beam out onto the water.

She smiled to herself, amused at how her father had begun fussing over Angelita's traveling alone on Lighthouse Road. Before, he may have worried about her just as he did about his daughter, but he had not spoken of his fears aloud.

Now? He again had two women who loved him to give him more reason for caring, for worrying.

Gathering the skirt of her dress, Eden ran toward the lighthouse. "I shall keep him company for a while," she whispered to herself. Somehow she just could not bring herself to stay in the cottage alone this evening. While she was alone she could not help but ponder Zach's fate—and her and Zach's future.

"Perhaps I need my father's company even more than he needs mine," Eden said, rushing up the steep stairs of the lighthouse.

Zach paced the floor of his upstairs guest bedroom, each of Joshua's raspy breaths tearing him apart inside. He peered down at Joshua and swallowed back the urge to cry out with remorse when he looked at the bandage at his right shoulder, where the arm had been removed.

Blood seeped through the bandage, drying in ugly, dark-red blotches against the white fabric of the dressing. It was an ugly reminder that the arm had been gangrenous and had been removed, and that his friend's life lay in the balance. Perhaps there were too many battles left for his friend to fight. A fever was now raging through him, weakening him even more. He had lost consciousness during the surgery and had yet to regain it.

Zach's gaze went to Sabrina. She sat at Joshua's bedside and was smoothing cool compresses over his fevered brow. She was singing softly, a song that Zach did not recognize. He went to her and laid a gentle hand on her shoulder.

"Sabrina, he's going to survive," he said. "He's survived many tragedies in his lifetime. This time will be no different."

Sabrina's dark eyes rolled slowly up to Zach. She flashed him an angry look. "Masta'

Zach, this time is different and you knows it," she said. "My man's fightin' fo' his life and you knows it."

A deep pain reflected in her eyes as she looked down at the bandaged shoulder. "Masta' Zach, he ain't no whole man no mo'," she murmured. "He'll wish he was dead, fo' sure, when he sees that his body ain't the same. I ain't known him for too long, but long enough to know he's a proud man."

She rolled her dark eyes slowly back up again. "He'll see hisself as worthless," she said, swallowing back the urge to cry. "Why, he won't be able to help you out no mo'. He'll feel helpless and disgusted with hisself. How can we make him feel different, Masta' Zach, when you knows as well as I that a darkie is considered worthless if he ain't able to work for his masta'?"

Zach turned his eyes away. He stiffened his back, knowing exactly how Joshua would feel once he regained his strength—if he ever did. Never had Zach seen such a proud man, black or white. Joshua might well not be able to cope with a body that was not whole. It would be up to everyone else to convince him that he was still valuable as a friend.

Turning back to Sabrina, Zach drew her to her feet. He took her hands and looked sternly down at her. "You say that you love him," he said. "And you know that he is dear to me."

"Yassa, masta' Zach," Sabrina said, nodding.

"Then there's no reason in hell why Joshua should come out of this thing feeling helpless and worthless," Zach said, squeezing Sabrina's hands. "I won't allow it. You won't allow it. Do you understand, Sabrina?"

"Yassa, Masta' Zach," Sabrina said, her eyes wide. "I understands."

Zach looked toward the window, seeing that night had fallen. He glanced at Joshua, then looked down into Sabrina's eyes. "I got permission from Judge Pryor to take only the time that was needed to see Joshua through the surgery, but I can't take any longer," he said. "I'm going to be leaving Joshua in your and Tom's hands. Until I return, it will be up to you two to see that Joshua recovers, both mentally and physically. If God is willing, I won't be gone for long."

"I understands, Masta' Zach," Sabrina said, sniffling as tears threatened to spill from her eyes. She suddenly flung herself into Zach's arms. "Oh, Masta' Zach, do come home again real soon. Sabrina don't feel safe at all with you gone and with Joshua so sick. I'm afraid of that blacksmith. You say he's not dead. What if he comes back? What does I do?"

Zach patted Sabrina on the back and then held her away from him. "Sabrina, Tom is going to be here," he reminded her. "He's going to be instructed to keep an eye on you. And while I'm gone this time, you'll be staying here in the big house. I dare any man to trespass in my house. Tom'll see to it that no intruder gets the chance to."

Sabrina's eyes danced and her lips quivered into an anxious smile. "You means it?" she asked. "I can stay here in yo' house?"

"If you like, stay here in the room with Joshua, or take the room adjoining," Zach said, smiling down at her. "When I return, I'll see to it that you stay here in the house permanently. You'll become my wife's personal maid."

Sabrina clasped her hands together before her and sighed. "Miz Eden's maid?" she sighed. "Oh, Masta' Zach, I do so thank you."

Zach went to stand over Joshua a moment longer. "Old friend, don't you let anything else happen to you while I'm gone," he murmured. "We've a few more miles to travel together, you and I. Do you hear?"

It tore at his heart that Joshua could not respond. He touched his burning cheek, then turned around and walked on past Sabrina, out into the corridor. He had one more person to reassure before riding on into Charleston. Eden. He had to bid her a sad farewell, but assure her that he would be gone for only a short time. This time he knew that he must direct his ship toward Pirate Jack's island. Too many things depended on his carrying out Judge Pryor's orders. Too many lives depended on it.

Outside, Zach shouted for Tom to saddle a horse.

"Lad, it seems I've another sea voyage ahead of me," he said, as Tom brought the horse from the stable.

His red hair blowing in the breeze, Tom held a hand out to Zach. "Sir, I'll make sure everything is all right here," he reassured him, as Zach accepted the firm handshake. "You just hurry back. I look forward to working with you when you return."

"And return I will," Zach said, shaking Tom's hand. "Lad, we have a bright future together here at my plantation. You won't have cause to dwell on your past. It's the future that counts. And, lad, yours is going to be the brightest."

Preston held his brass telescope steady as Eden directed the beam slowly across the dark waters, the moon only a small white arc in the black sky.

"Damned if I can see that elusive ship again," Preston said, scowling.

"Are you certain you saw it?" Eden asked, herself following the light of the beam with her eyes.

"You know that if I said I did, I did," Preston said in a low rumble. "And since I did see the damn black pirate ship lurking in these waters, I don't want you going back to the cottage alone. You know Pirate Jack must be dangerous, or the Navy wouldn't be cooperating with Judge Pryor by going to so much expense and trouble to rid the seas of the bastard." He lowered his telescope and placed it on a ledge. "Judge Pryor even chanced losing a friendship to rid the seas of the damned pirate—mine."

He went to Eden and drew her into his embrace. "I think it would be best, Eden, if you snuggled up in that chair in that corner over there and slept here tonight," he said softly. "There's no need to take chances with the likes of those pirates so near."

He held her away from him and looked down into her eyes. "And don't say it," he said dryly. "I know all pirates aren't the same. Zach has proven that point. But Pirate Jack's reputation is no myth. His dirty deeds attest to that."

"You truly do see the goodness in Zach, don't you?" Eden asked, warmth flooding her. "It means so much to me that you do."

"There's a lot about Zach that has to be admired—and pitied," Preston said, nodding. Then his eyes squinted with alarm as he heard a commotion on the staircase. He eased away from Eden and grabbed a pistol from a shelf.

"What is it, father?" Eden asked, paling. She watched him as he moved stealthily toward the trapdoor. Her insides froze when she too heard movement below.

Then she breathed more easily when the memory of Zach's surprise visit that one night flashed through her mind.

"Father, don't be so alarmed," she said. "It's probably Zach. He promised to come and reveal his plans to me, if given a chance."

"Stand aside, daughter," Preston said, motioning with the barrel of his pistol. "I'm taking no chances. There's been enough excitement around here lately. I don't care to chance anything else happening."

He went to the trapdoor but he didn't have the chance to open it, for suddenly it crashed open and a man dressed in bright garb, sporting a thick head of gray hair, leaped out of it.

Eden gasped and grabbed for her father as she saw the old pirate's pistol lift and discharge, filling the air with the stench of gunpowder.

"Father! No!" Eden screamed. Panic seized her as blood spread on her father's dark shirt as he dropped his pistol and clutched at the right side of his chest. Her knees grew weak and she watched helplessly as her father crumpled to the floor, gasping for air.

Too stunned and frightened to move, Eden looked up at the pirate. Loops of gold earrings hung from his earlobes. He was an old man, his hands ragged and scarred, a sabre cut across one cheek, livid white. He wore a loose shirt open to the waist, with big gathered sleeves, and black leather breeches with a red sash around his waist. His high, wide-topped boots were black and shining. He held one pistol in his hand, another was thrust into his belt, and a cutlass was slipped into his belt alongside it.

Pirate Jack stood over Preston, his dark eyes gleaming. "If ye survive yer wound, ye can tell Zachary that I'll be waitin' for him on my island," he said in a deep, gravelly voice. "Tell 'im Pirate Jack left 'im the message."

Two other swarthy pirates rushed into the tower room. Pirate Jack looked Eden up and down. "Take 'er away," he commanded sharply. "Take 'er to the ship. Place 'er in my cabin."

Eden's face was awash with tears. She tried to fight off the two pirates, but they held her in a firm grip on each side and dragged her toward the trapdoor.

"No!" she screamed. "Please don't take me away. My father needs me. He'll die if he's left here. Can't you see? He's badly wounded."

She saw that her words were falling on deaf ears. She flinched and gasped with alarm when Pirate Jack picked up a chair and began smashing out all of the windows of the lighthouse, and then the precious lanterns that lighted the beam.

"You can't do that!" she screamed, struggling to get free as she was forced onto the first step. "Oh, my God. Why are you doing this? Please stop."

"This damn beam has spied me ship more than once," Pirate Jack said hotly. "It could lead the Navy ships to 'er. The beam rendered helpless, me ship can come and go as she damn well pleases."

"Now I see why you are hunted!" Eden cried. "You deserve to die."

Seeing the blood all over the outside of her father's shirt and how lifeless he lay, Eden made one last effort to get free. But the two men dragging her along tightened their grip on her wrists and yanked her on down the dark stairs.

"Father!" she cried, her voice echoing back at her in the small spaces of the tower. She fought with all her might when one of the pirates yanked her up and threw her over his shoulder as though she were no more than a sack of potatoes, then began running with her toward the ocean.

"You can't do this," she cried, looking up at the dark windows of the lighthouse. The old pirate was now running along behind them, his destruction obviously finished in the light-house.

She looked away from him, finding it hard not to tell him that he would soon die if Judge Pryor—and Zach—had anything to say about it. Once Zach discovered what had happened here tonight, the old pirate's life would not be worth anything. Zach would go hunting for him willingly.

They reached the water's edge, and Eden's breath was stolen away when she was tossed into a longboat, hitting the bottom with a loud thud. She cried out with pain and moved slowly up on one elbow, every inch of her beginning to ache.

"Row hard. Get us to the ship. Quickly. Someone is sure to notice that the lighthouse beam 'as gone dead," Pirate Jack shouted, settling down on the seat in the middle of the longboat.

As the small craft lurched out into the water, the pirates lifting their oars up and down in unison, drawing water beneath them, Pirate Jack reached for Eden and gently urged her up beside him.

"Ye'll not be harmed if ye cooperate," he reassured her. "Just do as I say and no one will lay a hand on ye. If any of my crew do, their lips will be slit and their ears removed. It ain't my intent to steal you away fer a playmate fer me women-hungry crew. I 'ave other plans fer ye, I do."

"What of my father?" Eden asked, shivering in the cool sea breeze. "Why did you have to shoot him?"

"Had I not shot him, he would've shot me," Pirate Jack said, shrugging. He patted the handle of his large pistol. "Now ain't that so, pretty lady?"

"You shot my father in cold blood and you know it," Eden said venomously. "Your time will come—and soon, I hope."

"I would say that ye are right," Pirate Jack said, his eyes looking haunted as if by some dark memory. Again he shrugged. "I know me days are numbered, but I could not let it 'appen to me at the hands of a mere lightkeeper. I do not want to go to my grave disgraced. When I die, I want it to be with honor, done by the hands of one like me." He looked over at Eden, his eyes wavering. "But of course ye do not understand at all what I am saying. Ye will just have to wait and see. It won't be long. Perhaps even tomorrow?"

Eden looked up at him, puzzled. He talked like a man who knew his fate, and by whom it would be sealed. Did he know about Zach and Judge Pryor's alliance?

Her whole insides ached, wishing her father had not become a pawn in this game of life and death between right and wrong.

As the longboat was being lifted into the great black pirate ship, her eyes moved to the lighthouse. She was stung with intense remorse when she saw no beam, only a nothingness in the night.

His cutlass shining in its leather scabbard at his left side, his brace of pistols heavy across his chest, Zach rode tall in the saddle along Lighthouse Road. He had hated like hell to leave Joshua, but he knew that staying with his friend would not help him to magically recover. Only time would tell what Joshua's fate was. If there was anything fair in life, his friend would recover and accept the loss of his arm. He would see that he still had Sabrina's undevoted love. He would see that Zach still regarded him as special.

Zach smiled to himself. Joshua would find a way to be of benefit to mankind. He had the strength of ten men. He had the knowledge of a hundred.

Yes, Joshua would find a way to compensate for the loss of his arm.

"And I'll find a way to avenge that loss, also," Zach whispered.

He wheeled his horse to a sudden halt and grew cold inside as he looked toward the lighthouse. He saw no beam. Only darkness. That meant only one thing. There was some sort of trouble at the lighthouse. Preston was too dependable to let the beam go out for even one second.

"Eden," he gasped.

He slapped his reins hard and rode off at a hard gallop.

Chapter Twenty-five

The midnight hears my cry.
— TAYLOR

Zach wheeled his horse to a stop in front of the lighthouse cottage. Seeing no candlelight at the windows made him tighten inside and his heart skip a beat. It was too early in the evening for Eden to be in bed.

As he quickly dismounted he looked up at the lighthouse, now realizing that not only was the beam not lit, but that there were no other lights either.

"Something has happened," he said, confirming his earlier fears. He took the steps up to the cottage two at a time. Yanking the door open and stumbling through the darkness, he felt his way to Eden's bedroom. When he discovered that she was not there, he became even more worried. If she was up in the lighthouse and all right, lamplight would be visible. If she was in the lighthouse without any lights, the chances were that she and her father had both met with some sort of mishap.

Making his way back through the house, his heart pounding, he rushed down the steps, drawing one of his pistols from its holster. Fumbling through the darkness inside the lighthouse, he climbed the narrow, steep stairs. Everything was too eerily quiet, the sound of his boots making contact with the metal stairs reverberating all around him. No voices could be heard overhead and there was still no signs of light.

"Preston! Eden!" Zach shouted, then scarcely breathed as he listened for a response.

"Damn," he whispered, fear mounting inside him. "Damn. Damn."

Breathless, he finally reached the top of the stairs. He could see the arc of the moon just ahead through the jagged broken glass of the window. He could hear only silence.

Reaching around through the trapdoor before pulling himself on up inside the tower room, Zach's stomach lurched and his voice froze in his throat when he found Preston's still body, then felt the wetness of blood on his clothes.

"Oh, my God," Zach groaned, slipping his pistol back inside his holster and pulling himself on up into the tower room.

He leaned over Preston and felt for a pulse

in the throat, then breathed easier when he found that it was there, and strong.

Zach turned and looked around the room, able to make out the destruction beneath the faint light of the moon. Eden was nowhere in sight. His gut twisted at the thought of her having been abducted again, for now he was certain that was what had happened to her.

Leaning over Preston again, Zach placed a hand beneath his head and lifted it gently from the floor. "Preston, can you hear me?" he asked breathlessly. "Eden! Where's Eden?"

Preston heard a voice coming from what seemed a deep tunnel. His throat dry, the pain in his chest severe, he slowly blinked his eyes open. With a trembling hand he reached for Zach, unable to make out his face.

Finally he remembered the voice that had just spoken to him, and recognized it. He grabbed at Zach's arm, clutching to it desperately.

"Zach." he said, his voice barely a whisper. "Eden. They . . . took . . . her away. . . ."

Zach leaned closer to Preston's face. "Who took her away?" he demanded. "Who? Where did they take her?"

"Zach . . . it was Pirate Jack," Preston said, his breath coming in short rasps. "He said . . . to . . . go to his island. He'll be waitin' . . . for you."

Zach was taken aback. "Pirate Jack?" he gasped.

"It was . . . Pirate Jack," Preston confirmed, coughing as a choking sensation grabbed at his throat. "He was old and . . . and had a sabre cut across his cheek." He closed his eyes and dropped his hand. "Forget about me. Go and find Eden. Zach, go . . . find . . . Eden."

The way Preston's words faded and the way he went limp told Zach that he had lost consciousness again. Desperation was rising inside Zach. He had to see to Preston's welfare, but all the while Eden was being taken farther and farther away on a ship.

"Pirate Jack?" he said, shaking his head disbelievingly. "Why would he?"

He knew Pirate Jack well enough to know that he never had gone into stealing women. There must have been some other reason that the aging pirate had done something so out of character.

No matter. Zach had to work quickly. First he would make sure that Preston was seen to, then he would go to sea and find that damnable old pirate.

Lifting Preston into his arms, Zach groaned as he descended the narrow stairs carrying him. He could feel blood rolling down his arm from Preston's wound. It seemed that not only had Pirate Jack come to abduct Eden, he had not stopped at shooting an innocent man, nor hesitated at totally destroying the lighthouse mechanisms.

"I'll go to the old coot's island and find out exactly why he did these things," Zach promised himself, glad to see the foot of the stairs at last. Perhaps it wouldn't be so hard now, as appointed executioner, to draw against his old friend—because he had suddenly become his enemy.

Rushing through the darkness, Zach took Preston into the cottage and placed him gently on the bed in his bedroom. He lit a candle, then ripped Preston's shirt away and examined the wound more carefully. He sighed with relief. It was not at all as bad as it had appeared to be. The wound was in the fleshy part of his abdomen just below his right rib, close to his side, and the bullet had gone clean through the flesh from front to back.

"You're one damn lucky lightkeeper," Zach said, sighing as he looked down at Preston who was once again regaining consciousness. "In no time you'll be back to tending your beam. That is, after you do some extensive repairs."

Preston woke suddenly and grabbed for Zach's arm. "Damn it, Zach, go and find Eden," he said raspily. "I told you to forget about me. Go. Now."

"I want to go after Eden just as badly as you want me to," Zach grumbled, leaning over Preston to speak into his face. "But, damn it, Preston, I just left my best friend, whose bullet wound had not been attended to promptly enough. I won't leave you until I get your wound cleaned and dressed. Then I'll go into town and send the doctor out for you. *Then* I'll go and rescue Eden. I promise you that she will be found and brought back." He rose to his feet and placed his hands on his hips. "You see, your daughter and I have made plans that I'll let nothing stop. We're going to be married."

Preston's eyes wavered as he looked up at Zach. Then he smiled slowly. "I think I shall give you my blessing without a moment's hesitation," he said. "You continue to prove that my first impression of you was right. You are one damn respectable, likable man."

"How you feel means a lot to me, sir," Zach said. "And if you did not approve of the marriage, Eden would never truly be happy with me."

Preston winced when a sharp pain shot through his wound. He laughed awkwardly. "That old pirate almost got this lightkeeper out of all of your lives," he said. "Thank God he was a bad shot."

"He's much better with a cutlass," Zach said, turning to go. He stopped when Preston spoke from behind him.

"Zach, when you go into Charleston to send the doctor to me, will you go and ask someone else to come with him?" Preston asked, breathing unsteadily.

Zach turned and gazed down at Preston. "Anything I can possibly do for you, sir, I will," he promised. "Who do you want me to go and see?"

"It wouldn't take long for you to go to Angelita and tell her of my misfortune, would it?" Preston asked, his eyes pleading up at

Zach. "While I am waiting to receive word of Eden, she will be a comfort at my bedside."

Preston's voice faded as his eyes slowly closed. "I . . . am suddenly so tired. Zach, please make haste with what you have to do here. Eden. You must find her. God forbid . . . anything has happened to her. God . . . forbid. . . ."

"Yes, God forbid," Zach whispered, then turned and left the room. As though in a daze, he hurried through the process of cleaning Preston's wound and bandaging it.

Driven, he mounted his horse and rode toward Lighthouse Road. He had a long night ahead of him and even a longer day tomorrow. He wouldn't get another wink of sleep until he found Eden.

"And, by damn," he growled to himself. "She had better not be harmed. . . ."

Stubbornly, with her chin tilted, Eden stood before Pirate Jack's massive oak desk in his private cabin on the pirate ship. Her heart ached with worry over her father, yet she would not show this to the pirate. It was important to let him see her strong and stubborn side. Perhaps he would admire spunk in a lady and not let any of his crazed pirates have their way with her.

Pirate Jack sat behind his desk. His ragged and scarred fingers drummed nervously on the desktop, the lines on his face deepening as he smiled slowly up at Eden.

"So ye are Zach's chosen, eh?" he chuckled. "I didn't think that young man would ever let himself fall in love. He rarely paid any attention to the many women who threw themselves at his feet from port to port." He locked his fingers together and leaned his elbows on the desk. "I guess he was waiting for ye, wasn't he?"

"How do you know about me and Zach?" Eden asked, her voice quivering, growing angry at herself for this weakness. "What is it to you whom he loves or doesn't love? He is no longer a part of your life. He left. You let him go. Why should you abduct me? You know that he will come for me. He will probably smile while killing you."

Raking his fingers through his shoulder-length gray hair, Pirate Jack rose slowly from his chair. He went to the porthole and peered out at the calm, dark sea. "Aye, he surely will, at that," he said, clasping his hands together behind him. "And if he does, my plan would have worked well. Ye were abducted so that he would follow through with the command given to him by Judge Pryor. Otherwise, he would have never gone through with it. And if not? He would either hang, or spend the rest of his days rotting in a cell."

He swung around and faced Eden. "As I see it, it has come down to this," he said, gesturing with a hand. "It's either his life or mine, and I am ready to give mine up, if it means saving his."

Eden took a shaky step backwards. She covered her mouth with a hand, gasping.

"Aye, ye would be shocked by what I say," Pirate Jack said, nodding. "Ye'll be even more shocked to hear what else I have to say. You see, I can look at this dilemma in another perspective. Perhaps it is best that I kill Zach, for I cannot help but believe that the authorities are lyin' to him about lettin' him go free once he kills me. What if they torture Zach and then kill him, once he has performed the deed of killing me for them?"

He turned his back to Eden and lowered his face into his hands. "I truly do not know which is the best way," he said, his voice drawn. "Should I kill Zach? If I did I would then turn the gun on myself. Our pirating days are over. Mine and Zach's days of camaraderie were over long ago. Now it must be made final. It must end by death—a mutual death."

"You can't mean any of that," Eden said, finally regaining her composure.

As Pirate Jack sank back down into his desk chair, Eden went to the desk and splayed her hands across the top, leaning her full weight against it. She put her face close to his. "You can't kill Zach," she softly cried. "You can't. You don't even want to."

"We shall see what happens," Pirate Jack said. "What will be, will be."

"He'll kill you first!" Eden snapped angrily, jerking away from the desk. She squared her shoulders and glared down at the old pirate.

"And then he will return to Charleston a free man. We will be married."

"And so your relationship has gone that far?" Pirate Jack asked, frowning up at Eden. "Even though ye know that he has been a pirate, ye will marry him?"

"He is a product of his past," Eden said, then her mood softened. "And I know that you turned his life around for him. Ironic as it seems, you are the one who gave him reason to live and trust again. How can you even think of killing him now? His life has truly just begun."

"I do not want to kill him any more than he will want to kill me," Pirate Jack said softly.

"Sir, you are wrong," Eden said, again leaning her face daringly close to his. "He will want to kill you now. You have abducted me and you shot an innocent man—my father. Zach will know that the world is better off without the likes of you. You have become an evil, contemptible man. You are no longer the kind man that Zach knew at the beginning."

Pirate Jack nodded. "Aye, things did get a little out of hand when life became borin' for me," he said, chuckling. Then his expression sobered. "But I do apologize fer having inconvenienced ye by bringing ye on this ship. And I do regret having to shoot yer father. It all became necessary."

"You even destroyed the lighthouse mechanisms," Eden said, her voice breaking. "The lighthouse is my father's pride and joy. If he recovers from his wound, I am not sure he will recover from the pain of what you have done to his lighthouse."

Feeling drained, Eden backed off and eased herself down into a plush leather chair. She laid her head back, sighing. "How did you know about Zach's assignment to come for you?" she said, her voice drawn.

"I have ways of finding out," Pirate Jack said. "I have my spies on land as well as at sea. News was brought to me about Zach being assigned to kill me. News was also brought to me of his interest in you. I saw the opportunity to kill two birds with one stone. I could abduct you to draw Zach to me, and I could destroy that damnable lighthouse beam."

He looked over at Eden, scrutinizing her. "Never fear anything while ye are aboard my ship," he said. "Ye'll be safe. As soon as I settle this thing with Zach, ye'll be returned home, unharmed."

"Sir, you just shot my father," she said. "How can you expect me to believe any promise of yours?"

"Because of my love for Zach," Pirate Jack said, rising from his chair. He went to Eden and gently took her hand and drew her up before him. "Because of yer love for Zach. It is my word that ye will not be harmed. My ship is headin' fer my private island. Ye will be very well taken care of there, by my wife. She will be happy to have company, if only for a short while."

Eden's eyes widened. "You have a wife . . . ?" she said in a near whisper.

"Aye, a beautiful wife of thirty-five years," Pirate Jack bragged, getting a faraway look in his eyes. The only woman I've touched in thirty-five years."

Eden was stunned, seeing a side to this pirate that she would have never expected. Suddenly she did feel safe, yet . . . should she?

Zach paced the floor of Judge Pryor's parlor. He stopped to stare down into the fire on the grate, then began pacing again. When footsteps entered the room, he spun around and faced the Judge, his jaw set.

"So you are ready to man the ship I have readied for you?" Judge Pryor asked. He gazed at Zach, puzzled. "Or is it something more? What's happened? Did your slavehand die?"

Zach turned to lean his arm on the fireplace mantel. Again he stared down into the dancing flames. "No, Joshua did not die, but when he realizes that he has lost an arm he will wish that he had," he said sourly.

"It's more than my slavehand that has gotten me lit with fire inside," he said in a hiss. "Pirate Jack has overstepped his boundaries tonight. He has not only attempted to murder one of the kindest men who walks the face of this earth, he has abducted the woman I love. I must board the ship you have assigned me tonight. I've got to go after Pirate Jack and rescue Eden. I think it just may be time to rid the earth of that elusive pirate."

Judge Pryor grabbed Zach's arm. "What are

you saying?'' he said, paling. "Preston has been shot? Eden has been kidnapped? How is Preston? Will he live?''

"Yes, he will live,'' Zach said softly. "I tended to the gunshot wound as best I could and I just moments ago sent Doc Raley out to check on his condition. He'll pull through. The bullet wound wasn't a fatal one.'' He jerked free of the Judge's firm grip. "But Pirate Jack's mistakes tonight will be fatal to him.'' He spoke into the Judge's face. "Lead me to the ship.''

"The ship is all ready for sailing,'' Judge Pryor said, rushing to the foyer. He grabbed a coat and hat from the hat tree. "This time the crew is made up of sailors from the United States Navy. They are so filled with determination, I see that this voyage will be a successful one.''

He turned and smiled at Zach. "Pirate Jack has made a major mistake by abducting Eden,'' he said smugly. "He's as good as signed his own death warrant.''

Zach's stomach lurched at the thought of killing his old friend. But Zach had never approved of murder and at this moment Pirate Jack could not help but think that he had committed murder tonight. When he had left Preston, it had been with the intention of letting the man die.

As for Eden, if she were harmed on Pirate Jack's ship, Zach's scruples wouldn't stand in his way.

* * *

Smoothing a damp cloth across Preston's brow, waiting for him to awaken, Angelita was torn with feelings. Tears streamed from her eyes when she looked at Preston's bandaged body, knowing that he had come close to being killed. When she thought of the danger that both Eden and Zach now were in, both far out at sea, vulnerable to so many things, she could hardly bear it.

Angelita sniffled as tears rolled across her nose and lips. Then her eyes brightened when Preston began licking his parched lips. "Angelita?" he whispered, his eyes slowly opening. "Is it really you? You've come?"

Angelita leaned over him, avoiding his wound. She twined her arms about his neck and placed her cheek to his. "Preston, I should have admitted to my feelings for you long ago," she murmured. "You should have, too. We've wasted so much time. Please, get well, Preston. I do love you so."

Preston lifted a shaky hand. He patted her back, then wove his fingers through her thick black hair. "When I get well enough to leave this bed, will you marry me?" he asked softly. "That is, if you truly want such an old man to wake up to every morning? You've had many young men who'd trade places with me. Are you sure you don't want one of them instead? They'd be much prettier, Angelita."

Angelita feathered kisses across his face. "Darling, you will forever look young in my eyes," she whispered. "And as for waiting until you are out of this sickbed, that isn't necessary. Let's get the preacher to come as soon as possible to say the necessary words. Now wouldn't that be a nice surprise for Eden when she returns?"

Preston framed her face between his hands. "You would do that?" he asked wonderingly. "You would marry me now?"

"Yes, now," Angelita said, giggling.

"But . . . Eden?"

"She would approve, Preston. She would be happy for us both."

"Send for the preacher then, Angelita. Let's not waste anymore time waitin' for anything."

Angelita hugged him softly. "Oh, Preston," she murmured, sighing with joy.

Chapter Twenty-six

She was a phantom of delight.
—WORDSWORTH

The breeze was warm. Its moist dampness seemed to wrap itself around Eden as if in an embrace. Standing on the deck of the old pirate's ship, she watched an island come into view. From this distance it looked no more than a huge, purple shadow along the horizon. But as the ship drew closer to it, Eden could see that it was a place so lovely that it might even be described as a paradise. It seemed a place that no one could fear, not even she.

Clutching her fingers to the railing, her golden hair rippling in the breeze, Eden peered toward the green jungle intermingled with valleys of lilac shadow. The heat of the day was drawing moisture from the earth, causing a mist to wreath the tangled mangroves along the sandy shoreline. Growing in great clusters, wild roses in a myriad of colors clung to the trees and grew in wild tangles across the land.

Even now, as the ship approached the island, the air was thick with the heady, sweet aroma of flowers.

"Drop anchor!"

The command made Eden jump with alarm. She looked at Pirate Jack where he stood only a few feet away from her, shouting out orders right and left. The scar across his cheek was more vividly white beneath the bright rays of the sun. His gold shirt with its long and flowing sleeves had not a wrinkle in it; his black leather breeches fit him like a glove.

Turning her eyes away, she fought back the fear that was growing inside her. She truly did not know whether to believe the aged pirate when he had spoken of a wife and a home. All that Eden could see on the island was a massive growth of trees and flowers. It appeared impossible to get past the beach. Surely the thorns of the roses would tear one's skin to pieces.

She flinched when she heard the creaking of chains as the anchor was lowered. Her every nerve tightened as a longboat filled with pirates was lowered over the side of the ship. She followed its movements with her eyes as it splashed into the water and then began making its way toward land, the men rowing hard and fast.

When the longboat was beached and the men had departed from it, Eden continued to watch, then drew back from the rail with surprise when suddenly they became swallowed up into the tangle of forest.

Soon they returned to the beach and waved their cutlasses, as though giving a signal.

"All is clear!" Pirate Jack shouted. "Those of you who have been given the command to depart may go. Others stay aboard. Keep watch on the island. Should Zachary arrive, let him pass. Let him come to my mansion. He's my duty, not yours."

Eden gave Pirate Jack a harried look, wishing she could look into his soul, to see his true intent toward Zach. Surely he had wrestled with himself during the week-long voyage as to what he would do once faced with Zach. She had been as torn, at times, over him.

But not now. She was at peace with her feelings about him. All that bothered her at this moment was the fear that Zach would not come out of this fracass alive, and that she knew nothing of her father's welfare.

She felt utterly helpless.

A strong hand on her arm made Eden's insides tighten. She glared at Pirate Jack as he ushered her along the deck toward a waiting longboat. "It's not necessary to manhandle me," she snapped, jerking away from him. "Where would I go even if I managed to escape from you? It seems you've brought me to the ends of the earth."

Pirate Jack smiled, his dark eyes dancing. "Soon ye shall see that ye have no cause to be angry over where I have brought ye," he said, again taking her by the elbow. "Let me help ye into the boat. From that point on, ye will be on yer own. I would like fer ye to enjoy yer stay on my island. Any woman would." He frowned down at her. "That is, unless she is too stubborn."

Eden climbed into the smaller craft. She sat down and stared icily up at the pirate. "How can you expect me to enjoy anything when I don't know how my father is, and I don't know what your intentions toward Zach are?" she said. "You are most surely daft, old pirate."

Pirate Jack chuckled as he clasped a hand over his cutlass and climbed into a seat opposite Eden on the longboat. "Aye, I have been called many things in me lifetime," he said, waiting patiently for several of his pirates to board the longboat. "Daft? I have been called insane." He shrugged. "And perhaps I am. But it matters not to me how I am labeled. I have had a lifetime of adventure. A lifetime."

"And, of course, that is all that matters in life," Eden said, hanging on to the sides of the longboat as the chain began lowering it toward the sea. "Your adventures and how to find more of them." She swallowed hard and looked away from him, her heart aching.

"Even if it includes shooting my father. Even if it includes killing Zach."

"How do ye think I have survived all these years with only one visible scar on me person?" Pirate Jack said in a growl. "I have defended meself. I shoot first. I do not wait until I'm shot at. Your father should've never aimed at me. He would have never been shot 'imself."

"Oh, yes, but he would have," Eden argued. "Once he saw you destroying his precious lighthouse, he would have pounced on you. You would have had to shoot him to get him off you. You were as good as destroying my father when you took it upon yourself to destroy his lighthouse beam."

"It is because of that beam that me ship was identified more than once," Pirate Jack snarled. "I should've removed it long ago. Zachary wouldn't 'ave been ordered to hunt me down and kill me. I would not be forced to turn my gun on him."

Eden turned cold inside, hearing how matter-of-factly the pirate spoke of killing Zach.

But weary of bantering with him, Eden clamped her lips together tightly. She clung to the sides of the craft as it splashed into the aqua-blue ocean. She looked from scruffy pirate to scruffy pirate as they each began drawing their massive oars through the water, soft spray settling on her face, cooling her.

Feeling nothing but contempt for the pirates, she gazed past them, watching the island grow closer. Eden inhaled the tantalizing aroma of roses as it became stronger. It was reminiscent of an expensive French perfume that Angelita wore on special occasions. The island itself was like something one might see in a painting, almost too fantastic to be true. Palm trees were thick. Roses and orchids grew in the moist thickets alongside streams that reached out into the ocean. The wind blew steadily in from the sea, riffling the palm fronds and stirring the bamboo brakes and the thigh-high guinea grass. A beach of snowy white sand edged the island.

Eden clung more tightly to the sides of the longboat as it was forced upon a spit of sand. She cringed when Pirate Jack left the craft and offered her a hand.

"Do not treat me as though I am a helpless ninny," Eden snapped heatedly back at him. "I can very well take care of myself."

She teetered as she stepped over the sides of the craft, then groaned as she splashed into knee-deep water, feeling the water seeping through her shoes. The moist, sticky air had already taken its toll on her, making her dress cling damply to her curves, and her hair hang in long, wet ringlets down her back.

Giving Pirate Jack a sour glance, she trudged on through the water and dropped the hem of her dress as she finally stood on solid, dry sand. She swatted at a mosquito as it began buzzing around her head, then with her chin held high, followed the pirates toward the tall grass and tangles of roses. She dreaded fighting the briars, but fortunately, a path led through the maze of palm trees.

Brushing her hair back from her eyes and swatting at another mosquito, Eden followed the pirates through an intricate network of passages through the palmetto forest. She ducked and leaned away from the rose briars; the fragrance of the roses was even more overpowering and sweet up close.

After traveling a short distance, Eden stopped and gaped at a wide opening just ahead in the forest. She could hardly believe her eyes when she saw a three-storied mansion with three great pillars reaching to its roof. Creeping and clinging rose vines decorated the walls. Shutters were thrown open at windows glistening beneath the golden rays of the sun. Mahogany, rosewood, and pine trees were clustered closely around the house, shielding it from the view of passing ships at sea.

"So ye are finding out that this old pirate does not lie?" Pirate Jack said, falling back from the other pirates to stand beside Eden. He took Eden's arm. "Come along. I would like for ye to meet me wife, Catrina. It's been a while since she's had a female visitor."

Eden glanced at Pirate Jack, awed by the many kinds of lives he led. Surely he was a man of multiple personalities. Such men were truly the ones to fear the most—they were the most dangerous.

Walking alongside him toward the mansion, she wondered which personality would emerge when Zach arrived at the island. For Zach would come. He would surely stop at nothing to find her.

Zach's shirt billowed out from his chest as the brisk breeze became trapped where his garment was buttoned only halfway to his waist. Standing at the bow of the ship, peering intently over the sun-drenched ocean, he watched for the first signs of the island that he knew so well. As a lad of fifteen he had chased butterflies there as they flitted around the roses. There he had momentarily forgotten his painful past and that he had become a pirate's ward. He had felt free on Pirate Jack's private island. He had been loved. Catrina had become a substitute mother, loving him as though he were her own. She had fought against him riding the high seas alongside Pirate Jack. She had wanted him to stay behind, protected by her loving care.

But she could rarely sway her husband when his mind was made up. She had learned to live for the few moments she had alone with her husband and her adopted son.

Zach inhaled deeply. Memories even more vivid of his times on the island were brought to mind when he got a faint whiff of roses across the sea, proving that the island was near.

Zach turned his eyes away from the ocean. "How can I do anything that will hurt Catrina? It is because of her that I have a measure of kindness towards humanity," he whispered. "Or will she understand? She surely has known all along that one day someone would have to stop Pirate Jack's marauding ways—Even if it is I."

Sabrina threw the shutters aside at the bedroom window, letting fresh air and the cleansing rays of the sun splash into the room. Her hair knotted up into a tight bun atop her head, her dress freshly laundered and smelling clean, her mosquito bites all healed, she felt whole again—except for the emptiness caused by Joshua's illness. She went back to his bedside and sat down to watch him.

She smoothed a hand over his brow, glad that it no longer was hot to the touch. Even the flush of his cheeks had mellowed and his dark skin showed a healthier color. The worst was over—except for when she had to tell him about his arm. Thus far, he had been too fevered and ill to even ask. He had slept almost continuously.

Sabrina's breath caught in her throat when she saw Joshua's eyes begin to flutter open. She leaned closer to him and placed a hand to his cheek. "Joshua?" she said, in a tremulous voice. "Oh, handsome man, is you finally goin' to wake up and speak to me? I'se been so worried."

Joshua licked his parched lips and looked through a haze as he opened his eyes. Then, slowly, he was able to focus on Sabrina as she sat at his side. "Little Momma, is it you?" he asked. In its weakness, his voice sounded foreign to him. He blinked his eyes. "Why such a long face?" He looked around him, seeing that he was not in his cabin, but in his master's house, even in his master's bedroom.

He looked quickly back at Sabrina. "Lord, woman, does Masta' Zach knows you brought me here?" he gasped. His gaze moved downward. He jumped with alarm when he saw the huge bandage at his shoulder. Then his mouth went dry and he felt a queasiness at the pit of his stomach. "I don't see all of me." His voice rose in pitch as he tried to raise himself on his one elbow. "Lordie, where's my arm?" Hysterical, he looked up into Sabrina's dark, teary eyes. "No, don't tell me. The doctor didn't remove my arm. I only remembers him. . . ."

Sabrina sobbed. She placed a hand to his mouth, stopping his frantic words. "You passed out, Joshua, before he got much cuttin' done," she explained, hurting for him. "Joshua, gangrene had set in. There was no choice. The arm had to be removed or you would've died fo' sure."

Joshua looked away from her, swallowing back the bitter bile that rose in his throat. He breathed heavily, battling an onrush of tears. "I be . . . only half a man now," he said thickly. "I be . . . worthless."

Sabrina moved to the bed and lay beside him on the side where his arm could anchor her to him. She snuggled close, clinging to him. "You be my man," she said. "That ain't worthless. And Masta' Zach loves you as though you were a brother. You mean the world to both of us. Don't let pity fo' yo'self ruin you. That's the danger here, Joshua. Self pity. It can fester like an open wound inside you, if'n you lets it."

Joshua smelled her sweetness. He burrowed his nose into her hair. "Help me, Sabrina," he pleaded, no longer able to hold the sobs inside. "Oh, Lordie, help me accept my loss."

Sabrina hugged him tightly. "You is gonna be all right," she whispered. "Handsome man, you is gonna be fine. Sabrina will make it so. Cry it all out, handsome man. Then you'll be better. You'll see."

Angelita stood beside Preston, a bouquet from Eden's garden in one hand, her other arm locked through Preston's. Attired in a dress frothing with lace at the low-swept bodice and at the hem, where it mingled with the many layers of lacy petticoats, Angelita smiled radiantly at the preacher.

Though it was just a week since he'd been shot, Preston had been determined to get married on his feet and not in a sickbed. Attired in only a loose shirt and a pair of breeches, he stood beside Angelita, scarcely believing that she would actually have him. Through the years he had admired her from afar, but had rarely let himself dwell on wanting her. She had always seemed the sort of woman who could never settle down with one man, while all along, she had secretly been wanting him.

That they had finally accepted that neither age nor anything else mattered if it kept them apart, was still beyond comprehension.

"Do you, Angelita Llewellyn, take this man to be your lawfully wedded husband?" the preacher asked, holding his opened Bible between his hands.

Angelita, her dark hair long, crisp and curly, her face radiantly pink, looked up at Preston. "I do," she murmured, smiling adoringly up at him.

The preacher cleared his throat and looked at Preston. "Do you, Preston Whitney, take this woman to be your lawfully wedded wife?" he asked, smiling stiffly.

Preston smiled down at Angelita. "I do," he said hoarsely. "I do very much take this woman to be my wife."

Angelita giggled softly.

"Then I now pronounce you to be man and wife," the preacher said, slamming his Bible shut. He again cleared his throat. "You may kiss the bride."

Preston turned to Angelita. He framed her face between his hands and lowered his mouth to her lips. Everything within him melted when he kissed her. Surely he had never loved as much as now. It was as though Angelita were a candle, he the flame. He felt all aglow.

"Ah-hem," the preacher said, shuffling his feet impatiently. "I've other calls to make. I'd appreciate payment so I can be on my way."

Preston drew himself away from Angelita

but still feasted his eyes on her as he fumbled in his pocket for his money. Withdrawing several bills, he didn't even count them, but handed them to the preacher. "The ceremony was nice," he said. "Thank you."

"Think nothing of it," the preacher said. He tucked the money in his pocket and offered Preston a hand. "Congratulations, Preston." He nodded toward Angelita. "Both of you be happy."

"The happiest we've ever been in our lives," Angelita said, smiling sweetly up at Preston. "Won't we, dear?"

The preacher eased his hand from Preston and, smiling, stepped softly away from the bride and groom. The banging of the front door jarred Angelita and Preston into realizing that they were finally alone. They stared a moment longer at one another, then suddenly Angelita tossed her flowers aside. She eased into Preston's arms. "My husband," she whispered. "You are truly my husband."

"It's about time, wouldn't you say?" Preston said, chuckling. "Think of the wasted years just lookin' and wantin' one another. It took a shock like you seeing me walk for you to jump into my arms and show your true feelings. What if I had never given you cause to get so excited over me? Would you have gone forever without giving me that wondrous first hug and kiss?"

"Oh, Preston, you always seemed so unapproachable," Angelita said, sighing. She looked at him. "I thought you wanted to be left alone. I thought you were still pining for your wife. How was I to know that you could love another? That you could love me?"

"Well, we both know now and we are man and wife," Preston said, holding her hands. He smiled down at her. "One thing is missing, though."

Angelita cocked an eyebrow up at him. "Oh?" she murmured. "What?"

"I won't be able to carry you across the threshold," Preston said, chuckling. A pain shot through his side. "Nor will I be able to make love to you on our wedding night. My dear, will you still love me as much tomorrow if I neglect you so tonight?"

"Darling, I shall always love you, no matter what," Angelita said. She slipped an arm around his waist and began walking him toward the bedroom. "You know that I was against your even getting out of bed for the ceremony. Come along. I'm taking you back to bed now and I shall sleep in Eden's until until she returns."

Preston gave her a fierce glance. "No wife of mine is going to sleep away from my bed," he growled.

"But what if during my sleep I accidentally bump against your wound?"

"I'll chance that to have you in bed with me."

"It will be so strange," Angelita said, laughing softly.

"What, darling?"

"Sleeping with a man."

"I'm glad to hear you say that."

"What?"

"That it will be strange sleeping with a man."

"And what's so strange about that, Preston?"

"It's just that now I know that you've never slept with a man before."

Angelita paled. "Tell me you didn't mean that," she said softly.

"There have been so many admirers, Angelita. What was I to think?"

"None has ever so much as touched me."

Preston reached for her and forgot his wound as he swept her into his embrace. "I'm sorry," he said, his eyes wavering. "I should've known better."

"No, you shouldn't have," Angelita conceded. "I did give people cause to gossip. I was foolish."

Preston touched her cheek gently and kissed the tip of her nose. "Well, there will be no more cause for gossiping about you, because you are my wife," he said flatly. "Anyone who says anything against you will have to answer to me."

"We'll be wonderfully happy, you and I," Angelita said, sighing. She looked up at Preston, eyes wide. "And it will be wonderful living away from my aunt. I've hired a nurse. She is now responsible for my aunt's welfare, not I."

"And that's the way it should be," Preston said. He held Angelita to him as he walked to his bed. He eased down onto it, then gave her a quivering smile. "It's going to be damn hard having a wife and not being able to take advantage of it."

Angelita helped him remove his breeches, then smoothed a blanket over him. "We have a lifetime of loving ahead of us," she reassured him. "A lifetime."

Eden walked beside Pirate Jack across grass that had been trimmed, then down a graveled path lined with pink roses, and then up a steep staircase to the veranda that reached across the entire front of the house. Her footsteps became unsteady when a woman opened the large oak door and stepped out onto the veranda, excitement bright in her eyes as she looked past Eden to the old pirate.

Eden was in awe of the creature who ran on past her. Though surely in her mid-fifties, Catrina was a vision of loveliness with her flowing, fiery-red hair, angel face, and trim figure. Her green satin dress, cut low to reveal magnificently large breasts, rustled as she lunged into Pirate Jack's arms.

Eden turned and watched the reunion, touched. Catrina wound her arms around her husband's neck and kissed him sweetly, straining her body into his.

Then Catrina stepped away from Pirate Jack and turned her eyes to Eden. Strangely, there was no jealousy in their depths.

"John, why is she here?" Catrina asked, raking her eyes over Eden. "Very rarely have you brought women to the island. Only when I have asked for company, and then it was women I have known from other islands that I have become acquainted with over the years."

"There is a reason," Pirate Jack said, placing his arm around his wife's waist. He guided her up the stairs, past Eden. "I shall explain." He looked over his shoulder at Eden. "Take a look around outside, or come on in and ye will be shown to yer room. Whatever pleases you."

Eden placed her hands on her hips. "Whatever pleases me?" she said icily. "How can you say that? Being here does not please me at all and you know it."

Pirate Jack waved a hand casually in the air. "Ye shan't be here for long," he said, walking his wife up to the veranda.

Eden stared openly at them as they went inside the house. She was in awe of this lovely woman married to such a lowly pirate, whose reputation preceded him everywhere he traveled. Was she not aware of her husband's unlawful activities? She even called him John instead of Jack. Was that a way for her to hide from the truth?

Sullenly, Eden followed along after them. She had no desire to explore the island. Though filled with the lovely, heavenly aroma of roses, she did not crave getting lost among them. Nor did she wish to venture off, in case Zach arrived soon to take her away.

But could Zach truly kill the old pirate? She saw too much about the man that could draw a person into liking him. Or into being fooled into it, as his lovely wife must have been.

Chapter Twenty-seven

Drink to me only with thine eyes.
—JONSON

In a state of awe, Eden sat at a grand dining table. A chandelier, dripping with pendants, hung over it, casting dancing shadows from at least a hundred candles. The table was set with expensive china and crystal goblets. Several servants were bringing in a feast of a dinner, and even Eden found the aroma tantalizing.

She smoothed her hands over her lap, feeling the wondrous touch of satin against her palms. She glanced down at herself, adoring the pale blue dress that Catrina had lent her. It nipped in tightly at the waist, where gathers flowed from it. Its bustline was low and tiny designs of orchid irises had been embroidered there by the hand of a talented seamstress—Catrina herself.

Diamonds, also Catrina's, sparkled at Eden's throat and earlobes. Her golden hair was drawn back from her face, pink roses pinned in it above each ear.

She had seen herself in the mirror of her assigned bedroom and felt that she had never looked more beautiful.

But it was wasted in this place, despite the kindness being showered her by all the servants, Catrina, and even Pirate Jack.

It was as though she had stepped into another world.

One that knew no pirates, no unhappiness, no pain.

"And did your bath relax you?" Catrina asked suddenly from across the table.

Startled, Eden jerked her head up. She gazed at Catrina, feeling a strange sort of bond, though she had just met her. "Yes, very relaxing," she said, recalling how stunned she had been when a lavish copper tub had been brought to her bedroom, followed by many servants carrying vases of hot water. Perfumed oils that had made lucious bubbles in the water followed. A maid had even come to wash her hair.

"We try to please our guests," Catrina purred. She straightened her back, causing her magnificent breasts almost to spill from her pale green silk dress decorated with tiny white embroidered roses. Emeralds sparkled at her throat and earlobes, and in her upswept red hair. Her sensually shaped lips were bright with color, as were her cheeks. Her green eyes sparkled at her husband.

"But we don't have guests often enough to suit me," she pouted. "John leaves on long excursions far too often and I am left to pass my idle time with embroidery work."

Eden was finding it hard to get used to Pirate Jack as "John," just as she was finding it hard to adjust to his civilian look this early evening. No one would ever guess that the man was a pirate at this moment. His gray hair had been neatly trimmed to hang just above his collar and it was sleeked back from his face. He wore normal clothes—an elegant brocaded waistcoat, dark trousers, and a shirt with white ruffles at the throat and cuffs. He even spoke with more eloquence in the presence of his beautiful wife.

Yes, Eden was beginning to understand how Zach had taken a liking to Pirate Jack. He had been so vulnerable at that age, and unloved. He had needed someone to cling to, to look up to. The pirate had just happened to be there, to fill that need.

"Did you and—uh, John ever have children, Catrina?" Eden asked.

Catrina picked up a fork and toyed with it, avoiding Eden's steady gaze. "No, no children," she murmured. "It seems that I am barren."

Eden's eyelashes fluttered nervously. She glanced away from Catrina, spreading a napkin on her lap as the final tray of food was placed on the table. "Oh, I am sorry," she said softly. "I shouldn't have asked."

"Zachary filled that void in my life," Catrina volunteered, looking slowly up at Eden. "When he was small, there were times when I felt that I truly had a child, a wonderful son. But when he grew older and was drawn to the sea and began sailing alongside John, I grew used to his absence as well as to my husband's."

"I didn't know," Eden gasped. "Zach never told me."

"I am sure he would prefer not talking of his past," Catrina said. She lifted a glass of wine to her lips and sipped from it, then placed it back down on the table. "Though I tried to brighten his life, I am not sure it helped erase the pain of his childhood before he came to be a part of my and John's life."

"I hope to help him forget the ugliness of his past," Eden murmured, nodding a thank-you as a servant refilled her wine glass. "I am sure he does not include you when he refers to his past as ugly. After meeting you, I cannot help but be certain that he sees you as part of his life that was wonderfully sweet."

Catrina smiled. "It's very kind of you to say that," she said, lifting her fork in her delicate hand. "And when are you and Zach getting married? John told me only that you plan to."

Eden looked quickly at the old pirate, trying to understand at least a little about him. He had shared small talk with his wife about her as though he had never met her father, much less shot him. He had talked of her upcoming marriage with Zach as though it was a certainty, even though he must be planning to kill Zach.

She glanced at Catrina, trying to see beyond her innocence. Surely she knew why Eden was on this island. She had to know that she had been forced, and why.

Yet Catrina could sit there and share small talk with Eden as though it were a normal everyday thing to do. Was she conditioned to put on this front because of the same sort of experience in the past?

Surely Eden was not the only guest who had come unwillingly to the island.

An uneasiness began to swell within her. Would she ever leave the island alive?

A voice spoke up suddenly behind Eden, causing her heart to skip a nervous beat. She dropped her fork onto her plate with a clank, then turned around and gaped openly at Zach, who stood at the dining room door.

Zach repeated himself, leaning casually against the frame of the door. "Eden, aren't you going to answer Catrina?" he repeated. "Tell her when we plan to get married."

Eden scarcely breathed, stunned that Zach could get into the mansion so easily, so quietly. He wore a brace of pistols across his chest and a dangerously pointed cutlass at his hip.

"Zach!" she gasped, paling.

"Zachary," Catrina gasped, her hands at her throat.

Eden wanted to go to Zach and embrace him, but she could feel the tension in the room tightening and remained in her chair.

Her eyes followed him as he sauntered into the room and gave Catrina a gentle kiss on the cheek.

Eden was eager to ask Zach if he knew of her father's fate. But his being there did not mean that he had come because of her. He had been ordered to kill the old pirate long before her father had been shot. Perhaps he didn't even know about her father.

Yet, he did not seem surprised to see her there. Oh, surely he did know about her father and had answers she was dying to know!

But for now, she must share in this little game that he was playing with Pirate Jack and his beautiful wife.

"Catrina, how are you?" Zach asked, his eyes revealing his respect for her.

"Zachary," Catrina said, rising from her chair. She fell into his arms, hugging him tightly, and whispered into his ear, "Oh, Zachary, why did you come? You know the dangers. John has told me what happened. Please leave. Leave now. Or one of you will surely die."

Zach gave her a fierce hug, then stepped away from her. He went to Pirate Jack and clutched a hand to his thick shoulder. "And you?" he said. "How are you faring?"

Pirate Jack's cheeks became inflamed with color as he looked at Zach, their eyes meeting and holding. "As ye see, I am faring fine," he said hoarsely. "And ye?" His gaze swept over Zach's handsome face, seeing the bruises. "But, of course, I see. It wasn't pleasant fer ye in jail. Ye see, I know everything, Zachary. I know about yer imprisonment and that yer comin' here was by force. But, of course, ye know that I do. I have abducted yer woman to draw ye here."

"Old pirate, your aim was poor," Zach said dryly. "Seems the lightkeeper will live. He gave me your message and so I am here."

"And so you are," Pirate Jack said, nodding. He looked more closely at Zach's bruises. "Damn the man who marred your face like that," he growled. "Damn him."

Zach sat down beside Eden. "Bruises heal," he said. "But what of the heart? When I said my good-byes several months ago, we knew that I would return."

Tears silvered Eden's eyes. Zach had found her father and he was not dead. She had prayed over and over again for his welfare. Her prayers had been answered. Now would they also be answered for Zach?

"But, of course, we had no idea that I would return to fight a duel with you," Zach said smoothly, pouring himself a glass of port as a servant placed a tall-stemmed glass before him.

Gasps reverberated around the table. Zach avoided looking at Eden, knowing what her reaction to what he had said would be. Even Catrina. Both women loved him devotedly.

"Sir, do you agree that would be the best

way to settle this thing forced upon us?" he asked, his voice drawn. "You have a handsome pair of dueling pistols. We may as well put them to use."

Pirate Jack reached for the bottle of wine and poured himself another glass. He had already consumed several tankards of rum on the ship before arriving on land, and his mind was beginning to reel from its effects. But it was a way to accept where life had brought him. Either he would die, or Zachary would.

Pirate Jack took several quick swallows of wine, emptying the glass. "A duel it will be," he said, pouring himself another glass and downing it. "Tomorrow at sun-up. I shall see that the pistols are readied tonight."

Eden's insides were trembling. Her hand shook as she reached for her glass. She almost choked on the wine as it trickled down her throat, burning it. Out of the corner of her eyes she saw a plate being placed before Zach. She stared at him as he began piling all sorts of food on it, as though this was an ordinary meal, shared with ordinary people, during an ordinary supper hour. She could hardly bear to sit and watch, much less eat.

"These ribs are very tasty," Zach said, smiling at Catrina who sat pale and drawn, watching him. "Do you remember that this has always been my favorite?"

Catrina nodded, dabbing the corner of her eye with a handkerchief, removing a stray tear.

"Catrina, are there many butterflies among

the roses this spring?" Zach asked, diving into the buttered peas, eating like a starving man. "Catrina, do you remember chasing the butterflies with me when I was young? Weren't those the days?"

Catrina nodded again, choking back a sob.

Eden looked, wide-eyed, back and forth across the table.

Preston was having trouble sleeping. He rose up on his elbow and looked over at Angelita. He touched her cheek thoughtfully, absorbing the softness of her flesh into the tips of his fingers. Slowly, he moved his fingers along her face, down the slender column of her throat, and then lower, where her breasts lay just beneath the sheerness of her nightgown.

Slipping his hand down into the gown, he cupped her breasts, fire with the need of her heating up inside him. It had been so long since he had made love to a woman. He had forgotten how soft a breast could be. He had forgotten how sweet a woman could smell. And this woman was his wife. His wife.

Turning on his side made him wince with pain, reminding him that though he had a beautiful wife, he was not able to perform as a husband. Aware of the dangers of arousing himself too soon, he withdrew his hand—but it was not soon enough for Angelita not to have been awakened by his gentle exploring of her body.

Turning to him, she smiled. "I want you as

much," she whispered, touching his cheek gently. "Perhaps tomorrow you will be stronger and the pain will be less in your side. Perhaps then, my husband, we can find paradise together."

Taking her hand, kissing its palm, Preston smiled at her. "This will be your first time with a man," he reminded her. "I shall be gentle."

Angelita nodded slowly. "I know," she murmured. "I know."

"Angelita, there is something else that needs to be said," Preston said, easing his hand from hers. He closed his eyes and groaned as he tried to position himself more comfortably on the bed. Angelita straightened the pillow behind his head, then smoothed the blanket across him as he stretched out on his back. "Though Eden is gone and we're not sure about her welfare, I still cannot wait to get repairs started in the lighthouse. And it might help me get my mind off worrying about Eden if I get involved in the repairs."

"But you can't leave this bed again until you are better," Angelita fussed, sitting up. She drew her hair back from her shoulders. "You shouldn't have gotten up even for the wedding ceremony. You shan't even attempt to climb those dreaded lighthouse steps."

Preston laughed softly. "No, I don't think I shall attempt that just yet," he said. "But I know someone who can. He worked with me before. He's good with his hands. He has knowledge of all the mechanisms of the lighthouse beam. He will know what parts to order and what parts to make himself."

Angelita frowned over at him. "I know who you are talking about and I am against his coming here," she said. "You know that he attempted to abduct one of Zachary's slaves, and he shot another. Gossip has spread all over Charleston about how the one slave was thrown into jail because he used a whip on Smitty, and about how Zachary managed to get the slave released. How could you want such a man as Smitty around here? He is a dirty, despicable man."

Preston kneaded his brow. "Yes, I know all of this," he grumbled. "And there are others that I could hire to help me, but Smitty is the fastest. In no time flat my beam would be reaching out to the ships again." He looked at Angelita, his jaw firm. "I must at least give him a try. As you go into Charleston tomorrow to check on your aunt, will you stop and ask Smitty if he will help me?"

Angelita sighed. "If you wish," she said, giving him a troubled stare. "If you wish."

Filled with many tumultuous emotions, Eden lay in her bed, moonlight spilling across her from the window. The sound of the waves washing up on the beach through the trees was peaceful, lulling, yet Eden could not relax. In a sheer peignoir that Catrina had lent her, she rose from the bed and began pacing back and forth in the dark room. Where was Zach? As soon as the evening meal was over, he had been swept away by Pirate Jack, talking over old times. It was as though there was going to be no duel. It was as though Eden did not exist. How could Zach and the old pirate act as though things were normal? And why hadn't Zach come to her and explained about her father? Why was he ignoring her?

"Why, Zach?" she whispered, throwing her head back in frustration. "Why?"

Eden tiptoed to the door and leaned her ear against it, listening for any sounds in the other rooms of the house. But she heard nothing. The silence was almost deafening.

Wrenching herself away from the door, Eden marched back to the bed and resolutely plopped down on it. She closed her eyes, trying to force them to stay closed. But her troubled thoughts kept drawing them open again.

The creaking of her door as it began to slowly open made Eden grab a blanket and pull it up just beneath her chin. Her heart was hammering; she hoped it was Zach, but it could be anyone—even one of Pirate Jack's swarthy friends sneaking in to have his way with her.

"Eden, it's me," Zach whispered, closing the door behind him. He stepped into the light of the moon. "Darling, I'm sorry if I frightened you."

Eden threw the blanket aside. She jumped from the bed and flew into Zach's embrace. Sobs tore from inside her as she looked up at him, imploring him with her eyes. "My father

—Zach, it's been sheer agony waiting for you to tell me of his welfare," she softly cried. "Tell me. Is he truly all right? Why, oh, why did you make me wait so long to find out? What have you been doing?"

Zach gently framed her face between his hands. He leaned down close to speak softly to her. "Darling, your father's wound was slight," he said softly. "He is going to be fine. I saw to it that Doc Raley was sent to look after him. Angelita is with him too. I am sure you have no cause to worry."

He swallowed hard. "I had no choice but to delay coming to you tonight," he further explained. "Jack was drinking too heavily. I had to make him stop. I stayed with him until Catrina put him to bed. If there is to be a duel between us, I want it to be a fair one. I don't want to get the first shot off because my old friend is too drunk to take a steady aim."

He lowered a kiss to her cheek. "Darling, I am sorry I was forced to neglect you," he whispered. "Please forgive me?"

Eden took Zach's hands and kissed both palms, then looked up at him through misty eyes. "You so amaze me," she said. "You could have let Pirate Jack continue to drink, knowing that would give you the advantage over him tomorrow morning, yet you could not. That says so much about your character. You are so good, Zach, so kind."

Zach laughed softly. "Some would call me stupid for stopping the old pirate from drinking himself mindless," he said, walking her toward the bed, his eyes feasting on her loveliness in the moonlight. "Perhaps I am. We shall see. Tomorrow we shall see."

"At least the news about my father is good," Eden said, sighing. "But I knew that it would be. My prayers are hardly ever left unheeded and I said plenty for my father." She fluttered her eyelashes nervously as she looked up at Zach. "And for you, also, my darling—I will be saying many more through the night for your safety tomorrow."

"As for tomorrow, I've brought you something," Zach said, slipping his hand inside his breeches pocket. He withdrew a tiny, pearl-handled pistol and laid it on the nightstand beside the bed. "This is for you. You keep it with you at all times, especially tomorrow. Should anything happen to me, protect yourself, Eden."

Eden grew pale as she stared down at the pistol. "Zach, just looking at that pistol frightens me," she murmured. "I can't bear the thought of being put in the position of having to use it. Tomorrow—"

"Enough about tomorrow," Zach said, running his hands up and down Eden's bare arms. His eyes grew dark with passion as he gazed at her. "You are a vision tonight, Eden. You are like a fairy princess in that peignoir. You are so pretty, you look unreal."

Eden held the peignoir out away from her, then let it flutter back down, to cling to her flesh. "Catrina has been very kind to me," she murmured. "She lent this to me and also that adorable dress that I wore to dinner."

"Once we are married you shall have all sorts of lacy fineries," Zach promised, his hands now cupping her breasts through the soft silk of the garment.

Eden sucked in her breath as a sensual tremor soared through her. "Oh, darling, we will be married, won't we?" she whispered, her pulse racing. "You will be sure nothing happens to you so that will be possible, won't you? You are my life. My life."

"We will be married," Zach said firmly. His fingers went to the hem of the peignoir and began slowly lifting it. "Tonight we shall pretend that we already are. May I spend the night with you, my wife?"

"Yes, my husband," Eden whispered. "Yes . . . yes."

Raising her arms, she let Zach pull the peignoir over her head. Silkenly nude, she felt a soft melting energy warming her insides as she looked up at Zach. Their eyes met and locked in an unspoken understanding, promising ecstasy.

Chapter Twenty-eight

Sing me a sweet, low song of night.
—HAWTHORNE

His clothes shed, Zach lowered Eden to the bed. He sculpted himself against her pliant body, fitting perfectly into the curved hollow of her hips. Their bodies jolted and quivered as he pressed himself into her yielding folds.

Only vaguely aware of making whimpering sounds, Eden responded to him, thrusting her hips toward him. Magnificently filling her, he thrust himself deeper, then began his easy, rhythmic strokes. Desire raged through Eden. She twined her fingers through Zach's hair and drew his lips close to hers.

"We are the only two people in the universe tonight," she whispered, her breath ragged. She ran her tongue across his lips, inhaling the smell, the taste of him. "I want you, Zach. I need you."

"Eden . . ." Zach whispered, his voice quivering. "My Eden."

He enveloped her in his arms and kissed her savagely. Desire filled him, drenching him with its warmth. His hands cupped her breasts. Feeling their softness, he groaned against her lips. He felt her growing passion in her hardening nipples against the palms of his hands.

Then he drew away from Eden. His lips began showering kisses along the slender column of her throat and moved down to her breasts. As he inhaled their nipples between his lips, Eden's gasp of pleasure echoed through him.

Then Zach's tongue made a wet, sensual descent across her trembling body. He flicked his tongue into her navel, eliciting a giggle from her.

His eyes on fire with building passion, Zach moved lower. He parted the golden fronds of curls at the juncture of her thighs and flicked his tongue against her throbbing center. Eden gasped and inhaled a shaky breath of pleasure.

Eden looked down at Zach through hazy eyes, her pulse racing. Feeling no shame over sharing this way of lovemaking with him, only that it was he who was sending her into a wondrous sort of rapture and not she to him, she placed her hands to the back of his head and urged his mouth closer.

As his tongue and lips paid homage to her, she closed her eyes. She tossed her head back and forth wildly, feeling an electric current flowing from his mouth into her. The spinning sensation flooded her whole body, blotting out everything but the moment, the pleasure, the bliss of being with Zach again.

But soon, fearing that she was about to go over the edge into total ecstasy, she urged his head away. Coaxing him to lie on his back, she began giving him the same sort of pleasure that he had just generously given her.

Zach closed his eyes. His heart pounded as Eden's lips and tongue played across his powerful chest, causing his nipples to harden painfully as her teeth nipped at them. His blood quickened when she made a wet trail across his abdomen, then ran her tongue along his satin hardness. He groaned between clenched teeth as her mouth closed over him and loved him in this special way. He began a slow thrusting movement, her tongue almost driving him to madness.

But soon, fearing that he was about to go over the edge into total ecstasy, he urged her head away.

Drawing her into his arms, he turned her around and straddled her. Without hesitation he thrust his hardness into her. He pressed harder and harder into her valley of softness, mindless with the mounting pleasure that was blinding him to reason, to time and place.

Eden whispered Zach's name, filled with wondrous desire that was building into something almost undefinable. She clung to him. She rocked with him. She was delirious with sensation. Each plunge of his magnificent hardness within her assured fulfillment. She tried to hold back, to savor these sensations as long as she could, but suddenly a surge of tingling heat flooded her. She cried out with rapture, every cell in her body affected by the joy of release. . . .

Zach held her trembling body in a tight embrace. He kissed her heatedly as he plunged over and over within her, filling her with the warm wetness that was spilling forth from within him.

Ecstasy sought.

Ecstasy found.

He moved his lips to brush a soft kiss against her cheeks. His body grew quiet, his breathing sharp and ragged.

"Don't let me go," Eden whispered, cuddling close to him as he moved to her side. "Zach, sleep within my arms tonight. I . . . so fear for tomorrow."

"Shh," Zach encouraged her softly. "Remember? We weren't going to talk about tomorrow."

"But, Zach, tomorrow is a reality," Eden argued softly.

"Tomorrow isn't a reality until tomorrow," Zach said, kissing her brow. "Now go to sleep, darling. I shall hold you. You will be a dream in my arms, a dream that is mine alone."

Eden snuggled closer. She sighed and closed her eyes. With Zach's breath warming her cheek, she felt herself begin to drift. She had not realized just how tired she was.

But this had been a day of days!

Eden awakened with a start. She bolted upright in bed, her eyes wide when she discovered that Zach was not there, as promised.

Breathless, fear gripping her, she looked toward the window. The moonlight was gone. Instead she saw the first traces of morning along the horizon, as streamers of black were replaced by a magnificent sunrise.

Panic seized Eden. She grew coldly numb inside. "No!" she cried. "He couldn't have gone without me. Oh, surely he wouldn't. I want to be with him. What if he needs me? I won't be there!"

Her heart pounding, she jumped from the bed and seized the first dress she found in the wardrobe and thrust it over her head. With trembling fingers she fastened the snaps, then pushed her feet into her shoes.

Not even bothering to brush her hair, she grabbed a shawl and rushed out into the corridor.

Then she stopped and looked back into the bedroom at the pistol on the nightstand. Recalling Zach's concern for her welfare, she rushed back into the bedroom. Grabbing the pistol, she slipped it into the pocket of her dress.

Stone silence met her in the hall. She looked from side to side, a sense of relief stealing over her. Surely everyone was still in bed. Surely Zach had just risen earlier than the others to go outside, to ponder over this thing that lay before him. She must go to him and tell him again that she loved him, no matter what happened. She would be at his side forever. She was soon to be his wife.

"If fate only allows it," she whispered harshly, heading for the winding staircase. "If fate only allows it."

Still hearing no sound, not even the servants preparing breakfast, Eden ran out to the wide veranda, then stopped as something grabbed at her heart. Only a few yards from the house, all of the servants, all of Pirate Jack's crew, and Catrina were witnessing the beginning of the duel. Zach had let Eden sleep, to protect her from the sight.

"Lord, no," she cried, whipping the skirt of her dress up into her arms and rushing toward Zach. Her shawl slipped from around her shoulders and fell to the ground. In her haste, her hair whipped around her face, stinging her flesh.

And then she was only a few feet away from Zach when Catrina grabbed her and held her back.

"You must not interfere," Catrina said, her voice emotionless. "This is between Zachary and John. Only Zachary and John. There is nothing you or I can say or do to stop it. If you try and interfere, you will only delay the inevitable. It is our duty as women who love them to learn never to interfere when it comes to fighting for their honor."

Eden jerked and pulled against Catrina's hold, but could not get free. "But honor has nothing to do with this!" she cried. "Let me go. I can't bear to see this happen."

"You have no choice," Catrina said, grasping more firmly to Eden's wrist. "Either watch and be silent or I shall have one of John's crew remove you and take you back to the house until the duel is over."

Pale, Eden stopped struggling. She gave Catrina a sour glance, then shook herself away from her. "You'll be sorry," she snapped. "You will soon see that this should have been stopped. The man you love will die."

"Yes, no matter which of them dies, the man I love will die," Catrina said, looking sadly at Eden. "You see, I love them both. With all of my heart, I love them both."

Eden looked at Catrina, suddenly aware of just how much this lady did love both men. Oh, Lord, she would lose a love however this duel ended. Eden had no feelings whatsoever for the old pirate, except for a loathing brought on by his having shot her father so cold-bloodedly.

No. She would not be filled with any remorse if the old pirate was shot. His reputation was known far and wide. These past months, he had left a trail of blood behind him. Eden wondered if Catrina was aware of that—or was her love for him blinding her to the truth?

Eden placed her hands to her throat when she looked slowly over at Zach. His attire was hidden beneath a long, black cloak. All that was visible was the mighty dueling pistol held in his right hand, the barrel pointed toward the ground. His back was to Pirate Jack.

Eden then looked at Pirate Jack. His back was to Zach and he wore the same sort of cloak and he carried the same dangerous weapon, also pointed toward the ground.

Tears splashed from Eden's eyes and her heart thudded against her ribs as Zach and Pirate Jack began to take slow, calculated steps away from each other. She could tell by the movement of their lips that they were silently counting the paces.

Eden screamed when they turned suddenly and fired their pistols, the twin blasts filling the air with sparks and the stench of gunpowder.

Feeling faint, Eden looked from Zach to Pirate Jack, and turned pale when she saw the bullet hole scorched through Pirate Jack's cloak and blood spilling from his left side, below the waist.

Pirate Jack crumpled to the ground, a strange look of dismay on his face, distorting it. Zach angrily tossed his pistol aside. He turned and began to walk away.

Eden looked from Zach back to Pirate Jack, then everything within her grew cold when she saw Pirate Jack slowly slip his hand inside his cape. Withdrawing a pistol, he aimed it at Zach, with the obvious intention of shooting him in the back.

"No!" Eden tried to scream. But no sound

would surface. Fear had claimed her ability to speak. But not her ability to think. She suddenly remembered the pistol in her dress pocket.

Without much conscious thought, she reached into her pocket and withdrew the pistol. Tears rolling down her cheeks, she aimed the firearm at the old pirate, and before anyone even had time to notice the threat she posed, she pulled the trigger.

The discharge knocked Eden to the ground. She sat there for a moment, stunned. Screams swirled around her, and she watched as Catrina rushed to Pirate Jack. He had dropped his pistol and was now clutching at his heart, where Eden's bullet had entered.

"John, oh, John!" Catrina cried, cradling her husband's head on her lap. "You were going to shoot Zachary in the back. Eden had no choice but to shoot you. Darling, you are the one who always said to fight with honor. How could you have forgotten that code today, when Zachary's life lay in balance? You would have shot him willingly, John. And in the back? Why? Oh, why?"

Eden was too numb even to feel Zach's hand when he placed it on her waist to help her up. She barely felt his embrace when he drew her into his arms. But his words brought her back to reality.

"Thank you, darling," he whispered. "Thank you for saving my life."

She grew limp as tears flooded from her eyes. She stared numbly down at Pirate Jack, dazed over what had just transpired. "I . . .

actually . . . shot a man," she whispered. "I've never before . . ."

Zach gave her a slight shake. "Eden, snap out of it," he said. "You had no choice. You had to shoot him." He looked down at Pirate Jack disbelievingly. "He was actually going to shoot me in the back."

Eden blinked back tears of relief. "Zach, you left me!" she cried, tearing herself away from him. She doubled her hands into tight fists at her sides. "Had I not awakened, you would be there on the ground dying, not Pirate Jack. I was the only one who saw fit to stop him when he raised his pistol to shoot you in the back. Lord, Zach. What if I hadn't awakened? What if I hadn't been here to stop him?"

"I was wrong," Zach said. "I tend to forget just how strong you are."

He smiled admiringly at her, but then his gaze moved back to Pirate Jack. He could not deny the slow ache in his heart for his mentor. He would have never thought their relationship would come to this. The damned old pirate would have shot him in the back. It was hard for him to comprehend that Jack was capable of such a contemptible act.

Zach had found that, after wounding Pirate Jack in the duel, he could not finish the job by killing him. He had decided at that moment to go to Judge Pryor and tell him that he could never do it, even if it meant having to rot in jail for eternity. He could not wound Pirate Jack and then stand over him and finish him off with another bullet. That would be a cold-blooded act. He was not capable of such fiendish behavior.

He had not wanted Eden to be involved in such a way with this thing, either. But because of her, true justice was done today.

Sweeping an arm around her, Zach led her away from the bloody scene. He flinched when Catrina let out a mournful cry and knew that to mean that the old pirate had taken his last breath.

Over his shoulder, Zach saw the pirate crew running into the forest. They no longer had a leader. Who was to say what would happen to them now? It was well known among the pirate community that once a leader was slain, the pirate crew would disband and go on their separate ways.

"Zachary!"

Zach's spine stiffened. With Eden still at his side, he stopped and turned. He looked at Catrina as she rushed toward him.

"Zachary, what am I to do now?" Catrina cried. "Where shall I go?"

Zach glanced over at Eden, then moved away from her. He drew Catrina into his arms and hugged her comfortingly. "You are coming with me," he said hoarsely. "When I was a child, you took me in and cared for me as if I were your own. Now it is my turn to care for you. You will live with me and Eden. I have a spacious house. You can have a corner of it all to yourself and can embroider to your heart's content."

Zach looked over his shoulder at Eden. "Darling?" he said softly. "Do you approve?"

Eden nodded softly. "Yes, of course," she murmured. "I understand your love for this woman. Please do bring her home with us."

"Go and pack your most precious belongings, alert the servants to do likewise, and let us leave this island as quickly as possible," Zach said. He looked back at Pirate Jack's body lying on the grass. "While you're packing I will see to John's burial."

Catrina reached a hand to Zach's cheek and touched it gently, then wrenched herself away and ran toward the house. Eden went to Zach and hugged him. "Your kindness continues to overwhelm me," she murmured.

Zach's eyes filmed with tears. "Eden, you may find this strange, coming so shortly after Pirate Jack planned to shoot me in the back, but, darling, I learned so much compassion from him," he said, recalling the earlier years when they had sailed the high seas together, to take from the rich, and to give to the poor.

Yes, he had learned much from the old pirate, and most of it good.

The sun was lowering in the sky when Smitty rode up to the lighthouse cottage and dismounted. He looked up at the sky, frowning when a great bolt of lightning flashed its wild streaks down into the ocean. A scud of dark clouds was rolling quickly toward shore. He could smell rain. He could see it off in the distance, blurring the line where the sky and sea met.

Grumbling, knowing that he would probably have to ride back to Charleston in the rain, he stomped up onto the porch and knocked. Earlier in the day Angelita had come and told him that Preston needed him. He was eager to help the sonofagun because they had worked together many times before on the lighthouse mechanisms. Preston was honest and paid him promptly. But Smitty was glad he wouldn't have to run into Eden or that Zachary fellow. Preston had been shot at the same time Eden had been abducted, and gossip had it that Zachary had gone after the pirate responsible.

He snickered to himself, thinking that everyone had probably seen the last of Zachary Tyson. The old pirate that he was chasing was well known to be merciless.

The door swung open. Angelita wiped her hands on her apron as she stepped aside. "Please come in," she said stiffly, always repelled by Smitty's downright loathsome ugliness. Bald, his face pinched and lined, he smelled as ugly as his drab clothes were dirty and greasy. "Preston is waiting in the bedroom. He still isn't up to getting up and conversing with you in the living room."

Another great bolt of lightning and an ensuing crack of thunder made Smitty jump with fright. "Can't stay long," he growled. "If I'd known a storm was brewin', I'd have waited until tomorrow. These last storms have been fierce."

Preston appeared at Angelita's side. Shirtless and wearing only a pair of breeches, he clutched at his wound. "No need for you to come in, Smitty," he said, wincing when a sharp pain cut through him. "Just you go on ahead up in the lighthouse while there's some daylight to see by. You'll find pen and paper there. Make a list of all that's damaged. I'll depend on you to see that everything is put back in shape. You're good at that sort of thing."

Smitty smiled smugly. "Glad you think so," he said, puffing out his chest proudly. He looked down at Angelita. "I see you've taken a wife. A good choice, this one. I've had my eye on her for a spell, but she ain't never given me the eye back."

Angelita gasped and paled, then turned to Preston. "You know you shouldn't have gotten out of bed," she scolded, changing the subject. "Now get on back in there. Do you hear?"

Preston chuckled. He drew her to his side. "In time, little one," he said. "In time." He nodded toward the lighthouse, flinching when a zigzag of lightning danced around it. "You'd better hurry along and get done what has to be done. I don't like the looks of this storm."

"Don't have to tell me twice," Smitty said. He mocked a half salute and ran down the steps.

Preston and Angelita clung to one another, watching Smitty go into the lighthouse. They could hear his footsteps on the metal stairs as he ascended them.

Then suddenly the whole world seemed to fill with white light as several flashes of lightning and crashes of thunder raced across the land and around the lighthouse.

A scream from the lighthouse made

Angelita and Preston jump with alarm. They gave each other wondering stares, then, forgetting his wound, Preston left the porch and made his way toward the lighthouse.

Stunned, he stopped when Smitty suddenly appeared at the door, all black and charred as he fell outside, on the ground.

"Oh, my God!" Angelita cried, rushing to Preston's side.

"Don't go any closer," Preston said, grimacing at the sight of the dead body.

"What happened?" Angelita said, her whole body trembling.

"It must have been those damn metal stairs," Preston said thickly. "They became charged with electricity from the lightning again. This time it was deadly."

Angelita turned her eyes away and buried them in Preston's bare chest. "Is he dead?" she whispered.

Preston nodded.

"It could've been you," she sobbed. "Oh, God, it could've been you."

"Well, it's never going to be me again," Preston said determinedly. "Now that so much work has to be done on my lighthouse, I'm going to do something that should've been done long ago. I'm going to have a more effective lightning conductor installed. I'm never going to have to worry about those blasted metal stairs again."

The rain started to fall in torrents. Preston hovered around Angelita, and led her back to the house.

Chapter Twenty-Nine

Eyes full of starlight, moist over fire.
> —EASTMAN

The sails of Zach's ship were drawing in the fair, soft wind, the canvas snowy white against the brilliant blue backdrop of sky. The waves were white and fleecy, spraying softly over the bow.

Eden stood beside Zach at the rail, the breeze gently caressing her face. She circled her fingers around the rail, steadying herself against an occasional lurch of the ship.

Looking at the far horizon, she watched lightning playing against dark clouds, wondering if the storm was over Charleston. If so, all ships at sea in the storm were in danger, for the lighthouse beam was not there to guide them—nor was the usually dependable lightkeeper.

She had to wonder how her father was faring. Had Zach told her the truth when he had said that her father's wound was not fatal? Or had he been trying to spare her the truth with a temporary lie?

She would not press him for answers. She knew that he was fighting his own private battles within himself. Though Pirate Jack had deserved to die, Zach was torn clean through with the loss. She could tell by the torment in his eyes. Surely he was silently reliving the more pleasant times with the old pirate.

"I wonder how Joshua is faring," Zach suddenly said, surprising Eden. He had not been thinking of the old pirate at all. His mind was on a true friend, one who had proven his trust and devotion to Zach.

"He's a strong man," Eden said, snuggling close to him. "I'm sure you have nothing to fear. He will come through the surgery just like new."

"With only one arm?" Zach said scornfully. "If it were me, I would wish I were dead. I only hope that Joshua's constitution is stronger." He looked down at Eden, his eyes wavering. "But perhaps Sabrina can convince him that he must not give up the will to live. A woman can work wonders with a man, you know."

"If the woman loves the man enough, she can," Eden said, standing on tiptoe to give

Zach a soft kiss on the lips. "I shall always be here for you. Always."

"As I will, for you," Zach said, looking into the distance at the play of the lightning in the heavens. "Damn. That must be some storm. I'd hate to have to fight another such storm at sea. I hope it breaks up before we get closer to it. That lightning is deadly."

Eden snaked an arm around Zach's waist. She gazed admiringly at his attire, seeing how handsome he looked in his pirate clothes. His dark hair was drawn back from his face and secured with a leather thong. His bright red shirt with its great, flowing sleeves was billowing out from his chest, caught by the wind. His leather-clad legs revealed the play of his muscles and the bulge at the juncture of his thighs to almost shameful proportions. He wore a pair of shining black leather boots, his brace of pistols, and his cutlass worn at his left side.

Zach's attention was drawn down into the water. He peered over the side of the ship, making out the shape of at least fifteen whales. They were pilot whales, swimming as though in escort of the ship a mere six feet beneath the ship's hull. As the first contingent passed under, others took their places. There had to be more than a hundred whales in the herd.

"Eden, take a look," Zach encouraged her, pointing.

Eden turned and followed his gaze. She

sighed, in awe of the sight. "There are so many," she said. "And they are so close. You would think they would be afraid of the ship. Instead, they seem to enjoy being close to it."

"Some whales are just curious, while others rub right up against a ship," Zach explained. "Some surface beside a ship, circle, or even lie gently beneath the hull so that the water disturbed by their great flukes will eddy up around the vessel."

"They are very interesting creatures," Eden said, watching the mammals dip into the ocean, then reappear again. "Ugly, yet beautiful at the same time."

"So many people are ignorant of what a whale truly is," Zach said, brushing back a wisp of Eden's hair that blew into his eyes. "They are thought to be fish, while in truth, they only superficially resemble a fish. They breathe air and suckle their young."

A loud cry from the crow's nest overhead rang suddenly in the air. "A sail. A sail. Ship approaching starboard," the lookout warned. "Ship approaching starboard. It bears the flag of a pirate."

"What?" Zach gasped, jerking his eyes starboard. He withdrew his brass telescope from a loop at the side of his breeches and swept the horizon with it.

The pit of his stomach felt suddenly empty as he spied the ship. "No," he said in a near whisper. "It can't be. It's Pirate Jack's ship. Could it even be the ghost of the old pirate at

caressing her back. "Nothing can be allowed to happen to you. Nothing."

Eden gave him one last hug, then wrenched herself away from him and ran toward the companionway ladder. As she began descending it, she heard him begin shouting his orders to his crew.

"All guns are to be double-loaded with shot!" Zach shouted. "Sling the foreyards in chains to prevent them from being cut away, and set up two powder chests, one on the forecastle and one on the poop. Run out four six-pounders on the quarter-deck and set up a swivel six-pounder in the closed quarters so that we can sweep the deck if the pirates manage to come on board."

Zach stood at the ship's rail and watched the black ship move closer. "They will fight to their death," he murmured to himself. "They've decided to avenge Pirate Jack's death and they'll be riding his ship as though he were there, shouting out orders. It's got to be their last voyage. It's got to end. Today."

When the black ship came into range, Zach gave the orders for the firing to begin. The cannons drew back, belched and roared. A swivel gun fired scattering shot and old spikes and nails at the black ship.

Answering fire began with the pirate ship's broadside. Zach's ship shuddered as a cannon ball crashed across the bow, scraping it and scattering wood splinters into the air.

"That was a close one," Zach shouted. He

ran along the deck, encouraging the sailors at the cannons. "Fire. Fire. Don't give 'em time to load their weapons again."

Turning with a start, Zach smiled when he saw the results of his orders. Three great shots went through the black ship's sides. The last shot smashed into a powder chest, exploding with a great boom.

Zach's crew gave a loud shout and redoubled their efforts. They poured a withering fire into the pirates. Black, thick smoke swirled over their deck. The screams of the maimed pirates rose into the air, as grenades scattered along their deck, spreading death and destruction.

"Cease fire!" Zach shouted, having had no return fire from the pirate ship for several minutes. "Aim a cannon across the bow in a warning to surrender."

"Let's sink 'em," one of Zach's crew shouted.

"Yeah, let's sink 'em," another shouted. "They're a worthless lot, all of 'em. The world will be a better place without 'em."

"It may be," Zach said. "But I am an honorable man and an honorable man gives all ships a chance to surrender. See that that warning shot is fired."

The boom of the cannon made the deck shudder beneath Zach's feet. He watched for a white flag to be hoisted up in place of the pirate's flag, but soon discovered that was not the way the pirates wanted it. All hell seemed to break loose as firing commenced from the black, devil ship. Before it was over, the port side of Zach's vessel had been shot through and much of the rigging had been damaged by more than a thousand rounds of shot. Eight of the crew had been killed and sixteen wounded, among them the chief gunner, the quartermaster, and the boatswain.

Pale and unsteady, Zach shouted out his final order, determined not to see the pirate ship left in the water once his crew was through with it. He had been foolish to hesitate at sinking the damned vessel in the first place.

"Give it everything you've got!" he cried. "Sink her to the bottom!"

Zach's remaining crew shouted and cheered. They didn't hesitate at sweeping the pirate vessel with a nine-pounder loaded with a maiming mixture of partridge and double chain shot. The blast caused havoc when it struck the pirate ship, and a terrible outcry could be heard from the men on ship. Amid a black swirl of fire and smoke, the pirate ship tumbled over on its side, spilling men from its deck. It seemed that the ocean opened up, like a huge mouth, and belched as it swallowed the ship and its crew whole.

The crew of Zach's ship ran up onto the poop in great excitement. They danced and hugged one another. They cried. They cursed.

Zach stood at the rail, feeling a strange sort of emptiness assail him as he looked at the debris popping up to the surface from the destroyed ship. He knew that he should be jubilant. Instead he was sad. For many years he had been a part of that ship. He had seen the world. He had become a man while riding the seas on that ship. He had . . .

"Zach?"

Wiping tears from his eyes, Zach turned and looked down at Eden as she approached him. He opened his arms to her and held her close as she moved into his embrace. "It's over," he said thickly. "Darling, it's really over."

Eden sighed.

As Zach's ship limped into Charleston Harbor, the hull groaned and labored both fore and aft; the remaining masts nodded and swayed. Some of the crew were still stuffing caulking by the handfuls into opened seams, others were resetting the shrouds.

Eden was tense as she looked at the pier the ship was moving toward. Would Judge Pryor keep his word? Now that Zach had done his dreaded chore for the Judge, would Zach truly be free of any further demands? Or would he be thrown back in jail?

"Darling, you look as though the burden of the world is on your lovely shoulders," Zach said, searching Eden's face. "You should be happy. Our life together begins the moment we set our feet on solid ground. Though many lives were lost in the effort to be free, the fact is, we are free now. The past, including Pirate Jack, will remain past. Never let us speak of it again. We shall live for the present. We shall live for the future. Be happy, Eden. Not everyone is given a second chance in life. But we have it."

He turned away from her for a moment. "Drop anchor!" he shouted.

Eden gave Zach a silent stare, not wanting to voice her doubts aloud to him. She did not want to take away from his moment of victory. He had fought. He had won. She should be thanking God over and over again that he had come out of it alive. That she had.

Turning her eyes back to shore, she froze inside when she saw Judge Pryor there, flanked by armed guards and Sheriff Collins. She began to tremble as the gangplank was run out to the pier. She became breathless with fear as Judge Pryor walked up the plank, the sheriff and the guards behind him.

Zach turned toward them. He squared his shoulders and extended a handshake of welcome to the Judge. "Sir, the deed is done," he said. "Pirate Jack is dead. He lies in a grave on his island. His whole crew lies dead at the bottom of the sea."

Judge Pryor refused the handshake, clasping his hands together behind him. He forked an eyebrow as he silently studied Zach, then Eden, then Zach again. "What proof do you have?" he asked flatly.

Zach took a shaky step backwards. He paled. "Proof?" he gasped. "You did not say that I must return bearing proof of my victory. Surely my word is enough."

"I don't think so," Judge Pryor said icily.

"You admired the old pirate. I even doubted that you could kill him. Again I ask you. Give me proof."

Eden was aghast at the Judge's demands. Anger welled up inside her. She stepped up and spoke into his face. "Sir, if you must know, I shot the pirate, myself," she said, lifting her chin. "Now what more proof do you want? I give you my word that he is dead."

Judge Pryor frowned down at Eden. "Eden, do you truly expect me to believe that you could shoot anybody?" he said, chuckling. "This just shows to what lengths you would go to protect this man, to tell such an outlandish lie as this."

Another voice, lilting and soft, spoke suddenly from behind Judge Pryor. "What she says is true," Catrina said, walking toward him. She clutched at a shawl around her shoulders, her red hair blowing gently in the breeze. "Eden shot John, my husband, known to you as Pirate Jack. If she hadn't, my husband would have shot Zachary in the back." She blinked back a tear. "Now what more proof do you need than the word of a wife who has lost a husband? If he were alive, I would not be here. I would be with him, or in my lovely home, patiently awaiting his arrival." She held her head high, fighting the urge to cry. "He is dead. My John is dead."

Judge Pryor's mouth went agape, taken aback by not only what the woman admitted to so freely, but by her downright loveliness.

Never had he seen a woman so ravishingly beautiful. And she had been married to the damnable pirate? Surely there was much about the pirate that he had kept hidden from the world.

Zach went to Catrina. He placed a soft kiss on her cheek, then put an arm around her waist. Then he placed his other arm around Eden. "Let's go home," he said, ignoring the Judge gaping openly at them. "I think the Judge needs no further explanations. I think Catrina has said it all."

Zach rented a horse and buggy, and soon they had left Charleston behind and were heading down the lane that led to Eden's cottage. She was breathless with excitement. She could hardly believe that she would soon be seeing her father again. For a while, during the fight at sea, she had thought never even to see land again.

But now, if her father was truly all right, her every dream was going to be allowed to come true.

Night was falling with its velvet backdrop of sky. Eden looked up at the lighthouse. A keen remorse flooded her senses when she did not see the dependable beam searching out over the waters. She would never forget the night that it had become disabled.

As Zach drew the horse and buggy to a halt in front of the cottage, Eden took another look toward the lighthouse, and her insides froze when she saw a charred body lying just outside the lighthouse door. It was so disfigured, there was no way to identify it.

"My God!" she cried, scrambling from the buggy. She picked up her skirts and began running toward the body, then stopped when a familiar, loved voice wafted through the air.

It was her father's voice. This charred body was someone else.

Spinning around, she saw her father move out onto the porch. She looked at the bandage at his right side, then back up into his eyes.

Blinded with joyful tears, she rushed to him and embraced him. She could feel his heart thundering hard against her cheek as she hugged him.

"Father, oh, Father, I was so worried about you," she cried. "I wasn't sure if you truly were safe. Zach could have just told me that to spare me. But you are. You are."

Tears streaming down his cheeks, Preston held Eden away from him and looked her up and down, as though wanting to reassure himself that it was truly her, alive and unharmed. "And you?" he said, swallowing back a lump in his throat. "You are well also. Thank God."

He looked at Zach, then broke away from Eden and shook his hand. "Thank you," he said hoarsely. "Thank you for bringing her back to me."

Zach chuckled. "I told you I would," he said, winking at Eden. "Anyhow, I couldn't leave her on that island in the middle of the Atlantic if I was going to make her my wife.''

Angelita moved out onto the porch. She looked from Zach to Eden, not knowing who to go to first. But, having been without Zach for all those lost years, she rushed to him first and hugged him. "Zachary," she cried. "I can't believe you're all right. Are you truly here? Are you here to stay?"

"I'm not going anywhere for a long time, Angelita," he said, gently kissing her brow.

She looked at Eden then and broke away from Zach to hug her. "Eden, I'm so happy to see you," she cried. "And wait until you hear!"

Eden laughed softly, easing from Angelita's excited grip. "Hear what?" she asked, seeing so much more sparkle in Angelita's eyes than she had ever seen before.

"Your father and I, we . . ."

Preston went to Angelita and snaked an arm around her waist. "We got married," he said, smiling down at her. "Now I couldn't have this pretty thing's reputation ruined by her stayin' here day and night carin' for me and my wound, could I? I made it all legal. She's my wife. My sweet little wife."

Eden's mouth opened with surprise. Then she smiled brilliantly. "My best friend is now my stepmother?" she said, then went to Angelita and her father, hugging first one and then the other.

Zach went to Preston and extended a hand. "Congratulations, sir," he said, clasping

Preston's hand warmly. "I believe you made a wise choice. And my sister deserves a man like you. I think you'll both be happy."

Drawing his hand away, Zach looked over his shoulder at the charred body. "Damnation, Preston," he said. "Who is that? What happened?"

"Well, it seems I sent Smitty up the stairs in my lighthouse to see what needed repair at just the wrong time," he replied. "He was on the metal stairs when lightning charged them with electricity. It happened earlier this evening. I didn't have the energy to take him back to town and I sure as hell didn't want to give the chore to Angelita." He forked an eyebrow. "I don't guess you'd do the honor?"

In Zach's mind's eye he was recalling all the trouble Smitty had caused him. He smiled slowly at Preston. "Seems you did me a favor by sending the man to his death," he said. "I guess I can do you a favor by taking him off your hands. Tell you what. I'll cover him with a cloth, if you'll give me one to use, then come back later and take him away. Right now I'm anxious to get to my plantation to see how friends are faring there."

"It's a bargain," Preston said. "Angelita, hon, would you go and fetch me one of the older blankets out of the cupboard?"

Angelita gave Preston a quick kiss and disappeared back into the house.

Eden took Zach's hand. "Darling, I'd like to go with you to your plantation," she said softly. "I don't think I'm ready to let you out of my sight just yet."

"After tomorrow you'll own every inch of me," Zach said, drawing her close. "Preston, do you think that preacher you used could perform another wedding out here on Lighthouse Road?"

Preston's chest puffed out with pride. "I think it can be arranged," he said, smiling from Eden to Zach. Then his smile faded into a frown. "You never said. Did you manage to find Pirate Jack?"

Eden paled, not sure if her father should hear the true account of the old pirate's death. He might be too shocked to discover who actually pulled the trigger.

"Yes, and he is no longer a problem," Zach said simply. He looked down at Eden with dark, tormented eyes. "Nor shall he be a topic to be discussed in our presence again." He looked over at Preston. "I'm sure you'll have no problems with that."

Preston patted Zach on the back fondly. "No problem at all," he said, nodding. "No problem at all."

The long avenue of oaks was a welcome sight. Zach slapped the reins harder against the horse's back, the buggy wheels grinding into the pebbled lane as it moved closer to the grand mansion.

Zach looked past Eden, who sat at his side, and stared at Catrina. She was sitting so still.

Since she left the ship, she had been withdrawn. "Catrina, you will be happy here," he assured her. "I promise you and I have never broken a promise to you, have I?"

Catrina smiled faintly. "Sweet Zachary," she said, sighing. "Please stop worrying over me. You have other responsibilities. You will see. I adjust easily." She lowered her eyes. "Surely I shall even adjust to missing my John."

Zach swung the buggy around. Stopping before the wide veranda of his stately mansion, he looked up at the windows glowing with lamplight. He looked quickly toward the door as it swung open, and recognized Tom in the shadows.

"Zach?" Tom called, then rushed on down the stairs. "Zach. My God, it is you!"

Zach leaped from the buggy. "It's good to see you, lad," he said, patting Tom on the back. Tnen he looked past Tom when Joshua's bulky figure filled the space in the door, leaning into Sabrina's embrace.

"Masta' Zach?" Joshua said, then broke away from Sabrina and wobbled down the stairs, feeling lopsided without one arm to help him keep his balance.

Zach felt tears burning at the corners of his eyes. He went to Joshua and threw an arm around his back and hugged him, avoiding touching his bandaged shoulder and side. "Goddamn, it's good to see you, Joshua," Zach said, choking with emotion. "If you had died—"

"But I ain't dead," Joshua said, sniffing as tears rolled down his cheeks. He stepped away from Zach and looked him up and down. "And you ain't dead either. Did you do it? Did you find Pirate Jack? Did you kill him?"

Zach glanced over at Eden, then back at Joshua. "Let's just say he's dead and leave it at that," he said. He looked at Joshua again, then smiled at Sabrina as she snuggled up beside him. "You kept him alive, did you, Sabrina?"

"I sho' nuff did," Sabrina said proudly.

Joshua laughed softly. "She did more than that," he said. "She done tol' me I still worth somethin' in life. You see, as she explained to me, we'll have us a son and he'll be my right arm. Or maybe we'll have a dozen and I'll be luckier than mos' men. I'll have a dozen right arms."

"Well, now, I'd say that's pretty good calculating," Zach said, laughing. He reached for Eden and drew her to his side. "Now, darling, doesn't that sound like a good idea? Do you think I could use a dozen right arms?"

"Are you asking if we could have a dozen children?" Eden asked, her eyes wide.

"Well, perhaps not a dozen, but a few?" Zach said, his eyes twinkling.

Eden laughed softly. "Now that sounds reasonable enough," she said. "Just as long as at least one of them is just like you."

Zach lifted Eden up into his arms and swung her around, warmed with happiness.

Chapter Thirty

So deep in love am I!

—BURNS

Five Years Later. . . .

The clatter of small feet rushing up the stairs of the lighthouse and mischievous giggles made Zach draw Eden proudly to his side as they moved up the steep stairs behind Timothy, their four-year-old son, and Joshua and Sabrina's four-year-old, Ezrah.

"You best slow down, boys, or you'll go tumbling down much more quickly than you're trying to climb these stairs," Zach shouted. "Timothy. Ezrah. Do you hear me?"

"Yes, sir," Timothy responded, giggling.

"Yas, suh, Masta' Zach," Ezrah responded, also giggling.

Eden strained her neck to look up at her

461

son. His hair was midnight black just like his father's, worn to his collar. His knee breeches met tight stockings, worn under sleekly polished brown leather shoes. His collar was a mass of frills, though he constantly fussed against wearing "girl's clothes."

Though she could not see her son's eyes, it was as though she were looking into them now, so green they mirrored her own. His round face was blemished by only a scattering of freckles. His delicately shaped lips and deep dimples gave her a look into his future. Oh, but the women would go mad over him!

She looked at Ezrah, who held onto Timothy's hand for dear life, always showing his fright of the steep stairs of the lighthouse. Otherwise he was a bold, eager boy of four with smooth, dark skin, and could hoe a garden better than most adults.

He was the first son of the three already born to Sabrina and Joshua. He had become his father's right arm. He had become Zach and Eden's son's best friend.

A baby's soft cries made Eden smile. "Just like I told you," she said. "Angelita is up in the lighthouse room with father. This must be father's day for losing some sleep so that he can take the time to clean his Fresnel lens." She laughed softly. "Sometimes I think he's going to work his fingers to the bone to keep that lens sparkling."

"He's damn proud of that lens of his," Zach said, tensing as he watched Timothy reach the top of the stairs and tug and pull to get himself up into the room with his grandfather and aunt. He breathed easier when the boy disappeared from sight into the small room, Ezrah scampering along behind him.

"Until Heather was born, the boys liked to hear father tell them all about his Fresnel lens," Eden said, reaching to pull herself up through the trap door. "Now all they want to talk about is the baby."

Zach followed along after her into the small room. He straightened his back as he looked at the boys standing before Angelita, who held her four-month-old daughter on her lap, each touching the baby's soft, delicate face. It had taken Preston and Angelita longer to have their first child, but Angelita was now already pregnant with her second.

Zach looked at Eden's loosely fitted dress that swelled away from her body, also swollen with her second child. Life had been good to them these past years. Zach's plantation was thriving, and he had enough field hands to sow and reap his crops of cotton and indigo. Joshua oversaw it all for Zach, having finally forgotten his handicap of having only one arm. So strong and robust, even without one arm he was still more man than most.

"Father, the lens looks so sparkling clean," Eden said, inspecting it. A part of her missed being the assistant lightkeeper, but though she still dirtied her nails working in her flower garden, she had not missed the stain the oil had left beneath them. Dirt washed out. Oil didn't.

But she was glad that her father had finally hired someone as capable as she had been to assist him so that he could spend more time with his wife and daughter.

"It was damn nice of Judge Pryor to go to the Lighthouse Board and speak in favor of the Fresnel lens for me," Preston said, wiping his hands on his handkerchief.

His eyes softened as he looked from Zach to Eden. "But you didn't come here to see the lens," he said. "You've brought Timothy for us to watch while you go into town to see your aunt." He looked at Ezrah. "It's nice of you to include Ezrah. He enjoys visitin' as much as Timothy."

Angelita folded a blanket more snugly around Heather and rose to her feet, carrying her small bundle in the crook of her arm. "Zachary, it is good that you have finally decided to go and see Aunt Martha," she said. She looked up into his dark, brooding eyes. "She isn't going to last long. I think you'd rest much more easily if you were to say your good-byes."

"I guess I've waited long enough," Zach admitted.

"Well, I had just concluded that you had decided not to go at all," Angelita said, placing a hand on Eden's and squeezing it reassuringly. "But even though she treated you badly, she is your aunt, and it may ease your mind if you do go and see her."

"If she hadn't hung on so long, I guess I wouldn't have gone," Zach grumbled. "But it's as though she's hanging on for a purpose.

Perhaps it is to see me. She's always been a stubborn old lady."

"A very stubborn, sick lady," Angelita corrected.

"I have managed to put my past behind me," Zach said, frowning. "And now to have to face up to it again by looking into her eyes? In them I shall see my past—the past with her that was so intolerable, even after I had gone. She sold me into slavery. How can one ever forgive such a heartless act as that?"

"No one is asking you to forgive," Angelita said softly. "The last link to your past will be broken once you make your peace inside your heart by going to your dying aunt to let her look upon your face for the last time."

Eden turned to face Zach. "Darling, what she says is true," she encouraged him. "Let's go. Let's get it behind us."

Timothy came to Eden and tugged on her skirt. "Can I stay with granpa and Aunt Angelita?" he begged.

Ezrah came and tugged on her arm. "Can I stay, too?" he begged, his dark eyes wide and black, as though they were all pupil.

Eden stooped to her knees and engulfed both boys in her arms. "Yes, you can stay. Both of you," she said. "But behave yourselves. Do you hear?"

"Yes, ma'am," the boys said in unison. Eden kissed them both on their round, velvety cheeks, then rose and locked her arm through Zach's. "Coming?" she asked, smiling softly up at him.

"Oh, Zach—before you go," Preston said,

his eyes twinkling at Eden. "What'd you think about Sefton losing the election? Seems he's back to being a judge and forgetting his political aspirations."

Zach chuckled. "Seems his schemes did him no good, after all," he said. "Now instead of being called Governor Pryor, he's being called the Mad Judge. He doesn't bat an eye at ordering hangings these days."

"Someone will slip a noose around his neck while he's sleeping if he doesn't change his ways," Eden said. "Come on, darling. Let's get your chore behind you."

Zach nodded. He patted both boys on the head and started down the stairs to their waiting horse and buggy. His heart beat soundly as they rode closer and closer to Charleston. In his mind's eye he was recalling so much that he had managed to put from his heart. He had never wanted to allow himself to hate anyone. Not even his crazed aunt.

But, damn it, it had been so hard not to hate her.

He dreaded seeing her again, for surely too many troubled memories would overwhelm him. Surely hate would overpower his feelings of pity for the dying woman. He did not want that.

Not at this moment in time, when so much of his life was filled with love.

The nurse left the room and stood in the corridor as Zach and Eden moved toward the bed in the room lit dimly by candlelight. The only sounds in the sickroom were short, raspy breaths, and an occasional cough. The air smelled of strong medication.

Zach's knees and the pit of his stomach felt weak, as if he were still the little boy that he was when he last saw his wicked aunt. He was recalling her flashing, dark eyes, her shriek of laughter, her scornful look as she scolded him.

He sucked in his breath as though feeling the flick of the whip against his bare bottom. It was as if it was only yesterday when he was punished for being alive.

Cold sweat covered Zach's body as he moved to the bedside and willed himself to look down into the face of his aunt. He gasped when he saw no resemblance to the woman who had haunted his midnight dreams throughout the years. He grabbed at Eden, steadying himself as she swept an arm reassuringly around his waist.

"It's going to be all right," Eden said softly. "Darling, take a good look and see the face of the woman who can no longer harm you. Now do you see? The woman of your past is no longer alive. She has been replaced by this mindless creature who has no recollection of ever even knowing you, the boy she mistreated. Look at her and walk away, free. Finally, you can truthfully say your past is behind you. Every bit of it, my darling."

Zach swallowed hard, looking down at his aunt. Her eyes stared up at him, sightless. Her skin was stretched tautly across her bones, her lips purple as she struggled for every breath. A blanket was drawn up to her chin, yet her arms lay over it, her gown covering her flesh except for her hands. They were hardly more than a skeleton's, all curled up and knotted. Her gray hair was sparse, the pink of her scalp showing through the strands.

Her eyes blinked and her lips began to move as she slowly lifted a hand toward Zach. But instead of saying anything, she began to scream.

Zach and Eden grabbed each other and clung together as his Aunt Martha continued to scream, over and over again—then grew suddenly quiet.

The nurse rushed into the room and checked Aunt Martha's pulse, then gave Zach a relieved look. "She does this," the nurse said, sighing heavily. "Always afterwards I expect her to be dead, but she isn't. She has more will to live than anyone I've ever encountered."

Zach reached for a handkerchief and blotted his damp brow. His heart was thudding inside him. "For a moment I thought she recognized me," he said. "I thought I made her scream."

The nurse straightened her back and placed a gentle hand on his arm. "No, she didn't recognize you," she murmured. "She recognizes no one. And she didn't scream because of you. As I said, she does this all the time. I'm used to it."

The nurse turned and looked down at Zach's aunt. "The poor thing," she said. "It's as though something is tormenting her terribly when she screams like that. Maybe the devil is there, hovering over her. I pity her. She would be better off dead."

Zach slipped his handkerchief back inside his pocket and locked an arm around Eden. "Yes, I believe she is being tormented by something in her past," he said, his voice drawn, quite sure of what it was. No one could treat a child so unjustly and not pay for it, even if it took many years for justice to be done.

"And, yes, I can find it in my heart to pity her, also," he said to Eden, walking her away from the bed and through the house. "You see, I believe she is never going to be free of her ugly past. I'm much luckier than she. I am finally free of mine."

They stepped out into the fresh air, magnolia blossoms sweet along the walk as they went to their horse and buggy. They rode along the oleander-lined streets into the promise of sweet tomorrows, blessed with love.

"Let's go home, darling," Eden said. She placed a cheek on his shoulder as he snapped the reins, sending the horse through the narrow streets.

"Home," Zach said, his eyes calm, his heart singing. "Ah, Eden, that has such a wonderful ring to it."

"Our home," Eden said, smiling up at him. "That sounds even better."

Zach threw his head back in a happy laugh. He had searched for so long for the happiness that he had found with Eden, that she had promised him from their first embrace. And she was not the kind of woman to ever let him down.

CASSIE EDWARDS . . .
ROMANCE AT ITS FINEST

Fans of Cassie Edwards will love **Secrets of my Heart,**
a favorite in Leisure's classic romance collection.

SECRETS OF MY HEART. Orphaned on the long trail
West, Lenora Adamson found her savior in rugged
James Calloway. Convinced that she had met the man
she would one day marry, Lenora gave herself to him
body and soul, not realizing that James was a foot-
loose wanderer who could be tamed by no woman.

_____2525-6 $3.95 US/$4.95 CAN

SWEPT AWAY WITH SANDRA DuBAY

"Wonderful escapist fiction. It fulfills all her readers' fantasies!"
— *Romantic Times*

WHERE PASSION DWELLS. Lovely and spirited young heiress Raine McQuaid had always taken it for granted that she would one day marry Patrick Thorndyke and unite their families' vast plantations—until she met devastatingly handsome Adam, Viscount de Burgh.

_____2245-1 $3.95 US/$4.95 CAN

BY LOVE BEGUILED. Lysette's marriage of convenience began with deep misunderstandings on both sides. Yet within her vulnerable heart a hidden love smoldered into a flame of passion for the husband she had learned to adore.

_____2330-X $3.95 US/$4.95 CAN

FLAME OF FIDELITY. Lovely Fidelity Fairfax inflamed the desires of every man she met. But another woman's jealousy drove Fidelity to seek refuge in America, where it seemed the love she sought awaited her.

_____2415-2 $3.95 US/$4.95 CAN

_____2441-1   BURN ON, SWEET FIRE. $3.95 US/$4.95 CAN

_____2555-8   SCARLET SURRENDER. An autographed
                bookmark edition. $3.95 US/$4.95 CAN

_____2561-2   FIDELITY'S FLIGHT. $3.95 US/$4.95 CAN